IGNITE THE STARS

IGNITE THE STARS

MAURA MILAN

ALBERT WHITMAN AND COMPANY
CHICAGO, ILLINOIS

Library of Congress Cataloging-in-Publication
data is on file with the publisher.

Text copyright © 2018 by Maura Milan
First published in the United States of America
in 2018 by Albert Whitman & Company
ISBN 978-0-8075-3625-4

Printed in the United States of America
10 9 8 7 6 5 4 3 2 1 BP 22 21 20 19 18

Cover artwork copyright © 2018 by Craig White
Cover model: Jessika Van
Design by Ellen Kokontis

For more information about Albert Whitman & Company,
visit our website at www.albertwhitman.com.

For my dear friend David

YEAR 8922 OF THE UNIVERSAL CHRONOS

The photo on the wanted banner had no eyes, no ears, no nose. No face. Just a helmet with a crimson feather etched through the middle of its visor, slashing down from the forehead. Everyone knew that feather.

They feared it.

And when they closed their eyes to dream, the name echoed in their nightmares.

I. A. Cōcha.

I. A. Cōcha.

CHAPTER 1

IA

SHE WAS SEVENTEEN, and her life was about to end.

The girl pushed back strands of her tangled black hair and pressed her forehead flush against the glass window. Outside were twenty starjets from the Royal Star Force, the military fleet of the Olympus Commonwealth. A shimmer of panicked whispers flittered around her, and she realized the other passengers had seen the squadron coming their way, too.

The girl glanced over her shoulder and caught sight of the Elder moving through the crowd of Tawny refugees, trying to quell the growing panic.

"Why the mif is the RSF here?" she called out to him.

The Elder shook his head, his lips drawn into a tight line. "If Deus is on our side today, Girl, they'll wave us by."

The passengers on the ship called her "Girl," which was fine by her. After traveling with them for a month, she didn't know their real names either. Her dark hair and golden skin stood out in this crowd like a crooked screw on a brand-new sheet of metal. The twenty-seven Tawny refugees on the ship all had milky complexions and hair as blue as the deepest ocean. That was what happened in the All Black. You got mixed up with all sorts of different people just trying to survive.

The RSF starjets knocked into the transport ship's hull, and the ship pitched forward. The girl heard the screech of metal scraping against metal, of screws twisting and connecting. The RSF had sealed its docking bridge to the transport ship's air lock.

The Elder held a hand up, attempting to ease the wave of anxiety passing through the crowd. "The air-lock door will hold. They won't be able to board without permission."

The girl held her breath, praying he was right, wishing that door was made from the strongest vinnidium steel instead of salvaged antique metal.

A tinny voice came through the speakers. "The Royal Star Force requests entry to your vessel."

Fear ripped through her. What were they searching for? Weapons? Contraband? She swallowed, her throat tight. The Royal Star Force had a reputation of being rougher out in the Fringe territories. Olympus had no problem taking everything from the many people of the Fringe—their homes, their water, their fuel, and their planets.

The Elder rushed to an intercom speaker and pressed a thumb to a red sensor. "We are outside Commonwealth territory. This ship is not subject to your jurisdiction. Be kind and pass."

But there was no response. Only a gentle hiss permeating through the small holes of the intercom speakers.

Silence settled, and then came light taps on the metal, one for each hinge on the entry door. From all her years traveling in the All Black, surviving scuffles against pirates and black-market traders, the girl knew what that sound meant.

"Take cover!" she screamed.

A dull tone reverberated from outside, followed by a loud boom. The doorway flew inward, carving a hole in their ship. Passengers scattered as twisted pieces of metal flew their way. Even with a veil of smoke hanging over them, the girl heard the shuffle of footsteps and armor, and she knew. The Royal Star Force was boarding.

The Elder grabbed her shoulder. At such a close distance, she saw the gray hairs speckled throughout his navy-blue mane and the age spots dappling his cheeks. But despite his years, his eyes were bright as starlight.

"Best to stay out of sight." The Elder pulled her away from the windows, and she was swallowed up by the crowd. Around her, everyone's shouts merged into one, and she felt her lungs compress as bodies drew tightly together. The smoke settled, and small orbs fixed with camera lenses flew out from the docking tunnel. It was the Commonwealth's media; they had sent their little Eyes to film and broadcast this entire thing. One camera drone buzzed by so close that it tousled her hair. She glanced at each Eye, watching them change position to find the perfect angle to capture the passengers' distress.

It was then she realized: this wasn't a routine search.

"Where is he?" a thick voice bellowed from the other side of the threshold. A formation of officers emerged from the docking bridge, followed by a large figure. The girl recognized him from the broadcast streams: General Adams, a war hero celebrated throughout the Commonwealth. The medals on his chest—shaped like golden stars and silver olive branches—jingled as he walked.

"Where is I. A. Cōcha?" he growled.

As if on cue, Commonwealth holoscreens appeared around them. On the screens was a Wanted banner, one she had seen over and over again, plastered on interstellar gates, projected on travel hubs—anywhere people could see. The banner had an image of a helmet, a red feather painted across its helm like a stain of blood.

General Adams was after I. A. Cōcha, a monster with many names: the Sovereign of Dead Space, the Rogue of the Fringe Planets, the Blood Wolf of the Skies. Cōcha was the most dangerous criminal in Commonwealth history.

General Adams surveyed the faces of the Tawny refugees. "I don't care much for guessing games. I know he's here. Send him forward."

The girl stayed hidden, waiting for someone to speak. The tension among her fellow travelers thickened, but even with the surmounting pressure, they nodded knowingly to one another, a secret agreement to stay silent.

"So be it." Adams motioned for his soldiers to come forward. All fifty of them were armed with laser pistols lethal enough to burn everyone on the ship to ash. The general's blue eyes glinted like a newly polished dagger. "I'll just have to shoot all of you."

General Adams raised his weapon at the nearest Tawny, a teenage boy. Adams would kill him, just because he could.

The girl's heart raced, rage boiling inside her. Surging forward, she grabbed an orb from her side pack and threw it down. A translucent-green energy force field spidered upward to the ceiling, creating a protective wall between the passengers and the RSF.

Across the barrier, General Adams grimaced. "Who are you?"

The girl slammed her palm against a button on the collar of her suit. Her helmet slid on, smooth and automatic. Upon its brow was a blood feather, shining in the darkness. To many, it instilled fear, but to her, it inspired hope.

The general's eyes widened in recognition. "I. A. Cōcha."

Ia stared him down. "It's pronounced *Eye-yah*. You don't spell my name; you say it."

Gunfire erupted, and the air was filled with a flurry of bright-blue energy blasts. They showered around her, absorbing right into the protective wall of the force field.

This type of force field was called a Carpion shield, designed to block any bullets coming from the other side of the protective wall, but any gunfire originating from within would pierce through. Ia grabbed the energy pistol holstered in her boot and aimed. Shot by shot, her bullets soared through the shield and toward the soldiers. Her aim was precise and clean. But there were too many of them, and she didn't have enough of a charge to pick them all off.

She checked the orb at the base of the shield. The meter showed 50 percent strength. The shield was strong, but it wouldn't last. If she wanted to survive this, she had to act quickly. Ia ran to the overheard bin above her seat and grabbed her pack.

She turned back to the Tawnies. "You have a choice," she told them. "You can get to the escape pods, or—"

She threw her pack onto the floor, revealing her stash of weapons. No more shields, but she did have more than enough guns.

"This is our ship," the Elder said, stepping forward. "We fight."

Ia pulled out her favorite hand cannons and tossed them to him.

"Aim for the quartered shield." It was the symbol of Olympus, a red-and-white shield embroidered on every RSF uniform, stitched on the chest pocket right at their hearts. The perfect target.

She quickly distributed the rest of pistols to the others in the group, and soon they were firing across the force field.

The Tawnies had terrible aim. Their rounds burst the pipes, dinged the softer metal of the ship, and hit everything but the RSF officers. The Elder and his group weren't warriors. They were civilians.

Ia glanced again at the meter on the Carpion orb. It was at 35 percent. At the state they were in now, they weren't going to win. She had to call in an even bigger gun for that.

She blinked inside her helmet, accessing the ArcLite, a communications system that spanned the known galaxies. A holo-image flickered onto a small panel on the right side of her visor. She sighed in relief at the sight of Einn Galatin's face. It was like hers. Black hair, golden skin. But her brother's cheekbones were more pronounced. Sharper, more angular. And his eyes were a different color, a stormy gray instead of her coal black. An image of two white hearts cast side by side was pinned prominently onto his collar. Their father always told them it was their family symbol. It meant loyalty, a word wasted on the father who had abandoned them long ago, but very fitting for her brother. Einn was the only person she could ever count on.

"Where the mif have you been, Ia?" Her brother crinkled his forehead. He did that when he was angry.

It had been months since she'd seen her brother. With the end of the Uranium War, the Commonwealth's leaders had increased their efforts at hunting down the criminals on their Most Wanted list. Ia had gone into hiding, hoping the heat on her would eventually die down. It never had.

"I'm in some deep mung, Einn. The Bugs found me."

That was what everyone on this side of the galaxy called the officers of the Star Force: Bugs. Ia had spent her whole life swatting them down, but no matter how many she killed, there were always more who took their place.

"What?" Einn asked. "How?"

"Don't know. I cloaked my signal with Alary tech, but that miffing general still knew I was here." She grunted, firing another round across the force field.

Her brother's eyes darkened. "Get yourself out of there."

She shook her head, beads of sweat dripping down her forehead. "It's not that easy. There are innocents onboard. Tawnies." She kept her eye on the firefight, watching the Tawnies as they attempted to defend themselves. Their firepower and skill weren't even close to being enough. "We need your help."

"You don't have to save every refugee who crosses your path."

"Einn," she whispered. "Please."

Her brother shook his head in resignation. "Ping me your location. Try to hold them off until I get there."

Her heart leaped. "I owe you one, Brother."

"Just survive. That's all you need to do."

Ia nodded. "May your eyes be open, Einn."

Her brother said the words as though they had been programmed into his heart. "And your path be clear."

It was their farewell, the lines they spoke to each other before they parted at each mission. A secret prayer to keep them safe.

As he signed off, Ia reminded herself that he was right. She had to get through this. She would find a way. They didn't call her the Blood Wolf of the Skies for nothing. With their viselike jaws and mighty wings, Lavisian blood wolves were vicious contenders in the Dead Space betting pits. And just like those fierce creatures, if anyone backed Ia into a corner, she was going to bite right down to the bone.

Ia took aim, gunning down as many RSF soldiers as she could.

One down.

Then another. And another.

Ia smashed her palm against the butt of her pistol, but her ammunitions chamber hummed to silence. She was about to ask someone to toss her another gun when she realized the gunfire on her side of the ship had gone quiet. Their ammo had run out. They had nothing else to use to defend themselves.

She breathed heavily, her eyes shifting from the never-ending fire coming from the Star Force's side. Each bullet further drained the strength of her shield.

The media's Eyes flew to the front lines, pointing straight at her.

"It's over, Cōcha," General Adams hissed. His white teeth reflected the lights of the cameras. "I don't even need to wait until that flimsy shield of yours runs out. I can just gas this entire ship and end it now."

Ia's heart pounded deep inside her chest. She glanced back at the Tawnies. This was a passenger ship, which meant there would be only one grav suit, maybe two. They'd never withstand a chemical attack.

"I see you figured it out." The general's voice interrupted the zigzag of her thoughts. "You have enough air in your helmet for what? Two hours? All these Tawnies will be long dead by then." His quiet calm slashed like a razor into her skin. "Or you can surrender."

Ia gazed out the window. Five more RSF battleships had joined the others, completely surrounding the Tawny ship. Each one of them was big enough to house fifty starjets. Even if Einn was on the way, he wouldn't be able to break through them.

General Adams turned to one of his lieutenants. "Get the gas ready."

Ia heard cries of panic from behind. She glanced back, her eyes landing on a Tawny woman holding her child and shielding his eyes so he wouldn't have to see their fate. The Elder stroked her hand, trying to keep her calm.

Ia took a deep breath as a decision shook her bones. General

Adams might have won, but there was still something she could do.

"I'll surrender. On one condition…" Ia said.

"Name it."

She dropped her pistol, nozzle clanging sharply on the floor. "Take me, but only me."

A smile slithered onto General Adams's lips. "Done."

Ia ripped her helmet off, her eyes searing into the general. "We have a deal."

The general looked back to the one of the officers. "Tell the ships to clear a path."

The Elder looked over at her in alarm. "What are you doing, Ia?"

"You helped me," she whispered, just loud enough that the Elder could hear her. "You didn't have to, but you did." She glanced at all the Tawny refugees. There were twenty-seven of them, enough to fit into the two escape pods built into the ship. "Get to the pods. My brother will find you." She looked back to the Elder, and she paused, her heart heavy with guilt. "I should have told you who I am."

"We knew, Girl. You can't outsmart a Tawny."

"Then why take me in?"

His eyes shone at her. "Not all the stories of I. A. Cōcha are bad ones."

All this time, they'd known who she was, and they regarded her the way she always wanted to be seen. Not as a monster, but as a person, just like any other.

She fought back tears. "Thank you," she said. Then she jutted out her chin, telling them to go. The shield wall blocked the Star Force from the starboard side of the ship where the escape pods were located. In her head, Ia counted to thirty, giving the Tawnies enough time to get to the pods.

At the end of her count, she put her pistol on the floor, and with her foot, she tapped the Carpion orb. The shield flashed green as it deactivated. The soldiers punched through the fading sheen of the force field and surrounded her, their pistols pointed at her head.

As she raised her hands in surrender, she felt a brush of air as cameras whizzed around to film her at all angles. One of them stopped, hovering in front of her, blasting its bright white light into her eyes. She squinted at the lens.

After today, everyone in the known universe would know Ia's face. And no matter where she went, she would no longer be safe.

Mif. This was going to suck.

The soldiers grabbed her arms and bound them behind her back. As she struggled against the binds, she turned to the windows. One of the escape pods had cleared the blockade as promised, its silhouette now a mere speck in the distance. Ia sighed in relief.

But just as the second pod was about to pass, a RSF battleship closed in, blocking the pod's escape. Her gut twisted. She had been a fool to think the general would keep his side of the bargain.

"You agreed to let them go," she screamed, lunging toward the general. Before she could dig her shoulder into his chest, someone kicked the back of her thighs, forcing her to kneel.

A young soldier approached the general, whispering low,

yet loud enough for her to hear. "What about the other escape pod, sir. Should we pursue?"

"Don't waste your time," General Adams told the soldier and then nodded over at Ia. "She's the one we want."

Still seething, Ia whispered a silent plea, praying Einn would find the first escape pod. He would see that those Tawnies were safe. And after that, he would come to rescue her. Guns in both hands, he would board the ship they were in and shoot the general right between the eyes.

The general noticed her glare. He crouched to face her. His rough fingers gripped her chin so she couldn't look away. "You lost, Cōcha. What do you have to say for yourself?"

If she couldn't escape and she couldn't kill him, she decided to do the next best thing. Like a viper, she sprung her head forward, her aim sharp and certain. Her forehead cracked the general hard in the nose.

Seconds later, the hard grip of a pistol smacked her in the back of the head. She fell forward, catching a wonderful glimpse of blood dripping down the general's lips and chin. Before she slipped into unconsciousness, she smiled.

If she was going down, she was going to do it one way and one way alone.

Gloriously.

CHAPTER 2

BRINN

BRINN TARVER PUSHED through the burgeoning crowd. The Provenance Day Parade was in full swing, and she wanted to get a good spot for the air show.

"Wait up," her fifteen-year-old brother, Faren, cried out from behind.

Brinn turned and a lock of brown hair fell over her eyes. She'd dyed it last night, and the sharp smell of chemicals still lingered in its strands. Her fingers fumbled, trying to set the stray wisp of hair back in place. She waited until she spotted her brother's unmistakably round face. Like everyone else in the crowd—and everyone celebrating the parade in the other territories—the two of them were adorned in the colors of the Olympus Commonwealth. Faren wore a red hooded sweater with a white brimmed hat, while she was dressed in a white blouse and red cardigan.

"What took you so long?" she asked as her brother neared.

Faren's eyes were glued to his holoscreen. "The Poddi

championships are about to start! I can't miss the tip-off."

"Celebrating the birth of our Commonwealth is way more important than that silly game."

"Are you serious?" Faren wrinkled his forehead and looked at her like she had spouted gibberish. "Wait. Don't even answer."

Brinn laughed. Faren knew Provenance Day was her favorite holiday. Their mother and father had stopped going to the parades, but it had become a special day for both Brinn and her brother, one meant just for the two of them.

They wiggled their way to the front of the crowd. Brinn had noticed a couple familiar faces, fellow students from primaries, and waved politely to some of them as she passed. It was a simple, empty gesture, something that made them look at her for a second and then move on to another face.

A few feet away was Angie Everett, the most popular girl in her school. Angie seemed to have found her prey for the day, laughing at a refugee girl across the street because her long, braided hairstyle was out of fashion.

From the moment the Uranium War started until the Armistice over a year ago, the war had displaced huge populations of people all across the Fringe. Some of them chose to drift, to stay in the Fringe. But others had decided to seek sanctuary within the Commonwealth, leading to its current refugee crisis.

Judging by the refugee girl's long, flowing attire and the markings that encircled her eyes, Brinn recognized her as a Makolian. She stood with a few other refugees around Brinn's age. While many of them were dressed in the red and white of Olympus, they still wore clothes that were distinct from their planetary regions.

"Her outfit is so offworld," Angie said loudly. She didn't even have to point and laugh; her friends did it for her.

As Brinn watched, she couldn't help but think how things could have been different for them. If the Makolian girl and her ref friends were smart about it, they'd be able to avoid detection. It was easy. Sometimes all it took was a little hair dye to blend into the crowd.

She glanced over at Faren's brilliant brown hair, a slightly lighter shade than hers, and reached out to ruffle his coarse locks. Much to his protest, she had helped him touch up his roots two days prior. No one in their school knew that both her and her brother's hair were a different color all together. A very different deep navy blue.

Only one refugee population was known for that color: Tawnies. Brinn wasn't a child of the war; her mother hailed from Tawnus but had married into Citizenship before the war broke out, and Brinn and her brother had been born right here on Nova Grae. Even so, Brinn had to be careful.

If Angie or anyone else in school ever discovered her secret...She didn't even want to think about it. All she needed was to stay off their radar for a few more days until graduation. She'd gone to huge lengths to make very careful mistakes on all her tests to hide the fact that she had an IQ beyond genius level. It wasn't just the bullying she feared. It went beyond that. If she was ever outed as a Tawny, she could be denied admission to the universities, and no one would hire her once she was ready to enter the workforce. She might be a Citizen, but that didn't matter—the prejudice still existed.

Around her, everyone cheered as a large holoscreen floated

down the street with the portrait of Queen Lind and her wife, Queen Juo, the ruling matriarchs of the Olympus crown family. Behind that screen floated large holoportraits of the military's celebrated leaders, including Captain Nema, the man leading the successful colonization effort in the Fringe, and General Adams, whose bloodthirsty tactics had produced several victories during the Uranium War.

"It's the same faces on those screens every year," Faren said with a yawn.

Brinn shushed him. "These people are the pillars of our society."

"Maybe you should go into politics," he joked.

Brinn laughed. "Mom would kill me."

Their mom wanted Brinn to be a history scholar, but Brinn still had her application for Nova Grae University sitting in her drafts folder. She knew she'd be good at it. History was all about memorizing dates and names, cataloging old battles and ancient treaties. But she didn't know if it was something she wanted to do for the rest of her life. Besides, she wanted to travel. And if she decided to study history, she'd be stuck on Nova Grae for the next four years—something she wasn't exactly excited about.

"You know what Mom always says…" Faren took on the high-pitched tone of their mother's voice. "You need to use that brain our ancestors gave you."

Brinn furrowed her brow. She was always amazed at how careless Faren was about talking about their lineage. She glanced at the crowd around them and lowered her voice. "Keep it down. You don't know who'll hear."

Just then, a holographic banner rounded the corner at the end of the street. Enlist in the Royal Star Force. Your strength is in the Commonwealth. In bright-yellow letters.

The RSF enlistment banner only meant one thing.

Brinn tugged at her brother's sleeve and pointed up into the shimmering blue sky. "The air show is about to start."

Two RSF starjets, white like doves, swooped through a plume of clouds, racing alongside each other until they were faster than sound itself. A deep boom shook the ground the moment the twin jets broke the sound barrier, causing the smaller children around Brinn and Faren to wail out.

But the noise didn't bother Brinn. She envied the flyers in those jets. At least they were heading somewhere.

After watching the twin jets fly toward the horizon, she looked back down from the skies and noticed that no one else was watching. A chilling hush swept across the crowd as dings pulsed on people's holowatches, and soon everyone had their eyes on their holoscreens. People were frozen, like time was standing still.

Brinn looked over to Faren, who was also gazing down at his screen. "What's going on? Did the Poddi championship start?"

Faren tilted his head up. His eyes were round with a strange, nervous excitement, and he pointed up at the large floating displays in the middle of the parade. All of them had switched onto the same news stream with text scrolling across the screen. RSF capture outlaw I. A. Cōcha appeared in bold yellow letters. The words cycled over and over on top of footage of Commonwealth starjets circling around a black traveling ship.

The crowd erupted into a thunder of cheers. Brinn grabbed Faren's hand to make sure she wasn't dreaming. And when she felt his fingers squeeze hers, she knew it wasn't a dream at all. No, it was real. The legendary outlaw had been captured. Brinn thought about the time Cōcha destroyed their system's interstellar gate, along with others across the Commonwealth. It caused panic all throughout the territories and a huge crash in the economic market. It was a day that everyone on Nova Grae wished to forget, watching the arches of their gate explode in the upper heights of the sky.

And today was yet another one of those momentous days. But instead of it being filled with hushed, fearful whispers, they would remember the cheers, the pride, the raised fists in the air. This was a day that would define her for the rest of her life. Energy crackled through the crowd, in the spaces between one person and the next. It was something that connected Brinn to everyone at the parade. No, bigger than that. It linked her with every Citizen in the Commonwealth.

Faren looked over at her and laughed.

"What?"

"That look on your face." Faren flicked his holowatch and brought up a camera screen, turning the view so that the two of them were on the display. "I don't even have to tell you to smile," he teased as he clicked the capture button.

He slid the photo over to her, and she studied it. The joy on her face. Usually, it would make her feel self-conscious. But today, it only made her smile wider, so her teeth showed, and she laughed.

Faren was better with humor and emotion than she was. He was an open book. But unrestrained feeling was difficult for her. It was something she'd inherited from her mother. It connected her to the Tawnies, to the unwanted history that flowed through her veins. But the smile on her face showed that she could break away from that. That there was a different part of her. She had always wanted that sense of brotherhood with her fellow Citizens. To completely belong. And she felt it now.

The news anchor's voice rang crystal clear throughout the street. "We've just received a report that RSF has released new footage."

Everyone quieted, and like the people around her, Brinn held her breath so she could take in every detail, etching all the images into her memory. The screen cut to black. Brinn edged forward, squinting as she tried to make out the images on the darkened display. The iris on the media Eyes adjusted, and details bled in. In the center of the frame was a girl with black hair, disheveled and cut short to her shoulders. A purpling bruise bloomed on her forehead, but despite that, the girl looked confident and strong, her mouth set in a grimace, as if she was about to spit into the camera lens itself.

Was this girl...

No way. Brinn always had a specific image of I. A. Cōcha in her mind. A tall man with a face full of a scars, a mouthful of missing teeth. And much, much older. Not a girl just like her.

"Deus," Faren said breathlessly. "Are those Tawnies?"

On screen, the Eyes flashed their lights on the people in the background, sitting behind I. A. Cōcha. The bright lights washed out their faces, but despite the dirt and grime, the color of their hair was unmistakable. Different. A Tawny blue. Just like her mother's.

Brinn's eyes fell to the group of refugees across the street, and her heart dropped when she saw there were also Tawnies in the crowd. This wasn't going to be good.

Soon, she noticed people staring at them with eyes narrowing into angry slits, transferring their rage from the screens above to what was standing before them.

"Criminals!" someone cried. "Dirty Mungbringers!"

Brinn flinched. *Mungbringers.* A cruel nickname that people had called Tawnies since the start of the Uranium War. The war began when the Tawnies had refused to accept the Olympus Commonwealth's invitation to become a part of their territories. The Commonwealth invaded, and the surrounding Fringe planets retaliated. War broke out, with huge losses on both sides. And though the Commonwealth prevailed, everyone still faulted the Tawnies, which was the main reason that Brinn hid her lineage.

"Go back to where you came from, Mungbringers!"

"You Mungbringers started the war," another yelled. "And now this!"

What started as a celebration was now turning into an angry mob.

People pushed closer, and Brinn was pulled along with them. She grabbed Faren's shoulder, trying to protect him from the surge of the crowd. "We need to get out of here."

Faren turned to face her. "Should we do something to help them?"

She cast one last look at the fear in the Tawnies' eyes, matched in the expressions of the Tawny outlaws being projected on the screens above.

Brinn shook her head. "No."

And she pulled him away from the crowd.

* * *

They walked down the sidewalks. Their house came into view, angular and gray like all the other cube houses in their residential sector. The door was already open, their father, Charles, standing in the doorway. The expression on his face was fraught with worry. Their mother, Brinn noticed, was absent from his side.

Their father ushered them inside and closed the door, blocking out the excited clamor spilling in from the streets. Their mother, Ana, swept toward them. Her navy-blue hair was pinned up into an elegant updo. When Brinn was a young child, she remembered her mother's hair dyed a rich mahogany, but before Brinn started early primaries, her mom decided to let it grow for some reason. It started with her roots, and now every strand bore the unmistakable navy of Tawnus.

Brinn had begged her to keep away from their schools, so her father was the only person who came to Parents' Day. Her mother knew her natural hair color would mark her in public, that she'd be heckled and cursed even during a short trip to the grocery store, so she usually stayed home. Despite all this, her mother kept her hair blue anyway.

Brinn had asked her mother once why she never dyed it back to brown. *So I can remember*, her mother had replied. To this day, Brinn never understood.

Maybe it was because Brinn had no idea what Tawnus was like. She had never seen it. She didn't even know its history, because it wasn't *hers*. Her father had dragged their family to the museums and historical sites of Nova Grae every summer since they were toddlers. The history she knew was that of the Olympus Commonwealth—of its monuments and heroes. And she couldn't name a popular Tawny figure, even if her life depended on it. Instead, she grew up watching famous Olympus stream stars like actioneer Gava Gable and Faren's favorite, Kinna Downton.

Brinn was technically half-Tawny, but in her eyes, she was a Commonwealth Citizen through and through. *Only* a Commonwealth Citizen.

"Thank Deus, you're safe." Her mother exhaled. "There might be a riot."

"Did you look outside? It's not a riot. It's a celebration." Tension crackled in the air between them. It was just like her mother to see today as a day of warning.

Sensing the shift in tone, her father stepped in between them. "Everyone's tired. Maybe it's time we all get to bed…"

But Brinn ignored him.

"The Royal Star Force just captured the most wanted criminal in the known territories," she explained to her mother.

"And we should applaud them?" her mother asked, scoffing. "For capturing a child."

"That girl is the same person who held High Governor Malo for ransom, the same person who destroyed our nearest gate so we didn't have supplies for weeks."

Brinn felt Faren at her side, tugging her sleeve so she would stop, to ground her from all the anger charging up inside her. But it wasn't enough.

"And what about them?" Her mother pointed to the holo-screen in the living area, replaying the footage from Ia's capture, showing Tawnies taking up arms. "Are you so quick to condemn them? Those are my people." Her gaze shifted to Faren and then landed on Brinn. "They're *our* people."

Brinn almost wanted to laugh. Being Tawny was the reason why she needed to be careful every day of her life, the reason she pretended to be someone else entirely. And now the Tawnies were harboring the most wanted criminal in the universe and killing Star Force officers?

The smile that Brinn wore on the streets had been soured, replaced with an expression more defiant. She felt like there was a line between her and her mother, something that could never be erased.

The words spilled out of her mouth. "They're *criminals*, Mom."

Brinn's mother was not a violent person. That was why it surprised Brinn when her mother's hand came down across Brinn's cheek with such force that she fell to the ground.

Faren knelt to help her up, but Brinn pushed him away. She massaged the sting on her cheek, feeling the pain resonate from the surface of her skin to deep inside her core.

Her father was at her mother's side, whispering into her ear to try to calm her down.

But he couldn't undo what had been done.

At that moment, a deep boom shook the ground. Brinn recognized the sound, and she looked out through the windows at the night sky crackling with fireworks, blazing red and white with hope. She saw the two twin jets from the air show earlier, flying through the clouds, ready to break the sound barrier once again. Brinn thought back to the overwhelming pride and camaraderie she'd felt when they had announced I. A. Cōcha's capture. If the Royal Star Force was able to catch the most fearsome criminal in the known universe, then there was no limit to what they could accomplish.

Her mind calmed with realization. There was a reason why her application to Nova Grae University was still sitting unsent. Being a history scholar was her mother's dream for Brinn, but it wasn't her own. History was an examination of the past, but there was no hope in the past, only sadness and despair. All she wanted to do was look ahead where the future was bright and blinding. And hers.

Without taking her gaze from the sky, Brinn spoke the words so everyone could hear, "It's not perfect, but I believe in our Commonwealth." Then she looked back at her mother, eyes brimming with a new sense of purpose. "I'm joining the Star Force."

CHAPTER 3
IA

THE ROOM WAS a large metal box. Totally bare except for a tubelike holding cell in the middle.

That was where they kept her. Like an animal in the zoo.

Ia sat inside, waiting, observing. She didn't dare touch the walls of her prison. Even a slight zelimeter of contact would knock her out for a whole week. The Star Force used contact shields on all their cells. She'd found this out two years ago when she broke Einn out of a high-level prison. She could still remember the smell of electrified flesh. She'd had to blow up the conductors deep underneath the prison itself so he could break free.

And now, how was she going to get herself out of this one? Surveillance cameras were mounted in each corner of the room. All Eyes were on her.

She tilted her head, getting a view of the ceiling and lowered her left eyelid enough to activate the artificial eye mod grafted onto the back of her retina. She had gotten the implant a year ago at a starship colony deep in Dead Space. Deus, was it expensive! She had to sell off her favorite energy gauntlets, but having an eye mod in her arsenal was worth it. It allowed her to make proper measurements and switch to thermal imaging, along with a lot of other fun perks.

A light vibration fluttered over the surface of her eye as numbers swelled in her vision. She focused on a single point above her, letting the measurements readjust. 10m.

Too high.

Even if she was able to climb up there, she would still have to get out of the handcuffs trapping both of her hands. When they'd cuffed her, the first thing she spotted was an escape sensor hidden along the rim of each brace. If she attempted to pull her wrists away from each other, the sensor would trigger a line of metal spurs to shoot down from the palm of each unit, shredding the flesh on her hands. She really didn't want to get fitted with robotic limbs when this was all over.

The Commonwealth was taking ridiculous precautions to keep her contained.

But she would figure it out. Eventually.

With nothing else to do, she thought about her life before her capture and the people who were important to her. There was Einn, of course. He meant everything to her; she didn't know how her life would be without him. But she also had a crew of Drifters and deviants who helped her do all the impossible things she set out to do. Like her comms expert, Trace, who was unmatched in decrypting stolen messages and in a totally different league when it came to delivering terrible jokes. And then there was Vetty, her engineer and her second-in-command. It was hard to forget that roguish face, with his strong jaw and dimpled chin, his bright-green eyes and tangle of curly hair. He always made her blush when he looked at her, even months after they had broken up.

Before she and her crew had parted ways last year, she had ordered them to dock in the Midas Belt just to stay off grid. It was a good decision. After the Uranium War ended in an armistice, the Commonwealth had put all of its war resources into tracking down her and the other Most Wanteds. The risk was too great, and she didn't want to put her crew in too much danger.

She'd rip the eye mod out of her socket if it meant she could be with them again.

A soft whirr echoed throughout the metal room, and a door in the far wall slid open. General Adams stepped inside. Even with the low light, she spotted the brand-new medal—a bloodstained star—pinned on the pocket of his chest.

General Adams's voice boomed, echoing against the metal walls. "Who knew that the great I. A. Cōcha would turn out to be a seventeen-year-old girl?"

Ia sighed. "I did. I knew." She ignored the scathing look he threw at her and asked, "Who tipped you off to my location?"

"Why are you so sure we had help?"

Ia cocked her head in his direction. "Because Bugs aren't that smart."

"The day of your capture, we received a message. Completely untraceable. You must have a lot of enemies, Ms. Cōcha."

Her mind flicked through her memories, trying to identify anyone who would betray her. She knew there were people who wanted to hand her in, but they never did. Because if they indeed stabbed her in the back, she would more than likely survive. And when she returned, the first thing she would do was kill them. And it wouldn't be a clean death. Oh no, it would be dirty, until all she could see was red.

General Adams turned to a thin wisp of a man standing behind him, dressed in a large, black robe like the Grim Reaper himself. His cloak blended so thoroughly into the shadows of the room that Ia almost hadn't noticed him.

"Let's get on with it," Adams said.

The man stepped up, adjusting the laurels around his head. Ia's eyes widened in recognition.

Not the Grim Reaper, she realized, but a judge.

They were going to sentence her. She had been certain they'd televise everything to the masses, from her sentencing all the way up to her execution. But surprisingly, the media and its floating Eyes were nowhere in sight.

The judge focused on her. "Ms. Ia Cōcha, you are charged with high-level criminal actions against the Commonwealth of Olympus, including theft, smuggling, assault, and first-degree mass murder."

She frowned. The Commonwealth always loved listing her "crimes." Every time they did a news story on her, it was all the same. They vilified her. Sure, she killed people, but those people had killed hundreds before she got her hands on them. It was a bloody, bone-breaking kind of justice, but it was still justice.

General Adams clasped his hands behind his back. "If it were up to me, you'd get the death penalty. But since you're a minor, there is now a question of ethics. So Ms. Cōcha, you have a choice."

"How charitable," she muttered.

The judge continued. "You are being sentenced to 120 years in prison on Moon 42."

"You can't be serious" she blurted out. Moon 42 was a penal colony filled with rapists and sexual deviants. They would tear her apart. She did what she could to stop the shiver of fear inside her.

"Or"—whatever it was, it had to be better than Moon 42— "you can choose a twenty-year interim with the Royal Star Force of the Olympus Commonwealth, to begin immediately with two years of training."

She had been wrong. This option was a hundred times worse.

"You want *me* to be a Bug?" Her voice echoed through the metal room. "You destroyed my planet. I lost my home and my mother. Why would I join you?" The RSF had led a war that destroyed civilizations; their greed created chaos. They were everything that was wrong with the universe.

General Adams leaned in so his eyes reflected the blue of the contact shield between them. "So what is it, Cōcha? Which do you choose?"

The answer was obvious. "Neither."

"I figured you might say that." The general stepped back, his arms crossed, the index finger of one hand tapping lightly on the Commonwealth quartered shield embroidered onto his sleeve. "I'll give you more time to think about it."

Ia watched as he trotted out of the room, the light jingle of his medals souring her silence.

* * *

The next morning, Ia woke up groggy, her head in a fog like she'd been drugged. But instead of rubbing circles at her temples, she grabbed at her chest. Because the pain there was... Well, the best word for it was *memorable*.

It felt like a handful of needles had stabbed her in her heart, a cold chill radiating outward from her left side. And then she felt the squeeze, like someone had made a fist around that tiny muscle in her rib cage. She punched above her breast where her heart would be, lightly at first. And then harder, because the pain was getting worse.

She fell to her side, her back arching to relieve the pain, but it was still there.

A full thirty seconds later, she felt her heart pulsate inside her, like a rusty old engine finally sputtering on after several tries.

"Thank Deus," she murmured, her body shaking even as she hugged her arms across her chest. After a few breaths, she was back to normal, and her heart felt like her heart again.

But then, five minutes later, it happened again.

And again.

And again.

* * *

It had been a week of torture. There were hours when it didn't happen at all. Other times, the heart trauma was a tiny blip, brief as fluttering eyelids. But that day, the pain came at her swinging. For one whole minute, her heart stopped, and exactly at the sixty-second mark, it pumped again. Like clockwork. Very unnatural clockwork. She had ten minutes to rest before the cycle restarted. Whatever they had put inside her knew her body's limits exactly, ebbing Ia to and from death's grip. It kept her stuck inside a painful, vicious loop, pushing her not only to the brink of death, but also to the brink of insanity.

Above her, the cameras hummed. They were her only companions. Watching. Always watching as she grew tired, weaker.

Her heart paused yet again. She coiled into a ball, holding her breath to try to quell her shaking body. *No more*, she wanted to cry, but when she spoke, the words came out a jumbled mess.

At the far wall, past her cell, the door opened. Footsteps pinged in staccato toward her, and it was only when he was at the edge of her cell that she saw the general's face, awash with blue light from the contact shield surrounding her enclosure.

"What did you do to me?" Her voice was so weak it bled into the hum of the lights above. "An implant?"

He smiled. "The first of its kind. It can track your location, and as you already know, it can do other things."

Her heart's pause was at forty seconds when she found the energy to roll up on her knees as if in prayer, staring up at the man towering before her. His harsh features, his stitched brow.

"Kill me," she pleaded.

General Adams plucked something out of his inner pocket. A silver oblong orb. He swiped at the orb, and she gasped as her heart twitched back to life again.

"We're not going to kill you," the general said. "That would be too humane."

Her voice trembled inside her throat. "What do you want?"

"The offer still stands, Cōcha. Train at our academy. We can ship you out to Aphelion in a week."

He stood, eyes burning into her as he waited for her response. And she hated every second of it. Because she knew she was a trophy to him. Something he had captured to display for all the universe to see. Her body was so weak she could barely hold herself up, but her eyes didn't waver, still holding on to her defiance. She wouldn't live as the Commonwealth's pawn, a weapon to wield at their disposal.

"I see you need more time to consider," he said when she had failed to produce an answer. The general tapped on the silver egg-shaped remote in his hand, and the pain began all over again. Ia fell to her side and watched him walk back toward the door, each footstep spanning a lifetime.

She had no other choice.

"Wait," she said so he could hear her. "Wait…"

CHAPTER 4
KNIVES

APHELION'S FLIGHT DECK was busy with activity as everyone readied the grounds for the new cadets, but Knives ignored it all and hurried down the tarmac toward his jet. If he wanted to get a flight in, he needed to do it within the next five minutes—a geomagnetic storm was scheduled to hit later that night.

A lock of sandy-blond hair fell over his eyes, but he paid it no mind, barely looking up as engineers in orange suits scurried around him, fixing up the refurb training jets. No one wanted the new batch of cadets to die while training on their first day.

"Flight master," Headmaster Bastian Weathers called out. "A word, please."

At nineteen, Knives was the youngest flight master in RSF history. It wasn't a position he'd wanted straight out of the academy, but after suddenly turning down a high-ranking spot on his first colonization campaign days before its launch, he was grateful to have a job at all.

Knives turned to face the headmaster, once his teacher, now his boss. He was probably there to lecture Knives about how to encourage the new cadets. *Let them grow*, Bastian had already told him. A thousand times over and over, like a sputtering radio unit.

"We need to talk about tomorrow."

"I know you're worried since it'll be my first day on the job, but seriously, Bastian, it'll be fine," Knives murmured as he continued toward the prep track. Above him, his 504 Kaiken hung in the rafters. With its long, sleek frame, the jet was a milestone in aerodynamic engineering. Fifteen years ago, they were used as racers. Now, they were obsolete. But even so, the metal beast was fast. He knew his father could have bought him a new model, fresh off the assembly line, but the Kaiken was the first thing he'd purchased himself. Who cared that he still had two years worth of payments left?

Knives pressed a few buttons on the console next to him, triggering the holding track to lower his jet for prep.

Bastian was still behind him. "I must warn you. This class will be unique. Since the broadcast, the number of applicants has soared."

Everyone knew what "the broadcast" meant. It was a historic event, a day the entire universe stood still just to watch I. A. Cōcha unmasked and captured. It made everyone want to be a hero.

"There are more of them this year. So what? Not all of them are going to last." Knives wasn't going to go easy on them. He was going to work the new cadets until they ran home, crying to their parents. Until they had nightmares of him. Because he knew what they all wanted to eventually become. A general. Like his father. He felt pity for them, that their dreams weren't their own.

If Knives applied himself, perhaps he could be as good as his father, but what was the point? His sister had tried, and as much as he wanted to, he'd never forget what happened to her.

"It's more than that," Bastian said. "I've received word of a late registrant. A celebrity of sorts."

"Please tell me it's Kinna Downton." It was a joke, but who was he kidding…Of course, he wished Kinna Downton, the famous and beautiful stream star, was a prospective cadet.

Bastian rolled his eyes. "No, it's not."

"Then I don't care." Knives tapped at his holowatch, initiating a program to warm up the engine of his jet. He'd be spacebound in two minutes, if Bastian would ever stop talking.

"She's a high-security registrant. Goes by many names. The Rogue of the Fringe. The Sovereign of Dead Space. The Hunter throughout the Wasteland. The Blood Wolf of the Skies…"

Knives rolled a ladder up to his jet, ready to get into the cockpit. "Who?"

"The one and only Ia Cōcha." Bastian pronounced every syllable. Loud and clear.

Knives stopped in his place. "Oh."

Bastian raised his hands. "I know. I know. You're wondering what on Ancient Earth a high-level criminal is doing at the academy."

Knives shrugged. "Even if she's a criminal, Ia Cōcha is one of the best pilots of our generation. What's left to teach?"

"You're not going to teach her. You're going to try your best to keep her on a leash. General Adams specifically made this request."

Knives clenched his fist. Of course this was his father's idea. He was always trying to test him, make him rise to the miffing occasion.

"Tell the general that I politely decline. This is a Star Force issue." He had told his father that while he was at Aphelion, he had absolutely no interest in getting involved with anything outside the academy. But his father never listened.

"No, Knives. She will be at the academy, so this is *our* issue. Do you understand?"

Knives stiffened at Bastian's tense tone. "Yes. I do."

Bastian nodded in approval and handed him a silver remote, shaped like a tiny egg. Knives looked it over, feeling the weight in his palm and the chill of the metal against his skin.

"What's this?"

"The leash," Bastian answered, and he turned to walk away.

Knives looked back down at his holowatch and checked the time.

"Mif." He sighed.

He needed to be in the sky fifty-six seconds ago. He glanced out the opening of the flight deck and stared at the purpling night. A trail of shimmering green light snaked across the sky. The geomagnetic storm. If he flew through that, his jet would be fried.

Now stranded, he looked back down at the silver remote in his hand and made a fist. It felt like a bomb, ready to go off and ruin his entire year.

CHAPTER 5

IA

IA WAS ON A SHIP TO APHELION. Even among the
Dead Spacers and criminals, Aphelion was famous. Everyone
knew that it was Olympus's first Star Force Academy, respon-
sible for training some of the RSF's most celebrated captains
and generals.

Its location was one of their most guarded secrets. Ia had
discovered that not even the Commonwealth's own Citizens
knew, right after she had tortured one of them for information and got nothing. She couldn't even find a name of a star
system to point her in the right direction.

With her hands still bound, Ia was harnessed inside a storage cage, now a makeshift prison cell for the duration of the
trip. There were no windows within her viewpoint. All she
saw was the general glaring at her from across the bars of her
door, the sound of his breathing whistling against the thrum
of the ship.

"We're here." The general's sudden announcement broke

the silence, which gave her a start. She was still on edge from being pushed to the brink of death every fifteen minutes while she was imprisoned. Her head wasn't running on all thrusters. And her face was another problem, she realized when she finally found herself in front of a mirror before their journey. The pain from the forced heart tremors was so immense the blood vessels had ruptured in both her eyes. Even now, they were still red where the whites should be. She was miffing scary to look at, but not in a way she was proud of.

She felt her feet pitch underneath her and noticed they were descending.

Two days of travel. And finally, they had landed. Somewhere.

The fact that they traveled for so long meant that Aphelion was far from the Commonwealth's most populated centers. That was the only clue she had, and it told her nothing. They could be anywhere.

The general opened the storage cage, undid her harness, and led her to the entry deck. The metal ramp lowered to the ground. Slowly, slowly, until sunlight blasted at her face. The air outside was freezing. The chill cut straight to her bones, even with the thermal balancing fibers woven throughout her suit.

The world outside was white with snow. Their ship had landed on a platform high upon the cliff of a mountain. Jagged peaks surrounded them, shielding their location from anyone who dared to follow. There were no man-made structures where they stood, but Ia spotted a cargo shaft that could only lead downward to sublevels hidden within the mountain itself.

It was a clever place to build an academy.

Ia glanced at the general. "What's your game? Why here? I'm a *criminal*."

General Adams clasped his hands behind his back. "This isn't a game. It's better to have you in here working for us instead of out there making alliances with someone worse."

"Who's worse than me?" she sneered. Because there wasn't anyone. She was the beast that everyone feared.

"You really don't know anything." His tone was different this time, not angry with spite, but cautious like he was keeping something from her. At this point, her pride had swelled too fat, and she couldn't ask. So, she pursed her lips and spat at his feet.

His hand landed hard in between her shoulder blades, shoving her down the ship's ramp. She stumbled forward into the packed snow. She stared down at her fingers, growing red against the ice.

"Thank you." Her eyes met the general's, wishing nothing more but to razor blade the smug look off his stone-cold face. "I will *so* enjoy running rampant in your academy. I'll eat your useless cadets alive, and it'll be easy without you here."

General Adams clicked his teeth, unfazed by her threat. "I'm not an idiot, Cōcha. I assigned someone else to watch you while I'm gone. And he's me, but younger and faster…though maybe not as smart. He will, however, have one of these."

He plucked the silver remote from his pocket, balancing it between his forefinger and thumb for her to see. She cringed, knowing all too well what that little thing could do.

Through the swirl of snow, she spotted a growing sliver of light coming from the cargo shaft as the elevator doors opened and figures from inside approached. Two guards, followed by an older man dressed in a black, fur-trimmed hooded over-coat. His eyebrows were thick and white, and his skin was a warm shade of brown. A boy with fair complexion followed behind him, wearing a RSF flight suit and a brown leather bomber jacket. From the light scruff dappling his jawline, she could tell he was around Einn's age.

The new party trudged through the snow and stopped before them.

"Headmaster. Flight master," the general said, addressing both of them respectively. She figured that the older man was the headmaster of Aphelion. And the boy, he was the flight master? He looked much too young. "She's all yours," the general said and then turned back to face her. His words bit through the cold. "Remember where you are, Ia. This is the Commonwealth now."

If anything, they were the ones who should be worried. Sending a known criminal to work with the Royal Star Force, where she could see all of their weaknesses. She could even sell the information to the highest Dead Space bidder once she managed to escape, which—from looking at this place—wouldn't take too long. Even so, she was still cautious about their motives for bringing her here. They wanted to keep her away from someone, but she had no idea who.

Hands gripped at her arms. Ia sized up the two academy guards beside her. One had impeccable posture and an abnormally symmetrical face, while the other had stronger features, very spare eyebrows paired with a sharper nose. This one was larger than the other, but soft and out of shape. Out of the two of them, he'd be easier to overpower. But then she saw that they were armed. Plus, there were the headmaster and the young flight master to worry about. Now wasn't the right time to attempt her escape.

The headmaster stepped forward, kindness in his eyes. "Welcome to the Star Force, Ia." He looked over to the general. "General Adams, would you switch over the print locks on her handcuffs?"

The general stepped forward, his breath swirling into heated clouds in the small space between them. He grabbed her cuffs, angling them so he could access the display on the side. The general pressed his thumb on the sensor, resetting the print lock, then nodded for the flight master to step forward.

The young flight master looked her up and down with his cold blue eyes. "You're shorter in person," he whispered under his breath as he pressed his thumb down on the sensor so it would recognize his print.

Her eyes narrowed at him. One day, he would realize that deadly things also come in small packages.

But then she realized something.

"Faster. Stronger...maybe not as smart," she repeated and looked over to the general. "This is him, isn't it?"

The general said nothing, so Ia turned back to the boy and examined him. His blond hair was long, like he was outgrowing a military cut, but his face was unmarred minus the slight scar along his jawline. His skin lacked the cuts and injuries that came from actual fighting experience. If he was in charge of watching her, escaping would be easy.

Suddenly, his eyes flicked up from the scan, and he noticed her staring. He glared at her, his irises crystalizing into a more frightening blue, like cracks upon a frozen pond.

The cuffs beeped. The new print lock was scanned and active.

"It's done," the general said.

"Well, then," the headmaster began and swept his arm toward the cargo elevator. "Shall we? We don't want to be too late for the Welcome Assembly."

When they were in the cargo elevator, she looked back outside, peering through the gusts of snowfall. She saw the general watching her from the entryway of his ship.

"This isn't over," she yelled, loud enough that the wind would carry her words. "I'll take this thing out of my chest, and I'll be coming for you."

The general roared with laughter, then pressed a button on the frame of his ship, triggering the ramp to raise. Soon, all she could see of him was the contempt nestled in the darks of his eyes. She was his prisoner, a dog on a leash, and if she ever ran, all he had to do was yank at the chain.

Ia closed her eyes and prayed for Einn to save her.

When she opened them, she caught a glimpse of the ship retreating beyond the salt-gray clouds before the elevator doors slid closed with a rumbling thud.

The ground hummed underneath her feet. She made a quick inspection of her surroundings. The elevator had high ceilings and was wide enough to fit a row of five starjets on the platform. There was no control board, which meant there would be no other stops on the way down and no way for her to reverse the direction of the elevator midway through its descent. She spotted two cameras on the opposite corners of the elevator and a row of vents on the ceiling, before her gaze landed back on the cuffs digging into her wrists and hands. If she could get out of these cuffs, she'd be able to steal their pistols and escape. But only print scans would unlock them. It would be difficult to do, but not impossible.

The headmaster turned to speak to the flight master, and Ia's guards were both a step in front of her, facing forward.

None of them would see, if she was careful.

She stretched the muscles of her hand, flicking her thumb to scratch at the tip of her index finger. Her skin grew warm as a spongy, light pink gel formed on the surface of her fingertip. She thanked Deus her imprinting system was still equipped. Before finding herself on the Tawny ship, she was on a mission where she had to break into a slaver's vault. Slavers always kept their goods under heavy lock and finger-imprinted key. Sponge imprint tips—or "Tips," as everyone in Dead Space called them—were an absolute must, as rare as they were. She'd had to call in a lot of favors in order to find a reliable dealer. Poor-quality Tips usually warped the imprints and, more often then not, burned right through your skin.

Ia looked down at her thumb, where the Tip had shifted back to her natural flesh color. It was ready to go. All she needed was a clean print.

A few feet away from her, the headmaster thumbed through a faded leather journal. She stared at it, wondering why anyone chose to record anything on something as archaic as paper.

He looked up from his pages, his gaze resting on her. "I know this may be different for you, working where there are rules and orders. Due to the seriousness of your past crimes, we've decided to take away a few of your privileges for your own safety and the safety of your peers. At least until you've fully assimilated."

The headmaster handed the journal over to the boy.

"Flight master, please continue."

The boy glanced down and then quickly exchanged a surprised look with the headmaster as if it was the first time he had ever seen the document.

The flight master began to read. "You will have no guns, weapons, or any type of ammunition. You are prohibited from any connection with the ArcLite to prevent you from getting hold of your crew."

A wrinkled line formed in between her brows at the mention of her crew. Einn knew about her capture, but as for the rest of her crew of misfits, she hadn't the slightest idea if the news had actually reached them.

"Hand sanitizer, gum, lipstick, and anything else that can be used to craft explosives will be confiscated from your person." The flight master's cold voice echoed around her, and Ia was instantly reminded that she was no longer in the company of friends.

"And one more thing," the boy said. "You will be bound twenty-four hours a day. Except during lessons and scheduled meal hours."

"So when I go to the bathroom, you'll be wiping for me?"

"If that's what you want." The boy looked up from the journal with a daring grin on his face, which only made her want to rip his throat out.

"Anything else?" she asked.

"I know you're trying to figure out how to escape," the boy said smugly. He pointed up at the ceiling. "Those vents are welded down with a solid layer of pure vinnidium and sealed with five inches of concrete. The ceilings are thirty meters high, impossible to get to unless you have a windpack." He shrugged. "I dare you to try though. It will make things more fun."

She sneered at him. Didn't he know it was dangerous to poke a stick at a sleeping beast?

Just then, the elevator hit a bump, dropping a few feet. She stumbled forward, her knees hitting the floor.

Ia held her bound hands up to the flight master. "A little help?"

The boy grabbed her hand, clutching onto her fingers, and hoisted her up.

She simpered, softening her voice to sound like that Kinna Downton that all the boys loved. "Thanks."

As she did so, she felt his fingerprint set upon the derma-gel on her Tips.

She thought back on the boy's dare. *Try to escape*, he had said.

Well, things were about to get much more fun.

CHAPTER 6

BRINN

BRINN STOOD IN THE MIDDLE of Aphelion's flight deck, her jaw still slack from the sheer size of it all. It was three times the size of the sports arena back home. The mountain's black, petrified walls domed around them like a huge wing, protecting and camouflaging them from any wandering eyes up on the surface.

She saw her shuttle parked against the far wall, right next to other shuttles that had arrived from pickup sites scattered around the Commonwealth, some traveling from much farther away than Nova Grae. She couldn't imagine that; it'd taken them eleven hours of travel to get there. And she still wasn't sure where *there* was—the cabin windows had been blacked out, keeping Aphelion's location a secret.

The cadets were organized in very neat rows in front of a makeshift stage, a white podium positioned in the middle. In front of the podium hung the Olympus Commonwealth's quartered shield. Like the other cadets, Brinn wore a charcoal-gray jumpsuit, issued to her upon registration. Her feet were adorned with regulation leather boots, metal capped on the toe and heel.

A small group of second-year students stood at the front watching them. They wore the same uniform, but instead of a green bar, an orange patch was stitched across each of their chests to denote their second-year status. When the new cadets had first arrived, this same group of Second Years had greeted them, giving them a short tour of the flight deck, which consisted of pointing out that the wing on the opposite side was restricted for only second-year cadets. From their tone and responses, it was clear that there was a firm divide between the new cadets and the senior classes.

A holoscreen floated above the stage with images of the Star Force's most noticeable accomplishments, including footage of Captain Nema fighting off hostile life-forms on the new colonies to the recent gunfight between General Adams and Ia Cōcha.

But by the second or third loop, Brinn started looking around the group. There were cadets from everywhere in the Exo sector—from the desert planet of Nion to the terraformed supercities on Hearth. And no other Tawnies in sight.

It was a clear reminder that while she was away from home, Brinn still had to be careful about exposing her identity, especially with anti-refugee sentiment growing strong among the public since Ia Cōcha's capture.

"Brinn?" a familiar voice called out.

Brinn looked over to see Angie Everett in the crowd.

Angie moved closer and raised a perfectly groomed eyebrow. "I was like, 'Those broad shoulders look so familiar.'"

Self-consciously, Brinn pulled in the tips of her shoulders, trying to make them look smaller. Angie wasn't smart, but she was good at making people feel like complete mung.

"What are you doing here?" Brinn blurted out.

"I enlisted," Angie swept her hands across her flight suit. "Obviously."

How had she managed to miss Angie on the shuttle? There were two tiers of seating, and Brinn had been one of the last cadets to board. It was possible that Angie was sitting out of view on the top floor.

"I think we're the only ones from our school here," Angie said, moving over to stand right next to Brinn. Brinn froze, gripped by panic. She had spent most of her years in primaries avoiding Angie, and now here she was.

"My dad is running for the Council this year," Angie continued, a note of bitterness laced into her crystalline voice. "He thought it would be fitting for his eldest daughter to join the very institution that had caught the most notorious criminal in the known galaxies. It'll guarantee a lot of votes." She peered up at Brinn. "What's your reason?"

Brinn gawked at her. Angie had never asked her a real question before. *Why don't you mif yourself? Why the mif are you even here?* Those were the type of questions Angie usually asked people.

"The same as most," Brinn answered carefully. "I watched that broadcast, and I knew."

"How simple," Angie sighed. Brinn prayed to Deus that Angie would grow tired of her company and move away. But she didn't. She remained fixed in place.

Brinn noticed everyone's eyes on one particular cadet with black hair and an unmistakable dimpled chin, standing in the front row. Nero Sinoblancas was the heir to the Sinoblancas family, one of the oldest families of the Olympus Commonwealth, with ancestors that could be traced back to Ancient Earth. They owned Sino Corp., the largest conglomerate in the known galaxies, which drew in more revenue each year than the royal family.

He was surrounded by cadets who looked just like him. Perfect faces, genetically modified for proportionate features. A regal sloped nose. Round eyes with long lashes. But surprisingly, no more dimpled chins. There were rumors that the Sinoblancas family had patented that genetic modification to keep others from copying it.

Nero scanned the group, sizing up all one hundred of the first-year cadets. Brinn recognized the look in his eyes—like Angie when she was trying to find an easy target. It was strange that Angie hadn't set out to join him.

When Nero's gaze landed on their row, Brinn looked over to a random corner, then to her feet. Finally, her gaze turned up to the starjets hanging from the revolving storage track above.

"Relax. He's already moved on to the next row," a deep voice said beside her.

Brinn turned to face a tall, muscular boy with dark-brown skin and a face made of angular lines. From where she stood, she could see the copper in his eyes, the color of summer leaves before they were about to fall.

"I wasn't worried..." she replied, even though she really was.

"I knew kids like him in primaries. We called them sloggers. Right, Cammo?"

A pale, lanky boy leaned forward at the sound of his name.

"Yeah, sloggers. Just like the nasty bit of grime at the bottom of an oil tank," Cammo said with a grin, showing off the gap in between his two front teeth.

"We had them at our school too," Brinn said. She wanted to gesture toward Angie, standing next to her, but decided it was best not to.

The taller boy stuck out his hand. "I'm Liam, by the way. From the Helios Cluster."

The Helios Cluster was a mining colony upon a large asteroid. He had probably arrived on one of the other shuttles.

She took his hand. "I'm Brinn. From Nova Grae."

"I've always wanted to go there. Be planet-side for a change."

She was shocked by his answer. Nova Grae wasn't a prime destination. It was a minor system that distantly bordered Rigel Kentaurus, the Capital Star System of the Olympus Commonwealth. "There are better places to visit out there."

"Well, it's better than living on a floating rock."

Brinn watched him nervously, feeling something tight inside her chest tug loose.

On her right, Angie had leaned in, her golden hair cascading off one shoulder like a waterfall. She eyed the two new boys and smiled. "I'm Angie. I went to primaries with Brinn."

And then Angie's eyes narrowed, zeroing in on the top of Brinn's head. "Brinn, your hair…"

Brinn's eyes widened as the blood drained from her face. No, please no. She combed her fingers through her hair. She had touched up her roots the morning of her flight, but was it possible that she had missed a few blue strands?

But then Cammo laughed. "It's sticking up."

"Oh." She let out a sigh, silently cursing herself for letting her guard down with Angie. "I slept a lot on the flight so…" She retied her ponytail, trying to smooth any stray strands behind her ears.

Liam angled his head, watching her. "You missed a piece."

He reached a hand to the top of her head, and she stiffened, her eyes focusing on the deck as he gently pulled a stubborn piece back into its place.

"There," he said.

She cleared her throat, but even so, her voice stumbled upon itself when she spoke. "Thanks."

"Attention," one of the Second Years ordered. And immediately everyone looked to the stage. Five instructors filed onto the platform and stopped in a line behind the podium.

One of them, a ruddy-faced man dressed in a three-piece suit stepped up to the microphone at the center of the stage.

Before he could say anything, the Second Years clapped their hands to their sides.

"Attention!" Their collective voices echoed through the flight deck as they synced up their salute. The first-year cadets followed their lead. As if they belonged to one mind and one body, they stood straight, their fists pressed against their hearts.

The man took off his glasses and began polishing them. "Good evening. I am Marik Jolinksy, your history professor. I know that you all must be tired from your travels, but the headmaster is running late with a prior engagement. If you could just wait for one…"

Just then, a sharp whirr buzzed from the far end of the flight deck where a vertical rail jutted upward, its gears activating as the platform lowered.

"Ah, there he is," Professor Jolinsky announced, balancing his glasses on the bridge of his nose. Everyone, including the staff, turned their heads to the cargo elevator as it settled with a deep metallic thud. The doors slid open, revealing the headmaster standing in the center of the lift.

Brinn had researched him before her arrival. Headmaster Bastian Weathers was a celebrated Commonwealth scientist, notable for his work in dimensional and multi-universal physics. Behind him was a young man who Brinn guessed was another member of the Aphelion teaching staff.

And then…

"Holy Deus," Brinn whispered under her breath.

Time stopped the instant she saw her. Even though the skin on the girl's cheek was bruised and her eyes were bloodshot, Brinn recognized that face.

Ia Cōcha.

The cadets, who had been of one body and mind, had broken from their salutes, fists off their hearts and mouths open, murmuring in unspoken terror. Their whispers swelled to a shattering panic, like waves feeding a tsunami.

Liam looked over at Brinn. "What the mif is that criminal doing here?"

"I don't know," she whispered as the headmaster led Ia Cōcha onto the stage. He approached the microphone, his expression cool and calm.

"Simmer down. There is no reason to panic. Ms. Cōcha will be studying here from now on."

Brinn's jaw went slack. Around her, everyone had started to inch back, trying to put as much distance as possible between themselves and the most wanted criminal in all the Commonwealth. "We came here to catch people like her, not work with them," she heard someone grumble in the row behind her. Anger and betrayal swelled through the crowd, and a girl near Brinn burst into tears.

"I understand you may all be concerned, but from now on, we are all fighting on the same side. I expect you to treat your colleagues with respect. And I mean everyone." The headmaster's hand opened to gesture at Ia Cōcha, who was eyeing them all like a vulture at carrion.

Everyone was too busy avoiding her gaze. No one else realized Ia Cōcha had already freed herself from her handcuffs.

CHAPTER 7

IA

THE HYDRAULICS on the locking mechanism hissed, and the cuffs dropped to the floor. Ia was free.

She looked up as one of the guards pointed his energy pistol straight at her. With a swift kick, she knocked the weapon out of his hands, and it slid far out of reach. She quick-stepped forward, grabbing the guard by the neck, then swung him into the other guard who was barreling toward her. The two of them toppled to the ground. Ia quickly snatched a knife and a grenade from one of their packs.

Screams echoed around her. The cadets crowded together, eager to veer out of her way. But before she could take off running, she caught a flash of movement and felt someone's shoulder buried deep in her side. Ia crashed to the deck, so hard the impact rattled her lungs. She rubbed at her rib cage, growling at the person who'd attacked her. It was the flight master.

In the distance, she saw the headmaster stare at them. "Knives! Apprehend her at once."

Ia's lips quirked. "Knives, huh? What is that? Some sort of nickname?"

"Knives *is* my real name," he said, then pounced toward her. She rolled out of his way. All the while, she sized him up, watching his reflexes. The lazy slump in his shoulders was gone, replaced with quick shifts of movement—from the balanced angle of his feet to the flexed muscles of his arms, waiting to react to whatever move she would make. He was more agile than she had thought he would be. And by the dogged look in his cold, blue eyes, she knew he wasn't going to back off. She would have loved to go up against him in the battlefield, but not today. Instead, she pulled the pin off the grenade she'd nicked and flung it at his feet.

It exploded, not with fire, but with plumes of smoke, thick enough to shroud their eyes. It wasn't lethal, but it gave her more than enough cover to buy some time. There had to be a way out somewhere. The starjets were locked up above. It would take too long for her to steal one. So she ran, her boots hitting hard against the pavement. She couldn't see ahead, but she followed the yellow lines painted on the tarmac until she felt the ice-chilled air from outside whip toward her face.

An exit.

Ia stopped at the edge of the runway, surveying the outside world. Snow cascaded from high peaks, swirling through the gap before her. This place was built into a mountain, which meant the only way out was down into a rocky chasm. She wouldn't survive a fall from this height.

Behind her, the flight master charged through the clearing smoke. He would be upon her in seconds. He'd wrestle her to the deck or use that damn silver orb to stop her heart and end her life.

She didn't like those options.

If today was the day she was going to die, she would meet Deus on her own terms. Her eyes sharpened into focus, and she took her mark. Her muscles activated all at once, and she ran like hell to the end of the runway, where the sky opened up and the world was once again a large and beautiful place.

With arms wide open, she jumped.

As she plummeted, Ia screamed with glee, the sound echoing through the icy chasm. The cold air bristled bitterly against her face, but she kept her eyes open. She squinted her left eye until she heard the soft buzz of her eye mod activating. Numbers rushed across her vision, calculating the depths of the chasm.

1,045 meters.

Mif, that's deep, she thought.

It also meant she still had time.

As Ia fell, she twisted her body to face the mountain and unsheathed the knife she had stolen. With both hands, she plunged it straight into the thick layer of ice and snow blanketing the mountainside. The knife dug through the thick layer of ice, slowing down her fall. The vibration shook through her, creating a sharp ache from her fingers to her forearms. Her arms were too drained of strength to hold on for much longer.

She scanned the white expanse around her.

There. Her eye mod anchored onto a small cliff about three paces long. It wasn't big, but it would do. A number flashed before her. 20 meters.

Ia brought her legs up, kicking off the side of the mountain. She dove, arms clapped straight along her sides as she aimed for that tiny ledge. The wind cascaded across the skin of her suit as her body sliced through the chasm. Her left eye counted down the distance 15m. 10m. 5m.

She raised her arms over her head and tucked in her knees. Then, contact. She hit the ground, the impact crashing into her bones. She curled her body into a ball and rolled to keep her joints from shattering.

She made it. But there was no time to pat herself on the back. Like a cat, she was back up on her feet.

And then a voice called out to her. "You shouldn't have run."

Above her, through the swirling snowfall, she saw those same cold, blue eyes trained on her again. Ia glanced at the contraption Knives wore on his back.

Great. A windpack.

Knives soared down toward her, expertly navigating the gusts of the chasm, and landed nimbly on the ground before her. He tapped the button in the middle of his chest, turning off the fans on his pack, and raised a pistol at her. At this range, he'd hit her where he aimed. Right through her skull.

Ia sized him up. The only option she had was to fight him, and she was going to make sure she was the only one left standing.

She charged.

Knives fired his pistol. Ia dodged low, then lunged upward toward his chest, her blade slicing at his face. The flight master blocked her attack and grabbed her arm, trying to wrestle the knife out of her grip. Ia twisted her body, twirling out of his grasp, and kicked him in the back of his knee. He stumbled forward, out of control on the ice underneath his feet. His arms scrambled outward as he fell over the edge. Out of Deus's good graces, he managed to grab hold of the rocky ledge of the cliff.

Ia walked toward him, her stride regaining her usual confidence. Towering over him, she stared down at the boy's face, now red and strained with effort. Right now, he was barely a threat. Hell, he'd never been one to begin with.

She crouched down. Her fingers flew to the windpack's locking mechanism near the back of his neck, and with a beep, it unlatched. She slipped the windpack off him and placed it around her chest. At this point, she could have pressed her heel against his fingers until he simply let go.

But she wasn't finished with him. Not yet.

Maintaining a safe distance, she lowered herself into a stable stance as she reached over the cliffside, patting down his flight suit for a certain silver tracker.

She knew she was being ridiculously daring right now, but sometimes you had to do stupid things to survive. Beside her, Knives grunted, making no move to pull her over; he was too focused on keeping himself alive.

"Where is it?" she asked, her tone almost frantic. Her hands dove into his chest pocket, and she finally felt the smooth, curved metal against her fingertips. She snatched it out, looking at the silver device in her hands. Her fingers, now trembling, closed around it to keep it safe.

With the tracker in her possession, her fate was no longer

set in stone. It had become a moldable, wonderful thing. Her eyes squinted through the wind. She needed to find a path through the converging gusts of wind above.

"You won't make it," Knives said. "The competing jet streams will knock you right into the rock wall. You'll die."

Ia laughed, her voice once again filled with the braggadocio of her old self. "I cleared the Harix Corridor in fifteen seconds. I can manage." She held her hand up in a lazy goodbye.

"Only fifteen seconds?" he taunted. "I know someone who flew that same corridor in ten."

"You're full of mung," she said, turning away, immediately dismissing his claims. The Harix Corridor was filled with enough asteroids to tear a jet into a hundred pieces; it took skillful maneuvering to cross that safely. She was unmatched in that department. She didn't have to prove it to him. Ia was walking off, ready to disappear, when harsh laughter filled the chasm.

"Or maybe"—his voice bit through the wind—"you're not as good as you think you are."

She stopped dead in her tracks, her pride flaring from the depths of her being. "Do you know who you're talking to? *I* am Ia Cōcha. Blood Wolf of the goddamn Sky, Sovereign of..."

She turned around, startled to find the flight master in front of her. He'd climbed off that ledge when her back was turned.

His hand swiped forward, slamming something into the side of her throat. What was it? A knife? But there was no blood. She felt her mind slipping, and her thoughts grew muffled. *Run away, run away,* she told herself. But soon she couldn't even recognize the words tumbling through her head.

Something wasn't right.

Her eyes fluttered hazily. She slumped to the icy floor and saw what was gripped in his hand. Not a knife, but a syringe.

What a clever boy, a clever boy with the cold, blue eyes of Neptune.

"You're smarter than he said you'd be," she said, her voice slurring. She tried to hold on to reality, but the drugs were singing sweet lullabies into her ear, and her thoughts became a wonderful mess that soon simmered down, down, down into black.

CHAPTER 8
KNIVES

KNIVES CROUCHED over the girl, her body curled into the snow like a brushstroke. She was rambling. Something about how she wanted to go home. And about a brother who'd shoot and maim him. And how she really wanted some peanut butter.

She pushed at Knives's cheek gently. "Dummy," she whispered at him. Then, finally, she was out cold. Knives stood over her, waiting for any sign of consciousness. He tapped her in the center of her forehead. Nothing.

Thank Deus. He'd thought she would never shut up.

Knives pried the silver tracker from her slack fingers, returning it to a more secure chest pocket on his suit, then slipped his windpack off her and readjusted it over his shoulders. He gathered her in his arms, and with a push of a button, they were in the air. It took him a while to adjust to the additional weight, but after a few seconds, he figured out his balance. For a small girl, she was remarkably heavy.

As they rose through the chasm, the wind whipped her

black hair back and forth like a tempest. Why didn't she tie it back like all the other female cadets? But she was different from the others. Not by appearance alone, but by the fierceness of her will. This girl was...

Before he could place the word, her head rolled so her cheek nestled close to his chest. Knives glanced at her to see if she was still asleep. It was meant to be a quick peek. Once he saw her eyes were still closed, he should have looked away to focus his attention on navigating the wind. But he found himself staring. And as he continued his flight up the mountain, he kept telling himself that this was the face of Ia Cōcha, the most dangerous criminal in all the galaxies.

He finally figured out the right word to describe her.

That girl was *trouble*. Big trouble.

"Good work, Knives," Bastian called, waiting on the runway with a slew of guards. The cadets had been cleared from the tarmac.

"This is way above my pay grade," Knives said, glaring at the headmaster over Ia's limp frame.

Bastian peered at the girl in Knives's arms. "Is she conscious?"

Knives shook his head. "Out like a light."

"Take her to the private med bay," Bastian said. He waved for the two guards that had accompanied them at Ia's drop-off to follow behind him.

Knives walked out of the flight deck and into the main corridor that led to the academy campus. He took a roundabout way to the private med bay, trying to stay away from the classrooms and the canteen so the other cadets wouldn't see them.

The private med bay was meant for highly invasive procedures. Surgeries and amputations—something that never happened on Aphelion, at least not since the war reached armistice. Because the bay had a sealed-off, fully sterile room, it was the perfect place to keep Ia until she regained consciousness.

Once he passed the Archive library, Knives stepped through the entrance to the private med bay, the bluish UV lights above causing him to squint in the brightness. The two guards trailed in after him.

A med borg, female like all the other medical borgs at the academy, stood waiting with a pleasant smile at the door of the operating room.

"Open the door," he told her.

"You Need To Change Into A Med Suit For The Sterile Environment," her voice said lightly, each word its own steady syncopation.

"There's no time for that," Knives said sternly. "Just open it."

The med borg pressed her hand against the sensor, and the door slid open. A rush of sterilizing air blew out at him, tossing his blond hair back and forth. He located the bed in the center of the room and set Ia down lightly. Knives rolled his shoulders, wincing at the ache in his muscles. Not from carrying her, but from the beating he'd taken from her back on the mountainside.

He watched her body rise and fall slightly as she breathed in and out. How could such a small girl pack such an intense punch?

His eyes went to her hands, delicate when relaxed, but then he noticed her fingers, specifically the tip of her thumb.

He grabbed her hand in his, rotating her thumb from side to side. There was a patch of raised skin, like it had been grafted on. He felt the tip, and unlike real skin, it was spongy to the touch. So this was how she got out of those cuffs.

He turned back to the med borg.

"She has some foreign material on her fingertips," Knives told her. "Extract it."

The med borg nodded. "Anything Else?"

"No, just let her rest," Knives said as he made his way back to the doorway.

"And what about us, sir?" Aaron, one of the guards, asked.

"Keep watch over her," Knives said. "I really don't want to be jumping off a cliff to chase after her again anytime soon."

Aaron nodded stiffly, his pronounced manner very typical of a borg. He was a new prototype, an advanced model with an evolved AI and enhanced physical detailing. The epidermal textile used for his skin was more elastic than the other models, pocked with tiny pores to give the skin its realistic appearance.

The other guard, Geoff, stared at Ia through the observation window, his jaw slightly agape. He had a holocomic up, and he was glancing back and forth from the comic to the girl beyond the glass. The specific panel he was looking at was of I. A. Cōcha, rendered as a tall, hulking man with giant biceps and muscular thighs as big as his own body.

Noticing Geoff's distracted state, Aaron cleared his throat. "You heard the flight master. We need to keep watch."

Geoff looked up apologetically and quickly swiped away his screen.

"I've been a fan since issue one," Geoff murmured. "But she's not at all like in the comics."

Knives knew what Geoff was reading. It was a black-market holocomic, depicting all of Ia's adventures. In this series, I. A. Cōcha was a hero of sorts. Knives had read it too, while he was researching her. He'd found every article and bit of source material on her. Because of his eidetic memory, it didn't take him long to digest everything. He remembered every single date and detail like a photograph that materialized every time he closed his eyes, starting with the day she appeared on the scene five years ago. Mif, he thought, she was only twelve when she hijacked the Sinsia fruit caravan?

He waved a hand as he walked off. "When she wakes up," he said, "you know where to bring her."

Knives marched out of the med bay, ready to be rid of the responsibility. But with each step, the weight of her still remained. All this, he thought, and it was only the first day.

CHAPTER 9
BRINN

BRINN SLID HER TRAY down the serving counter. On the other side, an articulated metal arm slopped down a slimy orange ball in the middle of her plate. Brinn stared at her meal but didn't bother to speak up. They were on a planet where resources were scarce and the land was frozen in ice. Of course the food wasn't going to be good.

She walked out into the spacious canteen, lined with rows of tables where the First Years sat in heated discussion. All around her, the beep of holowatches filled the room as cadets rushed out into the hall to take their incoming streams.

Brinn found a place at an emptying table and was about to take her first bite of the mystery slop when Angie slinked down into the seat across from her. Brinn sat alert, unsure how to process her presence. She had avoided Angie throughout primaries, but now here she was.

"My dad's miffed," Angie said. "I asked if he could talk to someone about sending Ia off to prison where she belongs, but there's nothing he can do." Angie nodded over to Nero, who was pacing up and down at the far end of the canteen, gesticulating wildly while conversing with someone on a holoscreen. "Apparently Nero's uncle is going straight to the Queens about it."

Brinn shook her head and grabbed a spoonful of orange goop. "But that won't do anything. The Queens don't have any governing power. That's the first thing anyone learns in civics class."

"Tell *him* that." Angie clacked a pink fingernail onto the metal tabletop. "*Why* would the Star Force do this? Why would they decide to bring her here and endanger our lives like that?"

Angie eyed Brinn, as if she was waiting for her response. It was strange that Angie wanted to actually have a conversation with her, but Brinn was also wondering these things. She let out a sigh. "I don't know. All we can do is trust that they have a plan. I mean, it's the Star Force. They didn't become the most powerful military in the universe by making mistakes."

At the table next to her, a frantic cadet was in the middle of a holostream with her family, her mother demanding that she return home immediately. Angie leaned over the metal tabletop and looked Brinn in the eye, her expression now serious. "So are you staying?"

Brinn groaned at the thought of calling home and seeing her mother's face on the holoscreen. She couldn't tell her mom that she was giving up. That wasn't going to happen. Ever.

So she nodded. "I'm going to stay and do my part."

"Patriot!" Angie teased, resting her chin in her palms. "You and my dad think exactly alike. He wants me to do the same." Angie snorted.

A crisp two-tone bell trilled throughout the canteen, and a message flashed on the large holodisplays in the middle of the room. Curfew at 2200.

Brinn glanced at her holowatch. That was in ten minutes.

"Great." Angie got up. "I don't even know if I can sleep tonight."

Brinn grabbed her food tray and her duffel bag. "Come on. Let's find our rooms."

After they got rid of their trays, Brinn and Angie shuffled into the hallway along with the other cadets, following the signs for the dormitories. They stopped where the hall branched into two separate paths.

"What room are you in?" Angie asked.

Brinn flicked through the messages in her holoscreen until she found her room assignment. "G-372," she read and then spotted an arrow for rooms G-350 through G-400 pointing to the hallway on the right.

Brinn was about to say goodbye to Angie when her holowatch beeped. She glanced down at her wrist. In bright-orange letters, the word FAREN scrolled through the small black square of the screen. Brinn was raising her hand to dismiss the stream when Angie angled her head over.

"Is that your younger brother?" she asked. Despite Brinn's warnings, Faren was part of the Junior Poddi League at primaries, so most people, including the popular crowd, knew him.

"Y-yeah," Brinn stuttered. "I'll call him back."

"Just take it," Angie said and then reached over to boldly tap the answer icon. A small, bright screen projected in the space above, displaying Faren's cheerful grin. His jaw dropped when he saw Angie's face.

He waved his hand meekly. "Hello," he said.

"Hello, little Tarver," Angie said with a grin. Even now, Brinn couldn't tell whether that smile was predatory or benign. Brinn waited for Angie to accost her brother, to needle him with intrusive questions.

But then Angie looked over at Brinn. "I'm sure you have a lot to tell him." She turned, waving her hand in goodbye. "See you tomorrow, if we're still alive."

Brinn said good night and watched Angie as she disappeared into the other hallway. A scene like this would have never happened in primaries. Angie would have ignored her, and Brinn would have been perfectly fine staying out of her sights. But now, after all that had happened, Brinn realized it was nice to know that she wasn't alone on Aphelion. Even if the other person was Angie Everett.

She looked back at her holosteam, taking in Faren's shocked expression.

"Angie Everett's a cadet? What did she want?"

Brinn looked behind her to make sure Angie was no longer in sight. "Somehow she's decided we're friends."

"If she finds out…" He was talking about Brinn's Tawny heritage.

"I know," she said, reading the room numbers as she walked. "I'm being careful."

"So tell me about the academy. Did you meet Captain Nema?"

"No," Brinn answered.

"Oh," Faren said, sounding disappointed. He angled his head in quick thought. "Well, did you get to fly a jet?"

"No," she answered yet again, waving it off. "We have testing tomorrow to find out what departments we'll be sifted into."

Faren crinkled his eyebrows and leaned closer to the screen. "So you just sat around and had a boring first day?"

"Today was definitely not boring," Brinn answered as she turned into another hallway and spotted two guards standing in front of one of the rooms. One of them, the smaller of the two, was standing at attention, but the other guard had pulled up a stool. She furrowed her brow. The last room she had passed was G-371, which would make this room…

Brinn glanced over at Faren. "I'm going to have to call you back." She tapped her watch, cutting off the holostream before Faren could even answer.

A series of questions rushed into her head. Was she in trouble? Where had she seen those guards before? What were they doing in front of her room? She hurried to the door and tapped her hand against the scan near the entrance, anxious to get inside and hide.

The door slid open, and Brinn froze. Her mouth gaped as she watched Ia Cōcha's limber frame balance on top of the center table, attempting to pry open a vent in the ceiling with her fingertips.

Numb from disbelief, Brinn dropped her duffel bag on the floor. It landed with a loud thud, resonating throughout the empty spaces of the room.

Ia turned her head and eyed Brinn up and down, mugging expertly like a criminal. "Hey, roomie."

CHAPTER 10

IA

THE SMALLER GUARD, Aaron, leaned his head into their room, and once he saw Ia on top of the table, he rolled his eyes. Aaron was a borg, but his construction was like nothing Ia had ever seen. The detailing, from Aaron's expressions to his complex speech patterns, was light-years more advanced than the few Borgs she had seen in the Fringe. Most of those had no skin at all.

"Cōcha, how many times do I have to tell you?" Aaron asked. "The only reason you're not cuffed right now is because we've cement-locked all the vents. There's no way out."

Her other, larger guard, Geoff, slinked in with a bashful smile. On their walk to the room, Geoff had peppered her with hundreds of questions about her career, and from that, she quickly found out that he wasn't just a guard—he was one of her *fans*.

"I see you two have met," Geoff said. "Cadet Brinn Tarver meet Cadet Ia Cōcha." He waved back and forth between them as if he wanted them to shake hands.

"What the hell is going on here?" Brinn yelled. "What are you waiting for? Cuff her! Bring her back to where you all keep her!"

Where they were keeping her, it turned out, was here. After Ia had been knocked out by the flight master, she'd woken in the med bay. They'd spliced off her Sponge Tips, but Ia had been delighted to find that they hadn't discovered her eye mods or any of her other secret toys. After she'd dressed, the two guards had escorted her to this room.

"Cadet Tarver." Geoff inched closer to the skittish girl, seemingly trying to make himself appear as nonthreatening as possible. "All Aphelion registrants are required to stay in the dorms, including Miss Cōcha. But don't worry. We'll be right outside in case anything happens."

As the guards exited the room and the doors slid closed, Ia turned to her new, unfortunate roommate and shrugged."What a day. Right, Tarver?"

Brinn didn't answer. Instead, she scooped her duffel bag off the floor and rushed to the bathroom, locking the door behind her.

Ia stared at the bathroom door until she was sure Cadet Tarver would not be coming back out and then turned her attention back to her previous task. The vents might be cement-sealed, but there had to be other ways to get out. Ia flipped up the beds, examining the hinges for any loose wires or screws, but everything had been custom molded to attach seamlessly to the wall. There was nothing to pry loose, nothing to get her fingernails into.

She jumped onto one of the mattresses, hoping the bed

frame would snap away from the wall with her weight, but it held firm. Damn Olympus and its solid manufacturing skills.

Ia hopped back down onto the floor and focused her attention on the round table and stools in the center of the room. With all her strength, she kicked her foot forward, aiming at the tabletop. It didn't move, but Ia did, ricocheting backward until she skid to a stop on the floor.

"Cadet Cōcha." A male voice hummed through the room.

Ia sat back on her haunches and glanced from corner to corner to find the source of this voice.

"Who am I speaking to?"

"I am the Monitor for this dorm room. An AI program designed to assist your studies and integration into cadet living."

"Great." Ia combed her fingers through her ash-black hair. "Get me access to the ArcLite."

"You do not have security clearance."

All right, so they blocked her from the ArcLite. They'd told her they would, so that was no surprise. But maybe there was some way to outsmart the Monitor.

"Any direct lines to this room then?" she asked.

"There is one that exists."

"Connect me."

In the center of the room, a screen flashed with the words: Contacting the flight master.

"Disconnect!" Ia jumped up and screamed, "Now!"

She had two things to do while she was here: get this miffing heart tracker out of her chest and escape. As far she could tell, General Adams and the flight master were the only two people in possession of the silver remote. General Adams was offworld, which meant she had to snatch the remote from Knives. She'd taken it before, so she could do it again. She would just have to be craftier this time. But tonight, she didn't want to deal with him. She hated to admit it, but he made her nervous. Unbalanced.

"You sound distressed," the Monitor observed. "Shall I play a music stream to calm your nerves?"

"No." She waved her hand in the speaker system's general direction. "Just some peace and quiet will be fine." Ia sat so long in silence that the lights, thinking there was no one in the room, dimmed down, shrouding her in darkness.

How was she going to break out of this place? Aphelion was built so deep in the mountain that even if she set off a bomb, the place would be a little crumbly, but still intact. The only real exits were through the cargo lift and the end of the runway. But the cargo elevator had no control box inside it. Even if she found a way inside, she wouldn't be able to make it go up, not without finding the actual cargo controls in Aphelion's massive campus. As for the runway…Well, she'd tried that and failed. It was going be a massive pain in the ass to break out of this place, so maybe her best option was to find someone to break in.

Like Einn.

But without access to the ArcLite, she needed another way to connect to him.

Ia clicked her eye mod on, switching it to thermal view. Fiber wires ran hot, and even in this cold environment, they would be giving off some sort of heat. Her eyes scanned the four walls surrounding her, sifting through a flood of blue.

Then her eyes stopped at a bundle of red wires, glowing like a torch in the night. There it was. A landline, hidden behind the wall near Tarver's bed.

But just like everything else in the room, the walls were solidly made. There were no panels to punch into. No weak spots to wiggle her way in. That wall was the only thing getting in between her and her brother.

But it was just a wall, Ia told herself, and walls were made to be knocked down.

And once that happened, she would connect to that landline and contact Einn so he could break her out of this high-tech Bug Hole. Ia thought of her brother, of that glorious feeling of standing beside him while this entire place burned to the ground. She fell asleep with a smile on her face.

CHAPTER 11
KNIVES

KNIVES WAS ANNOYED. His stomach was grumbling. And instead of heading to the canteen to satiate his late-night hunger, he was on his way to the conference room.

Why on Ancient Earth were they calling a meeting at this time of night?

He passed his hand over the sensor to the conference room. The door slid open in time for him to catch Professor Marik Jolinsky slamming his fist on the long, white table in the middle of the room.

"This is getting out of hand. More than half of the new class have already elected to transfer to another academy."

"What are you griping about, Marik?" Knives asked as he slouched into a nearby chair. Bastian was also present, as well as the other instructors. Even the general was holostreaming in, his image shifting from blue to regular skin tone as his holo warmed up.

"You saw them earlier, Knives," Marik continued. "Those

cadets were scared out of their minds."

Ah, Ia's escape.

Even now, Knives was still reeling from it. It was a miracle that he'd even caught her. The thought of it unnerved him. How was he ever going to keep up with her? She was reckless and brilliant, which only meant he had to be equally as reckless and brilliant.

But he didn't want to.

Before Ia arrived on Aphelion, Knives had taken this flight master position as an easy ride through the rest of his contracted fifteen years of service. It was supposed to be simple. Wake up, teach class, stay out of his father's way, and do the bare minimum.

This was not the bare minimum.

"Where is your head, officer?" the general barked, noticing Knives's dwindling attention. Always the general, and never the father. Even as a hologram, General Adams's presence was overpowering. Knives found the best way to counter it was with a large dose of apathy.

He shrugged. "I'm hungry."

The general let out a very audible sigh and motioned for Marik to continue.

"Might we consider sending her to a less prestigious academy?" Marik asked. "Nauticanne Academy back in Rigel Kentaurus perhaps."

"That won't do. Their perimeter has too many holes. Aphelion is the most secure training grounds in all of Olympus," Bastian pointed out. "It's our best option."

Professor Meneva Patel cleared her throat. "I'd like to point out that she's already escaped once. Or did all of you already forget?" Professor Patel was the smartest person in the building, and because of that, no one wanted to cross her. "What will we do if it happens again?"

Knives felt everyone's attention turn to him. He sighed. "Then I guess I'll have to catch her again."

The general's voice edged into the conversation. "Flight master, do you have anything to add on Cōcha?"

Of course he did. He had a whole list. "She's undisciplined. Arrogant. Impossible to talk to. But she's also…" He wanted to use the word *talented*, but he decided against it. "She's cunning."

"Ia Cōcha may be a criminal, but she's quite the young lady." Bastian clasped his fingers, clearly trying to remain diplomatic. "There are things brewing out there that go beyond anything we've handled before. Ia may be a force the Commonwealth needs right now. She has the wits, the skill, and more importantly, the audacity."

General Adams faced the rest of the staff. "I need to speak to Bastian in private. You are all dismissed."

Metal chairs clanged against the brushed concrete floor as everyone readied themselves to step out. Knives was already at the door when he heard his father's voice.

"Flight master, you may stay."

Rolling his eyes, Knives turned back to face him. "Is my presence really necessary? The canteen is about to close."

The general extended a hand to an empty seat, so Knives had no choice but to sink back into the stiff, white chair.

As the last instructor left the conference room, Bastian swiveled to face the general. "Erich, are things really that dire out there?"

"Slaver activity is up. There are reports of a slaver nation going after both refugee camps and new colonies."

"Strange," Bastian commented. "Most slavers know better than to tangle with Olympus."

"We're sending more warships, but it's impossible to fend them off. It seems as if there are alliances forming. It's a good reason for Ia Cōcha to stay here with us. If she joined forces with them...they'd be unstoppable."

"But who's leading these attacks?" Bastian asked.

"We've gone down the Most Wanted list. Our suspicions point to Goner, but it's not like him to coordinate something so grand. All this activity could suggest a new presence. Whoever it is, it appears he's amassing slaves for a large attack."

"A large attack? I doubt it," Knives blurted out.

The general angled slightly toward him, his eyes as sharp as a hawk's. "Explain."

Knives traced a pattern on the tabletop, trying to escape his father's withering stare. "Slaves can't fight. It would take years to mold them into a force that could go up against the Commonwealth. If this group was planning an attack, they'd be enlisting mercenaries and Dead Space murk. We have enough enemies out there to form a decent-size army against us. And if they're not organizing an attack, they're probably building something...something very big."

Knives glanced up, only to see the general lace his fingers together and furrow his brow. At least his ears weren't red, a sign he was angry.

Bastian hummed in response. "To build something large-scale, one would usually acquire borgs, not slaves."

"But this isn't the Commonwealth we're talking about," Knives reminded Bastian. "We may have the largest borg workforce in the universe, but not everyone else can afford them."

The general paused as if he was considering this, but then turned to Bastian.

"I am trusting you with Cōcha. We may need her insight in the days ahead."

"Good luck with that." Knives laughed. "She sees us as the enemy. There's no reason for her to help us."

Bastian turned to the general. "Agreed. We're keeping her handcuffed like a criminal. She won't be willing to confide in us if we act like we can't even trust her."

"Fine." General Adams responded with a wave of his hand. "You can remove her handcuffs. We have the heart implant in her for a reason." His eyes flicked up to meet Knives's gaze. "Don't be afraid to use it."

The general stood up, straightening his sleeves and adjusting the collar of his coat. He looked over at his son and nodded. "Good work," he said, his voice resonating throughout the conference room.

And with that phrase, Knives realized the general had tricked him into doing what he had no interest in doing. Work. And for the Star Force. This was a RSF problem, not an academy problem. Knives was firm in drawing the line between the two, but his father was always quick to pull him back over it. His father didn't understand the betrayal Knives felt, that stain growing inside him. Instead of leaving the system that had killed Marnie, the general kept on, each month gaining a new medal, a new honor, while his daughter decayed underneath the cold, hard ground.

"I thought we had an understanding," Knives reminded his father. "No official Star Force business for the duration of my term."

"I remember," the general answered, pointing at the quartered shield on Knives's flight suit. "But you're still an officer, whether you like it or not."

General Adams ended his stream, fading away before Knives could raise his voice.

Knives felt the heat rush to the tip of his ears, furious he had inherited such a ridiculous physical trait to begin with.

Like father, like son.

CHAPTER 12
BRINN

EVEN WITH THREE inches of metal and a locked door protecting her, sleep didn't come for Brinn. She lay on the hard bathroom floor for a few hours, blinking in the darkness and listening to the banging coming from the other side of the wall.

What was Ia doing out there?

Around 0200, Brinn placed her ear against the cold metal door. The noise had quieted down. Maybe Ia had given up and finally fallen asleep. Or, Brinn thought, perhaps it was the opposite, and Ia had escaped, leaving a bloody trail in her wake.

At some point during her tumble of thoughts, Brinn drifted off, tossing and turning occasionally, her knees banging against the toilet.

She woke in the morning, and with each blink, she cringed, remembering the reality of her situation. That there was a good chance Ia Cōcha was still outside that door. Brinn cupped her hands under the running faucet and splashed cold water onto her cheeks. She inspected herself in the mirror, groaning at the unsightly dark circles that had appeared underneath her eyes.

Out of habit, Brinn checked her roots. She squinted in front of the mirror, and her eyes widened in discovery.

A fist banged on the other side of the door. "I need to use the bathroom. Wake up."

"Hold on," Brinn yelled, but the banging continued. She kept her eyes on the navy-blue strand dangling in the midst of her tangled mane, not wanting to lose sight of it. With discerning fingers, she plucked it out.

"Hurry up!" Ia cried against from outside the door. "If I go out here, you're cleaning it."

Brinn quickly combed her hair, trying to smooth out the tangles, and then threw the offending blue strand and her comb back into her duffel bag. Tapping the lock sensor with her elbow, she opened the door to find Ia standing there waiting for her, her eyelids still heavy with sleep.

Brinn glanced into the dorm room, which still looked impeccable despite all the banging she'd heard in the middle of the night. "What were you doing out here?"

Ia nodded at the bathroom. "What were *you* doing in *there*?"

Brinn ignored her and crossed the room to the closets. She slid one open, amazed that the door was still on its hinges. "Whatever you were up to last night, it was loud."

She threw her duffel bag in the corner of the closet. She turned, and Ia was right in front of her. The tired look in her eyes was gone, replaced by something else. Something more predatory. The girl was short, but her presence filled the room. Brinn shuffled backward, but Ia snaked toward her. "I think you already know we're not going to be friends."

Back in primaries, Brinn would smile to disarm bullies. But she couldn't smile at Ia, nor could she look away. There was something unhinged in Ia's gaze, happy at the chaos she created around her. Before she knew it, Brinn had her back up against the wall. There was nowhere else to turn. She was cornered and vulnerable, a mouse staring down the mouth of a lion, a fearsome creature from Ancient Earth. Ia's fingers curled around Brinn's shoulder and leaned in, so close that Brinn could see the punishing depths of her eyes.

"I'll be out of here soon enough. Do me a favor. Just stay out of my way until then." Ia's grip loosened. Brinn pushed away from her and ran across the room. She punched the sensor so that the dormitory door slid open. Outside, the two guards were waiting. The larger guard was in the middle of drinking a bottle of caffeine when he saw her.

"Is she ready in there?" he asked.

But by then Brinn had already run too far away to answer.

* * *

By the time Brinn stopped running, her thighs were sore. She was far from danger, so she stopped in the central atrium, leaning over to catch her breath. She was furious that Ia had threatened her, but even more, Brinn was furious that she'd let her. Doubt wiggled its way into her brain like a parasite, and for the first time since she arrived, she wanted to go home, to where things were safe and familiar.

Why had she come here in the first place? she wondered.

Looking up, she saw a large statue displayed in the middle

of the room. Strips of metal had been melded together, warped into the shape of a raised fist. It was an old relic, she knew because of its color, oxidized into a lustrous green with time.

Upon its wrist were words.

Of Progress.

Of Prosperity.

Of Proficiency.

It was the motto of the Olympus Commonwealth.

And instantly, Brinn's doubts evaporated like a mirage.

There was a reason she'd come here, she reminded herself. She'd wanted to be a part of something big, a movement she believed in. It was why she'd left her home and family.

And that reason, like the fist before her, was as firm as steel.

The Star Force brought order where there was chaos. Right now, the chaos came in the shape of a small, snarling girl in the middle of Brinn's dorm room. But chaos could take other faces and other forms. And when that happened, Brinn would be ready. She would know how to face down the darkness because she had already stared right into its frightening black eyes.

With bright new confidence, Brinn took a step forward. There was work to be done.

CHAPTER 13
KNIVES

KNIVES SURVEYED the First Year canteen. The new class, which had been at one hundred at their arrival, had dwindled to half that amount. Knives laughed. Cadets were usually fighting to make their way into Aphelion's prestigious training grounds, but now everyone wanted out. He saw it as a stroke of luck. Today was the testing day. Fewer cadets meant fewer exams to grade.

He made his way to the one corner of the room that was completely empty, save for one girl. Instead of eating her breakfast, Ia Cōcha was hunched over the table, resting her forehead against its cool metal surface. The same guards as yesterday stood watch behind her. Per Bastian's suggestion in their meeting the night before, Ia's hands were unbound to foster the feeling of mutual trust. On the table was a tray of food, but all the portions remained untouched. Knives didn't blame her. He had spent two years eating the canteen slop. One of the perks of working there was the fresh selection of imported fruits in the instructors' lounge, like the banana he held in his hand.

Knives slumped into the empty chair in front of her. "You're still here? I thought you'd escape by now."

Ia angled her head up and then groaned at the sight of him. "You," she muttered.

"I see I've made an impression," he said as he peeled his banana and took a bite.

"You stuck me with a syringe. That's the type of thing a girl doesn't forget." Then her lips quirked up in sudden mischief. "I also didn't forget that you're named after a kitchen utensil. I mean, what kind of deranged parents name their offspring Knives?"

Knives was about to answer when he realized one crucial fact: Ia didn't know his deranged parent was the same deranged man who had captured her. He offered up a silent prayer in thanks. Knives hated when people found out about his father.

Two years ago, when Knives was still a cadet, Bastian had mentioned his pedigree in a lecture. Knives had made Bastian promise to never bring up his illustrious family again in the academy environment, but the truth had already spread.

That simple revelation instantaneously changed how everyone looked at him. Those who despised him tried to become his friends, and others who doubted him suddenly respected him.

Now that everyone he'd trained with had graduated, he was free from all the looks, all the whispers. Perhaps a few of the Second Years knew, since they were lowerclassmen when Knives was in his last year as a cadet, but for the most part, they had their own separate classes. There was a good chance that Ia and the rest of the First Years would never find out about his famous father.

Across the table, Ia clasped her hands, laying them flat on the table. Her chin balanced gently on top of her knuckles as she looked at him lazily.

"Knives, Knives, Knives," her voice trilled, wispy and completely out of tune, as she tested out the sound of his name. "It's not the *worst* I've ever heard. Although it's definitely up there. I once knew a guy named Goner. He tried to murder me. So you two have a lot in common."

He shot her a look like she was crazy. She *was*.

Knives crossed his arms. "Judging by the fact he's still alive and on the Most Wanted list, I see you had it in your heart to forgive him."

"Goner." She groaned. "You know he thinks we're rivals? If I bothered killing Goner, it would prove to him that I agreed we were." She rolled her eyes. "In any case, his name is exquisitely bad. It's punishment enough." A laugh bubbled out of her. The sound started loudly and slowly, and then grew faster like a boulder rolling down a hill.

Knives snorted. He had never seen anyone laugh so wholeheartedly.

As Ia's laugh dropped out, a word rumbled across the canteen. *Jumper. Jumper.* Knives glanced around the room, watching as the majority of the cadets chanted in unison. They were calling out Ia for launching herself off the runway yesterday. One voice was louder than the rest, leading the class in its fury. Who was the idiot trying to start a fight with the Blood Wolf?

Knives recognized him sitting in the center of a group of boys sneering in their direction. Nero Sinoblancas.

Knives's gaze drifted back to Ia. Her eyes were focused on a scratch on the tabletop as though she had tuned everything out. But her shoulders were tense, and her nostrils flared.

He reached his hand forward but stopped it halfway between them.

The movement caught Ia's attention, and her head snapped up at him.

He nodded over to the jeering cadets behind her. "Don't let it get to you."

Her eyebrows drew together. "It's not."

Knives studied Ia's face. This was a girl who had hijacked supply fleets, devised complex air maneuvers against his father's battalion, and by her actions alone, had accrued an 898 billion NøN bounty. But now as he watched her, Knives couldn't help but feel a little sorry for her.

A metal chair screeched across the floor, and Nero stood. All at once, the chitter of conversation died down to quiet.

"Hey, Jumper." Nero's voice was full of venom. "Do us a favor. Maybe actually kill yourself next time."

Knives saw the tension in Ia's jaw, the small vein rising softly against the smooth skin on her forehead. He opened his mouth to say something to calm her, but he wasn't fast enough.

Ia was up, rising like a demon from the underbelly of hell.

Nero didn't have a chance.

Her hand was at Nero's neck, and with incredible ease, she slammed his head hard onto the cafeteria table, the sound echoing through the canteen.

"That wasn't very nice." She spoke quietly, but the anger in her voice was sure.

"You're just like the Refs. A parasite. A waste of space." The last words were a struggle for Nero. His face had grown pale, now inching toward blue from asphyxiation.

Like everyone else, Knives was frozen in place, wide-eyed and waiting for what was coming next.

"Oh, I see. You think you're worth more than me." She pinned his hand down, clutching one of his fingers. A wave of screams erupted from the boy's mouth. A maniacal glee flooded her face as she savored his pain. "How much do you think your parents will pay for you? How much are all your fingers worth?"

Knives charged toward them, his hand grabbing Ia by the shoulder.

The muscles in her back shifted at his touch, and she swiveled to face him, her free hand already set in a fist aimed in his direction. Maybe it was a defensive impulse, built up from all the years she had survived in the All Black. Or maybe, Knives thought, she actually wanted to hit him. He didn't have time to find out which one it was.

He snatched the silver heart tracker from his chest pocket. Remembering his father's directions, he held his forefinger and his thumb on both ends of the egg-shaped device to activate it. A red light flashed upon its surface, and he tapped it right in the center.

Ia's punch fell midswing, her body's weight tipping forward until she was on her knees. Her shoulders slumped, and soon she was writhing on the ground, resting her weight on her forearms. Her hair hung around her face like vines, swinging as her body trembled.

This girl was a child of violence. She had suffered and survived. That was a part of her, but what about the girl who had teased him five minutes ago? Where did she fit in? Was she a mirage, a mere trick of the eyes? Did that person really not exist at all?

Knives fought the impulse to help her up. Instead, he turned to her guards. "Make sure she gets to her first test."

CHAPTER 14

IA

EVERYTHING WAS THERE. Navigational panels. Engine displays. Pressure gauges. Throttle levers. And, of course, the control wheel.

Ia's heart throbbed, but not from the forced heart failure she had been subjected to less than an hour ago—which hurt like mung. This time her heart was singing inside her from the thrill of being back in the pilot's seat.

The main display was black when she heard a buzz. A flash of code blinked in on the screen, and immediately afterward, the outside view opened up, spanning all around her, as bright as the world itself. White LED lights twinkled in front of her, marking the path of a runway.

The control panels were up and running, numbers flashing on the main monitor.

5

Ia's hands raced forward. She flicked the switches in front of her, activating the dual engines.

4

One hand on the wheel, and the other hand on the throttle.

3

"Rear thrusters on," Ia called out. A slight vibration rumbled against her back as the thrusters activated.

2

She pushed the throttle lever forward, allowing more fuel to power the rear thrusters.

And 1.

The lights flew past her as the jet zipped down the runway until all she saw was a black expanse.

She was flying.

And not even the muted pain of her recovering heart could keep her from yipping with glee. This was the first time she had flown since her capture. Zigzagging between stars, she dipped her jet along the orbit of a nearby moon, feeling the tug and pull of its gravity. She tested out the beautiful engine that carried her, trying to push it as fast as it could go. It was almost as quick as her own starjet, *Orca*. Almost, but not quite.

Loud beeps stung at her ears. And the words Begin Course Simulation blinked onto the screen.

Then she remembered where she was.

That this was all a simulation, a series of constructed images stitched together to fool her head and eyes.

This was just a test. A stupid test.

A streak of competition flared within her, knowing they would rank her with the other cadets, with those tyros—Dead Space slang for newbies who had no idea what they were doing. Even if this wasn't real, she was going to conquer this sim. It would allow her some sense of happiness to know she was better than all the Commonwealth flyers on this Deus-damned planet.

"Computer shields to one hundred." The shields flashed blue as they activated. It was only for show. She knew she wasn't going to need them.

The mother of all asteroids tumbled toward her. Large chunks of ice and rock splintered off, colliding with smaller asteroids.

She was going to need the extra power. Her voice rang out through the cockpit. "Mid thrusters."

"Activated," the computer called back.

Her jet reached the outer edge of the field. She pivoted, dodging each piece of rubble that came her way. She broke through a flurry of debris. But she wasn't in the clear yet. There was still the big one. It crashed toward her like a behemoth in the darkness.

Keeping one hand on the wheel, she grabbed the two side-by-side throttle levers. One was for the rear thrust, and the other for the front. She punched them forward, feeling the simulation pod tilt as it tried to re-create the motion. The jet flew head-on at the mother asteroid, and she saw it winking at her like a giant icy eye.

Ia flew faster and faster, until the engines were overheating. WARNING. The word was all over her screen. Light flashed as bold and red as the blood pumping through her veins.

"Collision imminent," the computer's voice trilled through the metal pod.

Ia kept her eyes on the navigational meters. 1000 meters. 500 meters. 200 meters.

She was so close she could see the cracks in the asteroid's crust.

50 meters.

Her hand flew to her side and yanked at the air brake right next to her, triggering an additional set of thrusts in the front. It gave her enough resistance. With both hands on the wheel, she pulled. The nose of her jet pointed up, straight up, so that she was now vertically traversing the height of the asteroid. Higher and higher.

Ia gazed into the All Black, basking in its embrace. Once she cleared this last obstacle, it would all end. The view would fade, and the pod would right itself into reality.

For now, she kept flying, staring into the darkness.

"Simulation complete," the computer sang into her ear, and an emptiness rattled her heart.

The pod readjusted, rotating back to its original axis. It settled back into its locking position. Ia fixed her face, trying to hide the sadness inside her. The simulator pod opened. With a grin stretching from ear to ear, she looked past the cadets until she found Knives's arrogant blue eyes, as cold as the planet she was stuck on.

"So that's the hardest thing you can throw at me?"

CHAPTER 15

BRINN

BRINN YAWNED BEFORE she stepped into the First Year common room. She had spent the night once again on the bathroom floor, and her neck was stiff from the way she'd slept. She'd fallen asleep hearing Ia bang something against the wall in the main sleeping quarters, followed by a yowl.

The First Year common room was filled with red L-shaped couches where cadets chatted, cheered, or consoled. To an outside observer, it would appear to be a normal day. But it wasn't. This morning would decide the rest of Brinn's adult life.

After a full day of tests yesterday, including a flight simulation and two written exams, their scores had been analyzed and their placements already decided. Whatever department she was assigned to would dictate her classes for the next two years.

There were three categories to be sifted into. Flyers. Engineers. And comms.

The flyers were self-explanatory. They were the pilots. The

heroes. Brinn would be lying if she said she didn't want to be placed in this group. Everyone wanted to be a flyer.

The largest group was the engineers. They did almost everything. While the flyers worked on their aerial maneuvering, the engineers figured out how to keep the vehicles in the air. There were several divisions within the engineers themselves. In addition to ship maintenance and engine duties, some engineers might be sectioned off to advance in hydroponics, armaments, or borg technology. Engineers could do anything. Except fly.

Then there were the communications specialists, experts in language and culture, the Commonwealth's intergalactic anthropologists. More importantly, they served as the eyes and ears of the Commonwealth. They knew about every transmission, legal and illegal, that slipped through the ArcLite.

In the center of the common room, three large holoscreens hovered above everyone's heads, angled so everyone could see. Brinn rose on her tiptoes to get a better view.

Angie leaned in. "I already checked. You're an engineer."

At the sound of those words, the heaviness of the unknown lifted off Brinn's shoulders. Of course she was an engineer. It made the most sense; her rational thinking was better suited for the engineering track, and she didn't have the gall to be a flyer. She'd failed the flight simulation within seconds. In all honesty, it was a blow to her pride. She had never failed anything before. The only thing that made her feel better was the fact that not many had succeeded. Brinn had been there when someone did though. She remembered it, that ghostly image of Ia emerging from the simulator pod, steam leaking from the broken hydraulics system.

A lot of the cadets were furious, calling her a cheat, a show-off. But some of the cadets were uncharacteristically positive. From that test alone, Ia Cōcha had gathered a handful of fans. Brinn couldn't decide if she was one of them. She was impressed by Cōcha's skill. That was certain. But Brinn had quickly exited the room to forget the smug look on Cōcha's face. Like it was *so* easy.

Brinn stared at her ID number and placement glowing on the holoscreen, and reminded herself that this was all for the best. Being a flyer would call too much attention to herself. Putting herself in the spotlight wasn't exactly how she did things.

Brinn glanced over at Angie. "Where did you get placed?"

Angie ran her fingers expertly through her fine blond hair. "Comms unit. Just like I expected."

In one corner of the room, a group of cadets clapped each other on the back, grins plastered on their faces.

"Check out the flyers." Angie ogled them from the distance. "I can't wait to see them in their grav suits."

Brinn shifted so she could see their faces. She recognized a few of them. Among the pumping fists and high fives, she spotted Nero Sinoblancas, Cammo with his gap-toothed grin, and right next to him, almost exactly in the center of it all, was Liam.

The group was small. Only ten of them.

But hold on.

Brinn scanned the flyers, her eyes doing a loop as she tried to find a certain face.

Around her, a hush of murmurs simmered throughout the room. She turned to see Ia standing in the doorway of the common room, her eyes on the holoscreens floating above.

"Are you miffing kidding me?" she muttered, then charged out, her guards rushing after her.

Brinn looked back to the holoscreen, searching the list of names, until a curious line of data jumped out at her in bright-yellow lettering.

Name: la Cōcha.

Category: Engineer

CHAPTER 16
KNIVES

LIKE AN EXPLODING GRENADE, Ia burst through the large metal doors to the main lecture auditorium where Knives stood at the podium, a holodisplay of Eden's planetary makeup hovering above them. Heads swiveled toward her. She was interrupting his lecture, but he'd expected no less—she had no shame. She stalked down the stairs like a damning Medusa, her eyes trying to turn him to stone.

"You made me an engineer?" Ia yelled, her voice so sharp it made his eardrums throb.

Just as she looked ready to launch herself down the stairs at him, her guards grabbed her arms, pulling her out into the hallway.

Knives sighed and looked up at his classroom. "I'll be right back," he told his second year students. He had to handle this before she made even more of a scene.

The moment he opened the door to the hallway, Ia swung a balled fist at his face.

He ducked, dodging the edge of her knuckles.

Aaron and Geoff rushed over, trying to restrain her. She shrugged out of their grip, and with one look, she urged them to back off. They didn't dare grab her after that.

Knives stood up straight in challenge. "What's your problem?"

"I'm the best pilot in this metal hole in the ground. I know it. You know it. Geoff freaking knows it," she said, pointing a finger at her guard.

Geoff nodded sheepishly. "She's right. I do."

Knives crossed his arms and grimaced. "Your skills are on another level. I won't deny that."

"Then I should be a flyer." Ia stepped up to him and glared. "Give me a starjet." It was an order, not a request.

Knives rolled his eyes. "So you can escape again?"

"I belong in the skies," she shouted, "not living out my days stuck in the middle of a frozen mountain!"

Knives took a deep breath. "Our flyers earn their jets. The Commonwealth doesn't just hand them out, especially to Public Enemy Number One."

"Listen to me. I'm the Sovereign of Dead Space, a Warrior of the Fighting Planets." Ia dropped her gaze and let out a long breath. "Without a jet, I'm nothing."

"Wrong." His eyes remained trained upon her. "Those fancy titles mean mif. What matters is how you act and what you do."

"And what about you?" She jabbed a finger into his chest. "It doesn't make sense why someone so young, with so much potential, is floundering as flight master. There are rumors floating around that you turned down a pretty big colonization campaign."

Knives gritted his teeth, annoyed that his personal decisions were fodder for the cadets' gossip.

"That doesn't concern you." His voice sharpened like razor blades.

"Then it's true." She sneered. "You're always egging me to escape, but how about you? Whatever happened to you made you too scared to leave." She shook her head, and every single vicious syllable corroded through him as quickly as tarnish through silver.

A violent silence bridged the gap between them. Filled with unspoken words and the creak of buried histories. She was right, though he'd never admit it to her.

"Go," he ordered finally.

"With pleasure." She scoffed and stomped away.

Knives spent the rest of his lecture simmering from what Ia had said, how she had tried to pry things out of him as if he were a broken toy. When the last bell chimed, he shut down the projectors of the classroom, leaving the rest of the class in the dim. "All right, that's it for today. Dismissed, all of you."

He was the first to make a move toward the doors.

"Is there any homework?" one of his second-year flyers called after him.

"Yeah," he yelled back. "Don't bother me." And he stomped out of the room.

Thank Deus for the weekend. After everything that had happened these past few days, Knives was ready to fly the mif out of there.

* * *

Myth was an old space station two gates away. It was a place to refuel, to drink, and to place bets on whatever you fancied. And none of it was legal, which was why it was located in Dead Space territory. But Knives was willing to take his chances, since by Commonwealth law, he was underage. Dead Space joints never checked IDs.

The docks of Myth were busy with vessels, all in various states of wear and tear. His Kaiken was the cleanest jet there, and as Knives landed, he had to ignore the looks that came from the crews nearby.

Fortunately, he'd chosen to wear a less flashy outfit. Instead of his flight master's suit, Knives wore a crumpled gray thermal shirt and navy-blue flight pants, the same as nearly half of Myth's patrons were wearing. Once he docked, he fished out his brown leather bomber jacket and shrugged it on. The jacket had come with the jet; he'd found it in the cargo bin the day after he bought the Kaiken from the racing garage. There were no patches on the jacket, just worn cracks of leather on the elbows and the previous owner's name etched and fading on the chest. *Pete.*

Even though it was his first time there, Knives found the tavern easily. All he had to do was follow the smell of sweat and vomit. The tavern was built into the old captain's deck of the space station. It was dark from the burned-out circuitry, and the floors were sticky with old grease, but that didn't deter all the people shoved inside, trying to get their preferred bev. Slurred conversation pooled around him as he edged his way through the crowd, trying hard to avoid the path of spilled drinks.

Spotting an opening at the bar, Knives wedged himself in

between a tall man with robotic arm prosthetics and another patron with deep scars along her cheeks.

Knives caught the eye of the bartender. She was slender, with long, tangled brown hair.

"What can I get you?" she asked, leaning in to read the patch on his chest. "Pete."

"A bottle of whatever you have."

"The archnol here is made from old burnout," she warned. "Rad level is pretty high."

"I'm not that picky."

She smiled in response, and he noticed the way she looked at him, her eyelashes flickering in his direction. She grabbed a bottle from behind her and twisted the cap.

Knives swiped at his holowatch, accessing his wallet app for scanning.

"It's on me," she said, placing the bottle down.

He flashed her a grin, staring at her long enough to see the blush creep onto her face. He could have stayed there the whole night, flirting with her. But all he wanted to do was turn off his brain and be rid of any thoughts of Aphelion. He'd expected the first week to be difficult, but with Cōcha on the cadet list and his new teaching duties, he had been stretched too thin.

Weaving through the crowd, he found a column to lean against, angling his head to catch tidbits of news from the people nearby.

"The price of century coin is going up," a person with a bronze eye patch said. "If you manage to scavenge one, keep 'em."

"Did you hear about them Armada trying to take control of Dead Space?" a Dvvinn woman asked.

"Of course. Ia Cōcha's gone, so someone's gonna wanna move in on her territory," lisped a Dead Spacer with a mouthful of missing teeth.

Great, Knives thought—two gates away, and people were still chittering about Ia. She was like a ghost, haunting him wherever he went. He took a swig of archnol, letting the liquid burn down his throat, and continued listening.

"That bit'll come back and kill whoever takes her place, mark me words. Pity the munghead who tries."

Knives smiled to himself; he agreed with the man.

"Fierce lil' thing. I hope to Deus I'm here to see that," said the person with the lisp.

"You talking about the Scourge? She's a weaklin'. I beat her down pretty good, cornered her on the docks of Whiler."

Knives's ears perked to the man's story, and he inched forward, trying to get a look at him. The man was of moderate build and not nearly as tall as Knives was. Ia could have handled him in a second, no question.

"They say she's untouchable," someone chimed in.

"Oh, I touched her." The man leered.

Before he knew it, Knives was at the guy's back, clapping him on the shoulder.

The man turned. "What the mif ya think yer doing?"

"This." Knives's fist flew forward. The man fell to the floor, holding his palm over his left eye. Knives looked up to see the man's companions moving in on him. There were four of them, and he knew he couldn't fight them off. Not in this crowd. But he had no other option than to lean back and put his fists up.

A hand grabbed his sleeve from behind and yanked him away.

He swiveled.

It was the bartender. Leaning forward, she eyed the men circling in. "No fights, you scuzz. If you ruin the place one more time, I'm closing down the taps. I swear to Deus, I will."

The men grumbled, but they eased off. The bartender turned toward Knives, her fingers still around the fabric of his sleeve.

"What were you thinking?" she asked, her voice tense. Her breath smelled of minty vapor. "I should have let them kill you. There'd be one less idiot in the universe."

He gave her a look. There were too many hotheaded women in his life; he didn't have room for another one. "I'll be going."

"No." Collapsing onto a nearby couch, she motioned for him to join her. "Might as well finish your drink."

He sat down and let her observe him, her eyes brushing over his features. Her fingers held a small vaporizer to her lips. Smoke curled from her mouth, and the smell of mint drifted his way.

He guzzled his drink and wiped the remnants of the thick brew off his lips.

"Earlier, those men, they were talking about the Armada moving in?"

She laughed. "This is Myth, my friend. Dead Space was Cōcha's territory, but not anymore. A turf war is coming. Though really, it won't even be a war. It's gonna be a *taking*. The Armada are coming in strong."

"Who are they?"

"They're a slaver nation. They must have forged an alliance with someone big because they're running around Dead Space like they own the place."

Knives's eyes clouded over as he thought back to the meeting with Bastian and his father. They had mentioned slavers attacking Olympus's colonies. Could they be the same group threatening to take over Ia's turf?

He was about to ask when the bartender's fingertips fluttered to his neck, tracing the lines of his chin. "I don't see your kind often."

His eyes snapped up to hers, and she peered at him like she was hunting prey. "And what kind is that?"

She leaned in closer so that only he could hear.

"Bug," she whispered.

"I'm not—"

"Sweetling, you're too clean to be a Dead Spacer. Even in the dim, I can see that. But if you'd like, I can dirty you up a bit."

Even through the sheen of sweat and dirt, he could make out the delicate curves of her lips, parted just so. She was gorgeous; there was no doubt about that. His body leaned closer, wanting to kiss her, to breathe that exhilaration into his lungs. She drifted toward him. Her hair smelled like ash and grease and life, and he flicked his eyes up to hers.

"You're beautiful," he whispered to her as if he were in a trance, but then he shook his head. "I should get going."

The woman slouched back into the dusty gray couch. She took a quick puff of vapor, and her voice was harsh. "Don't tell me. You have someone waiting for you…"

"Yeah." He got up, adjusting his jacket. "Something like that."

Grumbling, he walked back to his Kaiken, parked out on the bustling docking bay. The landing platform was surrounded by an atmos field to protect them from the vacuum of space. The atmos field shimmered as jets came and went. Finally, there was a pause in the activity, and like a deep breath, the view became clear. Knives looked up into the All Black and buried his hands in his pockets. His fingers knocked against the cold silver metal of Ia's heart tracker.

How strange that such a little thing would link the two of them together. If he wanted to get rid of the burden of looking after her, he could throw it away, jettison it out into the dark abyss.

But instead, he left the tracker where it was, nestled safely in the corner of his pocket.

Try all you'd like, Cōcha, he thought. I'm not letting you go that easily.

CHAPTER 17
IA

THE TEAMWORK TEST—that's what their professors called it. The tests were semiannual examinations, simulations meant to assess each cadet's ability to work with others in high-stress situations.

Ia was with a small group. She glanced at the names flashing on the holoscreens above their separate holding stations. Liam Vyking. Cammo Talle. Reid Loiqo.

And then Ia's eyes landed on Tarver, standing in her own station across the way. The assignments were random, but by a stroke of fate, Brinn Tarver was also on Ia's team. There were dark circles underneath Tarver's eyes, a sure sign that she wasn't getting enough sleep in that tiny bathroom they shared. But Ia didn't give two mifs about Tarver's comfort. While they were in the room together, the two of them said nothing to each other. No "good night," no "have a nice day." And she was completely fine with that.

She glared over in Tarver's direction, but her attention was directed at Cadet Vyking, who was standing in the station beside Ia's. Ia grimaced. Puppy love.

What was so great about the Vyking kid? Yes, his jaw was strong, and his face was rather nice to look at. But he was almost a carbon copy of Captain Nema. A tall and younger-looking Nema.

The last time Ia got tangled up with the prolific captain, she'd left him turned about near the outer moons of Echo. She'd led him around like a mouse tempting a large and oafish cat. It all had ended when Nema forgot to calculate the gravitational pull of those oddly gargantuan moons and used all of his fuel trying to escape. She'd spent a marvelous hour watching him struggle. That was exactly what Ia liked to call fun.

This Vyking boy could be fun as well. But an annoying kind of fun. Like swatting a fly that pestered you all night.

Ia squinted up at the blinding lights. The ceiling was webbed with wires, leading from their pods to a main processing tower in the middle. From the far end of the room, a number of med borgs were making their way toward Ia's team.

One of the women stopped at Ia's station. Ia read the raised numbers across her neck and smiled at her, making sure to initiate eye contact. "Hello, 494."

The borg inched up to her, so close Ia could detect the glassy sheen of her eyes.

"Greetings," 494 replied as she placed a gentle palm on Ia's shoulder to ease her back into the long, cylindrical holding station. As Ia leaned back, her arms rested comfortably into grooved armholds that protruded from the sides of the cylinder.

Ia put on her sweetest voice. "I am so grateful for your

assistance, 494. And I can't help but mention that your outfit looks impeccable on you." 494 was wearing the same exact uniform as the other med borgs, but Ia was going out of her way to be complimentary. There was a way to persuade borgs to favor you. In a way, wooing borgs was a lot like charming people. All it required was a lot of eye contact and a lot of praise to trick the little bits of circuitry in their head.

The woman gave her a very pleasant but forgettable smile and pressed a button on the outer wall. The holding station tilted backward, only stopping when Ia was lying flat.

The borg held up a small piece of equipment, dangling from her dainty fingers like a mechanical worm. Glowing nodes pulsed all along the mechanism's vertebrae. It was a neural device.

With a gentle touch, 494 laid the device upon the crown of Ia's forehead until it curved to the back of her head.

"You Will Not Feel Any Pain." The borg's voice was like a lullaby as she pressed a button at the tip of the device. Ia felt a light tickle, and then she was somewhere else entirely.

Red warning lights flashed in her eyes. Alarms trilled. Electrical wires sparked as they fell from the ceiling.

She made quick note of her surroundings. They were on the captain's deck of a battleship. A large rumble shook the floor, and she knew instantly the ship was going down. Within ten minutes, it would all be over.

The other cadets flickered into the simulation. They all took a second to collect themselves and then burst into action.

But Ia chose to hang back. To observe. Because it would be so wonderful to see them fail without her help. It enraged her that she hadn't been picked to be a flyer. She knew she was better than everyone, and she was sure the Commonwealth knew this fact as well. They should've been honored to have her fly for them. They should've begged her to take the pilot's seat in their name. It was a ridiculous thought to have about your enemy, but she was *that* good. And they refused to acknowledge it. So let them perish.

Of course, the Nema wannabe was already calling orders. "Tarver, can you access the flight logs?"

Tarver ran up to the control panels, and her fingers flew, accessing the onboard system. Ia had never seen a person sequence so quickly.

A series of numbers flashed on the holodisplays as Tarver continued to navigate the ship's safety levels. From the screen, Ia already knew the problem.

And Tarver confirmed it. "It's a breach... I don't know where."

A computerized voice echoed throughout the metal interior. "Caution. Oxygen levels are at eight percent."

Ia knew the cabin would depressurize at five percent, but she wanted to see what these tyros would do.

"How long do we have?" Vyking called out.

Two minutes.

"Around two minutes and counting," Tarver said, echoing Ia's thoughts.

"We have to find the hole and repair it," Vyking ordered.

Ia crossed her arms. *Way to state the obvious, kid.*

She watched as Nema Jr. pointed to a female cadet with long messy braids. "Reid, put out an SOS." Then he turned to the other cadet in their group. "Cammo, stimulate the algae baths so we can generate more oxygen."

Wrong. This was all wrong. Everyone was doing exactly the wrong thing at exactly the right time. She loved seeing Bugs suffer, but this was beyond annoying.

"Oxygen levels are at seven percent," the computer updated them.

Ia took a deep breath. Seven percent was a good enough challenge. From her brief moments of observation, she'd scoped out the tech on everyone's suits. They were all equipped with tasers on their belts. A nonlethal model that gently lulled the nervous system, instead of shutting it down.

Ia charged forward, her fingers clasped around the grip of her weapon. First, she needed to eliminate the unnecessary use of oxygen.

She aimed her taser at the gap-toothed kid. Then at Reid, the redheaded girl with the braids. Finally, Nema Jr., the most satisfying of all. Electrical surges flickered like tiny fireworks along their bodies. She didn't even wait to watch as they fell to the floor.

But Tarver did. "What are you doing? That's against the rules!"

Ia hoped she'd made the right choice by keeping her conscious. Tarver had proven herself quick-fingered at the system controls.

"They're asleep," Ia explained. "Sleep lowers your individual oxygen intake. With three people down, it'll give us a couple more minutes."

Ia's eyes studied the monitors as she leaned on the control panel. "Scan the lavatories for breaches."

Tarver gave her an unwilling look, a very obvious second of hesitation. "Why would I do that?"

Ia glared at her. "About ninety-seven percent of natural breaches are caused by faulty lavatory receptacles."

Tarver's hands were on the onboard displays, flipping through the ship's layout. "You gotta be kidding me. Toilets? Faulty toilets?"

"More action and less chatting."

Ia swiped the screen and watched as the image rendered a 3-D schematic, rotating and unraveling it like peeling the layers of an onion. The animatic turned a corner, and there it was: the breach. Exactly where she'd expected.

"Close down that section of the ship."

Tarver typed. Error. She typed again. Error.

"I can't get into the system settings," Tarver reported. "There must be an admin lock on it."

"Then find a back door!" Ia slammed her hand hard against the metal console. She was furious. If her own Dead Space crew was there, they would have fixed this in seconds.

"You want me to hack in? That's a criminal offense."

"You forget who you're talking to. Do you want to pass this sim or not?"

Tarver turned back toward the control panel.

"Oxygen levels are at five percent." The computerized voice reverberated straight to Ia's spine.

She watched Tarver's multiple attempts, her fingers writing code that was close but not quite. She typed, then deleted. Typed more, and deleted again. Something was odd about the pattern, about her moments of hesitation. Like the cadet knew exactly what she was doing and undoing.

"Are you trying to fail?" Ia asked.

Tarver swiveled her eyes at her, a glimmer of shock on her face. But why was she alarmed?

Tarver's face changed like a chameleon. "I'm trying to—"

The word CRITICAL flashed across the screen. Ia shook her head. A *Warning* was doable, but in ship talk, *Critical* meant they were in dire circumstances.

"We're out of time." Ia reached for her last resort. Her fingers gripped the base of a helmet, calibrated to withstand pressure changes. Instead of bearing a crimson feather on the visor, it had the quartered shield of the Commonwealth on its helm.

She never in her wildest nightmares would have donned a Bug's helmet, but this was her only option. It was just a sim, she reminded herself. The helmet didn't mean anything to her. It never would.

So she slipped it on.

Tarver glanced at her, confused. "What are you doing?"

It was game over. In a few moments, this ship would self-destruct.

Ia tapped the button at her temple. Her visor slid slickly into place and balanced the pressure inside her helmet.

From the safety of her helmet, Ia looked Tarver straight in the eyes. "Thanks for trying."

Her fingers gripped the taser at her side. Without a single moment of hesitation, she raised her arm and pulled the trigger.

From this distance, the beam spattered onto Brinn Tarver's chest, and her body shook into unconsciousness. But Ia didn't see any of this. She was already out of the captain's deck, heading straight for the escape pods.

CHAPTER 18
BRINN

BRINN'S EYES FLUTTERED OPEN. The lights on the ceiling burned into her vision.

She struggled to sit up, massaging her eyes in the process.

A hand cupped her shoulder.

"Not too fast." Liam's voice was soft and steady. "I made that mistake and ended up vomiting."

Brinn glanced at him. His eyes were bloodshot, like he had been up all night. However, the gold and emerald flecks circling his pupils continued to shine, even in the awful glaring light.

Liam unzipped his hoodie and tossed it at her.

That's when she realized she was no longer in her jumpsuit. Instead of the slick polyaeriate material against her skin, she wore a loose tank top and gray cotton shorts. Her bare arms prickled with goose bumps. She glanced around and quickly realized she was no longer in the exam room—they were in the med bay.

She slipped into Liam's sweatshirt, still warm from the heat of his body.

Liam poured her a glass of water. She took it and sipped, the water cool on her chapped lips.

As she drank, she glanced around the room. Rows of medical beds were lined up against the walls, all empty. They were the only two left in the med bay.

"Cammo and Reid left an hour ago." Liam sat down on the edge of her bed. "I wanted to make sure you were all right."

But Brinn wasn't thinking of Cammo and Reid. Instead, Ia was the one who haunted her. The last thing Brinn had seen before she lost consciousness was the hollow end of Ia's taser gun.

"What happened with the test?"

Liam propped his arms behind him and leaned back, his weight shifting the cushions on the medical cot. "No idea. We were all knocked out. Everyone woke up with red eyes and a splitting headache."

A ball of anger flared her vision.

"Damn that girl." The words came out without thinking.

The right corner of Liam's lips tugged upward. "That's exactly what I was thinking."

A wave of embarrassment washed over Brinn. She shook her head in surprise. This wasn't like her at all. She was angry. And she couldn't control it, not like she controlled everything else in her life.

She jumped off the bed, her legs wobbling from the effects of the simulation. She technically hadn't been zapped by a taser gun, but because of the neural device they'd worn, her mind was tricked into feeling like she had actually been shot.

Regaining her balance, she made her way toward the med bay doors.

"Where are you going?" Liam called after her.

Enough was enough. Brinn was through dealing with Ia's antics. And she was completely over living with her. But there was only way out of that situation.

"There's someone I need to see," she said.

* * *

Brinn stalked down the hallways, the heat of anger flooding onto her skin. She stopped in front of a large metallic door gleaming with a slight green sheen. But before her knuckles rapped right underneath the placard bearing the headmaster's name, the door slid open. The headmaster stood on the other side of the doorway. His gray flight suit was crisp and clean, with not a wrinkle in sight, displaying the headmaster's insignia—a laurel wreath with a star in its center—pinned prominently on his chest. He wore an even-tempered smile as if he was happy to see her.

"Cadet Tarver," he said. "To what do I owe the pleasure?"

Brinn burst into the room, then waited for the door to slide closed again so they could have their conversation in private. "I refuse to room with Ia any longer." Her voice sliced through the air. "I need a reassignment."

Headmaster Weathers moved back to his desk and gestured toward a chair across from him. But Brinn remained standing, waiting for him to apologize, perhaps even tell her that all of this was indeed the result of some clerical mistake. That they'd never meant to force the fearsome Ia Cōcha on an unsuspecting cadet.

Instead, Bastian Weathers clasped his hands and placed them on top of his desk.

"To request a room reassignment, one would need to have a good reason. Has Ms. Cōcha harmed you in any way?"

Brinn stared at him, dumbstruck. She actually had to justify her decision? "Well, no. But she grabbed my arm really hard," she explained.

He motioned to her arm. "Are there bruises?"

She glared at him. It had been a week since that happened, and any marks had already faded. "No."

"Then there's no proof that you're in any danger."

She paced before his desk, raking her fingers through her hair, now tangled from the chaos of her day, then sank into the seat in front of him. She stared at her knees. "I don't think you're listening to me."

"I am," he assured her. "But I've been headmaster to Aphelion for more than fifteen years. I've seen cadets who start as enemies but end their training as the best of friends. And I think you of all people should give Ia the benefit of the doubt."

"What does that mean?" Brinn stared at him, caught off guard.

The headmaster cleared his throat. "Ms. Tarver, your loyalty to the state is unwavering despite your family's complicated history."

Brinn froze in her seat. Of course the headmaster was aware she was Tawny. He had access to her files.

His face was relaxed, and he looked her straight in the eye. "No one else knows, except for me."

Brinn's face flushed, and she looked away, uncomfortable.

"Everyone has a complicated past," the headmaster

continued. "But we don't run from it; we face it, accept it. That is how we all grow stronger. Don't you agree?"

It took all of her strength to nod. "But what if she won't change? She practically murdered us in the teamwork test. Doesn't that prove how heartless she is?"

"Before you judge, I want you to see something." Headmaster Weathers tapped on his holopad. Projections shifted onto the walls, and the room transformed around her. The office furniture, the portraits on the walls, even Headmaster Weathers were nowhere to be seen. Everything vanished behind the holographic world before her.

Lights flashed red into her eyes. And the shrill notes of warning alarms flooded her ears.

Foosht. Brinn turned around to see the double sliding doors open. Ia Cōcha stood in the doorframe, her obsidian eyes searing through the translucent visor of her helmet.

"You," Brinn uttered under her breath.

But Ia looked through her as if she wasn't there. Brinn crossed the room and waved her hands in front of Ia's face, but she didn't respond.

That's when Brinn understood. All of this was a recording. It was the teamwork simulation from earlier that day.

Ia's holographic image kept walking until she passed right through her. Brinn turned, following Ia to the navigational orb, skirting around the consoles, until Ia finally stopped in the center of the captain's deck.

There, lying on the metal floor, was an unconscious Brinn.

Over the rising screech of the emergency sirens, the computer's staccato voice chimed in an update. "Cabin will depressurize in sixty seconds."

None of this made sense. Ia should have been long gone by now. And where were the other cadets—Cammo, Reid, and Liam? None of their bodies were on the floor. What had Ia done to them?

Ia crouched down, leaning over Sleeping Brinn's oddly peaceful body.

And then she did something completely unexpected.

Ia hooked her hands underneath Sleeping Brinn's shoulders. She let out a guttural cry as she pulled, her muscles taut and straining through her flight suit. Sweat glistened upon her brow.

It was strange to see Ia struggle, to see that confident grin no longer wiped across her face. Ia Cōcha was flesh and blood like anyone, and even she had her limits. But despite this hardship, Ia never seemed to stop. She never seemed to give up.

Brinn followed Ia as she dragged Sleeping Brinn's body across the captain's deck. Within seconds, they were at the far end of the hall. Ia stopped. Yellow and black caution lines rimmed the double-sided doorway before them. A small circular window made of clear quadruple-walled plastic was built into the door. Brinn caught a quick glimpse inside and saw him.

Liam.

Brinn ran through the metal doors, her body slipping through the projection until she was at his side. Ia had placed a calibrated helmet on Liam. Brinn peered through his visor to make sure he wasn't hurt. She saw a slight rise in his shoulders. Up, then down. He was breathing.

She glanced around and saw Cammo and Reid, both in the same state. Brinn wondered why Ia had bothered. Why would she increase their chance of survival by equipping them all with calibrated helmets? She turned around and saw that all three of them were strapped into flight seats attached to the walls.

This wasn't a room at all. It was an escape pod.

Behind her, the door slid open, and Ia inched in backward, dragging Sleeping Brinn inside.

Overhead, the computer's calming voice called out, "Warning. Fifteen seconds until depressurization. All personnel must evacuate."

The lights in the main hallway flickered as the ship began to power down, channeling all of the remaining power into the escape pod.

Baffled by the turn of events, Brinn followed Ia's every move, waiting for her to do something *bad*. Inside her helmet, Ia's face was drenched in sweat, and with a hoarse, labored breath summoned from deep in her gut, she hoisted Sleeping Brinn into one of the seats.

"What are you doing? That's the last seat," Brinn shouted, even though the words wouldn't reach Ia. Because this had already happened. It wasn't a premonition of what was to come; it was actual truth, the irreplaceable, immutable past.

In one quick motion, Ia slipped off her helmet, and Brinn stood, her eyes growing hot as she watched Ia fix the headpiece onto Sleeping Brinn's head.

"Cabin will depressurize in five..."

Ia scanned the pod, doing a quick check on everyone's seat harnesses.

"Four…"

Ia rushed out of the escape pod, and the doors slid closed behind her. Brinn stayed on the other side of the door, watching Ia through the circular window. Was she rushing to another escape pod? Surely, Ia Cōcha had a plan to save herself. She wasn't going to sacrifice her life for them, for four helpless cadets who couldn't even save themselves.

"Three…"

But instead of running, Ia stood by the doors, her fingers flying across the activation panel.

"Two…"

Brinn watched as Ia finished inputting the launch code. Ia tilted her head up, getting one last look through the window. Gazing back at her from the other side, Brinn could see the triumph in Ia's eyes.

Without hesitation, Ia slammed her hand against the red launch button.

"One…"

Brinn squinted her eyes through an explosion of light and steaming exhaust. It was so bright that it burned. Yet none of that bothered her because she had just seen the unimaginable. Even as the veil of fumes dissolved around her and the dim of the All Black loomed, she recalled the changed look in Ia's eyes. This was only a simulation, and there was no real danger to this test they took, but Ia had done something selfless, so human. Brinn's eyes burned with shocking realization.

Ia Cōcha had saved her life.

The world went to black as the recording reached the end,

and one by one, the panels of the headmaster's office returned to reality.

Brinn's movements throughout the recording had left her standing at the far end of the room. She could sense Headmaster Weathers shifting in his seat, waiting for her reaction. But she remained staring at the wood grain on his wall.

"The ship was equipped with one escape pod," the headmaster said. "There was only one casualty in that mission."

Brinn took a deep breath. No, it couldn't be, she thought. Ia Cōcha was the most wanted criminal in the known territories. She hijacked resource ships, kidnapped Commonwealth officials, and killed anyone who got in her way.

The headmaster's voice pierced through the clamor of Brinn's thoughts. "Everyone is capable of good, Brinn. Even her."

CHAPTER 19

IA

IA STARED AT THE WALL by Brinn's bed, her eye
mod set to thermal imaging. The bundle of communication wires glowed red behind the metal wall. Connection to
the ArcLite was usually wireless, but there were ways to get
around that in an emergency.

She glanced underneath her bed at the collection of broken
bio-plastic sporks she had stolen from the canteen. Her guards
weren't warriors by any means, but they had eyes like hawks.
It had been hard sneaking anything into her room to use. The
utensils from the canteen were the only things she could slip
away unnoticed, wiggling one each day into the sleeve of her
flight suit. And one by one, she had broken them all.

There was a slight indentation on the wall near where the
wires were. A dimple. Ia figured that if she hit it at just the
right angle, with just the right amount of pressure, then perhaps she could gouge a small enough hole into the wall. But
today, like the previous times, the spork had shattered in her

hands. She threw the broken pieces on the floor with a grunt, then kicked her foot at the wall over and over again, screaming in frustration. And when she fell to her knees with exhaustion, she glanced up at that wall, seething at that damn little dimple. But still there was no change.

"You sound distressed," the Monitor observed. "Shall I play some music?"

"Fine," Ia said. Maybe it would spark some inspiration.

"Accessing classical music stream." The loud thump of double bass drums and aggressive guitar thrashed through the dorm room. It was music from Ancient Earth's first technological renaissance. Heavy metal, they once called it. Ia was a huge fan of the classics, but today it did nothing to elevate her mood.

She looked around the room, at the empty bathroom and the spare bed where Tarver was supposed to sleep. It was rare that Ia was left in the room all by herself for long periods of time. Tarver was usually locked in the bathroom, and when she did finally venture out to the main room, it was only to deposit her duffel bag in the closet before classes started in the morning. The second she returned, she would grab the bag and bring it with her into the bathroom for the rest of the night. But now Tarver was in the med bay after what had happened during the teamwork test.

Ia glanced at the closet.

She found Tarver's duffel bag on the floor of the closet space. Ripping open the clasps, Ia emptied out the contents. Basic clothing. All the necessary toiletries. A hairbrush. A lot of brown hair dye.

And scissors.

She examined the blades. They were blunt but had enough edge on them to make a mark. Not as a weapon. But perhaps as a tool.

She just hoped she had enough time to put them to use.

"Monitor, can you track down Tarver's device?" she called out.

"The device is currently in the North Wing."

The headmaster's office was in that part of campus.

Ia frowned. "How long has Tarver been there?"

"Exactly twenty-nine minutes and thirty-four seconds," the Monitor answered.

A long time. Ia hoped that whatever business Tarver had with the headmaster would last long enough for Ia to get ahold of Einn.

"Keep track of her," she said. "Let me know if she's headed back."

Ia clicked her eye mod on, switching it to thermal view, until she spotted the landline warming to red behind the wall. With sure and certain movements, Ia knelt next to Tarver's bed and thrust the scissors into that same dimple, creating a small hole. She wiggled the tip back and forth, using it as leverage until the wall panel clicked and the bottom corner popped open.

With no time to lose, she plunged her arms into the wall. Her fingers fished blindly, sifting through the empty, frigid air. Holding back a whimper, she overarched her shoulder to give her arm more length. Finally, her fingertips knocked against rubber-coated wires. She snatched at the bundle and fished it out. The wires wrapped around each other like a growing vine. Buried in the center, she found the thinnest one. She was about to cut through its protective rubber sheath when she caught sight of a faint metallic glimmer in the coating.

"Mif," she muttered. The wires were patched into a secure system network. If she cut through one, someone in Aphelion would know. She yanked her hand out of the wall and threw the scissors across the room, dragged her fingers through her hair, and uttered curses at Deus for deceiving her, for giving her hope when there was none.

Then, through the booming music, she picked up the Monitor's staccato voice. "Cadet Tarver is one minute away."

Ia's eyes scanned the room. The place was a mess. She needed to hide all evidence that she was trying to escape or else Tarver could go out there and report her to her guards, to that headmaster, maybe to Knives. And she really didn't want to hear the flight master laugh at her for once again failing.

On the floor, Tarver's duffel bag was splayed open, its contents still strewn all over. Ia's hands darted here and there, stuffing everything back inside.

She reached for Tarver's hairbrush lying in front of her. And stopped. With delicate fingers, she plucked out a strand of hair.

She stared at the curiosity of it. She was sure her eyes were deceiving her, but after twirling it in her fingers, there was no mistake.

It was half brown and half navy blue.

CHAPTER 20
BRINN

WHAT WAS ALL THAT NOISE? It sounded of distorted tones and thudding booms.

Turning the corner into her hallway, Brinn realized it was coming from her room. She pressed her hand on the scanner, prepared to find the room a total mess. She was surprised to see nothing was broken. Instead, it almost looked cleaner inside, shinier.

Ia Cōcha sat on her bed, her back against the wall, staring at her.

Brinn spoke. "Monitor, music stream off."

The song faded until they were left in a surprisingly loud bubble of silence. She glanced at Ia, remembering the recording she'd seen just moments ago at the headmaster's office. Maybe there *was* more to Ia than her crimes.

She decided to extend some sort of olive branch. So she spoke, her voice awkward in the glaring silence. "Still up?"

But Ia said nothing.

"We should get some rest. There's an early class tomorrow," Brinn rambled on as she moved to the closet. Before getting to bed, she had planned to do a quick touch-up on her roots. Her fingers fished through her duffel bag, sifting through her toiletries.

Wait. Where was her—

"Looking for this?" Ia interrupted.

Brinn's hairbrush dangled between Ia's fingers. Before she could say anything, Ia threw it over to her.

"You should have told me you're Tawny."

"What are you talking about?" She had to deny, deny, deny.

Ia held up a long strand of hair. Of Brinn's hair. "Your roots are showing."

Oh. My. Deus.

Brinn rushed to the bathroom. She leaned over the sink, her head as close as it could get to the mirror. Her fingers flew through her hair, parting it everywhere to check her roots. Her eyes zeroed in on a navy-blue stripe near her right ear.

Her heart beat fast as she tried to figure out what to do.

Behind her, Ia leaned up against the doorframe. Brinn swiveled around, and she knew how her own face looked right then. She was scared.

Then Ia paused, squinting in observation, and Brinn knew she had pieced everything together. "You lied on the teamwork test, didn't you? You could have hacked into their system in seconds."

It was true. Brinn had the final line of code figured out, but she took her time, typing it and then deleting it.

"I could have. But I didn't." Her legs were shaking so hard

that she was ready to fall to her knees, to beg and plead for everything to be as it had been just moments ago when her secret was not yet out. "Please don't tell anyone. I'm not even full Tawny."

Ia's usual smirk was gone. "You should be proud. The Tawnies I've met are the most brilliant minds in our universe." Ia leaned against the doorframe, watching her. "Why are you hiding who you are, Brinn?" It was the first time Ia had called Brinn by her name.

Brinn had spent her whole life fighting with her mother on this, so she already knew what to say. "You've seen how they are. People hate the Tawnies. They call us *mungbringers*." The Uranium War was now over, but still, when Citizens saw the Tawnies, it dredged up all their past associations with one of the deadliest wars in all of Commonwealth history. Brinn didn't even want to imagine how the cadets at Aphelion would react to a Tawny in their midst. They'd bully her, make her life so miserable that she'd have to go back home. She looked up at Ia. "If anyone here finds out who I really am…"

Brinn tried to decipher the look on Ia's face, but it had grown cold and calculating. What was she thinking right now? What was Ia planning?

Finally, Ia leaned in. Her dark hair swayed like a curtain across her face, but even so, Brinn could see the danger in her eyes.

"I'll keep your secret. But I need something in return." Ia nodded at the holowatch strapped around Brinn's wrist.

"No way," Brinn snapped. "If they find out I let you use it, I'll be tried for treason. Who do you want to contact anyway?"

Then Ia sighed, her gaze landing on the floor. "If you must know, I want to talk to my brother."

Brinn stared at her silently. She had expected that Ia would want to get hold of a criminal almost as awful as she was. A serial killer perhaps? Like the BroadStone Slasher that was terrorizing the mining colonies. But not her brother...

"Space is a gigantic place, Tarver. No matter how far you journey, your family is the anchor that brings you back."

There was a deep sadness in Ia's voice, and Brinn, for the first time, saw a speck of vulnerability in Ia's armor.

It would have been simpler to hate her, to believe aggressive weirdos like Ia were born alone, that they were brought into the world as orphans, with no parents or siblings. But now that she knew Ia had a brother, Brinn was struggling with one strange fact.

They had something in common.

Brinn unhooked her holowatch. "Fifteen minutes. That's it."

CHAPTER 21

IA

IA TURNED TARVER'S holowatch over in her hands, amazed at how easily Tarver had said yes. Tarver and her little secret had just fallen into her lap like an answer to her prayers. She thought about the number of failed attempts to pierce through that wall and the sad pile of sporks underneath her bed. Receiving favors for keeping secrets was sometimes the best way to do anything. Bribes, blackmail, tit for tat. Why hadn't she thought about it earlier?

Brinn hovered over her shoulder, her fingers touching the bare ring of skin on her wrist where her holowatch used to be. "Clock's ticking. Even though I don't have my watch, I can still keep track of time."

Ia unscrewed the back casing of the holowatch and glanced down at the tiny circuit board built into the frame.

Brinn's eyes grew round and wide, like a perfect circle. "I said you could use it, but I didn't say you could break it."

Ia shushed her. She needed to concentrate. What she was

about to do was somewhat delicate.

She disconnected one of the wires from the circuit board, pinching it in her fingers. At the pressure point, the fiber unhinged, curling away like a live worm and extending to five times its initial length. She snaked the fiber wire around the back of her neck. With her other hand, she lifted her hair, her fingers feeling for a tiny, hidden input jack buried in the base of her cranium, providing a direct link to her brain and a secure way for her to contact her brother.

She had gotten the cerebral implant almost four years ago and had nearly died from the procedure. But it was useful for times like these. Without hesitation, Ia guided the fiber wire straight into the port buried in the base of her neck. A jolt of electricity reeled her backward, and her eyes glazed over, allowing her mind to see.

* * *

Ia stood in the middle of a blinding white expanse. She called it the White Room, which admittedly was an uninventive name, but it had stuck. The White Room was a virtual construct she had created. The concept was simple. One mind was a closed system, but add another mind, and it became a unique network between authorized users. Because of its invasive nature, if someone died while connected in the shared virtual space, the person's brain functioning in the real world would cease as well. Luckily for her, only two people had access to this particular room.

Her.

And Einn.

The moment Ia connected, she knew Einn would get a

notification that the White Room was active. She only had to wait a few seconds until she heard his voice.

"Ia? Is it really you?"

She turned, and there he was. He had lost weight, his face more gaunt than usual. But it was still him—her big brother. Ia skipped up to Einn and wrapped her arms around him in a hug. She took a breath, taking this moment in. When she stepped back down to solid ground, her fingers darted to his hair, combing the stray black strands so they tucked behind his ears.

He wriggled away from her hands, yet his gaze never left hers. "I thought they killed you."

As always, he wore their father's pin—the two white hearts—on his collar, but that was the only thing that was the same about him. The shadows underneath his eyes were deeper and darker than before the Tawny raid, and she knew he had been torn apart by grief. Her brother was loyal to her, loved her. He would kill a million Bugs for her. An eye for a million eyes. That would be their punishment.

"Which base did they throw you in?" he demanded.

"They're keeping me at Aphelion."

Einn raised his eyebrows in surprise. "You're *not* at a prison base?" But then his eyes darted back and forth as if his mind was racing to put everything together. "If you're at Aphelion, does that mean you know where it is? I've been trying to figure out its location for years now. Everyone in Dead Space has."

Ia shook her head. "I didn't see our route here. I don't even know what planet we're on."

"Why on Ancient Earth did they drag you over there?"

"Believe it or not, they're trying to recruit me." Her face grew flush with both anger and embarrassment.

"Then let them," he said easily.

She snapped her head up and looked at him. "If that's a joke, it's not very funny."

Einn's features were still, as if he was hatching the beginnings of a plan. "We have an amazing opportunity here, Ia. You need to figure out where you are before I can even come break you out. But before then, you can familiarize yourself with their security layouts, their weapons development program."

Her face dropped. She knew what he was getting at. "Einn, I should be out there, with you."

"This is what we've always wanted to do, Ia," he reminded her. "They destroyed our home, our entire star system. And now you'll be able to find whatever you can to shut the Bugs down. Permanently. "

Deus damn him. Why was her brother always right?

A distant voice called out, one from outside the White Room. A voice from the real world.

"Ia." It was Brinn, her annoyed voice faintly reaching Ia's ears from the physical world. "It's been fifteen minutes."

"Einn, I have to go." Ia's hand flew to the raised knob at the base of her neck, but before she could leave, Einn placed a hand on top of her head, a loving gesture, something he did when they were both children.

"We'll see each other again. I promise. But in the meantime, play nice. Do you understand?"

She nodded. With his free hand, Einn reached for the back of his neck to tap out of his connection. His other hand was still on her wrist, his fingers still circling it lightly as his connection started to fade.

"May your eyes be open..." she said in goodbye.

But Einn was already gone.

* * *

Ia's eyes flickered back into focus. Her view of the dorm room skewed sideways, and she realized she had collapsed on her side. She plucked the fiber wire out of the input at the base of her neck. It tickled as it came out.

Tarver stood over her and pointed at her holowatch. "A deal's a deal, right? You'll keep my secret?"

"You have my word." Ia dropped the holowatch into Tarver's hand, leaving it in the disassembled state for her to deal with.

"A criminal's word," Brinn said scornfully. "Does that even mean anything?"

"Well, you'll just have to find out," Ia said. She could expose Tarver tomorrow if she wanted to, but it wouldn't be the right move. If she did that, she'd lose the only "in" she had in this whole academy, and she knew it would be hard to find another.

But Tarver didn't need to know that.

So for now, Ia would use this secret like a delicious carrot to hang over Tarver's head. In case she needed another favor down the road.

Ia slumped into her bed, trying her best to get cozy. She was going to be here longer than she'd expected. She had been a deplorable excuse for a cadet for a little over two weeks now. Because she hated that word. She hated what it meant— loyalty to this horrible Commonwealth. But if she was going to start needling her way in, then she should probably play the game. Doing homework. Listening to lectures. Slowly finding information. Bit by bit memorizing weapon plans.

She'd go along with being a cadet for now, until they'd all forgotten about the Blood Wolf within their ranks. Once their defenses were down, only then would she flash her teeth.

CHAPTER 22
KNIVES

KNIVES WAS INSIDE Bastian's office, waiting for the headmaster to return. Bastian had called him to meet for a short check-in on the beginning of the semester. Knives stared at the class photos lining one of the walls of Bastian's office. In the middle of the set, the photos had shifted from holographs to printed photos, the film grain dappling the faces of people in the image. That had been one of Bastian's decisions when he became headmaster. He loved the idea of paper, how the ink would fade and the paper would age. So finite, he would explain, just like life.

Knives stopped at a photo from the class that graduated a year before his and stared at a face that look almost like his own. High nose, thin lips, and dark, strong eyebrows. As he looked at his sister, he felt his breath leave him.

The office door opened, and Bastian entered. He stepped silently in line beside him. "Ah, Marnie. She was one of our best."

Knives tensed at Bastian's use of the word *was*. "Still is. I don't know anyone who can fly like her."

"Not even our new charge?"

Knives paused, thinking of the way Ia had flown during the flight simulation. She'd navigated around those crumbling asteroids without a slight moment of hesitation. There was a ferocity in the way she used that jet. Something he hadn't seen, not for a while. "Don't compare them, Bastian."

Bastian angled his head, observing him. "It's been four months, hasn't it? Since it happened," Bastian said.

Knives stepped away from the wall of lost memories, lost souls. "I don't want to talk about it."

"Then we won't." Bastian patted him on the back. "Are you adjusting well to your instructor duties? I imagine the transition might be difficult."

Knives wandered over to the plush green sofa at the opposite side of the room and plopped down on it, grabbing the wooden paperweight on the coffee table to distract himself. If he had been asked that question a year ago, he would have laughed. Taking a teaching position wasn't even close to being on his to-do list.

"I recite facts that I find off the ArcLite," Knives answered. "It's easy."

Bastian sat down in the armchair across from him. "Easy, yes. But is it what you want to do?"

Knives shrugged. "I'm here, aren't I?"

"Well, there are still other opportunities for you," Bastian mentioned casually. "For instance, the Serval Campaign still needs a captain."

Knives glanced up at Bastian. Placement on a Star Force campaign was something he would never entertain, and he thought Bastian understood this. But his father was another story.

Knives narrowed his eyes. "Did *he* ask you to bring this up?"

"No." Bastian's gaze softened. "Knives, when you turned down the colonization campaign, I didn't ask questions. After what happened with Marnie, of course you needed time to heal. To grieve."

Knives was on the verge of standing up and bolting when Bastian pulled up a file from his holopad and sent it his way. Knives glanced at it. It was his academy records from his past two years of training at Aphelion.

"High marks on all your exams, advanced cognitive skills due to your eidetic memory. Not to mention all the flying accolades you've accrued from your training. As much as I like having you around, it pains me to see you squandering your talent. Marnie was one of our best, and so are you. But you gave up before you could try."

Knives grunted and waved his file back to Bastian. "Because there's no point. Marnie trained like a beast. You can be good at what you do, but skills don't matter when you're marooned in your jet with only minutes of oxygen left." Knives banged the paperweight onto the table's surface with a loud thud.

"That's not going to happen to you."

Knives scowled. "You think I won't take on a campaign because I'm scared? They sent her on a mission with no backup. She died alone, Bastian. They forgot about her up there."

Knives was done with this conversation, and he was *done* believing the false promises the Star Force fed him all throughout his life. Why fight for them, when they would just abandon you? Now when he raised his fist against his heart in salute, he no longer meant it. Knives got up and walked to the door. He passed by her photograph. She stood in the third row, shoulder squared, fist on her chest like a good cadet.

He thought of what Marnie's life would have been like if she hadn't taken the path of an officer. She would have finally perfected her ramen recipe. Gone on to beat Knives's high score in *CometKaze*. She would have fallen in love, started a family.

And she would still be alive.

Knives took a deep breath, ready to step back out into Aphelion's halls, where Marnie had bragged about breaking academy time trial records, gave advice to first-year flyers still on their training thrusters, where she smuggled Knives up to the Nest for his first taste of archnol. It paralyzed him, the memory of her. It kept him here, haunting the halls for glimpses of his sister.

"You have to move forward, Knives," Bastian said, calling after him. "You know Marnie would want that for you."

He didn't want to explain it to Bastian for fear he wouldn't understand. There was another reason he had chosen this limbo. Generations of cadets had roamed these halls, and now there was a new flock. When he looked at these kids, he saw his sister, and he saw himself. Blinded by Commonwealth promises.

By the time he had figured it out, Marnie was gone, and he had no one.

It was too late for him, but not for them. One day, some of these cadets would open their eyes and see it. And when they finally did come to that crossroad, he would be there.

And unlike him, they wouldn't be alone.

CHAPTER 23

IA

EVERY MORNING, Ia woke up early, too early. Like at the crack of dawn early. And it wasn't by choice. Her guards were at her door at 0600 to escort her to her first class. The classes were back-to-back and ended at 1800—sometimes even at 2100, depending on her engine maintenance duties, which both first-year and second-year engineers were assigned to.

There really wasn't much free time except for eating hours. Sometimes she'd catch a glimpse of Knives dashing out of the canteen with an apple in his mouth, but he never stopped to talk. The other cadets avoided her like the plague.

Her spare time was usually divided into figuring out how to escape and working out. But now that Einn wanted her to scope out Aphelion's high-security training grounds and since he couldn't rescue her until she found out Aphelion's exact location, escape was off her to-do list, at least for now.

So she threw herself into her exercise routine. She was stuck here, so she could at least hone her body to the point where she could easily crack some skulls. One hundred sit-ups, one hundred push-ups, and one hundred lunges, mixed in with some core isometrics designed to strengthen her balance. Tarver hated it. Ia often caught Brinn glaring in her direction while Ia was in the middle of her routine. But at least then there was eye contact.

One night, after her exercises, Ia sat on her bed, rubbing the ache out of her limbs. It had been nearly a month since she arrived at the academy, and she was finally starting to feel strong again, building muscles that carved harder, sharper angles onto her arms and legs. And she was gaining some much-needed weight by gorging on bags and bags of delicious chocofluff from the canteen. She was beyond addicted.

As the days went by, Ia grew more and more curious about her roommate. She had forced Tarver into lending her ho-lowatch one more time by threatening to run out into the hall-ways and scream Brinn's secret at the top of her lungs. Tarver had begrudgingly complied, and Ia was able to give Einn a few more updates on Aphelion's layout. The highlight was that the academy housed a uranium core with enough power to fuel a whole planet for hundreds of years. That was all she could relay to him, since Tarver was as stingy with the time as ever.

Through their small interactions, Ia had discovered a few things about Tarver. That she had few friends. That despite her IQ, she aimed to be a mediocre student, and that out-side this dorm room, Brinn always thought before she acted. Within the room itself, Tarver was moody and uncomplacent.

Ia rolled to her side and peeked over at Brinn sitting on her own bed. Tarver had stopped camping out in the bathroom and started sleeping in the main room. She was dressed in a pair of sweatpants and a white cotton shirt with the quartered shield across the front, a shirt that Ia refused to wear, no matter how comfortable it looked. Tarver stared blankly at her holoscreen. Ia knew it wasn't homework, but just an excuse for Tarver not to look at her.

"What are you doing?" Ia asked.

Brinn didn't respond.

Did she not hear her? Ia was sure she said it loud enough; she had a habit of speaking like the world should hear.

"Are you just looking at a blank screen so you don't have to talk at me?"

Again, no response.

"We *are* roommates." Ia propped her head up on her pillow. "We might as well talk to each other."

Brinn shot her a look. "So you can blackmail me again?"

"No," she answered. "So we can relieve ourselves from this useless boredom."

Tarver's face twisted at the chatter in the room, and she made a point of putting No-Noise buds in her ears.

Ia sighed and then tilted her head up to the audio speaker in the center of the room. "Monitor?"

"Yes, cadet?"

"Pull up a game of Goma," Ia requested.

A screen materialized in front of her, displaying a diamond shaped game board, sectioned off from tip to tip. The goal of the game was to take control of the enemy pieces and territory. Ia clicked on a black piece and placed it in the middle of the board. She swiped the screen across the room so it landed directly in front of Tarver. If they were going to be angry with each other, they might as well have some fun with it.

Tarver stared at the screen and then shook her head, tapping on the display before sending it back over to her.

Ia smirked, looking over the Goma board. Brinn Tarver had made her first move, and it was a ballsy one.

* * *

They had already played through three games, all which Ia had easily won.

It was then that Brinn finally broke her silence. "You're cheating, aren't you?"

"It's called strategy."

Brinn buried her face into her pillow, letting out a muffled groan. "You're impossible."

"Shall we make it more fun?" Ia grinned. "Chocofluff to whoever wins?"

"Fine," Brinn said with a wave of her hand. "But my brain has the ability to predict the success probability of every move you will make. And this time, I'm not going to hold back."

* * *

Ia woke up the next morning, rubbing her eyes as she glanced across the room. Tarver's bed was already made, and she was nowhere to be seen. Ia's gaze settled on the middle of the room, and she grinned.

On top of the center table lay a bag of chocofluff.

CHAPTER 24
BRINN

IT WAS FINALLY FRIDAY, and Brinn's last class was on the flight deck. Their daily schedule was so packed that she couldn't wait for the next day, which was a free day. Most cadets used the day to socialize, maybe even go on dates, but Brinn just wanted to catch up on some rest, which could be hard with Ia sharing the same room.

The flyers started their training missions today, and the Aeronauticals—second-year engineers who had chosen to specialize in maintaining the training jets—and the first-year engineers were assigned to clean up after their mess. Brinn was in the hallway on the way to their meeting location when her holowatch beeped.

She swiped at her screen, pulling up the message. Her face paled as she read, and before she was done, she was already running, scanning the halls until she spotted Ia from behind, her familiar black bob swishing above her shoulders. She grabbed Ia by the elbow, then glanced behind at the guards before leading Ia a few steps away so that they wouldn't hear.

"I just got a message from the headmaster," Brinn said. "He wants me to come to his office."

"Don't look at *me*. I didn't say anything," Ia grumbled.

"Do you think he knows? Is there any way they could have found out about…" She pointed at the neural tap hidden underneath the hair at the base of Ia's head.

Ia glared at her. "No," she hissed. "The connection is completely private."

Brinn was on the verge of panicking. If they found out she'd helped Ia, she would be convicted of treason. The oxygen inside banged against her lungs, threatening to leave and never return.

She thought Ia would laugh at the state she was in, but instead Ia patted her softly on the back. "Relax. It's probably nothing."

Brinn felt unbalanced. It was one of the first times in her life that she didn't have a clear solution to a problem. Normally when she was unable to figure something out, she asked Faren for advice, but he wasn't there. And going to Angie for help would instantly burn the bridge between them. Here in Aphelion, there was only one person she could turn to. She looked over at Ia. "What should I do?"

Ia stiffened at the earnestness of her tone. But then her eyes focused. "A good friend once told me you can never outsmart a Tawny. Just remember that, and you'll be fine."

* * *

Brinn sat in a chair facing the headmaster's desk, her back straight and her hands clasped in her lap. He studied her, and she studied him, watching his brows knit into a vee, his jaw clenching into hard lines. She took a deep breath to keep herself from fainting in her seat.

"I just wanted to check in on you. How are things working out with Ia?"

Brinn stared at her fingers, trying to figure out the least conspicuous thing to say.

"She sings in her sleep," Brinn said softly. "It wakes me up in the middle of the night."

It had happened the first night she slept in the main room. As she lay awake, a tiny hum came from Ia's side of the room. Brinn lay on her side, observing Ia's dormant figure, convinced she would stir, but Ia's eyes remained closed, and the hum quickly turned into a tune, mournful and dissonant. Utterly unlike the songs of Olympus. It lasted for three bars when the melody descended into a gurgly snore.

Brinn had eased back into bed, a little baffled by what had transpired. Maybe there was some meaning to it? She spent most of the night sequencing the note progression, trying to decrypt whatever message could be hidden underneath its melody. It led her in circles until finally she decided there was no message at all. It was a sad song, and that was all it was. But every night from then on, she listened.

The headmaster leaned back in his chair, drumming his fingers upon his desk. "Ia singing in her sleep is hardly anything worth worrying over."

He scratched his chin with the pink rubber end of his writing utensil. Brinn was certain it was called a pencil, though she'd never actually seen one. He went on scribbling something into his journal while they spoke. From the brushstrokes, she could tell they were a series of numbers.

"And is there anything else odd that you'd like to bring up?" he asked while he wrote.

That was a question Brinn wanted to avoid completely. She stared at the headmaster's pencil as it erased one of the graphite scratchings on the page. Not scratchings, really. But numbers, math. Instantly, she remembered Ia's advice. *You can never outsmart a Tawny.*

Instead of answering his question, she tapped the piece of paper. "Don't," she said.

His hand stopped, and Headmaster Weathers's evergreen eyes rose.

"Don't erase that," Brinn said. "You still need it."

"Is that so?" His eyes darted along the string of numbers littering his page, but when he realized Brinn was peering at his work, he closed the cover.

"If you just tweak it so that X is a variable, not a constant, then the last part will work."

He gave her a look and then reopened his journal to peer down at his formula.

"If you want," she added, "you could simplify it even further."

The headmaster ripped out a blank page. He scrawled Brinn's name on it and slid it over to her. His other hand held out his writing utensil for her to use.

Brinn took it from him and leaned over the blank page. She started scribbling. It felt awkward to physically handwrite each symbol and number, and the lines didn't appear as neat as they would on a holoscreen.

She set the pencil down when she was finished. The head-master plucked the paper from her, positioning it at a readable angle. His fingers tapped on the page, moving from one section to the next. And then his eyes swooped up to hers. "How did you *do* this?"

"I suppose I see numbers differently than other people…"

His words burst out of him. "I've been trying to crack this wretched thing for nearly twenty years now. My experiments have only been able to transfer energy one way, but not the other. And without properly maintaining the balance, the whole thing collapses within minutes. But with this"—he tapped the piece of paper—"we can open a door that we can finally go through."

"What exactly are you working on, sir?" Brinn asked.

His expression fell as if plucked from a fanciful dream; then he peered at her like she was either precious or danger-ous. Brinn couldn't tell which one it was.

He tapped his pencil against the wooden desktop. It made a high-pitched ticking sound like an old-fashioned clock. "You're a very unique girl, cadet. Smart. *Observant.*" He paused, eyes flashing at her. "But for now, I kindly request you keep this between you and me."

Brinn shut her mouth and nodded.

The headmaster closed his notebook. "You're dismissed."

Brinn left the office, her worries now replaced with questions.

She was a girl who was used to secrets. Hiding her identity, then covering for Ia as she spoke to her brother. Now Brinn was charged with another one. She had seen those equations, and they played by a different set of rules. Whatever the head-master was working on was based on a new realm of science. It was something that went beyond the universe itself.

She just had to hope that they stayed as they were. Numbers. And nothing else.

CHAPTER 25

IA

IA STOOD ON THE TARMAC, staring at the Head Aeronautical, a Second Year who looked like he had just hit puberty.

"Everyone to your stations," the boy barked. "I want these jets cleaner than when they first got here."

Brinn was lucky. Ia would much rather be chatting up the headmaster instead of stuck doing deck duty. If she ever had the chance to have an audience with the headmaster, she'd have a field day, asking him everything she could about Aphelion. Like where it was located for starters.

But for now, she'd have to unearth Aphelion's secrets all on her own.

Ignoring the Head Aeronautical's orders, Ia wandered to the outer boundary of the tarmac. She had been focused on gathering intel. Sights, sounds, schedules, voices. Anything that would be helpful in either an escape plan or the complete decimation of Olympus. And now, finally, was the perfect time to take pictures of the flight deck.

Her left eye clicked into camera mode, and she took photos of all the jets and their storage order, making note of which ones were in better condition than the others. From close inspection, she noted the doors were locked with fingerprint scans. Every single one of them. She scratched her head. Well, then, she would have to cut someone's finger off.

She took a glance at some of the engines. Most of them came back steaming, which meant these tyros were riding too hard on their thrusters. As she cornered around the tail of one of the jets, a Second Year placed a hose in her hands. Ia stared at it, shocked.

That little scuzz expected her to wash the grime off this ship.

Grumbling, she clicked off her eye mod. She was the Sovereign of Dead Space, not a maid. Yet sadly, this tiresome task would be the most interesting part of her week. She twisted the hose on and pointed the water at the burned layer of debris gunked up under one of the wings.

It took her two hours to get the training jet spotless. No one helped her. Everyone else worked in teams, steering clear of her. Even the Second Year who was maintaining the engines of that same starjet kept his distance. By the time Ia was done, everyone had completed their duties and headed back to their quarters, leaving her in the sole company of her guards.

Suddenly, there was movement as starjets shifted on the hanging system above, rotating around the track in unison. The jets were in a different class than the training jet she had spent most of her evening polishing. No matter how much she scrubbed at the frame, it was still an ugly, clunky thing. The jets above looked dangerous, especially one particular white model, long and sharp as a blade. She watched as it lowered to the tarmac a couple meters away. It was a 504 Kaiken jet, with red and orange racing stripes still painted on the sides.

What was a racer doing here?

Ia glanced back at Geoff and Aaron, who were leaning up against the wall, immersed in a heated discussion on the correct way to clean their charge pistols. They wouldn't notice if she took a closer look. She crept around a line of parked training jets. And there it was, right in front of her.

She reached up, running her fingers along the smooth metal. It was in pristine condition. Whoever owned this jet took good care of it.

"What are you doing here?"

Ia turned and saw Knives. She had been wondering when they'd bump into each other. Every time she saw him, she looked him over from head to toe, wondering where he kept the silver heart tracker that day.

But the heart tracker wasn't the only reason she remained firm in her place. He would be useful in *other* ways. Tonguing the bio-metal node at the top of her mouth, she turned on her vocal synthesizer. Yet another toy in her bag of tricks that the academy had failed to confiscate from her. A short chat with him would secure several sample sets of phonetic syllables and generate an identical match. She'd be able to literally use his voice.

"Need a hand?"

He ignored her, sifting through the drawers of the standing toolbox.

A little bit of flirtation wouldn't hurt, and it wasn't like she'd mean it anyway. She just needed to get him to talk. Confidently, she angled her head so that she could catch his gaze.

But then his ice-blue eyes flicked up at her, bright like starlight, and her heart swayed. Perhaps the wiring they put insider her was acting up, she thought, entirely dismissing that uneven, fuzzy feeling that had left her speechless.

Knives stared at Ia, then rolled his eyes. "What's the catch?"

She shook herself out of her daze and placed one hand on her hip. "I like your ride. That's all." She patted the undercarriage of the jet. "You don't see them very often."

"You know about this model?" he asked.

She nodded. "Only that Vars Ferrini flew this exact racer to win the Allmetal Cup two years in a row."

Knives snorted and turned away. But Ia could tell he was impressed.

"Go get the fuel pods," he said finally.

"If I help out," she said, standing firmly before him, "let me sit inside."

There were two reasons why she wanted to scope out the Kaiken's cockpit. It could be a great escape vehicle later on, and also just to check it out, to sit in wonder at how spectacular this piece of machinery was.

Knives stared at the Kaiken, considering.

Ia held her right hand across her heart and pledged. "I'll be on my best behavior. Look, my guards are right there, watching me like hawks."

Off to the side, Aaron tapped his two fingers to his temple in salute, acknowledging that he had heard every word she had said.

"Fine," Knives grunted.

Ia smiled. "How many do you need?" she asked, moving toward the fuel shelves.

"Six."

Before Knives could even grab his tools, Ia had returned with a cart of fuel pods behind her and a pair of pliers held out in offering.

With another grunt, he grabbed the pliers and started switching out his old spark plugs for new ones. Ia opened the fuel latch near the tail of his jet.

Knives hovered in her periphery, studying every move she made. "You better not be sabotaging me."

"There are better ways to sabotage a person than to mess with their fuel." She held up a screw in her fingers. "For instance, I could run this over your window and weaken the glass enough to shatter at takeoff. You'd die instantly."

"You can kill me," he said, snatching the metal screw from her, "but leave the jet out of it. I'm still paying this thing off."

Chuckling, she heaved the last of the pods into the charge receptor. "Six fuel pods, huh? Where are you heading?"

She was fishing for information, and he seemed to know. His eyes narrowed.

"I'm your instructor. I don't have to answer you."

She glared at him. "Those ranks don't mean anything up in the All Black. One day, you'll see."

"You can say that if you ever get to fly again."

Ia winced, suddenly furious by his jabbing tone. He was right, but that didn't mean she wanted to hear it. "Are we done here?" She took her gloves off, ready to leave.

She walked back to her guards, balling her hands into fists. As long as she was here, she would never be able to go up in the All Black again, much less sit behind the wheel of another jet.

"Wait." Knives's voice echoed throughout the flight deck. "I thought you wanted to see inside."

She stopped and glared at him over her shoulder.

He pulled down the ladder to the cockpit and looked at her. There was something apologetic in his expression that chipped away at her anger.

She stormed up to him. "You better not be miffing with me."

Knives shook his head, then produced a pair of cuffs. "I'm not. But you have to wear these."

She gave him the side-eye, and then finally held out her arms. Being cuffed would be worth it to see the inside of this jet. All she needed were her eyes anyway, to get a glimpse of the panels and displays in order to know how to use the Kaiken for her escape if she had to.

After Knives bound her wrists together, she was instructed to sit in the front pilot seat of the narrow cockpit. Knives sat directly behind her, in the copilot chair—which was boosted to see outside and at the same time gave him a full view of everything she was doing. It would be hard to access any information from his logs or MOS or to even snoop through his side compartments to see if there was anything silver and egg-shaped inside.

The cabin was surprisingly clean. Even the windows were free of smudgy fingerprints. Not at all like her jet. She didn't go out of her way to keep her own ship, *Orca*, in mint

Ia's lips curled into a smile. She was home.

Once they breached the upper atmosphere, Knives disengaged the thrusters, the roar dying down around her.

"You still have time to back out, to save yourself the embarrassment," he said.

Ia leaned her head against the headrest. "Knives, for me, this isn't even a challenge."

He scoffed in disbelief. "Yeah, yeah. Let's get started."

She held her bound hands up. "This would be easier without my handcuffs."

Knives saw right through that. "You can manage," he replied.

Ia shrugged and swiveled forward. She centered herself in the driver seat as Knives hovered the starjet into position, aimed at a strip of wide, empty space.

"You should be able to hit max acceleration in no time with this baby," Ia said. "The question is, how long can you maintain the speed?"

Behind her, buttons clicked and meters beeped as Knives lined everything up, surely and swiftly.

She placed her fingertips along the middle of the steering wheel, feeling the engine hum. The gauges flittered to life as Knives eased onto the throttle, and the front thrusters kicked in.

Acceleration pushed against her body. The stars in the distance shifted from sharp pinpoints to blurs of light bleeding into black.

Deus, this ship was fast.

The engine revved up, and Knives engaged the rear thrusters. Ia cringed as she felt a slight jolt underneath her feet. The engine was struggling, being forced, instead of flowing into its cycle.

She turned to face him. "You're advancing the front throttle too quickly. It's throwing your acceleration cycle off."

Knives furrowed his brow. "I'm telling you, with an updated MOS and processor, I'll be able to monitor the cycle better."

She waved his response off. "That's just being lazy. Let's do another run, and I'll tell you when to punch the throttle."

"Front and rear engines on," Knives voiced to the MOS. He gunned the front thrusters, and she felt the familiar pulse of speed rush through her veins.

If it were any other time, the two of them would be in different starjets trying to blast each other into oblivion. A criminal and a Bug. But now, together they were just two pilots trying to answer an age-old question: *How could they go faster?*

Even though the engines were made of thousands of precisely cut parts, fine-tuned by engineers, each had its own personality. "Your engines have a higher pitched hum at the exact moment you should move on to the next thruster."

Through the metal frame, the engine whistled as it approached its peak.

"All right," she said. "Now!"

Knives pulled on the throttle, and with another surge, the starjet shot forward, pushing her back into her seat. The propulsion was heavenly. She felt it in her flesh. So smooth, with so much power. It was perfect.

She glanced over her shoulder. She laughed, seeing the energized grin on his face, and her eyes met his. "Your turn."

A small smile flickered onto his lips, one of childish glee.

Ia closed her eyes, shutting out everything except for the chatter of the engine. It started with a murmur of gears, of compression and building pressure. Until finally the engine itself sang out.

Now.

Knives triggered the afterburner, and the ship catapulted forward.

She sat back, her blood pulsing through her veins, feeling the thrill of the ride.

By the time she opened her eyes, Knives was already navigating them back to Aphelion.

Ia's heart ached at the thought of returning.

Out here, there were no strings holding them down. She scanned the blackness around her, orienting herself to the stars. In the distance, a light pulsed like a beacon. An interstellar gate, unmarked so she didn't know which one it was. But it was so close.

If only they could keep going, flying faster and faster into infinity. Don't stop, she wanted to say. Her lips molded around each syllable, but her voice was caught in her chest. She knew Knives would never grant her that wish, so there was no point in saying it.

CHAPTER 26
BRINN

"YOU LOOK LIKE MUNG," Angie said, grabbing Brinn after dinner Monday evening. "Ia problems?"

Brinn rubbed her knuckles against her eyes. It wasn't Ia problems, but Brinn nodded anyway just so Angie wouldn't ask any questions. Brinn's meeting with the headmaster had stressed her out, and remarkably, Ia was the one who'd helped her through it. After everything that had happened last week, all Brinn had wanted to do was curl up in her room and sleep, and that's exactly what she'd done—all weekend long. Apparently, it wasn't enough to wipe away the deep stress lines digging in between her eyebrows.

"Did you know Ia set fire to a whole Olympus comms station last year?" Angie rambled on. "The new colonies didn't get supplies for weeks. It was legit on the media. She would give me nightmares."

"She's not all bad," Brinn said, suddenly aware that she was coming to Ia's defense.

Angie gaped at her in shock.

Brinn shrugged one shoulder as casually as she could. "She's been teaching me how to win at Goma."

"The game old grandpas play?" It was meant as a question, but Angie's voice was very high, very sharp.

Brinn turned away, not wanting to see the judgment in Angie's eyes.

"Oh, Brinn, she's torturing you!"

"I think you have the wrong definition of torture. Besides, it's kinda fun."

"And I think *you* have the wrong definition of fun," Angie replied. Her eyelashes fluttered as an idea took hold. "Come on. I know how we can fix that."

Angie took Brinn's hand and tugged her through the halls until they lined up behind a group of cadets swarming into the First Year common room.

As they walked in, Angie waved hello to a few passing cadets, most of them boys, and found a free space on one of the couches. She sat down, motioning for Brinn to join her. Brinn stood there, staring at the empty seat before Angie pulled her down beside her.

A floating bev machine drifted by, and Angie held out a hand to stop it. "Two caffeines."

The machine produced two bottles from the drop chute in its center. Angie took a bottle of the orange beverage and handed the other to Brinn. Brinn took a sip and scanned the room. A handful of engineering cadets were having a debate about engine mechanics on another couch. In the middle of the room, Cammo gripped a Poddi, a compact blue force field ball, and tried to find a free person to toss it to.

"Over here," Liam called out nearby.

Hearing his voice, Brinn's eyes darted over to him. He stood by the long communal table where a group of female cadets, including Reid from their teamwork test, watched rapt with attention.

Cammo launched the Poddi, accidentally arching it too far. Liam had to sprint to the front of the room to catch it. As he turned to head back to the rest of his group, his eyes locked on to Brinn's.

Exactly 2.3 seconds, she counted. That was how long it took to break away from his gaze, which was one full second too long based on her natural reaction speeds. There was something about him that always slowed her down. By the time she glanced back up, Liam was already at Cammo's side, listening to another one of his jokes.

"All the girls are talking about him," Angie said, drawing out the words like they were taffy. "Liam Vyking is such a flooder."

Brinn furrowed her brow as she tried to figure out what Angie meant.

Angie sighed, realizing Brinn's confusion. "That means he's nice to look at, like he's flooding your heart."

Brinn watched Angie's gaze hover over Liam, and she felt a strange weight creep into her chest. Every boy in the world was in love with Angie; all she had to do was take her pick.

Then Angie's eyes shifted over to Cammo. "Honestly, I think his friend is way better."

Brinn relaxed.

"Go for another one," Cammo yelled as the Poddi zoomed overhead. Brinn's eyes followed its trajectory as it arched over Liam's head.

A hand came up, lithe and golden.

All at once, the room quieted. Ia Cōcha stood in the doorframe, palming the Poddi in her right hand. "Can I play?" she called across the room.

Cammo drew out a wide and undiscerning grin. "Sure."

And with that one word, the tension in the room ebbed away just a little bit. Everyone turned back to their own conversations. Ia tossed the ball back and forth with Cammo while Liam took a seat at the communal table among the same group of girls who were fawning over him.

A news program played on the screens floating in the center of the room. Mug shots flashed on the displays. They were the Tawnies captured the same night the Commonwealth took down Ia Cōcha. The group was on trial for harboring a wanted criminal as well as opening fire on Star Force officers.

Around them, Brinn heard people's whispers as they passed their own judgments.

"They should rot in jail for firing on us," someone said.

"They're refs. They don't even have rights," said another.

Guilty was the word she heard repeated the most.

Brinn glanced over at Ia to gauge her reaction, but she was too busy dazzling Cammo with a fancy-looking Poddi move to notice.

Onscreen, the news anchor stared into the lens with a neutral expression. "The trial has shed light on the refugee crisis within Olympus's borders, spurring an outcry for action."

The news program cut to recorded footage of a man standing at the podium. He had graying brown hair and was dressed in a silken black Commonwealth jacket, one that all government officials wore, except that this jacket had golden rope looped on the shoulders.

Beside her, Angie groaned. "My dad's on the media again."

"That's him?" Brinn asked. "So he got elected to the Council?"

Angie crossed her arms, slouching low in her seat. "Yeah, and Nero's been a massive mung about it. My dad and his uncle are on opposing sides." She rolled her eyes, spying Nero crossing the room.

"Hey, Everett, didn't know your family was leftist trash," Nero called as he passed by.

Angie made a face that Brinn had never seen before. "Just because my dad doesn't want to get rid of the Sanctuary Act doesn't mean he's a radical, Nero."

The Sanctuary Act protected the refugees that had been affected by the Uranium War. It established refugee blocks in all the major city centers within Olympus, giving them a safe place to live within the Commonwealth if they chose it. If the act was repealed, the blocks would be eradicated and the refugees deported. To where, no one really knew.

Above them, a montage of footage splayed across the screen. A huge protest filled the streets in front of the Council House. "No more refs! No more mungbringers!" the people chanted as they held long, wooden poles above their heads. Makeshift dolls swung side to side, hanging off the tips of the poles from nooses. The dolls bore the blue hair of the

Tawnies, or the silver markings of the Dvvinn, or the pointed ears of the Juorti. All refugee nations of the Commonwealth. The discrimination against the Tawnies was most noticeable in the crowd, with the word *mungbringer* stamped on several protest signs. While the footage played on, the room quieted as more eyes focused upon the screen.

A flash of blue flew through the air in a blur. The Poddi smashed into the bulb of the central holoprojector. The screens distorted and then blinked out.

"Oh, come on," groaned Nero.

"Oops," Ia said flatly. She stood with her arms crossed, her eyes simmering as they passed over the room. "My hand slipped."

Nero stepped forward. A handful of cadets gathered behind him. "You're just mad because no matter how hard you try, you'll never be able to save them. And no one else is stupid enough to think they deserve saving."

Ia narrowed her eyes, her neck muscles tensing. Brinn sized up the group. If a fight broke out, it would be seven against one. Ia was outnumbered, but Brinn was sure Ia would still win. Because Angie was right. Ia was the source of nightmares. There was no way a handful of tyro cadets would stand a chance against her.

But instead of throwing the first punch, Ia Cōcha left the room.

Brinn stormed after her, her anger growing with every step.

Why couldn't Ia just stay out of trouble? Maybe even blend in for a change? That was something Brinn did every day of her life. In a way, Ia reminded Brinn of her mother. Stubborn.

Headstrong. Pride bursting from her pores. They were both so infuriating.

Brinn expected the room to be trashed, but instead found Ia in the bathroom calmly washing her face.

"Why'd you do that?" Brinn demanded.

Ia angled her head, her face still dripping wet. "Do what?"

"Make a scene."

Ia grabbed a towel. "That was *not* a scene. You realize I could have snapped that kid's neck, right?"

"And you want points for that?"

Ia shrugged.

"You still broke the holoscreens." Brinn crossed her arms. "You know people actually wanted to watch what was on."

"That trial is just a bunch of propaganda." Ia snorted as she flopped onto her bed.

After everything that had happened today, Brinn wasn't in the mood to hear one of Ia's conspiracy theories.

"It's not propaganda," she replied. "It's called justice. They shot down our officers. The footage speaks for itself."

Brinn replayed the images in her head, of the Tawnies on that ship gunning down Star Force officers. She had seen it over and over again on the daily news streams. It was even used in the RSF recruitment videos.

"You think the Commonwealth would ever show themselves shooting first?" Ia scoffed. "Those Tawnies were just defending themselves. I would know. *I* was there."

"You're lying," Brinn hissed.

"I'll prove it." Ia held her hand out. "Give me your holopad."

Brinn wanted to laugh out loud. What kind of proof could

she possibly have? Brinn glared at her defiantly as she handed Ia her holopad. Ia undid the backing and grabbed one of the wires, linking into the input at the base of her head. Her eyes shifted back and forth as if she was trying to find something, eyelids fluttering rapidly, until finally she unplugged the wire and handed back Brinn's holopad.

Brinn glanced onto her home screen. There was a new file, sitting at the bottom of the display.

"What's this?"

"A recording." Ia's eyes rose. "Of the day I was captured."

Brinn tapped on it, and a holoscreen projected into the space in front of her. The footage was from Ia's point of view. She saw gray, rusted walls, the same background as the media footage she had become so familiar with. There was no gunfight. Not yet. But she knew it was coming. She waited for the first Tawny to load his weapon, but none of them seemed to be armed. That didn't make any sense. The Tawnies were the ones who fired first.

Hypnotized, Brinn watched as the Star Force officers charged into the rusty metal ship. She watched as General Adams walked down the line of Tawnies. Then watched as he grabbed at one of them, a boy a couple years younger than her, and pointed a gun right at his skull.

Brinn's eyes widened in horror. She looked down as the rest of the scene played out, staring at the smooth metal on the floor. She heard Ia's voice defending them, then the screams, the gunfire. Until she'd had enough. She swiped the screen away and stopped the recording.

Across the room, Ia watched her. "Believe me now?"

It was a fake, Brinn tried to tell herself. Over and over again. But she couldn't get past the image of the general raising his weapon. It was as if he was pointing his gun at her, ready to shatter the world she lived in.

"Why would you show me that?" she asked angrily.

"Because you need to start asking questions," Ia answered. "The Commonwealth doesn't care about the Tawny refugees. And that trial...it's all for show, Tarver. A clever setup just to get the Sanctuary Act repealed and all the refugees out."

Her words were like a sandstorm, each speckle of dust finding cracks and crevices upon a seemingly polished veneer. It painted a picture of a different truth, one that Brinn refused to see.

"It doesn't matter. I'm a Citizen. I'll be safe." She said it, but it was more for herself than for Ia. A repeal would only affect the refugees who've claimed sanctuary in Olympus. She was a Tawny, but she *wasn't* a refugee.

"You think that matters? You already said it yourself. People hate the Tawnies." Ia shook her head as if she was through explaining. "Do I have to crack that thick skull of yours for you to get it? Once that act is repealed, they'll come for you next."

Brinn's mouth opened, but the words didn't come. She sank down onto her bed. Putting on her earbuds, she turned on a random music stream. The song that was on was light and saccharine, but it did nothing to ease her mood. No matter how hard she tried to ignore it, one foul question circled over and over in her mind: What if Ia was right?

CHAPTER 27
KNIVES

THEY WERE FALLING ASLEEP. During *his* lecture. The series, called Mapping the Star Systems, was meant to educate the cadets about all of the existing Commonwealth territories. There were a lot of lists, a lot of coordinates, a lot of memorization. All useful information.

But also very boring. Knives remembered this class when he was a cadet. He'd fallen asleep during this lecture block as well.

The weekly evening class was a requirement for all academy First Years, which meant the auditorium was full of drooping eyelids. A deep, gurgly snore interrupted one of his sentences, not intentional, since everyone was too fast asleep to even laugh.

Knives clapped his hands against the podium, the sound echoing against the ceiling. Sleep-stained eyes blinked open.

"I get it," he said. "You're bored."

He tapped on his watch so the hologram projected above

him dimmed into black, and the only source of light pooled around him.

"Then let me tell you a story. It's somewhat of an academy tradition. Has anyone heard of a star system called Fugue?"

Eyes blinked at him in silence.

"No? None of you?" he asked. "I'll tell you why. Olympus doesn't want any of you to know what happened there."

Even in the dim, he could make out a number of cadets leaning forward in their seats. At least he was getting their attention now.

"Years ago," Knives continued, "Fugue was the next star system due for colonization. We had just completed the Wuvryr Gate, which was set to jump straight there. Everyone was certain it would be an easy campaign. The day came, and the colonial fleets made the jump, but after a few days, there were no reports, no transmissions. No one thought much of it, just that the fleet was too busy with their campaign to report in.

"Finally on the seventh day, a transmission came in. HQ was already in the middle of celebrating, knowing it'd be news of success. But when the Comms Lead opened the stream, there was only one short message.

Flee.

The cadets quieted, and he knew they were all listening. Even Ia watched him from her seat in the far corner.

Knives curled his voice into a willowy tone, feeling the tension in the air thicken. "To dismiss their fears, they told themselves the transmission was jumbled. Most likely, a longer message came before it, gone missing due to the weak connection. But the next day, comms received another transmission.

And this one had video."

Knives sped up the pace of his words, so each syllable fell at a running pace. "It was a simple security log, flipping through different angles of the ship's interior. The image was choppy, but it didn't matter. The color of blood is hard to mistake. Limbs, heads, torsos were scattered all over the cabin floor. Entrails hung from pipes in the ceiling.

"But the bodies weren't what troubled them the most."

His eyes scanned the auditorium. Some of the cadets hugged their knees up to their chests while others leaned against each other, clutching hands.

"The longer they stared at each image, the easier it was to see him." He pointed a finger up to a dark empty corner of the room, and he heard the squeak of metal as everyone shifted in their chairs. "There. A figure stood in the dark, staring not at the floor, not at the bodies, but at *them*. In the last seconds, it stepped forward, closer to the camera.

"And when it opened its mouth, there were no words." Knives tapped his watch, cuing up an audio file. "Only this."

A series of ghostly whispers hissed up into the high ceilings, rising with a haunting, pulsing crescendo. It was the sound of terror, of the unknown abyss.

When the audio waveform had finished, sinking the classroom into a frightened silence, Knives flicked at the light sensor. All the lights above flared on. His eyes scanned the cadet's faces, now pale and wide-eyed from the tale they had heard. Even Ia's face had blanched white.

Knives's lips curved upward. "Class dismissed. Good luck getting sleep tonight."

As the classroom emptied, he packed up his things. A holomap of the known star systems floated above him like a cloud. He was about to turn it off when a voice rose from the back row.

"Is that story true?"

He looked up and saw Ia staring at him, her arms draped over the seat in front of her, that smirk rippling across her face.

"Why do you ask?"

"I've never heard of a system called Fugue," she said. "And I've traveled all over the place. I bet I've even been to your home planet."

"I doubt it."

She jumped up from her seat and headed down the steps to the podium. "Try me. Where are you from?"

His brow furrowed at such a personal question. "Aphelion."

"Is that your final answer, or do you just want me to feel sorry for you?" Her voice was laced with humor. "How about I take a guess?"

She grabbed onto a control orb mounted on the lecture podium. Her fingers dragged across it, and above her the holomap shifted, zooming in to center on a star system and then another. Finally, she stopped on a system with nine planets.

It was Rigel Kentaurus.

She raised her eyebrows. "Am I right?"

He scratched the back of his neck. "Yes."

"Rigel Kentaurus, the central system of the Olympus Commonwealth." She tapped her finger on the podium. "It means you come from quite a powerful family."

She was right. Only the most influential members of the

Commonwealth lived in that star system. Governing leaders like the Royal Matriarchs, heads of major corporations, and the military elite like his father.

"And you?" he asked, eager to change the subject. "What side of the universe do you hail from?"

"You wouldn't believe me if I told you."

"I'm serious," he pressed on lightly. "I want to know."

Her hands spread against the orb on the podium, sweeping and circling until the map above fell on a completely dark space. Then she raised her hand, her index fingers jutting out like a gun, pointing into the black infinity.

"There," she said.

His heart sank. There weren't any planets there. All that was left was rubble floating around a shattered star.

"What is this place?" he asked.

"It was called the Maqronne system."

She raised her eyes to look at the empty map above her. "It was small. Only consisted of three planets. Broadside, Galatin." And then her gaze lowered to his. "And Cōcha."

His eyes widened. So that was how she got her name.

"It's a tradition from my father's side of the family to take the name of your birthplace. Our family hopped from planet to planet. Galatin was where my brother was born. And me, my planet was called Cōcha. It was where we stayed until..." Her voice trailed off as she stared off into the distance.

Knives remembered reading about the Maqronne system for one of his history classes. Over a decade ago, the tiny solar system self-imploded without warning. Every physicist and astronomer had their own theories, but since everyone from Maqronne was thought to be dead, no one could be entirely sure.

"Did you see it happen?" he asked.

"I wasn't there," Ia answered. "My brother and I stole a jet to search for our father right after he left. It was an impossible quest. But you know, when you're kid, you never want to believe you've been abandoned. Of course, we couldn't find him. We turned back, but by then, the Event had already happened. Our mother was gone. And so was our home." She paused, her face suddenly going red with anger. "All that was left was a bunch of space dust and Bugs sifting through the floating rubble."

Knives remained silent. He didn't know what to say. But now at the very least, her hatred toward the Commonwealth made sense. And instantly, it reminded him of everything that had happened to Marnie, how one simple heartless decision cost his sister her life.

"Miffing Bugs," he murmured.

She glanced at him, and then snorted. "Yeah, mif 'em."

His eyes traced the elegant line of her neck as she swiveled around to face him, her eyes sparking like collapsed stars swallowing up the surrounding light. She was a dark star, a black hole in the endless sky, and if he got too close, he would surely disappear.

He knew all this, but even then, he couldn't turn away from her.

There was no harm in looking, he told himself. There was never any harm in that.

CHAPTER 28

BRINN

IT WAS MIDWEEK, and Brinn was due at the headmaster's office in thirty minutes, leaving just enough time to stop by the canteen. He had been calling her to his office on a weekly basis for the past month to go over the mysterious equations in his journal.

She pressed her fingers over her eyelids, trying to rub the fatigue away. After her argument with Ia last week, she'd spent her nights watching the footage saved on her holopad. She played the image of the general raising his gun on that Tawny over and over. Even after watching it almost twenty times, it was still hard to believe. She was a Citizen, but would he shoot her too, if he had the choice?

When Brinn got to the canteen, she made a beeline for the bev dispenser. Taking a sip of fresh caffeine, she noticed a group of cadets sitting around a holoscreen.

Brinn edged toward the fringes of the group to see the screen, but lowered her bottle once she realized what was on.

The verdict for the trial had come in.

The judge, framed in the center of the screen, eyed each of the Tawny defendants. "For conspiring against the Olympus Commonwealth, I proclaim each of these defendants guilty. They are sentenced to jettison death one week from now."

Around her, the cadets erupted in collective applause.

"Take that, mungbringers," someone from the group whooped, while some of the other cadets stood on the chairs to cheer. Brinn stared at them. These cadets were her peers, her brothers and sisters of the Commonwealth. She should feel united with them, but a sliver of dread crept up her spine.

The footage panned down the line of Tawny prisoners, and as the camera settled on each face, the cadets booed. Brinn stepped backward, trying to sink back to the corners where no one would notice her.

Her eyes turned to the face that was projected on the display. It was the same boy from Ia's footage, the one the general had pointed his gun on. He couldn't have been any older than fifteen, her brother's age. But this boy was so different from Faren. Life and all its cruelty had made him that way. It had forced the boy's mouth into a hard line, molded his eyes into hopeless pits, painted scars where the skin should be soft.

And she knew now that this boy was innocent. That he wasn't the one who had fired first. Yet, Brinn couldn't say anything. She couldn't do a thing about it.

She backpedaled out of the canteen until she could no longer hear the news anchor's voice reverberating through the hallways. She pulled up her primary contacts and tapped on her brother's name, wanting desperately to hear Faren's voice. She wondered what he thought about the trial, and she still hadn't gotten a chance to tell him about what had actually happened on the Tawny ship before Ia was captured.

The stream connected, but instead, a woman's face flickered onto the surface of the display, her visage round, with soft wrinkles feathered at the outer edges of her wide eyes.

Brinn froze in the middle of the hallway. "Mom? Why do you have Faren's holo?"

Faren never took off his holowatch. He was too obsessed with tracking the Poddi League for updates.

Her mother's voice, which was usually smooth, was now pitted with cracks. "We're at the hospital."

Brinn felt a shock run through the entire length of her body. "Is everything all right?"

She noticed her mother's hair was uncovered, her navy blue tresses swept up into a tight, clean topknot. Everyone in the hospital would be able to see she was Tawny.

Brinn made her way to a more private corridor and glanced to make sure no one was there to hear. "Why are you with him? People are going to link the two of you together. They'll find out."

Her mother shook her head. "They already did. That's how this happened, Brinn."

"What?" Her eyes sharpened. There was no way Faren would have told anyone. "Is he there? Let me talk to him."

Her mother looked to the side as she spoke to someone off-screen, and then finally she slid the screen over to face Brinn's brother. Both of his eyes were black, his nose broken. The sight of him made her shake. She backed herself to the wall to find her balance.

"Hey, Fare. You okay?"

He nodded with a wince.

"What happened?"

"I got in a fight. They were picking on a Makolion boy in school. He wasn't doing anything wrong, just going to the bathroom. People cornered him. I had to stand up for him, Brinn."

She remembered the night of the Provenance Day parade, when the bystanders had turned on the refugees in the crowd. Faren had told her he wanted to help them. Brinn was the one who'd said no.

Her hands started to shake. Perhaps if she was there, none of this would have happened. "I told you to be careful."

"It's gotten bad here, with the trial and the Sanctuary Act hanging by a thread. There's so much hate."

"And that's why you don't get involved." She wanted to grab him by the shoulders, to make him understand.

He shook his head, and his voice was firm. "No. This is *why* we should get involved."

The image of the general raising his gun seared into her vision, but instead of the young Tawny boy on trial, she saw Faren's face. Ia was right. It didn't matter that she was a Citizen. Her whole family was in danger.

"Mom said they found out you're Tawny." She wanted to scream at him, but she couldn't, not in these hallways where everyone could hear, so her voice remained hushed yet sharp. "Seriously, Faren, you're just going to get yourself killed. How could you be so careless?"

Her brother looked up. "I told them, Brinn," he said. Even with the bruises, Brinn could see the deep-gray eyes that they both shared. "I don't want to hide who I am for the rest of my life. We shouldn't live like that."

Brinn felt the air in her lungs grow heavy, and all she wanted to do was lay her head on her brother's shoulder.

"You should rest." She heard her mother's voice offscreen. Faren smiled a farewell to Brinn before the screen flipped back to their mother.

"Is he going to be all right?" Brinn asked.

Her mother sighed as if trying to expel all her worries, but then she answered, her voice sure. Certain. "He's a Tawny. He'll survive."

But how could she be so sure? His eyes were black and swollen. He was beaten to a pulp. Brinn saw people like that on the movie streams, maybe even on the news, but not her brother. She regarded her mother, a face of steadfast calm despite everything.

"Aren't you scared, Mom?"

Her mother lowered her eyelids, thinking. "Do you know why I decided to keep my hair blue?"

Brinn thought about all the times she asked her mother why, and she remembered her answer. "As a reminder. Of everything that happened in the past. Of Tawnus. The war. Of all the people lost." All those sad memories.

"No, Brinn. That's not it at all," her mother replied. "It reminds me that after everything that's happened to us, we're still here. Our people are still alive."

* * *

When she met with the headmaster, Brinn was surprised to find he had no follow-up questions about Ia. Instead, he got straight to business and tasked Brinn with looking over a few equations. Numbers and patterns usually comforted her, but her mind was elsewhere, replaying her conversation with her brother and mother. Instead of feeling a sense of duty toward the Tawny people or betrayed by her own blind loyalty in the Commonwealth, she simply felt like she had been drained empty. Her sense of purpose was gone, as if all the direction signs had been uprooted and now she had to decide which way to turn. But all she could do was stand in place until she made a decision or until someone pushed her.

The headmaster, noticing her absentmindedness, excused her and sent her off with papers filled with the equations for her to finish on her own time. When she returned to her dorm, the room was empty.

Brinn placed her homework on the table and changed into a comfortable pair of black polymesh shorts and a light-gray tank top. When she was done, she sat down at the center table, her head in her hands. She couldn't stop all the questions crowding her head.

Brinn had always believed in Olympus and its ideals. *Of Progress. Of Prosperity. Of Proficiency.* It was the first part that haunted her. Her brother lying in a hospital bed after admitting he was Tawny. Was *that* progress?

Violence was an ugly thing. Usually she would tell herself that it was also a necessary one in order for the Commonwealth to be as powerful as it was. But she couldn't do that today. Because when she thought of Faren, she grew angry at herself for even trying to justify this in her mind. She couldn't patch things together, and now there was a hole she didn't know how to fill.

The door slid open, and Brinn pushed the palms of her hands onto her closed eyelids. She heard Ia enter, her boots clipping against the metal floor. The noise made Brinn's head thud harder.

"What's wrong with you?" Ia prodded.

Brinn angled her head so only one eye peeked out at her roommate. Ia sat across from her, taking a quick glance at the papers shuffled across the desk before grabbing for the open bag of chocofluff.

Brinn shook her head. She didn't want to tell Ia any of this. She would scoff at her and finish it off with a very smug *I told you so.*

"I don't feel well," Brinn answered instead.

Ia leaned forward and brushed her fingers against Brinn's forehead. Brinn glanced up at her. Ia could crack her skull open if she wanted to, yet here she was being gentle, being kind.

"You have a fever."

Brinn chuckled softly to herself. Of all the times, this would be when her body crumbled. "I don't even remember the last time I was sick."

Ia smirked. "I wonder why."

Brinn angled her head. "What is that supposed to mean?"

"Tawnies never get sick. Or, well, never *stay* sick."

Brinn stared blankly at Ia. She felt a thrum of guilt at just how much she didn't know about herself, but then she remembered what her mother had said earlier about Faren. *He's a Tawny. He'll survive.*

"Are you saying I can heal myself?"

"It'll take a toll on you, but it's possible. I've seen it before," Ia explained. "I fought a war with Tawny soldiers. They healed full plasma wounds to their heart tissue, lacerations to major arteries. One soldier I knew was caught in an explosion and lost his eye. It was the ugliest wound I've ever seen. The next day he showed up on deck with a face as smooth as a baby and a brand-new eye in his socket." Ia leaned in, her eyes wild. "You can do it too, you know?"

"Show me," Brinn said. If Ia was telling the truth, then Faren would be all right. His body would heal. "How did they do it?"

Ia shrugged. "I think you just have to will yourself to do it."

"That's not going to work. Look…" She pointed two fingers at her head. "Get rid of this fever, body," she commanded.

Ia's eyes met hers. "Give me your hand."

Brinn placed her palm on the tabletop. Ia scooped her fingers gently. "Do you trust me?" she asked.

"What are you going to—"

But before Brinn could finish, Ia gripped Brinn's forefinger and twisted it back. Her skin tore, and her bones snapped. Brinn screamed. The pain was so fierce that she almost tumbled out of her chair.

Brinn stared at her broken finger, trembling at the sight of bone poking through her flesh. Rivulets of crimson blood spilled out of the wound, dribbling down her forearm.

"You broke my finger." Brinn's voice shook.

Across the table, Ia stood with her arms crossed, offering her no assistance. "You needed more motivation. Now, do it. Heal."

The pain. It was all Brinn could think about. Her hands trembled, making it sting worse. She gripped her wounded hand trying to stop it from shaking, to stop the awful sensation from ripping up and down the nerves of her arm.

The Monitor interrupted. "Cadet Tarver, are you in need of assistance?"

Brinn opened her mouth to answer, but Ia beat her to it. "She's fine, Monitor." Ia turned her attention back to Brinn. "Stop screaming. Just do it."

She felt like she was going to faint. "I can't."

"Do I have to break another finger?"

Brinn shook her head. Ia stood back and nodded for her to get on with it.

Brinn drew in a shaky breath. How on Ancient Earth was she going to do this? Maybe if she treated it like something she had a better grasp on. Like numbers. And patterns. And codes.

And hacking.

She could hack into anything. Any network of any size. And the body was like a network. She closed her eyes, and her mind waded through the dark. There was a sound. Her heartbeat. Her mind grew closer to it until the beat grew crisp, and she saw everything.

Her blood pulsed inside her, rushing, always rushing.

And because of her thoughts, it pumped faster through her veins.

Too fast. Her body would go into shock.

Normalize, she thought. And it did. Her blood flow steadied, and with her next breath, her mind flashed through her neural system until she located the exact source of her pain.

With her mind's eye, she saw the damaged fibers of her muscles gaping open and the severed break in her bone.

It was like reading code. Binary. Concept-based. KovX code. Her brain was better than any supercomputer in existence, and she could read all of it. Now, that included the code inside her, from her DNA to her cells to the atoms that built her.

With all her energy, she focused, rearranging her internal programming to repair her bone and musculature. She opened her eyes in time to watch her finger fold back into place until all that was left was an open gash. Again, she concentrated, her mind rewriting the state of her skin cells, reconstructing it. The wound sealed itself.

"Nicely done, Tarver," Ia commended with pride, and then felt Brinn's forehead. "Looks like your fever's gone too." She draped a blanket around Brinn's shoulders and patted her on the back.

After seeing her body repair itself at will, Brinn felt calmed, knowing that her mother would show Faren his unique ability as well. She wanted to hear his voice, to talk to him about this skill that made them so unique, that connected them to each other. But her brain was too tired. Ia did say that healing herself would take a toll on her. All Brinn wanted was sleep. She felt hands around her shoulders, guiding her to her bed.

The mattress shifted as Ia sat down with her legs crossed at the corner of Brinn's bed.

Brinn's thoughts were a messy jumble, piling up inside

her. An unmovable mountain. It was on the verge of crashing down and burying her. She needed help.

Her eyes rested on Ia. "My brother's in the hospital," she said.

Ia's face twisted, her tone now severe. "What?"

"They found out he's Tawny."

Instead of lecturing her, Ia placed her hand gently on Brinn's knee. "I'm so sorry, Brinn."

"I feel like I'm losing myself," she whispered. "Was I wrong to come here?"

"I know I've done bad things. Regretful things," Ia admitted. "The only way you can live with your past is to recognize that every decision you make in your life will make you stronger. There's no such thing as right or wrong, Brinn. Not in this universe."

Ia reached over and gripped Brinn's hand like she had done just moments prior. Unlike before, her touch was gentle now, but still strong.

Brinn's eyes fluttered closed. That night, she dreamed she stood in the middle of a path, staring in one direction and then the other. Her foot came up, preparing to take a step. She woke before she could see where her foot had decided to land.

CHAPTER 29

IA

HER FIRST CLASS wasn't until after lunch period, so Ia spent the morning on her bed watching Brinn talk to Faren about discovering one of their Tawny traits. She envied Brinn at that moment, being able to talk to her brother whenever she felt like it. It was an everyday act, something people thought nothing of until it was no longer possible.

It had been a while since she'd contacted Einn, and she was starting to feel his absence, as though her connection to the outside world was fading away. She could demand to use Brinn's holowatch again, even threaten to tell her secret if she wanted to. But the more she got to know Tarver, the guiltier Ia felt about getting Brinn tangled in her own plans.

Brinn was in the middle of saying goodbye when Ia called across the room. "Tell him I hope he gets better."

Brinn swiped the screen into the center of the room. "You can tell him yourself."

Ia had heard a lot about him from Brinn, even overheard

them on the streams with each other in the past, but this was the very first time Ia has ever seen him. Faren waved at her on the screen. His eyes were bloodshot, but his face now bore no bruises, only the faint mark of a cut across his nose. Ia sat up, a smile somehow painted across her face. "Hi, Faren. You look well. Strong."

"I still feel awful," Faren said, drawing out a slow laugh. He didn't have enough strength, but his eyes focused on hers. The next words he said slowly but surely. "Thank you, Ia, for looking after my sister."

Brinn motioned for the screen, and it returned to her side of the room. "Bye, Faren. Miss you."

With Faren gone, the two of them were left. After a few minutes, Brinn swiveled around and stared at her expectantly. "Why haven't you made fun of me yet?"

Ia shifted in her bed. Brinn was right. She loved poking fun at Tarver, mainly because getting under her skin was so easy. But seeing her joke around with Faren, Ia remembered there was another person she liked to tease, and she immediately grew somber.

"You miss him, don't you?" Brinn asked. "Your brother."

"So you can read minds now?" Ia bristled.

"No, I can just tell," Brinn said, her eyes studying her roommate.

"I do," Ia admitted. Einn was her anchor. She felt lost, as though she had been washed away without him.

Brinn opened her mouth as if she was going to say something.

"What?" Ia asked.

Brinn played at the hem of her sleeve. "Well, do you want to talk to him again?"

Her question caught Ia off guard. She'd never thought Brinn would offer. The answer was stuck inside her throat, so she nodded, speechless.

* * *

"I'm failing all my classes," Ia said as she stared into the infinite white. Einn sat behind her. They were in the White Room, leaned up against each other, sitting back-to-back. Ia didn't realize seeing the letter *F* multiple times on her report card would make her feel like she was totally and completely worthless. It was just a letter, for Deus's sake.

The midterm exam questions were all about facts and dates. Memorizing wasn't her thing. She was certain she would have aced it if the questions were about surviving life-or-death situations. Why couldn't they have tested her on that?

"Well, I don't think any less of you," Einn said.

Ia was relieved to see him again, after more than a month of no contact. Fifteen minutes was all she had back then. Now Brinn trusted her enough to leave Ia with her holowatch while she went to the canteen to grab a quick dinner with Angie, which meant Ia had some time.

Ia turned and looked at her brother, finding comfort in his expressions, from his subtle grins to the crinkly laugh lines that gathered around his eyes. Since her arrival at Aphelion, she'd felt like her sails had been pointed in the wrong direction, and only her brother could direct her to her original path.

"I hate that this is my life now, where I have to worry about a pointless test score," she told him. "If any Dead Spacers found out, they would laugh."

"No," Einn answered, "they would think you're running a very elaborate con that only someone as clever as Ia Cōcha could think of. Did you find out anything we could use against them?"

She paused, realizing the weight of his question. Something about this felt wrong to her.

"Ia?" he said, interrupting her thoughts. She shook her head, trying to alleviate the feeling of guilt sinking into her. If she did this, she would be dragging Brinn deeper into her own plans.

Einn wanted her to find something that they could use against the Commonwealth. Weapons, intel, starship technology. It was easy at first, imagining how she could turn their own tech against them. But now there were other people orbiting her. Like Knives, and more brightly, there was Brinn.

Ia had to keep telling herself Aphelion wasn't her home. She didn't belong here. She needed to be with Einn, so she could be happy again. So she could smile like Brinn had with Faren just moments ago.

Swiveling around to sit beside Einn, Ia plucked out a strand of her hair and tossed it up. It shattered, breaking off into images, streams of data, basically everything she had collected while she snooped around academy grounds. Photos of blueprints, prototypes, even the pieces of paper filled with random numbers that Brinn had left on the table in their room.

The most notable finds were the goodies from the Armaments department. That place was a playground, filled with gadgets and advanced tech. AI-partnered missile launchers. Roaming area scatter nukes. One corner of the room was completely caged off, surely where they kept all the fancy stuff. Through the bars, Ia had snapped photos of boxes with different names. *Project Mech. Project Icarus. Project Perpetus.* All wrapped up in chains like Solstice presents.

"I managed to get photos during a mandatory tour of the department. There's war-grade weapons tech here," she revealed, "and did I mention the uranium core? It's massive."

Ia's eyes darted to Einn, trying to gauge his reaction. "Yes, you mentioned it last time," Einn said, looking everything over and pursing his lips. She knew that expression on his face. "Is this really all you've found?" he started.

She leaned in. "What's better than a uranium core?"

"There's something more dangerous than any weapon," Einn answered. "It's information."

"Information? Well, I'm pretty sure my guard, Aaron, is in love with one of my professors, if that's the type of stuff you're after," she joked.

Einn gave her an amused look. "I don't even know how to respond to that."

"See! That's how bored I am here. On top of that, the flight master won't let me fly, and my roommate is very close to actually beating me at Goma."

She wanted to slap herself for how silly she sounded. She remembered back when surviving a gunfight was her biggest worry of the day. Or finding out that half the NøN she'd stolen was counterfeit. Those were Dead Space problems. *Real* problems.

Einn gave her a moment to collect herself before asking, "Who's your headmaster?"

"Bastian Weathers. He's like a living statue. Do you know him?"

He scratched his jaw lazily. "I know of him."

"Brinn says he's really smart. She helps him with his impossible math problems sometimes. She's smart too, because she's Tawny. She never explained what they were working on. The numbers just look like gibberish to me." Ia knew she was rambling at this point and decided to change the topic. "How are the Tawny refugees from the travel ship?"

She was relieved the Elder and some of the people on that ship were able to find their way to Einn. She knew it must have been hard for him to leave his comrades. She felt it too. The guilt tore her up inside, watching the captured Tawnies day after day on the media streams. They were there because of her.

But that's what happened when you drifted. You lost people. Pirate scuffles, sickness, insufficient resources, radiation poisoning. There were too many things working against you. The only way to survive such a loss was to keep moving forward, to find another tribe and survive.

Was that was she was doing now? With the cadets she had come to know at Aphelion? She tried as hard as she could to push those questions away.

Einn nodded. "They're safe. That Elder though... He's a stubborn one. But intelligent. He helped me figure out a computer problem. Something was wrong with the processor." Einn scratched at the stubble on his chin and angled his head toward her. "Now tell me about your life as a student."

Her eyes widened. Oh, she had tons to tell. "Get this. Knives, he's that stubborn flight master I was talking about. He told this absurd scary story during lecture to freak everyone out. It was all about a monster that ate some star system I've never heard of. Fugue? Ridiculous, right?"

"Very." Einn smiled at her, then bumped her lightly on the shoulder. "It almost sounds like you're having fun there."

She waved her hands. "If I'm stuck here," she hurried to explain. "I might as well amuse myself."

"You should," he agreed. "Just don't forget where your priorities are. Once I get there, you'll need to drop everything and leave."

"That's if I ever find out where Aphelion's located."

"Sometimes things fall into your lap when you don't expect it. It'll happen. Eventually." He stood up, his long, limber frame like a stain in the expanse of white. He crossed his arms, thinking. Like the real conversation had only begun. "Escape routes... You have them planned?"

She had memorized all the hallways of Aphelion's campus in her head. If she was cornered, she'd know how to wiggle away. She'd recorded the flight master's voice and knew where all the Eyes were located and how to avoid them. A big perk of being an engineer was that she knew which engines were in the best condition, so she had already made a list of the best possible training jets to steal when it came down to it. The jets were print-locked. She may not have her Sponge Tips, but there were other, albeit more violent ways to get fingerprints. Aphelion was full of fingers, and she just had to break off one.

"I'll be ready," Ia said.

Einn looked at her, pleased. "Good. No loose ends?"

She thought of all the people she'd grown fond of while on Aphelion. There were her guards. Geoff was her number one fan. She didn't even want to imagine the look on his face when he found out she'd left. And even Aaron, with all his stiff borgy mannerisms, had grown on her.

Ia thought of Brinn, and how their strange dynamic had turned into an actual friendship. She hated the fact that she was going to miss her roommate, and she would worry about her. But Tarver was smart, and Ia knew she would be okay.

She could leave these people. And she would have to if she wanted to resume her life as the Blood Wolf and fly those skies again.

Then there was Knives. He would be right behind her, chasing her throughout the onyx sky. She could outfly him, easily. But no matter how fast she flew, he would be tied to her, gripping her heart, the shape of a tiny silver egg, in the pit of his fist.

"There is one loose end," she told Einn.

Ia had to get that heart tracker. Only then would she be able to fully break free.

CHAPTER 30
BRINN

BRINN WAS IN THE LIBRARY, studying the screens for the next history quiz, when a new dialog box popped up into her field. Her eyes widened as she read the words.

I know.

The hair on her arms bristled, and she stiffened in her seat. The username wasn't tagged, so she wasn't sure who sent it. Everyone's holos had to be registered with Aphelion admin, so whoever messaged her was doing it from an unapproved device. With jittering fingers, she waved a hand across the screen, closing it before anyone could see.

"Hey, Brinn."

Brinn glanced up as Liam sat next to her. She feigned a smile, but it was no use. The worry had already seeped into a crinkle of lines on her forehead.

He leaned in closer. "You okay?"

Brinn nodded. "Do you need something?"

Liam paused, probably from the tone in her voice. "Can I

share screens with you? My holo is fritzing right now."

Before she could answer, another message popped up in her field of view. Do you want to tell him? Or should I?

She stood up, surveying the room. The other cadets were either studying or chatting quietly among themselves. Who was sending her those messages?

"I'm sorry," she told Liam, as she grabbed her things. "I have to go."

"Oh." He looked confused—an expression she had never seen on him before—and then he shook his head, and he appeared calm and strong like he always was. "Next time then."

Brinn wanted to explain it to him, but she knew she never could.

She forced herself to walk calmly back to her dorm room. She told herself it was nothing, repeating that like a spell that would break a curse, but no matter how many times she tried, her heart kept on hammering inside her chest.

Focus. FOCUS. But she couldn't, not for the life of her.

Quick-stepping around the corner, she sprinted to her dorm room. Inside, the room was empty, and she felt a wave of relief rush through her. She didn't want to tell Ia any of it.

Because this wasn't a problem at all, she assured herself. She dyed her hair, aimed for B's in all of her classes, and kept quiet so no one would notice her enough to pick on her. There was no way this person knew the truth. She was too careful.

Brinn sat on her bed, hugging her legs close to her body. It was quiet except for the gentle hum of the lights above, when her watch beeped. She sat still, her skin prickling with goose bumps.

It's nothing, she said breathlessly to herself. Nothing.

Taking a deep breath, she looked down at her holowatch and tapped the screen.

The message materialized before her. It took only a few seconds to read it, but for a long time, the words burned into her.

I heard your talk with your mom. I know what you are, Brinn Tarver.

* * *

During their nightly Goma match, Brinn curled up into fetal position on Ia's bed and buried her face in Ia's pillow. She felt a tap on her shoulder and swiveled her head. Ia was sitting at the foot of the bed watching her, a Goma board floating in her periphery.

"You're dead, Tarver," Ia said. Brinn snapped upright at the phrase. Ia pointed at the Goma board. She had moved a black orb onto the far end of the Goma board, blocking the rest of Brinn's pieces out. She'd won the game.

"You seem distracted," Ia observed.

Brinn turned away, her gaze drifting down to the dull metal floor.

"Is it because of Vyking? Did he finally find out you love him?" Ia put emphasis on the word *love*, singing it out like an old children's rhyme.

Brinn sat up straight and glared at her. "No."

"Then what is it?" Ia asked as she poked Brinn's leg with her knee.

Brinn struggled with the words. "Someone found out."

The expression on Ia's face grew bleak. "Do you know who?"

Brinn shook her head.

Ia's shoulders slouched over her legs. The lights droned above them, filling in the gap in their conversation. "Maybe it's a blessing in disguise," Ia finally said.

"A blessing? You saw what happened to Faren."

"Yeah, but if someone comes after you, they'll have to get through me first," Ia said. She cracked her knuckles before curling her fingers into rocklike fists.

Brinn rested her cheek on her knees, chuckling softly at Ia's threats to mow everyone down. She was grateful that Ia was willing to stick up for her.

"Who'd have thought that I'd have the Blood Wolf of the Skies as my personal bodyguard?" she said.

"You're lucky I'll do it for free. My rate's pretty steep." Ia smiled smugly. "Anyway you shouldn't worry too much. If everyone finds out, it's not like you're going to get kicked out. The headmaster already knows you're Tawny."

"Getting expelled is the least of my worries." Among all the staff, the headmaster was the only person who knew about her Tawny lineage, and she was surprised how accepting he was. By working with him, she was able to use her brain like her mother had taught her to. But Brinn was convinced the cadets weren't going to be as easy on her. Look at what had happened to Faren.

Brinn hugged her knees tighter to her chest, trying to become as small as possible. Small enough to disappear.

"I'm envious of my brother, that he had the courage to tell everyone," she admitted. "But I'm not at that place yet. Hopefully, one day. But not yet."

She glanced cautiously at Ia, thinking she would press on

with the issue, force her into seeing what was the right thing to do. The expression on Ia's face was gentle and accepting.

"In the end, that's your decision to make. Not me. Not that scuzz who's threatening you. You get to decide when and where to come out with the truth. And when that day happens, it's going to be hard. But you'll have your parents, your brother. And you'll have me. I promise you won't be alone."

And Brinn believed her.

She remembered when she and Ia first met. Brinn couldn't even stand being in the same room as her. Now, she was turning to her for advice and support. Was this girl really the same person she'd seen up on the screens during the Provenance Day parade?

"Thank you," she told Ia, "for understanding."

"So what do we do?" Ia asked.

"Wait." Brinn took in a heavy breath, letting it weigh down her tiny frame. "And hope it'll all just go away."

Her gut churned angrily from worry. Brinn could hope and wish and pray all she wanted, but deep down, she knew this problem wasn't going to disappear that easily.

CHAPTER 31

IA

IA SAT IN PROFESSOR PATEL'S cybernetics class, only hearing disembodied words and snippets of sentences. *Transhuman reconstruction. Acknowledging artificial identity.* None of it was registering. Her head was crammed with too much stuff. Not numbers, facts, and dates that she had to memorize, but more personal things. Like Knives, and how he made her so uncertain about everything. When she told him about losing her home, that was the first time anyone from the other side had ever acknowledged how awful it was, how much it sucked. It almost made her *like* him.

She shook her head, trying to do away with the idea.

Ia's eyes shifted from one corner of the room to the next, scanning the back of everyone's heads to find that uninspired, ordinary shade of brown. Brinn had already missed three days of classes. It wasn't like Tarver to skip, and it wasn't like Ia to worry. She had tried to convince Brinn that it'd be better to stick with her usual schedule, to show that awful scuzz that it didn't bother her that this person knew her secret. But Brinn decided missing class was the best option. *Maybe he'll get bored*, Brinn answered her.

Ia knew those types of people never forgot, never moved on. They held on to secrets like they were weapons.

The three-tone bell chimed at the end of the afternoon lecture, and Ia was the first one out of the classroom. The next schedule block was study period, which Ia always spent in her room.

Aaron and Geoff waited for her across the hall. Geoff, as always, greeted her with bright eyes and a smile, while Aaron sneaked a glimpse into the classroom.

She grinned. "If you want to see Professor Patel, she's still in there."

Aaron swiveled. "Why would I want to do that?"

"Because," Ia elbowed him lightly. "You know..."

She was well aware that Aaron had developed a fixation on the engineering professor. But whether it was love or just a quirk to his program, she couldn't tell.

Aaron crossed his arms and glared at her.

"You're blushing," she pointed out.

With a humph, Aaron pushed past her. "Let's go."

As they shuffled away from the dispersing crowd, a voice called out to her. "Ia, wait."

Angie jogged toward her. Her lips were painted a blinding magenta, and her blond ponytail bounced like it defied gravity.

"Is Brinn all right? I haven't seen her the past few days."

Ia glowered at her. "I'm not Tarver, so don't ask me."

She swiveled to continue on her way. As she moved through

the passing crowd, a pair of footsteps *click-clacked* behind her, echoing her gait.

"Stop following me," Ia said without a pause in her step. Possibly sensing her shift in mood, Aaron and Geoff kept ahead to give her some space.

"I'm not following you," Angie answered. "I'm going to visit Brinn because her roommate won't tell me what's going on."

"You'll miss class."

"Don't care," Angie said.

Ia sighed and slowed her pace, allowing Angie to skip up beside her. Around them, the hallways emptied as everyone rushed to get to their next class.

"Is she sick?" Angie asked. "Should I bring her some soup?"

Ia snorted. "Why would you even bother?"

Angie arched an eyebrow and stared at Ia as if she was from a totally different universe. "Because that's what friends do. They bring food and tell jokes."

"Tarver doesn't joke," Ia said, her voice flat.

Angie tucked a loose piece of hair behind her ear. "I know, but she's good at listening to them."

Ia peered over at Angie. "Is that why you like her?"

"Yes," Angie answered. "Sometimes her reactions are so strange, they make me laugh, but not in a mean way. Not like before, at least. We were in primaries together, and I used to make fun of her a lot. I wasn't a good person back then."

"And you're a good person now?"

Angie's voice rang out in the empty corridor. "All you need is one person who thinks that you are. And those are the type of people you have to protect."

Ia bit the inside of her cheek, mulling over Angie's words. As they passed the simulation bay, Cammo leaned out from the doorway.

"Hi, Angie." His smile spread wide from one side of his face to the other. His cheeks flushed pink.

Angie turned to Ia. "Go on ahead. I'll catch up."

Ia left the two of them to flirt in private, and as she made her way farther down the walkway, she found the smile still lingering upon her face. It was so strange that she had to slow her pace and think.

She hated the Bugs. She knew she did.

But maybe she didn't hate all of them?

Angie spoke to her without a trace of fear, and Cammo always welcomed her with a grin. Both of them were *decent* people. Of course, Ia would shoot herself dead before she ever told either of them that.

Her dorm room was just around the corner, and as she made her way closer, she found Aaron and Geoff stopped at the end of the hallway.

"What are you two staring at?" Ia asked, but as she stepped up to them, her hands curled into hard fists.

The tap of footsteps echoed behind her, and her eyes widened. Angie was coming, and soon she would see. Spinning around, Ia rushed up to Angie, grabbing her by the shoulders before she could go any farther.

"You have to go. I'll tell Brinn you were looking for her." Ia angled her head toward Geoff. "Get Angie to her next class."

"All right. I get it," Angie blurted out when Geoff took a step toward her. "I'll leave, but I don't need an escort."

Ia watched as Angie made her way back down the hallway. When she was almost out of sight, Ia turned back to Geoff. "Follow her. Make sure she doesn't come back this way."

He nodded and rushed off without hesitation.

Ia backed up into their hallway. Aaron faced her, silent. The air in the corridor was still, and the lights above them didn't dare hum.

"We need to clean this up," Ia breathed.

Aaron nodded.

Ia rubbed her hand across her brow, hoping they were the first to see it, to read it. She turned back to her dorm room, to the word dripping red across her door.

Mungbringer.

The paint was still wet, probably brushed on no more than fifteen minutes before they found it. It took nearly an hour to scrub every stroke of paint away. Because it happened when lectures were in session, there was a good chance none of the other cadets had turned into their hallway and seen it, but there was still the problem of *who* did it.

Ia turned to Aaron, who was mopping the suds that had dripped to the floor. Pulling him away from the door, she whispered, "We need to find the person who did this, but I can't do this alone. Will you help me?"

Aaron adjusted his grip on the mop handle. "How?" He pointed at the Eye positioned at the end of the hallway. The lens was sprayed over with the same red paint. Whoever had done this had planned it all out.

"I know the academy can track holo devices," Ia said.

Aaron narrowed his eyes. "How do you know that?"

"Because I use Monitor to track Tarver's device when she's out of the room."

"You what?" Aaron raised his eyebrows in the most symmetrical fashion. "If the headmaster finds this out, I'll be turned to scrap metal."

She held up a hand in promise. "I won't tell him. So, will you help?"

"I'll look into the logs."

Aaron pulled his feet together and stood up straight. His eyes glazed over as shimmers of blue flickered across his irises like weaves of thread. It took only a few seconds. Aaron blinked.

"A holo device passed through here at 1642 this afternoon."

That was thirteen minutes before Ia got back to her room.

"Who does it belong to?" she asked, ready to hunt the person down.

"The device is currently not registered in our database."

She ran her fingers through her hair. That scuzz was smart enough to hide his tracks.

"Can you pinpoint its data signature? Where's the device now?"

Aaron's eyes washed over, filling with a sheen of data. Each millisecond that passed felt like hours. "The simulation bay."

Ia had already turned.

"Guard the door," she called behind her. "Make sure no one comes near the room."

"Wait," Aaron yelled after her. "I'm not supposed to let you run off on your own, Ia."

She wasn't thinking of escape, not now.

"Don't worry," she said, meeting Aaron's gaze long enough for him to understand that she meant it. "You can trust me."

When she got there, the simulation bay was quiet, minus the whirr and buzz of hydraulics. It was the first time she'd visited since the day of testing.

She walked down the middle lane, glancing around her. There were sixteen flyers, all locked in their simulation pods. It had to be one of them, but there was no way to know who owned the unregistered device.

As she rubbed her fingers across her brow, her eye caught sight of her fingertips. She spread her hands out before her, glancing down at the red staining the skin underneath her fingernails. That was it. That was how she would find this scuzzhole.

Her eyes jumped from monitor to monitor, each one streaming the interior view of the simulation pod.

She stopped at one pod, staring up at the screen, at long and spindly hands gripping onto the steering wheel, the index and middle finger stained an unmistakable red. Her eyes flitted to the top corner of the display where she read his name.

Nero Sinoblancas.

Gritting her teeth, Ia whispered, "Found you."

* * *

Ia sat at the table in the middle of their dorm, watching Brinn pace back and forth. Their room was small, so it took only a few steps before she had to turn around and march to the other wall.

"Are you sure it's him?" Brinn asked.

"It's Nero. No doubt about it," Ia said.

"Then there's nothing we can do."

"Look at you. You've been stuck in this room for days because of that munghead."

"Maybe we can change his mind," Brinn proposed.

"How? By politely explaining how much of a brute he is?" Ia caught her gaze. "He's not going to stop, Brinn."

"I know." Brinn leaned against the wall, her arms gripped tight around her chest. "What if we can use something against him?"

Brinn sat on the edge of her bed and pulled up a holoscreen.

"Now that's more like it," Ia said, scooting next to her.

Typing as fast as she could, Brinn ran search after search on several displays. All they needed was a tiny bit of information, a secret he wanted to keep as much as Brinn did hers.

After an hour, they turned up nothing.

"He must have scrubbed his ArcLite clean. There's nothing except boring news stories about their perfect, mundy family." Brinn tapped at one of the screens so it flipped for Ia to see. "Look at this picture. His two older sisters are the heads of the Intergalactic Charity Foundation."

Ia pinched the tip of her chin as she stared at the girls' faces. Then her head shot back up as she recognized a certain similarity with someone she once knew. And right now, it was the perfect card to play. "I have a plan. Tell him to meet you in the common room after shutdown."

Brinn gawked at her. "No way. That's like walking straight into an ashtigra's den."

"I know," Ia responded simply. "Luckily, you're not the one going."

Brinn paused. "The Sinoblancas family is one of the

most powerful bloodlines in all of Olympus. You can't scare them, Ia."

"I learned a hard lesson when I first arrived on Aphelion. No one is unbeatable, Tarver." Ia's expression grew mournful. "Even the mighty will fall."

* * *

Ia was seated on one of the L-shaped couches, her legs crossed and her eyes set on the door. Above, the holoscreens glowed silver, casting a ghostly tint onto the room around them.

At 0030, the entrance doors slid open.

"What are you doing here?" It was Nero, his body a slim, lean slash in the middle of the doorway. The loose black curls on his head were slicked to the side, showing off his perfect symmetrical face, complete with the dimple piercing through the exact center of his chin.

"Brinn couldn't make it." Ia smirked, allowing the silence to hang in the air.

"So you figured out it was me." Nero made his way into the center of the room, his long legs swinging toward her in a march. "You can beat me up, but that's not going to stop it."

Her eyebrow twitched. Out of all the Bugs she had ever met, Sinoblancas was one of the worst. "Why are you being such a mung? She's one of your Citizens."

His face grew red, from the tips of his ears all the way to the dimple at the end of his chin. "Everyone here is going to find out Brinn Tarver is a Tawny. It's our right to know—"

Nero's holowatch dinged, interrupting his rant. She sat back and watched him, noticing a crease burrow into his brow.

He narrowed his eyes as he glanced up at her. "It's a message from Tarver."

"Oh really?" she said innocently.

Before she'd left for the common room that night, Ia had asked Brinn if she could connect to her holopad once again. She needed to give her something. A memory.

"Well, go on," Ia continued. "Open it."

Nero touched the message screen, enlarging the attachment onto another display. From where she was seated, Ia could make out the details of the image.

Nero's jaw went slack. "Vetty..."

Ia got up from her seat, her eyes trained on the person in the photograph. His face was beautiful, with his thick brown hair tied back and eyes the color of sea-foam. His smile was never-ending, and he had Nero's dimpled chin.

"Vetty was a part of my crew. We were pretty close. He talked a *lot* about his past." Ia took a step toward Nero, so close he had to inch back. "I told Tarver all about him. She has her own copy of this too."

Nero's eyes snapped to hers. "You're trying to blackmail me."

"Think about the chaos your life would be thrown into once the public finds out a Sinoblancas is a Dead Spacer. Vetty's father, your uncle, would lose his Council seat. Suspicion would fall on the whole family. The entire Sinoblancas empire would crumble. I'm pretty sure the universe would be a better place, but you wouldn't want this to get out, would you?"

A stillness hung between them, and she watched Nero's face twist and shrivel as he tried to figure out his next move.

The lights in the common room flickered on.

"What are you two doing in here?" Knives stood in the open doorway.

Neither of them answered. Ia's eyes bore into Nero, and he hung back, unwilling to meet her stare. Perhaps he was realizing her threats were never the careless kind.

Knives walked into the room, surveying the two of them. "Sinoblancas," he barked. "Back to your dorm."

Nero rushed past the flight master. Ia made her way to follow him, her gaze set on the space where he had just exited. Knives's hand rested on her shoulder, stopping her.

"What were you two doing?"

"Let go," she snapped.

"Not until you tell me what you were fighting about."

Her lips curled into a snarl. "He's trying to expose a Tawny cadet in Aphelion."

"Well, it looks like he's too scared to do anything now." Knives pressed his lips into a grim line. "Good work."

Ia's head snapped up. "What?"

His gaze rested upon hers. "Not all of us have the same beliefs as the Sinoblancas clan."

Ia stood, speechless. It should have been easy to hate him, but he kept giving reasons not to.

There was an unspoken tension between them. She felt it even as he strode past her, throwing himself onto one of the couches. It emanated from her core and filled up her head, so that her cheeks felt numb. She knew the heat of anger very well, so it wasn't that. It was a *confusion*. A curious confusion. Like solving a mystery. She didn't want to stop until she got to the end, and even then, she wanted it to go on. To last forever.

He pulled down a control screen and started a new program on the central displays. Her chin tilted upward as an image faded up from black.

"Is this really why you're here?"

His blue eyes twinkled at her, warmer this time. Again, she looked away.

"Out of all the places on campus, the First Year common room is the coziest."

A flashy title sequence erupted onto the screen. "What movie is it?" she asked.

"The latest Kinna Downton one," Knives answered. "Supposed to be scary."

She noticed Knives hadn't told her to leave or go back to her room. She glanced at him, and he scooted over, making room for her on the couch.

To her, he was the Bug who had her little silver orb, but she decided to forget that, at least for now.

CHAPTER 32
KNIVES

KNIVES GRABBED HIS PACK, throwing in everything he would need for the night. A bottle of archnol, two ripe oranges—which had been Marnie's favorite snack—and a candle. He looked at his reflection in the mirror and combed his hair for the first time in a week. He wore civilian clothes, black insulated nylon pants and a gray long-sleeved thermal. It would be cold where he was going.

As he crossed his room to his door, Knives grabbed his brown leather bomber jacket from his table and slipped it on. He stepped out into the hallway and rushed down to the flight deck. When he got there, he passed underneath a line of jets hanging from the revolving track above, but instead of going to the Kaiken, he veered toward the storage bay, which was right next to the cargo lift.

As he crossed the tarmac, he spotted Ia throwing recharged fuel pods onto a cart. It had been a week since they watched the Kinna Downton stream together. He remembered every single moment of it, from the little gasps she made when the zombs invaded to how they'd bellowed in laughter at every over-the-top pun.

It was strange how *fun* that night had been.

"How many more of those do you have to do?" her guard Geoff asked.

She counted the empty pods littering the floor. "Maybe two more carts."

"Is it possible you'll be done before the Poddi game starts?"

Knives tiptoed away, knowing that if he interrupted, Ia would just draw him in. Even though he'd been enjoying her company lately, he didn't have time for her tonight. He already had his own set of plans.

But as he was about to get out of earshot, he heard her call out. "Look who's here." She waved to the exit. "Geoff, go watch that Poddi game. The flight master can take over for the night."

Knives stopped in his place. "What? You can't just relieve your own guard of his duties."

"And you can't make him work overtime night after night. Isn't that some violation of one of your labor codes? Right, Geoff?"

Geoff looked from one to the other as if he was unsure what to do.

"Right?" Ia asked again.

"Labor codes advise no longer than four hours of overtime per day, and I've been on the clock since five a.m.—"

Knives threw up his hands. "Fine. Geoff, you are free to go. And if you're placing bets, just make sure you give me a cut if you win."

Geoff grinned. "Thank you," he exclaimed, and then rushed away.

With hands in his pockets, Knives turned back to Ia. She was wearing her flight suit, and her hair was pinned back, making her face look rounder, less harsh than it usually was.

"Well, I guess it's just you and me," Ia said as she waved him over. "Wanna give me a hand? I gotta do these or else I'll fail another one of my classes."

He glanced over at his watch. It was almost midnight, and he needed to get to the Nest before the end of the day.

"Leave those there. I'll just give you the extra points," he said.

She wiped the back of her hand across her sweaty forehead. "Really?"

"Let's go." He didn't have time to explain, so he nodded for her to follow. "I have somewhere I need to be."

* * *

The storage bay was dimly lit. He led Ia through the maze of freighters filled with supplies and piles of replacement parts for the training jets. He made sure to walk at her side so he could keep tabs on her. He had noticed her eyeing the cargo lift as they passed it, like she was trying to slice right through it with the power of her mind. A reminder that even though they had become more casual with each other over the past month, he still had to be careful.

He walked in silence, his footsteps retracing the exact path he and his sister used to take whenever they wanted to steal away from class. He remembered the first time she took him here two years ago. Marnie had dragged him away after one of his drill practices, and they had run through the stacks of this same storage bay.

"Where are we going?" Ia asked him. Her eyes were everywhere, looking at the pipes, the crates, even the floor. Probably trying to figure out a way to escape.

He called her name, and she snapped back into focus, her head tilted in his direction.

"Can we make a deal tonight?" he pleaded.

Her eyes flashed. "Bargaining now, are we?"

He knew this was going to be a big ask, but he said it anyway. "Promise me you won't try to escape tonight."

She knit her brows together. "And why would I promise that?"

He swung his pack over and pulled the bottle of archnol out by its neck. "Do it, and this will all be yours."

To be honest, he had brought that bottle for his own consumption, but he was willing to make a small sacrifice in order to have some peace of mind for the rest of the night.

She pressed her lips together and then smirked. "Knives, you got yourself a deal."

He passed her the bottle, and her eyes brushed over the label. "Batical? That's a real brewery. I usually get my archnol from the Dead Space Market. If you aren't careful, you could drink too much and go blind."

"Well, then, Cōcha, I guess this is your lucky day." He remembered the long-lasting burn from the archnol he'd ordered from Myth, knowing how hard it was to get a good-quality batch so far from the Commonwealth city centers. The bottle in Ia's hands was even more special. It had been stolen from Professor Jolinsky's secret stash.

Knives turned the corner, passing a stack of spare wing parts, when he caught sight of a rusted metal door. It stood apart from the newer silver panels that had built the walls of Aphelion. He crossed over and pulled it open for Ia. "After you."

She narrowed her eyes as she tried to look through the tunnel that lay beyond, and then glanced back over at Knives. "This night is only going to get more interesting, isn't it?"

"Hurry up," he said.

She clicked her tongue and went through. He followed behind her and watched the outline of her narrow shoulders disappear into the shadows. The air inside was frigid and dry.

Rocks skittered across the ground underneath their feet. The tunnel was drilled through the rock of the mountain, and metal beams supported the whole length from caving in. Ia's footsteps were steady and wide at first, but then she slowed to smaller steps. He bumped into her back and grabbed her shoulders to steady her, feeling the heat of her body despite the surrounding cold.

"I can't see anything," she complained. "If I fall and break this bottle, the deal's off.

He knew this path like the back of his hand; he was able to navigate it even in the pitch-dark.

"Just go forward," he instructed, but he gently held her shoulders to guide her, and she allowed him. Through the thin nylon mesh of her flight suit, he felt her shiver. From the cold or from something else? Before he could think anymore of it, he saw a patch of green light streaming in from the opening ahead.

They stepped through the archway and into a narrow circular space. The walls were made of the same rusted metal as the door at the tunnel's entrance, and they reached thirty meters high. The ceiling had a reinforced grated port with a window in the middle to let the light from outside spill through. From where they stood, they could see the green flashes of the geometric storm piercing through the atmosphere.

"Welcome to the Nest," he said, sweeping his hand through the air. Out of all the places in Aphelion, the Nest reminded him of Marnie the most. This is where they came to drink, to make fun of the professors, and to complain about their father. No one else knew of this place except for the two of them. It was their secret.

And now someone else's.

Ia stepped into the center and looked around, not realizing how precious this place was to him. He hoped it wasn't a mistake bringing her here.

The walls, though rusty, were smooth so Knives knew there was no way for Ia to scale it, and even if she did get up there, there was a double lock system. One required a print signature, while the other needed a real physical key, as rusted as the metal inside this place. And he had no idea where that was—maybe lost and buried with a previous headmaster.

Ia's gaze fixed on the port above, examining it, trying to figure it out.

"I know what you're doing," he pointed out. "We had a deal. No escaping."

"I wasn't going to."

"But you were planning how," he said, pointing at her. "I can see it in your eyes."

She batted at his finger. "Yeah, yeah. You know me *so* well."

He sat down on a boulder hugging the wall opposite of the entrance. Ia walked around the space, then stopped at a sign by the entrance, a coat of grime and dust obscuring the text underneath. Her hand came up to pick at the edging of the sign, and he called out to her. "What are you doing?"

Her shoulders tensed, and then she turned around and held up the bottle of archnol. "Nothing. Just looking for something to open it with."

He patted the boulder next to him. She crossed the space and took a seat. He grabbed the bottle and brushed his hand against the side of his boulder. His hands dipped into a familiar crevice denting the rock. He wedged the top of the bottle in the little nook just like Marnie had taught him and then twisted until he heard the lid pop open.

He handed the bottle back to her.

"Thanks," Ia said, and she took a swig. Her face twisted as she swallowed, followed by a delighted sigh. He reached for the bottle, but she pulled it away. "No way. We had a deal. This bottle is all mine."

"Fine," he grunted, then pulled the orange from his pack and started peeling it.

Ia took another sip. "So what exactly is this place?" she asked.

"It's the Origin Site," he said, throwing the orange peel on the ground. "The exact place the builder borgs landed around five hundred years ago."

"So did you boot the last inhabitants like you usually do?"

"There was no one else here except a giant herd of wultakus. They seem fine with coexisting." Wultakus were the local wildlife, grazing animals who ate lichen that grew on the permafrost.

Knives took a slice of orange and popped it in his mouth. Beside him, Ia's body shivered, and she hugged her arms close to her chest. Standing up, Knives took off his jacket and held it out for her.

She snatched it. As she threw it over her shoulders, Knives noticed her hands darting in and out of all the pockets.

"The heart tracker's not in there," he said. She was persistent; he would give her that.

"Can't blame a girl for trying," she shrugged.

He checked his holowatch. It was 2355. Only five more minutes until midnight. Above them, the geometric storm cleared, rippling away to reveal the stars in the faraway sky. Ia balanced the bottle in between her legs and looked up, not examining anything like she usually did. Just looking.

"What are you thinking about?" he asked.

She smirked. "I'm thinking about the first time we met."

He felt heat rise to his cheeks. "What about?"

Then she angled her head at him. "Do you really know someone who crossed the Harix Corridor in ten seconds?" Her tone grew serious. "It's been bothering me ever since."

He chuckled to himself and then nodded. "My sister, Marnie. She was grinning for weeks after it happened."

"Of course," Ia said. "When you find out you can fly that fast, you're invincible."

Invincible. He tiptoed around the word like it was a bomb. Is that how Marnie felt up until the end? Invincible? He couldn't tell if it was a blessing or a curse.

"Is that how you feel when you fly?" Knives asked.

"It's not something you feel; it's something you chase," Ia explained. "And once you're there, it lasts for one second. That's it. And then you're back at square one."

"Then why do it?"

"Why not?" Her eyes flashed with a sense of danger, the same look he'd seen whenever Marnie returned from a drill. He felt it too whenever he was in his Kaiken, but ever since his sister's death, he tried to push it away.

Knives came to the Nest to remember his sister, to dig up all the memories so he could bring her back to life, at least for one night. And here he was with a girl—a girl who was bold and smart, and who reminded him of Marnie in many, many ways.

"I think you should know by now that I have a big ego," Ia said, standing up, raising the bottle to the air, swaying slightly from the effects of the archnol. "So I challenge your sister. A race through that same corridor!"

"I would have liked to see that, but it's not possible," he said, eyeing her to make sure she wouldn't topple over.

"Sure it is. You can even lend me the Kaiken," she pressed on.

"Well, if she were still alive, she would have schooled you. Kaiken or not."

Ia lowered the bottle, taking a seat on the boulder right next to him. Her eyebrows rose, as if she had solved a great mystery. "So that's why you dropped out of your campaign? Is she why you decided to stay at Aphelion?"

He nodded. And then he waited for the slew of advice

that would surely come his way. *You're too talented to stay here*, Bastian always said. *Move on with your life*, his father tried to tell him. Knowing how opinionated she was, he was sure Ia had something to say about it as well.

But instead, her hand fell softly on his shoulder. She sat with him in silence.

All this time, he had been quietly grieving, pleading that Marnie would return. He missed her. Everywhere he went, he missed her. And feeling Ia's touch soothed him. It made him feel there was no shame in his grief.

Eyes stinging, he looked away.

His alarm rang, and he checked his watch. Midnight.

He stood up. Dropping to one knee, he pulled out the candle, placed it in the center of the room, and lit it. Slowly, the warm light of the candle's amber flame reached high up the walls, like it was asking for the sky itself.

Knives grabbed the other orange, placing it right next to the candle. There was a reason he'd brought two. One for him, and one for her. A birthday gift. A memory.

He looked back at Ia, who was sitting reverently, watching his ritual.

"She'd be twenty-one today," he told her.

Ia got up and sat down on the floor across from him. She handed him the bottle of archnol. "To Marnie then."

"To Marnie." Smiling, he took the bottle and took a swig, remembering the first time Marnie had brought him here. She'd laughed at him while he coughed at the first sip. But now, he was two years older. And the burn no longer took him by surprise. Not much could.

Except for maybe her.

He turned to look at Ia. Her eyes were dark and large, pulling in the light around her. He felt it, like a force of gravity. He didn't want to look away. He didn't want to blink. It was strange how she made him feel. Like his atoms were being rearranged into some new shape, a new composition of himself. The light from the flames gave her golden skin an even warmer glow. She lived in eternal sunset.

She saw him staring at her, and her cheeks reddened. From the archnol. But perhaps from something else. She dragged her finger against the etchings on the ground, and then immediately her body tensed, along with everything around her. From the rust on the walls to the infinite atoms splitting between them.

Her eyes came up to him, fierce like the first time he'd met her. What had happened? What had changed?

He glanced down at the markings at their feet. Marnie always wanted everyone to remember she was here, so she carved her existence right into the rock.

Marnie Adams, 8919—her final year at Aphelion.

Oh mif.

Ia was already up. "Are you General Adams's *son*?"

Time was running at a heightened speed. He couldn't even form the words.

"Answer the question."

He took in a deep breath. The only thing he could do was answer. "Yes."

She pushed away from him, but he grabbed her by the wrist, stopping her. "Ia, let me—"

"Don't." Her voice burned through him. "Just take me back."

With those words, the space between them crystallized. It grew pointy and sharp, so that all he could do was let go of her. As he walked her back to her room, he thought back to when her hand had been on his shoulder, and he had felt it for that one second.

Invincible.

But now he was back to square one.

CHAPTER 33
IA

THEY WALKED BACK to her room in silence, with Ia keeping two steps ahead and Knives remaining two strides back. Yet, it felt like more. Like they were light-years apart.

And when they were at her room, she turned to go inside without even a goodbye. By then, the buzz she had from the archnol had worn off, leaving all but the sting of truth and a blinding headache.

Knives's father was the person who had hunted her down for years like she was an animal, who had caught her and finally caged her. If she'd known Knives was his son, then she would have been more careful. She wouldn't have gotten too close. She was angry at herself for being such a fool. But thank Deus it had happened. It reminded her that she didn't belong here, and this was just another reason why she had to get out of this place.

Ia stepped inside her room and stood there, seething. Even as the door slid closed behind her, she remained planted in place. The bathroom door was closed, where she could hear the pipes creak from the swell of the water. Tarver was in the shower.

She scratched at the fabric around her arms, her eyes searing into the Commonwealth quartered shield embroidered onto her sleeve. Her flight suit suddenly felt tight and itchy. She couldn't breathe. She punched her fingers on the buttons on her shoulders, which loosened the elasticity of the material. The suit shrugged loose, and she flailed until it was off her. She keeled forward in her undergarments, tight black compression shorts and a black band around her chest. Using the center table to stable her balance, she glanced at the feathers tattooed on her forearms, a reminder that it was not in her nature to be caged. In here, she had grown weak and unsure.

Her eyes focused on Tarver's holopad, unguarded on the tabletop and ready for the taking. She thought back to when she had first stepped into the Nest. She had looked around, stopping in front of an old sign hanging near the entrance. It was coated with what may have been hundreds of years of dirt and dust. The text underneath was faint yet visible.

AG-9

Knives had said the place was an Origin Site, so that must be where they were. Too bad Ia knew nothing of a planet named AG-9. The Commonwealth must have stricken any mention of it from the Planetary Records, for extra security measures. And the name of planet meant nothing to her without the exact location.

But then she'd seen the line of numbers on the corner of

the sign, hidden by a layer of rust. She was picking at it when Knives called out to her, and she had to stop.

Thankfully, she had scraped off enough to see what it was. They weren't *just* numbers.

They were coordinates.

Ia might not have gotten that heart tracker, but she'd discover something better. Aphelion's exact location. One of the Commonwealth's most guarded secrets. The information was something that even her professors had been tight-lipped about.

Einn was right. Sometimes information was more dangerous than weapons.

And now Einn would be able to find her, and she knew the perfect little tunnel to break his way in.

CHAPTER 34
KNIVES

KNIVES TOSSED AND TURNED in his bed, and by the middle of the night, his sheets had gathered in a tangle around his feet. Everytime he closed his eyes, Ia's face seared in the darkness, the look of betrayal replacing the smirk that he had grown so familiar with.

A knock came at his door. Groaning, he tumbled out of bed. Who could it be? Immediately, his chest swelled, hoping it was Ia. He ran his fingers through his messy blond hair and prepped himself on what he would say if it was her. How he would apologize. And apologize. And apologize.

But when the door slid open, the headmaster stood in the hallway, which was stark and empty at that hour of the night.

Knives squinted at him. "Bastian, what is it?"

"Flight master, your assistance is required." The headmaster's voice was hurried as he glanced at the time on his holowatch.

"I know you're a workaholic, Bastian, but I'm off right

now," Knives said, rolling his eyes. "Can we talk about this in the morning?"

"It can't wait. I have to attend to some business offworld. We have to leave Aphelion immediately." Bastian pinched the bridge of his nose. "It's for the Star Force."

"Then I don't care. I told you. No Star Force work."

Bastian narrowed his eyes, his voice stern. "It doesn't matter. You're still an officer, and officers obey their orders. You have to go, whether you like it or not."

* * *

Their rendezvous with General Adams's cruiser, a state-of-the-art 64 Tachi, was scheduled for 1500 Planetary Time. Knives glanced at the clock on his console as he stepped out. It was 1535.

"You're late." His father's voice was even, but Knives could tell by how red his ears were that his father was trying to hold back his anger.

Knives stood at attention, glaring at his father as he laid his fist upon his heart. After nearly sixty hours of nonstop travel, he was ready to pass out, but as an officer, he had to wait for the general to return the salute.

Bastian looked over at him. "Knives, at ease, my boy."

With a huff, Knives slouched out of the stiff salute. General Adams grunted for them to follow. Knives fell into step behind them, but then turned back to his jet in confusion. He expected engineers to rush in and service it, but the cruiser's flight deck was quieter than usual. Not an engineer in sight.

Where was everyone?

He drifted through the empty hallways, noting the vacant

rooms they passed. There were no engineers, no comms, no flyers. He thought he would at least see a service borg somewhere, but there were none.

They stepped through an arched doorway and onto the captain's deck, as empty as the rest of the ship. General Adams made his way to the adjacent control room in order to look over all the maintenance systems.

When they were alone, Knives glanced over at Bastian, who had started pacing while poring over his thick leather-bound notebook. "Are we the only ones here? Where are the other officers?"

"This mission is above their security clearance," the general answered through the paned glass that separated the control room from the rest of the captain's deck.

Knives lowered his voice and looked to Bastian. "When you told me we'd be offsite, I didn't realize it was for some top-secret mission."

The headmaster continued reading. "If I told you specifics, you wouldn't have come."

"Bastian, you know I don't want to be here," he hissed.

Bastian raised his bushy white eyebrows. "But you're one of the most talented young men I know."

"Well, you don't know that many then," Knives grumbled.

"I'm the headmaster of a prestigious Star Force Academy, Knives, so yes, I do. And none of them have half the skill or know-how that you do." Bastian closed his journal and offered it to Knives. "So for now, use your eidetic memory and study this."

"Fine." Knives relented and started flipping through the pages. Display controls, layouts, system programs. Words like *Mirage*, *Dark Star*, and *Threshold* popped out at him. He scanned through each section, quickly memorizing everything. As he went on, there were pages that had been ripped out entirely. Which was fine. Less work was always welcomed in his book.

Most of it was gibberish, until he stopped at a set of blueprints. Why did they look so familiar? His brow furrowed as everything locked into place. It was a gate. But not an ordinary gate. Most gates were stationary structures, but this one had been fitted with ionic thrusters along its outer rim, which theoretically meant it could be moved. None of the gates he knew of did that. He wasn't sure it was possible.

"Have you familiarized yourself with everything?" Bastian asked. "These notes are highly guarded. Only two records of these are in existence."

Knives was about to ask why, when General Adams stepped back into the captain's deck. Without a crew, his father was busy doing all the duties that were normally beneath him.

"Lynk, how far off are we?" General Adams asked.

A series of interlocking lights floated together, forming the shape of a woman's head, an elegant torso, arms, and legs. Lynk was a Monitor, an advanced AI hologram programmed to assist this ship.

"The Wuvryr Gate is within activation distance," Lynk announced as she floated toward the navigation console in the center of the room.

Knives stared at his father, his mind still processing the words Lynk had said. *The Wuvryr Gate?* He rushed to the navigational orb, tracing his finger over the automated simulation of the ship's path. He scratched the back of his neck as the strangeness of their journey settled upon him. "Are these navigation paths right?"

"Why wouldn't they be?" General Adams snapped.

Knives ignored the look on his father's face. "Because it says we're heading toward Fugue."

It couldn't be. Fugue was a made-up place from a made-up story passed around late nights in the common room to keep cadets in line.

But as he peered out the observational windows, the Wuvryr Gate towered above them. It was old, and it was rusty, and it was *real*. Its circular frame stared back at him like a gargantuan eye, its metal arches rotating clockwise while white lines spun in the opposite direction inside it, a visual refraction of light and space. It was a wrinkle in the universe.

Usually, before a jump, one would catch glimpses of the other side, freckles of stars or belts of faraway white gases staining the dark blank canvas that linked the universe together. But standing there now...

He saw nothing.

The universe was full of stars, but their destination was devoid of them.

They crossed the threshold into the mouth of darkness. The dim glow of the holoscreens rescued them from the pitch-black. Lynk offered some further illumination, her blue holographic form trailing streaks of luminescence wherever she tread.

Knives placed a hand against the front window. Dark as far as his eyes could see. He didn't want to know what kind of monsters lurked outside.

Bastian stood next to him, peering out into the infinite abyss. A somber expression weighed heavy on his face.

"The stories don't get it quite right," he said, his voice breaking the eerie silence. "The Fugue system was a Commonwealth testing ground for new technology. But there was a meltdown, and afterward they shut down the site. For years, it was a ghost system. No one came in or out. But now, someone has taken interest."

"Is it true about the monster?" Knives asked. "Was there really something locked up here?"

Bastian looked over at him. "Depends on your definition of 'monster.'"

General Adams swiped up a document from his holopad. It was an activity log. "The motion sensor in the lower quadrant was first triggered sixteen rotations ago."

Bastian wore a grave look on his face. "We must make sure nothing's been taken."

"Taken? There's nothing out there but ghosts, Bastian."

"Yes, there is." Bastian gestured at the large gate circling the ship. "On this side of the universe, this gate is no longer called Wuvryr. Here, we call it GodsEye."

This was the gate from the blueprints. It was unlike any interstellar gate Knives had every seen. It was a monolith, big enough to fit a whole megaplanet in its center, which meant the gate could open the jump to something very big. Instead of floating vertically, it hovered horizontally above them. From the blueprints of GodsEye, he knew it had living quarters and a laboratory unlike ordinary gates found throughout Commonwealth territory. This gate was meant to house people as well as transport them. Another reason why it was so massive.

"Suit up," the general's voice grated against the stillness. "If someone broke in, find out how. See if anything has been stolen."

They were in Fugue, a place Knives had only heard stories about. *Scary* stories. "You want *me* to go out *there*?" he asked.

General Adams clasped his hands behind his back. "You're the only one here who's expendable, officer."

CHAPTER 35

IA

IA HAD NO IDEA where Knives was. He had been absent from his lectures for a few days. Good, she thought. She didn't want to see him anyway. She wished the day would come when she'd never have to see him and his cold blue eyes again. It would happen any moment now, she knew.

Yet, it had been three days since she gave Einn the coordinates. She had to believe he was on his way, but there had been no word from him. Not even a simple reply to her message. But she'd be ready when he arrived. She still hadn't secured the tracker, but she and Einn could find some way to disable that, once they were finally together again.

Ia grumbled, adjusting herself in her stiff lecture hall chair.

She tipped her head back to take in the fully immersive holoscene around her. A large, white Commonwealth starjet carrier careened peacefully through space. It was quadruple the size of any ship she had ever commandeered.

She furrowed her brow at the ship's familiar silhouette, feeling strange déjà vu.

"March 19, 8920. 1412 Planetary Time." Professor Jolinsky was setting the stage. His voice was wretchedly annoying. "The Fringe Alliance ambushed a Commonwealth Starjet Carrier, the *Ardor*, stationed in K-5 Neptune's orbit."

Ia grinned in the darkness. No wonder that ship looked familiar. She knew exactly where this was, and best of all, she knew what was going to happen next.

From behind her head, a fleet of "enemy" starjets, painted in black and navy camouflage, spiraled toward the Commonwealth carrier. Olympus gunheads took aim. Fast as lightning, the camouflaged ships zigzagged through the flurry of gunfire. They struck everywhere and all at once. Soon, the Commonwealth carrier was ripped apart from a fierce explosion, a sphere of blue light wilting in curls like a rose in the bitter cold.

Jolinsky's voice droned in. "Commonwealth historians have compared the battle of K-5 Neptune to Ancient Earth's historical Attack on Pearl Harbor."

No kidding, Ia thought. That battle was a bloodbath.

"The ambush was led by LiteSpars General Malcomme Storm and his Juno Battalion, who hid for eighteen hours behind the Chekhov moon—"

"Stop!" Ia shouted.

The holographic scene recoiled, as if burned by her voice, and the classroom reappeared. Ia met Professor Jolinsky's gaze as he stared bullets at her.

"That's all wrong," she said.

"Excuse me?"

With her legs propped up on her desk, Ia reclined backward, tilting her head toward the now-blank ceiling.

Using her hands, she set up the geography. "The Juno Battalion hid behind the Solaris moon, not Chekhov."

Professor Jolisnky crossed his arms. "Ms. Cōcha, must I remind you this is *my* classroom."

"Then get your facts straight," she said, her eyes digging into him.

He stepped away from the podium, his shoulders tensed like they were about to fight. "There is documented footage of a fleet behind the Chekhov moon."

She flicked her hands, waving his statement away like a fly. "That was a decoy."

"And how would you know all this?"

She leaned in away from the shadows, her face catching the light coming from the front of the auditorium. "Because that was the battle that gave me the nickname Blood Wolf."

The professor's face grew pale. "Are you saying you were the mastermind behind the slaughter of K-5 Neptune?"

Her eyes narrowed, and her voice evened. "You can't use the word 'slaughter' in war, sir."

The classroom erupted in protest. Professor Jolinsky raised his hands, trying to calm everyone down, but no one noticed.

Three rows away, a cadet stood, his face now so red it hid his freckles.

"My uncle died in that battle!" he screamed, charging at her. Reid, who Ia recognized from the teamwork test, rose to hold him back, but nothing could stop the growing outrage. It was like a fire had been lit.

"Murderer!"

"You deserve to die!"

Their shouts collided into a deafening wave, thudding heavy against Ia's eardrums.

Her voice broke through the cacophony, loud and true and filled with clarity. "You talk about the Uranium War like it's ancient history." Ia jumped on her desk and gazed down at them. "This war is not over. Every day Tawnies, LiteSpars, Makolions…millions of people and families die in the Fringe because of you and your greed."

A flurry of papers, pens, anything the cadets could get their hands on, flew all at once, like bullets at Ia's face. She was fighting a losing battle, but she didn't cower. She remained standing, and she would never step down.

Then her brother's voice whispered in her head, rising above her anger. *Play nice*, Einn had told her. *Play nice.* She was so close to being rescued; she couldn't start anything now.

Pounding an angry fist into her thigh, she jumped down and stormed out of the room.

* * *

Ia headed to the nearest empty room to cool off. Fortunately for her, it was the training gym. Aaron and Geoff insisted on accompanying her inside, but they changed their minds once she screamed curse after curse at them while hurling all the weights she could find in their direction. They retreated, standing watch outside the entrance. So for now, she was alone, punching the air, wishing it was Jolinsky's face.

She swiped at the space to her right, her three fingers pulled together, activating a holoscreen to pop up.

Run Fight Program. Y/N?

She tapped at the Y icon and cracked her knuckles. The fight dummy positioned itself into a blocking stance, then shifted into different positions.

A left jab came at her. She dodged, then aimed a counter-punch into an opening in the dummy's right side. Her field gloves activated, creating a small-radius force field at the point of contact. It was meant to cushion any blows to a living opponent, but since she was fighting a dummy, it was somewhat unnecessary.

A voice called to her from outside the ring.

"Hey, murderer."

Ia angled her head, trying to pick out the scuzz's face. It was Sinoblancas. No matter how much she threatened him, that mung never learned. But at least she was his target now, not Brinn.

"This is the flyers' ring."

She groaned. She was so angry, she hadn't noticed the flyers enter from the adjacent weight rooms at the far end of the gym. They must have been weight training when she first barged in there. Her eyes flicked toward the entrance doors, and she briefly contemplated calling out to Geoff and Aaron. With Knives gone, there was no one to keep the flyers in check.

No. This was nothing she couldn't handle. Rolling her eyes, she turned her back on them to resume her fight simulation.

Footsteps entered the ring.

In an instant, Ia twisted, facing Nero down. She grabbed him by the arm. Angling her body, she flipped him out of the ring.

Nero landed on the concrete floor and whimpered. The rest of the flyers gathered around, trying to help him up. All of them but Liam Vyking, whose eyes never left hers. His jaw was tight, and his brown eyes flashed with a glimpse of darkness.

He unzipped his hoodie and stepped toward the ring. Cammo grabbed his shoulder, trying to stop him. Vyking shrugged out of his friend's grip. He tapped at the top of a perimeter post, deactivating the barrier. He stepped inside the fight corner.

Within moments, the Vyking kid was standing in her periphery.

"I'll spar with you." His voice bit through the air, now thick with heat and sweat.

"Do you even know how?"

Ia didn't wait for an answer, continuing to throw punches at the HG dummy. She hoped her technique and power would scare him off. Instead, Liam Vyking circled around her and dodged into her fight sequence.

The sensors recognized this new body standing before her, and a hollow computerized voice echoed from above. "Exiting simulation."

The HG dummy vanished, and in its place stood Liam, adjusting the field gloves on his fingers before making quick but sure fists.

Ia swung at his face, giving him no time to react. He leaned out of the way, just barely getting out of her reach, her fist clipping his right shoulder instead of popping him hard on the nose.

She set her eyes on him, her nostrils flaring with anger.

"Don't waste my time, Vyking," she growled. She couldn't spar with him, not now. If this day ended in a bloodbath, they would throw her into a deep, dark hole where not even Einn could swoop in to save her.

Yet it was all *so* tempting.

"You think I'm that easy to beat?" he asked.

Yes.

Ia closed in, feinting with a right jab. Liam dodged left but straight into Ia's left uppercut. Her field gloves activated, creating a small force field before her knuckles could make contact. But the weight of the force field created a light impact, causing Liam to stumble backward. He dug his back leg into the ground, steadying himself, and then rose to his full height, looking down at her in defiance.

They were face-to-face, lips snarling, eyes darting to see who would make the first move.

"I can take it down a notch," she said, her voice steady and confident.

"No." He eased back up into a boxing stance. "Never."

He charged forward. His eyes were vicious as he swung a left jab to Ia's face. She raised her right arm, blocking his attack, but Liam circled around, striking her in the ribs.

Even with the field gloves, the hit was hard, and she keeled forward, her bones screaming. She fought off the discomfort, biting her tongue, not wanting him to see the pain racing through her body.

Ia rested her arm on her thigh, easing the side that had gotten hit. "You say you want to spar, but it feels like you want to fight."

"My father was stationed at K-5 Neptune," Liam said between breaths.

Ia knew she had gained more enemies by her outburst earlier that day. Now, there were people who didn't just want her dead; they wanted her to suffer, wanted nothing more than to rip her fingernails off one by one just to hear her scream. And Liam Vyking, she realized, was one of them.

"Is he dead?" she asked Vyking. Surviving that battle would not have been easy.

"Paralyzed. From the neck down." His voice sounded like a boy's.

Liam's father was paralyzed because of her orders, but she'd had no choice. The decisions she had made were for the good of the Fringe and any other planet fighting against Commonwealth control. She killed for everyone's right to their own independence. Those Bugs *had* to die for the sake of what she was fighting for.

She couldn't even look at the broken expression on Liam's face. It had been so easy for her back then, to be there on the battlefield, watching as all the Commonwealth ships burned. They'd always been the bad guys to her. But now that the smoke and dust of battle was gone, she was starting to see that they had suffered too.

Fine, she decided. She would allow Vyking this moment.

"Let's settle this." Ia ripped her field gloves off and threw them onto the floor.

Liam followed her lead. With both of their gloves thrown off to the side, Ia grew more alert as tension filled the empty space between them. She could sense the rage fuming off him, almost equal to her own. Even the bystanders outside the ring had quieted.

The two of them circled each other, like the opposing winds of a hurricane.

Ia knew she had to watch out for a left uppercut; she could tell by his stance that he favored his left side. He was tall and had enough muscle to knock her unconscious. No matter. She had gone up against larger, more dangerous men before.

But there was something in the look on his face that she didn't expect. An intensity that made him unpredictable. And by the way he squared his shoulders at her, she knew he had something to prove. People like that never knew when to quit.

Just like her.

Beyond the ring, Liam's fellow flyers cheered him on and called taunts at her to throw her off her guard.

Ia realized this was more than just a fight to Liam. He wasn't searching for vengeance; he wanted closure. He needed Ia. And in her own way, she needed him. His grief, his anger, his emptiness.

War was an awful thing. It left an impression on her cells, soured the blood flowing through her veins, leaving a rotten stench inside her that only she could smell. She didn't want to admit it was guilt, but it was, festering forever in her core.

Liam hit her in the stomach. She grunted in agony as she pitched forward. Coughing and gasping, she tried to reclaim the air that had been knocked out of her lungs.

"Fight back!" He rotated to the side and kicked her in the ribs. Ia tumbled down to the ground, her face red from the adrenaline of the fight. The pain was suffocating. But she needed to feel the guilt inside her, she needed to understand the hurt she'd caused. As she rolled to her side, she sputtered, her blood-flecked saliva glistening on the light-gray floor.

The small crowd around the ring cheered at Liam's near victory.

"Finish her off, Vyking," Nero shouted.

Liam's boots came into view, treading closer.

Instinctively, her knees came up to her chest, curling up into a ball to protect her stomach from any more injury.

He was going to kick her. She knew it. All the men she had fought were like this. They liked to kick people when they were down. She flexed her core, readying herself for the impact, but instead, Liam grabbed her by her collar and pulled her up to face him.

"You may be at Aphelion, but you're not one of us."

A moment of clarity settled upon her. She wasn't one of them. She understood his pain, but would they ever understand hers?

"You're right, Vyking," she said, her voice low. "Thanks for reminding me."

It was time to end this. She had momentarily faced the guilt inside her. For that she was grateful, but now it was time to put everything back in its place.

With the surety and force of the catlike Maguan from the Verdu Forests, she twisted her body, sweeping a leg at Liam Vyking's feet. His body crashed to the floor. There was confusion. Panic. But not from Ia. She jumped on top of him, bringing the weight of her knees down hard onto his lungs.

She watched his face for the exact moment of realization.

He was *never* in control.

In a panic, Liam's arms flew out, into her face, into her chest, anywhere just to push her off him. With each attempt, she pushed him back down.

The flyers were no longer standing by. They rushed the

ring in a flurry, calling for the guards. Before they could reach them, she leaned in, breathing in the scent of his blood, sharp like iron.

She needed to teach him a lesson. If these Bugs went into the All Black, they would face the darkness. They would face the monsters. They would face her, and they all needed to know one thing.

"It's brutal up there, Vyking. The sooner you learn that, the less you'll feel."

Ia raised her fist and, with finality, punched Liam Vyking right in the throat.

CHAPTER 36
BRINN

BRINN GRIPPED TWO CUPS of caffeine. Her steps neared the entrance to the comms lab, triggering the motion sensor. The door whooshed open, revealing the cramped quarters of the communications department.

Angie sat by the wall in her own audio cubicle. The whole room was packed with them, each equipped with noise-blocking and frequency-enhancing audio orbs arching over the workstation. Instead of paying attention to the scanning sequences being run on the equipment before her, Angie hovered over her hands, delicately laser etching intricate pink patterns onto each of her nails.

Brinn ducked into Angie's cubicle. Static hissed all around her.

Angie pointed at an orb speaker and then pressed her ear up against it. "Can you hear that?"

Brinn angled her head, trying to pick something out from the enveloping hiss. Nothing.

"It's just white noise."

"Are you sure?" Angie twisted the knobs in front of her to continue scanning frequencies. "I've been hearing this weird frequency fluctuation for a couple days now."

Brinn held out a bottle filled with orange liquid. "Here's your caffeine."

"Thanks. You didn't have to." Angie didn't even look up, her attention now turned back to her nail art.

Brinn set the cups down and pulled up dialogue screens from her holowatch. "Twenty-seven messages, all from you. Bring me caffeine. Caffeine please. Caffeine would be so crucial right now. If I didn't bring these, you wouldn't have stopped."

Just then, a man's gravelly voice rose through the radio static. "RSF408 go for JAG33."

"What are they talking about?" Brinn asked.

Angie waved her hand. "Sometimes a military vehicle will cruise close enough for us to get quick snippets of news. It happens all the time."

Angie leaned forward, turning a knob to boost the volume.

Another voice transmitted onto the stream. "JAG33, we are tracking a large freighter ship, arrival at Gemini Star System at 1700 Universal Time. We ran the ship through our database. It was licensed in the Mainas System but appears to be under new ownership. The Armada."

"Those slavers are getting ballsier by the minute. Were our suspicions correct?"

"Affirmative. They're building what appears to be an unregistered gate."

Brinn rubbed her forehead. *An unregistered gate?* That was

impossible. Only the Commonwealth had the resources to build and maintain interstellar gates. An interstellar gate in the wrong hands could mean a number of things. Black market trading, illegal deals, or worse—the start of another war.

Angie glanced up from her nails. "Pretend you didn't hear that."

Brinn looked around at a group of holodisplays arranged in one corner of Angie's orb. Each one depicted security footage of people marching in the streets, holding signs in protest. "Where is that?" Brinn asked.

Angie looked up. "That's on Nova Grae. Citizens are marching to get rid of the Sanctuary Act and eradicating the refugee blocks."

Brinn leaned forward, examining the signs they carried. *Kick them out. Refs don't belong. Ours, not yours.* "This is really happening?"

She thought back to what Faren had said about how things have gotten worse back on Nova Grae, but she didn't think it had gotten to the point where people might lose their homes. Thankfully, her family was safe. Since their father was a natural-born Citizen, their house was located in the Citizens sector of their town, but there were hundreds of families who lived in the refugee block near their home. If the protests succeed and the Sanctuary Act is repealed, all of those people were going to be homeless.

Brinn rubbed her fingers on her temples, shocked that she hadn't even known this was happening.

"That's awful," she said.

Angie stared at her, as if she was turning around the words

Brinn had just said. Brinn was sure that Angie was going to attack her for siding with the refugees, but then Angie sighed. "I know someone who lives in that block. My mom and dad weren't home a lot. I was pretty much raised by my nanny, Fiotée. She's Dvvinn."

All at once, everything she knew about Angie unraveled like a cut ribbon. "But you always picked on the refugees in our school."

"And I'm ashamed of all of it. After Ia's capture, everything changed. The rioting on the streets, the hate crimes reported on the media. I realized that words have power. They have points and edges that can cut deep, and up until then, I wasn't very careful with them. I was part of the problem," she admitted. "So when I found out my dad was going to run for Council and fight for the Sanctuary Act, I told him I would do whatever he needed to give him the best shot at the election. That's why I'm here. No one can accuse him of being anti-nationalist if his daughter is in the Star Force."

Brinn sat in silence. All this time, Brinn thought she understood Angie Everett. But she was wrong. There was more to Angie's story. There was *always* more to people's stories.

Brinn focused on the display screens, watching the images of people rioting in the street.

"It feels like everything is falling apart," Brinn said.

Angie's hand touched her elbow, her eyes widening as if she sensed Brinn's thoughts. "Whatever's broken can be fixed."

Brinn looked up at Angie. This was what she'd always wanted. She had felt it after the Provenance Day parade, that feeling of brotherhood and connection with all the Citizens who watched that broadcast. And she felt it again, but now it was more complex. It had a direction, a point to the arrow. The system was broken, and it didn't require a mere patch to set it right. It required *real* change. "You're right," she said. "We'll fix everything. From the ground up."

Angie smiled at her. It was a promise between them, the beginning of a movement.

Just then, a chorus of shouts swelled in from the hallway. They were screaming something, a phrase, but she couldn't tell what it was. As the chant grew louder, Brinn finally picked out the words.

"Kill her," they shrieked outside. "Jettison her!"

Brinn rushed out of the comms lab, turning the corner only to be stopped behind a crowd of people. Rising up on her tiptoes, she caught a quick glimpse of two med borgs marching through the sea of cadets.

She caught whispers of a name. *Vyking,* they said. *Liam. Vyking.*

Brinn's heart sunk to her stomach. She pushed through the crowd, expecting to see Liam with a bloody nose or some other minor injury. But a different face stared back at her, completely mangled. His nose was smashed, and clotted blood gurgled from his split lips. Deus, no. Was that really him?

The borgs pushed past her, rushing him to the med bay. Brinn stood as if the world had stopped.

A hand from the crowd grabbed her shoulder. Brinn spun around, seeing Cammo's face, blanched white from fear.

"Cammo, what happened?"

"I tried to stop him, but he wouldn't listen to me."

That's when she heard a familiar shriek, a sound so sharp it scraped against her spine.

Please don't be her. Please don't be her. She repeated this over and over in her head, like witchcraft.

But of course it was. Clawing and cursing as the guards peeled her away from the training gym.

Brinn charged toward her, pushing Geoff and Aaron to the side.

"What did you do?" she asked Ia.

"He was the one looking for a fight," Ia snarled. "I went easy on him."

"Why were you even fighting in the first place?"

There was something different about her. She wouldn't look Brinn in the eye. "Because of something that happened during the war."

"The war's over now."

"Brinn, I hurt and killed thousands and thousands of people. That decision haunts me to this day. It's not *over*. It will never be over, not for me."

Brinn's eyes widened. That was why the crowd was there, ready to rip Ia apart. They wanted justice. They wanted her blood.

Brinn grabbed Ia's hand, pulling her away from the crowd. "Come on."

Ia snatched her wrist away. "Don't get involved."

"Let me help you," Brinn pleaded.

"Why?" Ia's eyes locked onto hers. "It's not like we're friends."

Brinn felt a tear in her heart. "You're being cruel."

"Why would I—the most notorious criminal in the known

universe—be friends with a Bug like you?"

Brinn's voice quivered. "If that was true, then why would you cover for me? Why would you scare off Nero? Why would you even bother helping me?"

"Because I pity you, Tarver."

All Brinn could hear was thunder roaring in her ears. She shot a sharp look to both Aaron and Geoff. "Bring her back to the room, and don't you dare let her out."

CHAPTER 37
IA

IA WAS OVER THIS PLACE. Completely over it.

Shrieking, she splashed ice-cold water onto her face. She was happy Brinn wasn't there. Otherwise, her fist would have flown directly into her face. She couldn't believe the girl had locked her in her own room.

Mif Brinn. Mif Knives. Mif that Nema wannabe. Mif this whole entire place.

Einn was the one who had persuaded her to stay put in Aphelion, to be a good cadet until he came for her. But she was done waiting for him, and she was through playing nice.

She had never been the maiden who needed to be rescued. That just wasn't her. She was the Sovereign, the Rogue, and the Blood Wolf. She was Ia Cōcha, whose red feather was stamped onto her helm with blood.

She had a plan, and it was time for her to use it.

Ia punched her fist into the metal wall. Over and over. Until blood trickled down her wrist. Her right hand pulsed with pain as she cradled it to her chest. Taking a deep breath, she bumped the door's sensor with her elbow. It swished open, and she stumbled into the hallway.

Geoff was the first to reach her. "You're hurt!"

Aaron bent over her, surveying her wounds. "She's fine. It's just a cut."

Geoff glanced down at the blood staining the front of her flight suit.

"You clunkhead, this is more than just a cut." He turned back to Ia. "Let's get you to the med bay."

Geoff pulled Ia to her feet and guided her to the main vestibule, Aaron following from behind. It was dinnertime, so the halls were empty. Even angry mobs had to eat.

As they approached the med bay, its white and red doors slid open, the smell of bleach and antiseptic stinging her nose. A floatbed swept toward her. Geoff assisted her onto the foam-padded mattress as med borg 494 appeared.

The data flowed behind her eyes as she recognized Ia's face. 494 looked at Aaron and Geoff. "I Will Take Over From Here."

Geoff gave a worried nod and ushered Aaron out of the med bay to keep watch outside. As 494 guided her into the infirmary, Ia glanced over her surroundings. Floatbeds lined each wall, all empty except one, closed off by privacy screens.

The med borg stopped Ia's floatbed in a vacant corner. She pressed a button, and a privacy wall projected around them. The borg snipped the sleeve off Ia's flight suit.

"You Should Be More Careful," 494 chided, examining the wound on her arm.

Ia looked up at her, examining the borg's features. A slight downturn of the lips and a noticeable crease of the skin textile on her brow area. Yes, 494 was worried.

Ia found herself smiling, grateful for her concern. "Sometimes my temper gets the best of me." Placing a hand upon her chest, Ia continued. "I've been experiencing some pains in my cardiac zone. Would you be able to survey the area for me?"

"Affirmative."

There was one thing she had been aching to get rid of since she got here.

After treating the wound, the borg retrieved a circular screen from a drawer on one side of the floatbed and positioned it over Ia's chest cavity.

"There Appears To Be Some Fibre Wire Laced Upon The Exterior Tissue Of Your Heart."

494 swiped her fingers upon the screen, and the view of Ia's heart, the implant coiled around every bit of muscle, appeared for Ia to see. Ia reached out at the holoscreen, pinching the image so it zoomed in. The tracer was intricate, its wiring laced in and out of the muscle of her heart. She shuddered.

"Is there any way you can extract it?"

The med borg tapped on her screen. "The Power System Is Designed To Short Out If Tampered With, Causing Heart Failure. There Is A 99.998 Percent Fatality Rate."

Ia took a deep breath. It was bad news, but it was what she had expected. There was a number of biotech systems inside her that she had already adapted to. Now, she had to figure out how to live with the device inside her heart. They would track her, so she couldn't stay in one place for too long, always glancing in her rearview for Bugs on her tail. And even worse, she would have to live each day, each minute, each second thinking it would be her last. Because she didn't know when they would stop her heart permanently.

But Knives was nowhere to be found, and she hadn't seen the general for weeks now. So she had some time to get out of this place, maybe grab a drink at a Dead Space bar before they found out she was gone. At least then they'd kill her when she was in the All Black, where she belonged. Mif it all. That was how she used to live anyway, hanging out on Death's doorstep. She was just lucky he was never home.

"How Would You Like Me To Proceed?" 494 chimed in.

"Leave it," Ia answered. "I'll deal."

"Affirmative. Now, I Must Advise You To Rest So Your Body Can Repair Itself." The med borg produced a knit blanket and draped it over Ia's legs. "I Will Be At My Charging Unit If You Need Me."

"Thank you, 494," Ia said as she held her hand. The cyborg's fingers were warm, like a human's. The Commonwealth built their borgs well.

Ia watched as 494 left. Above her, the lights dimmed for a sleep environment, but Ia had no plans to rest. She listened until 494's activity died down outside, replaced by the soft drone of her charging unit.

With smooth movements, Ia stepped off her floatbed and made her way across the room. She had to pay a certain someone a visit. She stopped at the only other occupied section, and without hesitation, Ia stepped through the privacy screens.

There he was, as expected. She leaned over his floatbed, face-to-face with Liam Vyking.

With the help of medical, the swelling on his face had gone down, but that hadn't stopped his skin from purpling with bruises. The med borgs had even reset the broken nose she had given him. All her hard work gone to waste. His face would heal like nothing had happened. No scars, no marks.

She rapped a knuckle on his forehead until his eyebrows crinkled and his eyelids fluttered open.

"Rise and shine, handsome."

Liam's eyes shot open. At the sight of her, his hands whipped forward, grasping at her neck. Her neck muscles flexed to give her some time. She reached out and dug her thumbs into the largest, tenderest bruise on his face.

The pain was enough to distract him. His hold weakened, and she pushed him off her, pinning him down onto the floatbed.

"I'm not here to fight," she spat out.

"Then what do you want?"

She looked into his eyes and whispered, "Help me escape. I need a flyer's prints to access those jets."

"No way. That's treason. Besides, you'd never be able to fly out of this sector without clearance from the flight master."

She had suspected this. Knives had all the jets locked down to this territory, which meant the engines would disable before she got to the gate. Luckily, she was prepared. "Don't worry about that. Just get me onto one of those ships."

"You must really think I'm stupid," Liam said.

"You're right. I do."

He rolled his eyes in her direction.

"Those print locks need a full biometric hand scan. So you can help me." Her fingers clamped down on his wrists, and she dug her fingernails deep into his skin. "Or I can just chop off your right hand."

His jaw clenched. "Let's go."

She loosened her grip and stepped back as he slipped off his floatbed. Ia passed through the privacy shields, glancing back at him. She placed a finger to her lips, prompting him to move as quietly as possible.

494 was still in sleep mode. The hum of her charging unit echoed through the med bay. As long as they didn't wake her, they would be in the clear. They hung back, sneaking against the wall until they were at the sliding doors. Now they had to worry about getting past her guards.

"How May I Assist You?" a melodic voice chimed out from behind them.

Ia swiveled around to see that 494 had stepped out of her charging unit.

"We just wanted to grab a snack from the canteen." It was the first thing that popped into Ia's head, and there was no way 494 would buy that. There was no way *anyone* would believe that.

"Cadet Cōcha, I Am Aware Of Your History."

Ia stiffened.

"Based On Your Body Scan," 494 continued, "I Have Determined You Have An Affection For Sugars."

Ia's expression brightened. "You know me too well. I love desserts. But Geoff and Aaron are charged with monitoring my nutrition. If there was a way I could get past them..."

"I Understand." Ia could have sworn she saw a twinkle in 494's otherwise blank stare.

The med borg walked toward a storage room and ushered them in. She slid open a secret panel on the floor and flipped a switch that was underneath. Across the room, a small door slid open, large enough for them to crouch into.

It was an emergency exit. Ia grinned to herself. She knew charming a borg would have its advantages.

"This Will Lead To The Flight Deck," 494 instructed. "From There, You May Reach The Canteen, If You Still Have A Need For Sweets."

Ia grabbed 494 by the shoulders, pulling her close. The borg was stiff but allowed Ia to hug her.

"Thank you," Ia whispered.

"Be Safe, Ia." Her voice was low, but still sounded like a song.

Ia stepped into the dark tunnel. At the end of it was her freedom.

CHAPTER 38
KNIVES

IT HAD BEEN THREE DAYS since he left Aphelion, where it was nice and safe, and there was no danger of him dying, except in a sim, which he programmed anyway so he always came out of them alive. He had forgotten firsthand how dangerous the universe was, and now, gazing outside at the fragments of Fugue, he was about to jump right into the thick of it.

Knives's watch trilled, and a holoscreen immediately flew up before him. It was the general. "Ready onboard, officer?"

Knives had his grav suit on and his helmet locked into place. Life-support systems were running, pumping in a healthy supply of oxygen. He pressed a square yellow button, and the overhead canopy came down, pressurizing the Kaiken's cabin as it lowered into place.

"Affirmative," he responded, flicking the general's screen to the side. He didn't like the idea of General Adams watching his every move, every facial tick, every bit of sweat that ran down his forehead. Instead, his father was going to get an amazing profile view of his left shoulder.

"Ready for takeoff?" The general's voice echoed through the pit.

Knives chose not to respond. He went ahead, punching the rear throttle forward.

"Follow protocol, officer. This is a military procedure, not one of your joyrides."

Knives tilted his chin up so his voice would carry to the onboard computer's voice recognition. "Mute all screens."

General Adams was cut off midsentence, and all that was left was the glorious roar of his starjet's thrusters. The nose of the Kaiken aimed toward GodsEye. Knives scanned the structure for a point of entrance. Drilled into the lower right arch was a set of rungs that led to a hatch. Knives steered toward it, then flipped a switch triggering the magnetic anchors to secure the hull of his jet to the outer rim of GodsEye.

The visor of his helmet gleamed slightly, and a short high-pitched ring announced an incoming stream. Letters flashed. Bastian.

"Everything all right up there? How are you doing?"

"Oh, you know, admiring the scenery. I think I'll vacation here during Solstice break," he joked.

Bastian shook his head. "It wasn't always this way. Fugue used to be a beautiful system."

"I'll take your word for it, Bastian. So what now?"

"Use your memory of the layout and find your way inside. Download all the cam footage on the servers. GodsEye is a technology that could become dangerous in the wrong hands. We need to know who's been out here."

So that was why Bastian had asked him to memorize the blueprints in his journal. And if this place was really under high security clearance, they wouldn't want to deal with digital files. Not when Knives could remember everything and see it all so clearly in his mind.

"I still don't understand why you can't patch in remotely," Knives said, trying to find every reason to stay put. He *really* didn't want to go out there.

"The operating systems were built to be fully closed off. Everything's analog. The only access is manual." Bastian took a moment's pause. "This is no easy task. Do you understand?"

Knives sighed. "Why am I doing this, Bastian?"

"Because you've never let me down," Bastian responded without hesitation. "We need you."

"The things I do for you," Knives muttered as he flicked a switch, pushing the canopy open. He tilted his head up so he faced GodsEye. Its interlocking metal panels were so large that it was all that he could see. His gaze stopped at a red paneled square with a rotating dog lever, surrounded by metal rungs on each side. It was an access hatch. That would be his way in.

With the Kaiken anchored underneath the structure, Knives aimed a grappling line at the column closest to the hatch entrance. Securing the other end to his belt, he pressed a button allowing the line to tow him closer to GodsEye. He swung himself to the access hatch and turned the wheel of the lever, then kicked his feet against the metal and pulled. The hatch door swung open, and he shimmied into the gate.

Inside, the grav systems were off, so he remained afloat.

Along with everything else. Papers. Old emergency flight suits. Rusted chips of metal. But what took up the most space was dust. With the gravity disabled, at least it wasn't getting all over his suit.

"I'm inside," he told Bastian. "It's dark as mung in here."

"There should be a power grid in…" Bastian's voice was swallowed up by static. Knives tapped his watch, silencing the display.

Strange, he thought. The signal wouldn't give out unless there was another signal jamming it. He'd have to find it and disable it in order to get hold of Bastian, but for now, he was without Bastian's assistance. He would just have to figure everything out by himself.

Knives pushed off against a nearby pillar and floated down the hallway, trying to avoid any rough debris that could tear through his suit. The lights on his shoulders didn't reach very far, so he felt against the wall, using it as a guide. About fifty feet in, he grabbed onto a handle protruding from the wall and stopped himself before a window. It opened up to the view outside, so dark he could barely distinguish the cruiser's outline.

He was on the observation deck. Based on the blueprints, he knew the power grid should be there. Somewhere.

Near the window, he spotted a metal casing the size of one of Bastian's leather-bound notebooks. He steadied himself in front of it, freeing the latch. Inside were rows of tiny black switches, but his eyes were drawn to a larger switch set apart from others, red in color and covered with a flip-up glass casing.

Prying open the casing, he rested his thumb along the edge of the bright-red switch.

"Red's a good color," he murmured to himself. "Red is always good."

He flipped the switch and instantly dropped to the ground. Around him, everything else did the same. He sat up, his helmet completely covered in a layer of thick dust. He wiped what he could off his visor so he could see.

The gravity and air systems were now working. The overhead lights were still off, save for a trail of flickering emergency lights along the walkway, but it was enough.

He followed the path, knowing the server room was in that direction. As he walked, the air grew heavy, humidity fogging the inside of his visor. He ran a scan on the air content, and when he was sure that there was enough oxygen for him to breathe, he bumped his fist against a button at his collarbone. His visor retracted, making it easier for him to see, but not by much. A rancid stench began to darken the air, clinging to his skin, permeating through his pores. It was unshakable. A human smell, of rot and decay. His stomach wretched forward, and the bitter taste of bile coated his throat. Despite his body's complaints, he held it down.

He had no desire to figure out what had happened here. Whatever it was, it wasn't good.

Knives stopped in front of a door. He tapped on the sensor, and the door slid open. If he thought the smell was bad in the hallway, it was a hundred times worse across the threshold. Using his hands to shield his nose from the stench, he stepped inside. No matter how much Knives squinted, his eyes failed to adjust to the shadows. But at least there was some light. It came from the center of the room, streaming from the edges of an onboard console. The server, he realized.

Limp sacks, like bags filled with food supplies, were positioned around the console. But there was something strange about them and the way they slumped over.

As he stepped closer, his vision adjusted to the dark scene before him.

His knees grew weak, and he reached out, leaning his hand up to the wall to steady himself.

No. It couldn't be.

These things weren't sacks at all. They were corpses. Relatively recent ones, though starved for weeks by the look of it. They were nothing but skin, bone, and fraying dark-blue hair.

Deus up above. They were Tawny.

Knives knew the Tawny were shunned in Olympus, but that was nothing in comparison to what he witnessed now. These people had died in their own filth, each of them chained to their own chair for Deus knows how long. A white cable dangled from the base of each of their skulls, hardwiring them straight into the console they clustered around.

He tapped on his holowatch, opening up a stream to the cruiser. "I found something."

The display responded with a hiss of static and a garbled message from his father. "We...document...thing..."

Getting the idea, Knives accessed the camera function of his watch. A holographic screen floated in front of him, and he angled it parallel to capture a shot of the nearest body. The dead man's face was jaundiced, almost yellow in the pale light. His mouth lay open as if he had been caught in the middle of a scream. The man was older than the rest of them, his blue hair already turning gray. Knives took the photo quickly, not wanting to stare at his face for much longer. As he was about to move on to the next body, he saw something on the man's neck. A scar of some sort. His fingers darted out, pulling the man's collar away, and he saw a pattern of red flesh the shape of two hearts side by side. It wasn't a scar, Knives realized. The man was branded. A quick glance around showed others also marked with the same symbol.

He swiveled as he saw something. Movement. A shadow stretched toward him in the inky darkness. In that instant, he remembered the story of Fugue, of the monster watching from a darkened corner.

Knives stood frozen as a figure stepped toward the light. His face was covered by a black helmet, raised on each side to form sharp edges like small horns. He was dressed in a sleek black flight suit. The figure raised his arm, his pistol flaring orange, ready to fire.

"Hands up." The voice was low, male, and carried a smoothness to the syllables. "I've always wanted to say that." There was something familiar in the way he spoke. That vicious glee and troublesome mirth.

As the figure stalked forward, the light caught on two white hearts engraved onto his chestplate. Before Knives could ask who he was, what he wanted, the man's arm rose and fell, the pistol cracking Knives hard across the head. Knives crumpled to the floor, and for a brief second, he saw an expanse of glittering stars, so bright they burned into his eyes, smoldering like a million suns all at once. As he lost consciousness, he was thankful for the light.

CHAPTER 39
BRINN

ONE STEP.

Then another.

Brinn's feet kept moving, shuffling through the hallway around the canteen. Dinner period was nearing its end, but Brinn still hadn't grabbed anything to eat. Instead, her thoughts were stuck on the same three words.

I pity you. I pity you.

"Brinn?" A face drifted into her periphery, following her. He continued to speak, but her mind was still stuck. After a while, she realized it was Cammo's voice.

"You've been walking around the canteen for an hour."

The only response she could manage was a short grumble.

Cammo scratched his jaw. "I visited Liam earlier."

Liam. Her feet stopped, and she blinked. For the first time in their walk around the canteen, she looked at Cammo. It was strange seeing him without that crooked smile on his face.

"Is he okay?" Brinn asked.

Cammo hesitated, but she saw the truth in his eyes.

"You should go see him," he said. "I know it'll cheer him up."

"Why do you say that?"

"Because every time he talks about you, he smiles."

Her heart faltered. It didn't matter if Ia pitied her. There were other people at Aphelion who valued her, who would call her a friend, maybe even something more.

Brinn rushed down the hallway.

She turned the corner, then staggered. Geoff and Aaron stood at each side of the clean, white doors.

What are they doing there? They're supposed to be guarding—

"Where's Ia?" she burst out.

Geoff opened his mouth to respond, but she rushed past them. She knew the answer. Ia was inside.

Brinn tried to ignore the panic brewing inside her, but it was too much of a coincidence. Ia and Liam in the same place, moments after they had fought.

Inside the med bay, 494 stood in the center. Her face was blankly pleasant as she charged on her pedestal.

Brinn raced to the far wall, the only section that had been curtained off. She waved away the holographic divider, completely expecting her heart to shatter at the image of Liam's body broken in so many ways it'd be impossible to jigsaw him back together.

Instead, she saw *nothing*.

Only an empty floatbed with crumpled sheets.

She checked each section of the room. No one was there.

Sprinting back out into the hallway, her eyes shifted back and forth between Aaron and Geoff.

"Get all the guards to the flight deck. Ia Cōcha has escaped."

CHAPTER 40
IA

"DO WE HAVE TO DO THIS?"

Ia had Liam in a headlock. They were crouched at the end of the tunnel, ready to push out into the open.

"It has to look like you're my prisoner on camera," Ia said. "If you want to be charged with treason, I'll happily let go."

"I'm no good to you if I collapse from lack of oxygen."

She loosened her grip. It was fun torturing him, but he was right. She needed him in order to get out of Aphelion, and he wouldn't be much help if he was unconscious.

She kicked out the grate and peered out. Above them, star-jets hung on the storage tracks. The lights were dim except for the beams lining the tarmac. It was 2200 in the evening, and the flight deck was empty.

She adjusted her grip around Liam's neck and nodded to the Eyes at the ceiling. "Try not to smile too much."

Then she lunged forward, not wasting any time. She would have gone straight for the Kaiken, but with Knives gone, it wasn't available. Luckily from all the nights and nights of maintenance duty, she had a good idea which starjets were in better condition than the rest. But since she was an engineer, none of these jets would power up for her. Ignition required an approved biometric signature, a handprint. A perfectly good reason why Liam was in a headlock and being dragged across the tarmac.

After zipping through a maze of vehicles, she stopped in front of the seventeenth spot, deciding to take a training jet parked on the ground and not stored above in the hanging units. It was one of the older models, which she preferred, and from previous examination of the front and rear engines, she knew the jet would hold up well for a long-distance flight.

As expected, the side door was sealed shut. Ia shoved Liam over to the door's biosensor. "All right, Junior, do your thing."

Liam rolled up the sleeve of his flight suit and pressed his palm onto the sensor. The computer whirred and buzzed as it sifted through the cadet database for a match.

Hurry, she pleaded. *Come on, hurry.*

Finally, she heard a mechanical click as the door unlatched.

"Well, I'm glad to say this is goodbye," Liam uttered as he edged away from her.

"I wish." She grabbed his wrist tightly. "I need your pulse print to start the launch sequence. Once everything is up, I'll let you go."

Liam was about to protest when she interrupted. "You're lucky it's a pulse signature they need instead of a simple print. Otherwise, I'd have already snapped that thumb of yours clean off."

"You're disgusting," he spat out.

"A girl's gotta do what a girl's gotta do."

She dragged him toward the steering wheel. Liam gripped the thruster handle so his pulse would register.

All around her, the starjet whirred to life. She scanned all the gauges, making quick note of the fuel levels. Only one full pod's worth, but if she drove economically, it would be enough to get her to a refill station after the jump.

"All right, Vyking, you can go," she said, looking behind her, but Liam was already gone. She peered through the pilot window and watched as he ran down the tarmac. She couldn't blame him.

Setting her sights back on the task at hand, she scooted into the pilot's chair and navigated the training jet out onto the tarmac.

"So far, so good," she muttered to herself.

Out on the flight deck, bright warning lights strobed out in alarm.

Mif. She spoke too soon.

Behind her, a line of sentry borgs spilled onto the deck. Because of their mechanical limbs, they were fast.

Ia quickly activated her rear thrusters to thermal burn. She glanced at the back monitors, watching as a stream of high-temperature exhaust burst out the back of the jet, taking out a group of borgs nearing the tail. A part of her felt a twitch of guilt, especially after everything 494 had done for her. Hell, even Aaron had given her a new sense of borg appreciation.

But right now, the only thing that mattered was getting herself out of there.

Force field generators sparked at the end of the runway, and she knew her escape time had been cut in half. She needed to be on the other side of that force field before it came down. Otherwise, she'd be trapped.

Retracting the wheels of the jet, she set the mid thrusters to hover. There wasn't enough time for a runway takeoff. She had to blast out of there cold. It would be bumpy, less precise. But faster.

The force-field barrier started to seal, quickly forming to meet at the middle. Swiveling back and forth in her chair, she switched to ionic thrusters and, with both hands steady, she guided the jet upward, bringing it to a hover at the midpoint.

Her hands now on the drive controls, she felt the jet hum, and at that exact moment, she slammed the rear throttle forward at full speed. Using her left hand to steer, she eyed the force-field surface for the exact position where the barrier would come to a close. The hole was barely big enough for the jet to pass.

Ia yipped like a maniac as the jet punched through, the edge of the closing force field knocking her aircraft to the right, and she knew it had shaved off the tip of her wing. Not a big deal. She could compensate for the wing imbalance with proper steering.

Nope. Not a big deal at all.

Because she was alive.

Because she was rising up through the swirls of snow and breaking through the clouds.

Because once again, she could see the sky.

* * *

An hour later, the floating archways of this system's intergalactic gate appeared in the distance. The structure was unmarked, so she had no idea where it would lead her. It could drop her into the middle of a hostile system for all she knew, but Ia didn't care as long as she was putting distance between her and Aphelion. Ia hovered the jet to the side, transmitting a signal to the gate's network. All she needed to do was activate the usage code, and she could jump away from this sector.

An automated voice came in through the speakers. "Thank you for using the Birra Gate. Your vehicle's data signature is locked. Please provide vocal confirmation before your jump."

Her tongue pressed against a metal node at the top of her mouth, initiating the voice generator wired into her vocal chords. All the audio data she had collected was stored there, perfect for a day like this. That was the reason she sought out conversation after conversation with that cold-eyed weirdo.

Well, *one* of the reasons.

She cleared her throat, testing out the feel of Knives's voice upon her tongue. "This is Knives Adams. Requesting access for travel."

She watched as an icon swirled upon the transmission display.

Then, finally: "Vocal confirmation approved."

Ia let out a sigh of relief. She clicked upon the navigation display, setting her itinerary while the gate whirred into life, its concentric circles churning as it activated. She laid her hands on the thrusters, but before she went forward, she saw a shimmer in the distance beyond the gate. Another ship was approaching. How odd. It had found its way to this star system without jumping through the gate.

With her awful luck these days, it would turn out to be a RSF ship making a pit stop at Aphelion. It could even be Knives, returning from wherever the mif he was.

But wait—all Star Force vehicles had free access to interstellar gates, while everyone else was tolled for their usage. A lot of pilots sometimes decided to take longer routes to forego the charges. So if it wasn't Knives or any other RSF vehicle, then who was it?

Her eyes widened. Perhaps it was Einn, finally come to rescue her. She positioned the jet to get a better look. As the ship approached, she tried to make out its shape. Einn's ship, *Shepherd*, was long and shaped like a cross with a yellow stripe running right through its center.

But the ship that approached wasn't any of that. Whatever it was, it was coated in nonreflective black, making it almost impossible to figure out where the ship started or ended, at least from a far distance. It was relying on stealth, which meant it was here for reconnaissance.

A scout.

And based on the model of the jet, she knew they were bad news. All the pirates, slavers, and crime lords she knew used those stealth jets as feelers to see if there was anything out in the far reaches to take.

Why were they scanning *this* star system? There was nothing here.

Except for the academy.

And once AG-9 was scanned by this jet, others would follow. That uranium core Ia had told Einn about would light up on the jet's sensors. Aphelion wouldn't stand a chance.

Brinn wouldn't stand a chance.

Ia sunk back into her pilot seat, trying as best as she could to sweep away all her worries. No loose ends, her brother told her.

She powered up her jet and raced through the gate, away from Aphelion, away from Tarver and the rest of those poor oblivious cadets.

She didn't dare look back. If she did, she knew she might change her mind.

CHAPTER 41
KNIVES

KNIVES WOKE UP, the smell of death still surrounding him. Rolling to his knees, he discovered his hands had been bound together by a goopy adhesive. His helmet was gone, and so was his holowatch. He couldn't connect with the cruiser or the ArcLite. His captor had thought things through.

Knives's eyes trailed across the confines of the room until he saw him, leaning against the server console and sharpening a thin blade the length of his forearm. Behind him was a small box with a purple display screen broadcasting a blocking signal. So he was the one scrambling Bastian's stream.

His captor was of light build, but by the way he held himself, Knives could tell he was a confident fighter. To make matters worse, his suit was modded with a lot of tech. Exoskeletal armor, plasma charges on his wrists. His captor would not be easy to take down.

As far as Knives could tell, there were no name tags on

the armor, only those two white hearts emblazoned on his chest piece.

"Excuse the mess," White Hearts apologized, seeing Knives was awake. "I've been upgrading."

Knives seared a look in his direction. "You murdered them."

White Hearts glanced at the decaying bodies arranged around him like petals on a flower. "I merely put them to good use. The processor in this rust shack was dead, so I needed to whip something up. What's the old saying? If we put a few heads together—"

"You used Tawnies for processing power?" Knives spat out. "That's inhumane."

"Inhumane? Olympus nearly wiped out the entire Tawny civilization. I only acknowledged their strengths. Their minds are the key to making GodsEye what it should be." He pointed his blade in Knives's direction. "Do you even know what this place can do?"

White Hearts made his way toward Knives and crouched before him. "It makes all kinds of rips and tears." He drew his blade up and slashed it across the thick of Knives's bicep. Knives felt warm blood drench the sleeve of his suit, and he bit the inside of his cheek to block out the pain. He wouldn't give his captor the satisfaction of seeing him suffer.

It only made White Hearts lean in close.

"Black holes, worm holes. They're all very deep gouges in the fabric of space." Another slash trailed across Knives's chest, ripping through the thick poly-fabric of his suit. Then one against Knives's cheek. Knives's vision pulsated, dimming and brightening as his body reacted to the pain.

His captor leaned back on his haunches. As he spoke, he waved his knife around like a toy. "What was that story you all tell each other? Of a monster that ripped apart Fugue?"

Knives angled his head. Was his captor former RSF? How could he know about that?

"It's funny how stories come about, latching on to some speck of truth. You know who that monster really was?" White Hearts tilted his head to the side, the horns on his helmet spearing the air as he moved. "It was the man who created this thing."

At that moment, White Hearts tapped at the button on his collarbone, and his helm slid off. Knives's eyes scoured every detail of his face. He was young, the same age as he was, perhaps a year older. His skin was a light bronze, his eyes a marbled gray, and he looked so, so familiar.

"You're staring," White Hearts observed. "You look like you want to say something."

"Yeah. You talk too much."

White Hearts smirked and patted his shoulder, much like a friend would do. "You know, I think I can make good use of you."

Knives met his gaze, squinting as sweat dripped into his eyes.

White Hearts stood, motioning to a darkened corner. A red light flared from the black. Metal footsteps clanged toward him, and the red light came closer, closer, until Knives could make out the figure in the darkness.

It was a borg. And he was a goliath. It wore no skin or clothing, only the metal armor that encased its construction. All raw metal and circuitry. Its limbs and joints were basic, with only two strong articulated fingers on its left hand, enough to crush skull after skull if it had to. On its right side, there was no hand at all, but a plasma gun attached at the end of its forearm. This borg was a machine built for combat.

"Put him in the circle with the rest."

The borg grabbed Knives by the neck and lifted him up. His hands were still bound, so he kicked at the thing's body, but it was no use. It was too strong, and he was too weak.

He was going to die.

Knives groaned as he stared at the red light embedded in Goliath's head. Then suddenly, the light blinked like a closing eye, and its two metal fingers went slack. Knives fell to the floor, coughing as his airway opened. Looking up, he saw his father clutching a fistful of severed circuitry and kicking Goliath to the ground.

"Dad?" Knives coughed. "What are you doing here?"

"I knew something was up when your signal was cut. I docked here as soon as I could."

Knives caught the look in his father's eyes, and it felt like time had stopped. He recognized that expression, though he had seen it only once before, when he was four years old. Like most kids, he'd loved adventuring up trees. But one day, he fell off a weak branch and tumbled to the ground. He was banged up and bruised, a deep cut slicing across his chin. His father came running out of the housing pod with that same look on his face.

Knives's breath caught deep in his throat. To see his father worry…he didn't know whether to cherish or fear it.

Before he could decide, time caved in again.

A plasma blast split the air in half, hitting its mark. The

general staggered back, clutching the arm where the blast had hit, the plasma searing through his armor.

Fingers gripped onto Knives's hair, jerking his head back, so he could see the devil's smile on White Hearts's face as he stood above him. The tip of the plasma cannon dug into the nape of his neck, ready to blast his head clean off.

"Stop!" the general pleaded, lowering his weapon to the ground. His father's voice was hushed, almost human. "Let him go."

White Hearts paused. "And why would I ever do that?"

"I can give you information. You want to know how this place works. There's someone on my ship who can tell you."

"What's his name?"

"Bastian Weathers."

"Bastian…" White Hearts repeated. There was something strange about the way he said Bastian's name, tonguing the word like it was candy in his mouth.

White Hearts threw Knives down. He rolled to the side in time to see his foe cup his hands together. In between his fingers was a ripple. Knives blinked, uncertain of what he saw. The space around him wrinkled, like a thin skin over an unknown universe.

White Hearts leaned in so Knives could hear. "Rips and tears."

And like a piece of paper, White Hearts's body crumpled upon itself, warping and shifting, until all that he was disappeared like water down the drain.

He was gone.

"What on Ancient Earth…" His father ran to the spot

where White Hearts once stood. "I've never seen anything like that before."

Knives shook his head at what he had witnessed. A person couldn't just disappear.

The general located the blocking device that was garbling communication with the cruiser and turned it off. Almost instantly, a beep sounded on the general's holowatch, and a screen popped up, lighting up the dismal space. Bastian, red faced, perked at the sight of them. "Thank Deus, you're all right."

A nagging thought pulled his attention, and Knives remembered what White Hearts said about the story of Fugue, that there was no monster who destroyed this place. Only a man. Knives felt the blood rush from his face. He knew where White Hearts was heading. He grappled toward the screen. "Bastian, listen to me. You have to hide. Take your journal and hide."

A voice floated in, interrupting them. "But I just got here…"

The next moments were a blur. A series of images that took only milliseconds.

White Hearts grabbed Bastian from behind, his hand coming up to stifle the sounds of his struggle. A sliver of silver glinted in his other hand.

He drew it like a brushstroke across Bastian's throat.

Red spilled to his chest, and Bastian's body dropped.

With a lazy kick, White Hearts nudged Bastian's dead body to the side and plucked the notebook from the bloody floor.

He snatched Bastian's holoscreen, still hovering, still transmitting, and he looked straight into it, knowing very well who was watching.

"Thank you for your cooperation. May your eyes be open…" White Hearts's hand swiped along the screen. The general's display blinked to black.

CHAPTER 42

BRINN

"I DON'T THINK I'm good at this game," Liam said from his floatbed.

He swiped the Goma board back to Brinn, who was sitting in a nearby chair. Brinn looked at the pieces. They had barely started the game, and yet she had already predicted the next moves he would make. He could try, but he was going to lose. She closed out of the display while Liam watched her.

"Are you all right?" he asked.

Brinn shrugged. It had been two days since Ia's escape. At first, Brinn had been ecstatic, her reaction still stemming from the anger of their fight. But after a few hours, she had started to feel Ia's absence.

"It's quieter with her gone," Brinn said.

"She didn't belong here, Brinn," Liam replied.

Brinn studied the monitor hooked onto Liam's arm, watching the rise and fall of his heartbeat like waves of an ocean.

He was still recovering from the events of that day, his bruises now fading into gray.

"I guess you're right," she said.

But then a strange liquid pooled into her eyes, overpouring onto her cheeks. What was this?

She was crying.

Her mind rushed as she tried to control herself, to rein everything back in, but her body fought against her commands. No matter how hard she tried, the tears continued to fall. And that noise. She was sniffling!

She felt Liam's gaze, even through her wet eyelashes. It was as good a time as ever to retreat, but before she could turn, his fingers grazed her cheeks. They trailed delicately underneath her eyes, tracing each tear like they were words of a sacred spell. His hands guided her head to his shoulder, and she heard the air inside him hum.

"I thought she was my friend. Is that weird?"

"I'm going to be honest with you. Ia is the scariest person I've ever met." His fingers lightly touched the bruises around his jaw and neck, and then his eyes rose to Brinn's. "But she was always different when it came to you. Nice, even."

"Now that she's gone, I don't have many friends," Brinn said.

He reached for her hand. "Yes, you do."

She leaned back, catching a glimpse of his eyes, the specks of green and gold sparkling like gemstones in the remaining light.

Those eyes. She felt herself getting lost in him, and strangely, her hand came up to cup his jaw. Normally, her mind would have fought her on this, screaming for her to stop what she was doing at once. But right now, all was quiet inside, and she allowed herself to feel his skin underneath her fingertips. That was when she realized she had stopped crying. And how awfully close they were, his head angled to the side, and hers angled to the other.

Her holowatch dinged. Just in time for her brain to take over and steer her back to safety.

She laid his hand back on the bed and stood up. "It's late. You should rest."

He leaned toward her as if he was going to say something. But she turned and walked away before she could even give him the chance.

She shuffled back to her dorm room, now quiet with Ia gone. The room felt so different. The first night Brinn was on her own, she had cleaned up Ia's things, picking up Ia's messy pile of clothes and placing them in a container in the closet. She had wiped up the blood that had dried on the wall but left the small dent where Ia had obviously punched at it.

Ia's bed was still there, sheets left unturned and crumpled. The past few nights, Brinn had fallen asleep listening to the drone of the lights instead of the tune Ia sang out in her sleep. Brinn had it memorized by now. So tonight, she hummed it lightly. It eased her sadness, just by a little bit.

* * *

It was 0448 when the ground shook. Brinn rocketed up in her bed.

The lights inside the room pulsed red.

"Monitor, what's going on?"

But there was no response.

She hooked her hair behind her ear and listened. Footsteps. Voices.

Maybe some sort of prank? Someone must have pulled the emergency alarm.

Brinn jumped out of bed and pulled on her boots. She was still in her sweats, but there was no time to change. She ran to her door, placing her hand to the metal. Hissing, she jumped backward. It was burning hot.

With fluttering fingers, Brinn pressed her palm to the sensor. The door slid open but then stopped halfway. Through the small opening, she caught glimpses of smoke and fire. And of cadets running.

Worse than that, she heard their screams. Like they had seen death.

She caught sight of Reid running past her door.

"They're coming!" she cried.

She was almost out of sight when her feet came up from underneath her, and she fell forward. Brinn angled her head out of the opening, trying to see if Reid was okay. Something coiled around Reid's ankles, a thick plastic, so tight it tore into her skin.

Pulling her sleeves over her hands, Brinn gripped the edge of the metal door, still hot through the fabric of her sweatshirt, and pulled. It wiggled open a few more inches. That was all she needed.

Brinn slid through the narrow opening and knelt before Reid, her red hair plastered to her face from both sweat and tears. Brinn's hands darted to Reid's ankles, trying to pry off the cable.

"You need to go," Reid cried.

"Let me help you."

Reid pushed her away. "They're slavers! Save yourself!"

The coils grew taut, ripping Reid away from Brinn's grasp and dragging her back to the far end of the smoke-filled hallway.

Brinn skittered backwards in shock, not stopping until her back hit the wall behind her. She heard voices from across the smoke.

"This way," one of them ordered. "Her room should be in this hallway."

Brinn stood frozen as heavy footsteps thudded toward her. She saw the sheen of eyes, vicious as they savored the fear they created.

She turned on her heels and ran. She didn't dare look back; she'd be stupid to think they weren't following.

She found a group of cadets and joined them. They were a small group at first, but then grew by a few people at each turn. That's when Brinn realized how experienced these slavers really were. They knew what they were doing. They were herding them, flushing them toward the flight deck.

So when the crowd veered right, Brinn darted left into a separate hallway. The corner came up fast, and she turned.

Right into arms clad with armored steel.

Her heart banged hard in her chest as her eyes met her opponent. He towered over her, dirt and grease clinging to every angle of his face. He was one of them.

She pushed away, but his hands shot forward, gripping tight around her shoulders. He leaned in, examining her. The stench of his decaying teeth soured the smile that flashed across his face.

"We're looking for a girl," he said. "You look like a girl."

His hand smothered her mouth, and she gasped in the stench of his oil-stained skin. Brinn heard a loud crack, and the slaver's body slumped. Behind him, Liam stood, a metal pipe gripped in his hands.

Seeing his face, her heart leapt, and without even deciding it, her arms wrapped around him, as Brinn tried to steady the rhythm of her breathing.

"Thank you," she whispered.

More voices traveled toward them. "We need to hide," he said.

"The comms lab. It's close." She grabbed his hand and pulled him down the hallway, her footsteps quick and certain. The doors slid open at their presence, revealing a room thrown into chaos. Each comms station had been torn from the floorboards and gutted. Water poured down from overhead sprinklers, trying to quench a fire brewing in the corner.

Her hand came up, drawing her soaked locks to the side, and that's when she heard it. A cough.

Someone else was inside.

Brinn turned to Liam and placed a finger against her lips. He readjusted his grip on the metal pipe.

Brinn pointed over at a large pile of ruined components. Liam led the way, his pipe raised high. As they made their way around the cluttered heap, Brinn caught a glimpse of someone digging through metal. The nails on her hand were painted a distinguishable shade of pink.

Liam's pipe swung down, hard enough to break through bone.

"Liam. Stop!"

Just in time, he readjusted his aim. The blunt end of the pipe landed off to the side, crashing down into a pile of metal.

Angie swiveled around, facing them. "What the mif do you think you're doing?"

Brinn rushed forward, shushing her.

"We thought you were one of them."

"Do I *look* like one of them?" She looked at the grime on her hands. "Oh mung. I do, don't I?"

Angie sat back on her haunches, her eyes darting over the wire and circuitry before her. "I was trying to send out an SOS signal to HQ. But all of the comms orbs are destroyed. Even our holowatches are jammed. We're totally scuzzed."

"No, we're not. Give me some cover from the sprinklers." Brinn crouched next to Angie, who had found a small sheet of metal to hold over her as Brinn unlatched her holowatch and pried the backing loose like she had seen Ia do so many times before. She spotted a landline wire in a nearby pile and fished it out. With deft fingers, she twisted it onto the circuits of her holowatch.

A holoscreen popped up, a blinking dash waiting for her input. A number pad appeared on the lower right side, but all she needed to use were two buttons. 1 and 0. She was connected to the spire, one of many beacons that patched all of the ArcLite together. She typed in a series of rapid-fire commands, and in response, a scrolling screen of numbers cascaded down like a waterfall. Her eyes raced as she absorbed the information.

"What does it say?" Angie asked.

"It's telling me the codes to all RSF spires."

"Why would you want that?"

"We can't send out a visual transmission. But I can get each spire to ping out an SOS code with our coordinates to the closest Commonwealth vessel." Brinn typed in her last line of code and pressed Enter.

"I didn't know you were this smart," Angie remarked.

Brinn snorted under her breath.

Liam brought a finger up to his lip and angled his head at the entranceway. "They're close."

They all held their breath as footsteps passed outside.

"I think they're gone," Brinn said after a moment of measured silence.

Liam turned toward them. "We should get out of here before they circle back."

Brinn made her way to the entrance. The floor had become flooded as the sprinklers continued to spray overhead. She wiped her wet hair away from her face. Blinking through the drizzle of water, she looked over her shoulder to see Angie frozen in place. Brinn looked past Angie's tousled appearance, her drenched hair and the rips on her flight suit. There was something off about her. Instead of her usual confident self, Angie stood hunched over, wringing her fingers. Brinn's gaze fell to the speckles of red staining Angie's suit. Blood. And it wasn't her own.

"Angie..."

"I don't want to go back out there." Her voice was very small. "I was with Cammo. He was right next to me, and then he wasn't. He was trying to save me."

"What are you saying?" Liam's voice was tense.

Angie's eyes darted up for a second. And from the pained look on her face, Brinn knew...

"No," Liam sputtered, his face pale. "Not him."

Brinn felt the room spin. Cammo was *gone*. Easygoing, joke-cracking, endlessly enthusiastic Cammo. Her throat tightened, and she felt like throwing up.

Brinn swallowed her sadness and looked Angie straight in the eye. "We can't let them win." She extended her hand, offering Angie her strength.

Angie raised her chin at the sound of her words. Her fingers slipped into Brinn's hand. They were cold and clammy, but Brinn held them tight anyway.

Metal screeched behind her, and she spun to see the entry doors wobble open, catching only a glimpse of a slaver adorned with metallic skull headpiece. He stood in the archway, a smile on his face and his pistol pointed.

The nozzle strobed red. Air cracked at her ears. Her head whipped back, and all she saw were the panels of the ceiling and the flat rows of lights. Her feet were no longer on the ground because she was flying backward. With a loud thud, her head cracked against the floor, but that wasn't what hurt. Pain radiated from deep inside her rib cage, and she found herself gasping for air.

Outside of her direct line of vision, she saw flashes of limbs and metal. The sounds of struggle mixed with Angie's screams.

She tried to sit up, but it felt like a boulder was on her chest.

The hollow clang of metal cracked against bone, and she

heard a body crash to the ground. The clatter of the fight died away, and Angie's screams muffled down to panicked sobs.

But what about Liam? Where was he?

Fingertips padded against her cheek, and she tilted her head up. Hot tears seared the corners of her eyes when she saw him standing over the slaver's unconscious body.

He was okay. Liam was okay.

He smiled but then glanced toward her side. "Don't move."

Angie appeared behind him, a look of horror on her face. "Brinn, you're bleeding!"

Brinn felt pressure as Liam's hands pressed down against her ribs.

Gunshots echoed toward them, loud like bombs. They were getting closer.

Liam looked her in the eye. "Brinn, we have to get you up. It's going to hurt."

She nodded through the pain.

Liam pulled her up. The throb in her chest radiated outward, buzzing toward her stomach and knifing through her brain. She whimpered, tears wetting her cheeks.

Brinn leaned on Liam, while Angie took her other arm. They had made their way through the first stretch of hallway when they heard sickening laughter between the gunshots.

"We know you're out there," someone hooted. "Keep crying, so we can find you." More slavers joined in, snickering, high from the hunt.

Brinn felt Liam's grip loosen as he eased himself away from her, his absence like a hole in her side. It made her shiver.

"Cut through the canteen," he told them. "You and Angie need to run until you're safe."

What about you? Brinn wanted to say, but she didn't have the strength.

And then Liam was running. All she could see was his back as he headed toward the gunfire.

Angie pulled her into the canteen. "They're everywhere. There's nowhere to hide."

"I know a place," Brinn managed to whisper, thinking of the secure uranium core. Her breathing grew sharp and staggered. She jutted her chin toward the engineering wing, and Angie hurried them through a maze of tables to the main hallway. They passed through the Horticulture labs, then the Armaments facilities, until finally they stopped in a dark room with a set of elevator doors.

They just needed to get into the elevator, and they would be safe.

"They're here," she heard in the distance. She didn't have to turn to know the slavers had sniffed them out.

It took all of her strength to lift her hand. Seeing her struggle, Angie gently guided her palm to rest against the sensor. The scan lit up, warming at her touch. But it didn't open. She didn't have the access to get through. If she could hook into the sensor—

She froze. The cold nozzle of a pistol dug into the back of her skull. The slavers had found them. Brinn swallowed, closing her eyes, waiting for the trigger to click.

A woman's voice interrupted Brinn's thundering heartbeat.

"Put your weapon down. They're with us."

Brinn turned her head slowly. It was Ia's guard, Aaron, who held the gun, now lowered at his side. His face was clawed, the skin textile shredded off half his head. Professor Patel stood beside him. She held her arm where a gash had splayed her flesh.

"Professor," Brinn choked out.

Professor Patel glanced at Aaron. "Quickly, help them."

Aaron hoisted Brinn's other arm over his shoulder while the professor scanned her hand against the sensor. With a lurch, the elevator doors churned open. Shots fired around them, clanging on the floor at their feet.

Professor Patel shoved the three of them inside and rushed to the controls. The elevator doors closed behind them as a second round of gunshots fired, their bullets hitting the polycarbon of the door instead of their flesh.

As they descended, heat rose around them, making it hard to breathe.

The elevator thudded to a stop, and there it was. The uranium core, showering them with its energy. It was surrounded by an intricate set of hover pods levitating it high above the rock surface, and a network of piped vents siphoned cold air from outside onto the core.

At that moment, Brinn's knees gave out, and she fell forward.

Professor Patel's hands pressed hard against her ribs. "You're losing too much blood."

Brinn's mind grappled for other possibilities, other ways to survive this, but there was only one option. There was no way around it; they would have to see. This was not worth dying over.

Brinn closed her eyes and focused until she saw the blood pumping through her veins, the hemoglobin racing to clot the flow, and then her mind snapped to a stop as she located it. The plastic bullet was buried in her right lung, hidden in the rapidly collapsing cavity inside her chest.

With every ounce of energy, she willed her cells to create new cellular tissue. They bridged together while pushing the bullet out of her body at the same time.

The plastic bullet fell to the floor with a soft clink.

As her lungs renewed, she took in a deep and hungry breath. Her eyes fluttered open, only to see a mixture of shock and horror on Angie's face.

"What the mif?" Angie whispered.

Brinn collapsed to her side, her face angled to the glow of the uranium. Despite how powerful her mind was, it was far from a perfect system. She still needed to rest. And against her will, she closed her eyes while Aphelion fell. Her mind slowly faded away to an eerie lullaby, with the hum of the core as its melody, and the explosions upstairs as its drumbeats.

CHAPTER 43

IA

IA WAS OUT OF GAS.

Why?

Because she had decided to turn back.

Yep. Back to miffing Aphelion.

And in her haste, she had gotten stuck in a megaplanet's orbital pull. It was a bitch to get out of. She had used all of her fuel to escape its gravity, and now she was stuck floating around at the edge of some unknown star system.

The best she could do was signal for help and beg for some fuel. But the place was deserted. She had to wait.

Ia groaned. She'd been sitting for two days, surfing transmission channels, both the mainstream and Dead Space ones. But nothing was coming her way.

Her stomach growled, and her hands clutched down to her belly. She had already eaten all the food packs she found by the console, but she hadn't gone through the emergency reserves.

Ia turned off the grav system to save energy. She threw her

head back and drew her knees into her chest. Her weightless body somersaulted backward. Kicking her legs out, she pushed against the ceiling.

Maybe she'd find some chocofluff. On *Orca*, she always kept her backup supply stocked with berry twists, sugar drizzle, and lopti jerky.

Ia found the emergency reserves in an overhanging storage chest. She tore the plastic bag open, letting its contents stream out. Band-Aids, regen serum, H_2O jelly, adrenaline shots. But no chocofluff.

At least there was a calorie bar buried in the bottom of the bag. She shook it out of the plastic until it spiraled outward, and then plucked it out of the air with her fingers. Within seconds, the entire bar was stuffed in her mouth. It was dry and starchy, but it would occupy her stomach for the time being.

Ia arched outward, her arms stretched above her head. She would have been content falling asleep this way—and was well on her way to doing so when a beep resounded from the scanner systems at the head of the jet.

People!

She pulled herself to the front of the jet and hovered over the scanner screen.

There, right around the nearest planet. A starjet was heading her way.

She accessed the transmission interface, setting it to automatically jump onto the approaching vessel's system.

"Hi there," she said in her sweetest voice. "Could you spare a couple pods? I'm completely stranded." She tried to sound as helpless as possible to appeal to the other pilot's generosity.

No answer.

"I'll pay you," she pleaded. "I have NøN. Or Zeroes. Even century coins. I'll make it worth your while."

Again with the radio silence.

Seriously? That offer could have hooked even the stiffest of cargo pilots.

"Hello?" she asked one last time.

"Well, well…" A familiar voice crackled through the speakers. "If it isn't the Blood Wolf of the Skies."

Ia angled her head trying to pin down the owner of that voice. No, it couldn't be. A smile tickled at the edges of her lips.

"Knives?"

* * *

Ia stood in the middle of the training jet, waiting. The Kaiken was docked, and the chamber that bridged the two vessels was in the process of vacuum sealing and acclimatizing. Finally, the entryway unlocked, and she watched Knives as he ducked in, a rush of air blowing into his face as he stepped through. She couldn't tell if he was angry. In fact, his energy seemed muted.

"Before you pull out that heart tracker, I just want you to know that I was on my way back," Ia blurted out.

"I don't have time for this," Knives said as he entered the cargo deck from the regulation chamber.

Ia opened her mouth to say something, to tell him about the scout she had spotted heading toward Aphelion. But then she noticed how he carried himself. Slowly, carefully like he was injured underneath his fresh flight suit. He gingerly raised his hand to unlatch his helmet. She gasped. His face had changed, like he had been to hell and back, a ripe cut buried down the skin of one cheek.

He walked toward a nearby passenger chair and eased into the seat. His hands ran through his hair, slick with sweat. She lowered herself into the chair next to him, her eyes resting on his hands gripped between his knees. He was trembling.

"Knives, are you all right? Where have you been?"

He stared at the floor. "We were in Fugue..."

"Fugue?" A piece of a memory flashed in her string of thoughts. "The Fugue from that story?"

"We were attacked," Knives cut in. "Bastian's dead."

Ia washed her eyes over his features. No wonder he was so upset. She wanted to reach out to him, but she stopped herself.

"What happened?" she asked.

"When we got there, someone was waiting for us." Knives breathed. "It was unlike anything I've ever seen. He had a whole bunch of Tawnies chained to chairs, all dead when I found them."

"Sounds like a top-level mungwad to me." Ia knew people like that back in Dead Space. They loved torturing their prisoners, taking their time with it. She had obviously killed before, but she tried to make it quick. Merciful, even. At least compared to them.

"He branded them," Knives continued. He traced a finger against his neck. "Two hearts."

Her stomach dropped when he said those words. "Show me."

He glared at her like she was a serial killer.

"Show me," she repeated.

A photo screen hovered before her, and for a moment, she was too frightened to raise her eyes to look. It was a face she wanted to see again, but not like this. Now, the Elder's eyelids were swollen shut, a crust of dried pus cemented at the crease, and his lips, the same ones that smiled at her, were red with dried blood. Along his neck, an imprint branded the Tawny Elder's skin. Two identical hearts. Side by side.

A wave of dizziness swept over her, and her knees grew weak. "That's my brother's mark."

Knives furrowed his brow, his eyes digging into hers. "Your brother did this?"

"It can't be him," she stuttered. "He wouldn't have."

Knives tapped his holowatch, accessing his photo stream. Several holoscreens popped up before them. All close-ups of Tawnies. Their faces gaunt, their skin suctioned close to the bone on their skulls. Bruises and cuts spidered across their skin. They had been tortured to a point that they could no longer heal from their wounds.

Still, Ia recognized them. They were the people on the travel ship, the ones who helped her, and the people her brother had promised he'd protect.

Anger ripped through her, flaring like a hot fire. She wanted to shut out everything she saw. All she could hear was her heart, exploding like gunfire inside her. Thoughts, ideas, excuses popped up in her head, crashing like thunder to explain all of it away. Maybe Knives had faked the pictures to make her turn on Einn. Maybe the Commonwealth had killed the Tawnies, and they were trying to frame her brother for the crime.

Maybe...
Maybe...
Maybe...

Her head felt heavy as her thoughts fumbled into one another. It was a feeling she wasn't used to. It picked at her over and over until it exposed everything wrong inside.

Just then, a sharp tone broke the silence, rising in pitch until it fell down to start again. It was an SOS signal.

Knives staggered over to the transmission console, enlarging the audio pattern to extract the data from its wavelength.

He gawked at the contents of the message. "This can't be right."

Ia looked over his shoulder, staring at the coordinates on the screen. She knew where it was pointing.

"I passed a Dead Space jet on my way out," she said, rushing to the pilot's seat. She checked the fuel gauges. While the Kaiken was anchored to the training jet, Knives had transferred his fuel over to it. Thankfully, there was enough power now to fuel them and bring the Kaiken back with them.

"What do you think you're doing?" Knives twisted to grab her wrist, but he winced at his injuries.

"Getting you to Aphelion. You're in no condition to fly." She looked him in the eye. "Besides, I'm a faster flyer than you, and you know it."

The way he looked at her was different, as if they had time traveled back to the day they met. He didn't want to trust her.

"Why are you doing this?" he asked.

She took a breath, eyes forward into the All Black. "To remind myself I'm not as horrible as everyone thinks."

With sure and steady hands, she punched the thrusters up to full speed.

CHAPTER 44
BRINN

BRINN WOKE TO SILENCE. The explosions were gone, and it seemed like time had folded back upon itself. Angie peered over at her, a deep crease denting the skin between her eyebrows.

"Oh thank Deus above."

Angie motioned for Aaron to come over and help ease Brinn up. Brinn's legs wobbled underneath her weight, but soon she was able to steady herself. Her fingers felt around her rib cage, digging underneath a bandage that had been wrapped around her while she was unconscious. But there was no longer any wound. That was when she remembered how she had healed herself.

She opened her mouth to say something, but Angie interrupted her. "You don't have to thank me. I didn't do anything but wrap you up."

Brinn pointed at Angie's now-sleeveless flight suit. "But you had to ruin your nice outfit."

"Oh shush," she said as she gave Brinn's leg a tiny nudge.

"I'm glad you're not dead."

Despite the fatigue, Brinn felt a small smile flicker upon her face.

She stretched to the side, testing out her new flesh and skin. There was no pain, only a tightness she was sure would disappear once she moved around a bit.

"How'd you heal so quickly?" Angie asked. "Did your parents implant you with cybercells when you were younger? I didn't know you were rich."

Professor Patel stood in the distance, observing them. "I'm sure Cadet Tarver is too tired to discuss anything at length right now." She gave Brinn the slightest of nods. She knew, Brinn realized. And she would keep her secret. But was it really worth keeping, especially now?

Aaron stood in the elevator shaft and peered up through the dark cylinder. "I don't mean to alarm you, but it seems that someone is up there."

Brinn walked over to the opening of the elevator shaft and peeked upward. They were hundreds and hundreds of feet underneath the planet's crust, where they were safe from the slavers. But there was still the radiation. The core was so strong their skin had started to burn. They'd be dead if they stayed there much longer, but that might be better than facing whoever was up there. She angled her head and caught the sound of sparks tinkling against metal.

The metal screeched, and she could tell the doors had been pried open.

"Aaron," Professor Patel whispered. "Do you have your pistol handy?"

Aaron unclasped his holster.

A voice shouted into the darkness.

"Tarver, you down there?"

Brinn felt her heart grow hard.

What on Ancient Earth was Ia doing back here?

CHAPTER 45
IA

IA FLEW DOWN the elevator shaft, a windpack strapped around her chest. She touched down on the elevator landing and turned off the windpack, the blades of the fan slowing to a halt. She searched through the dark for Brinn's face, expecting a warm welcome. A hug, a hello. Anything.

Footsteps stomped toward her, followed by the sting of a palm against her face.

All right, that worked too.

"Why are you here?" Brinn shouted.

"To rescue you, you idiot!" Ia screamed back.

Brinn's face was red with fury. "Why don't you just head back up and leave again? I don't need your pity." There was acid in her words, an anger backed up by hurt.

A hesitant voice called out from above. "Uh...everything okay down there?" It was Knives. He had stayed above as lookout but must have heard them.

"We're fine!" they both screamed in response.

"Honestly, people are too emotional for their own good," Aaron muttered.

"Brinn," Angie cut in. "I know you're angry, but we can be angry upstairs. My insides are starting to cook."

"Agreed," Professor Patel said. She walked past them to a small panel mounted on the far railing of the platform. "If you must, you may fight on the way back up."

Professor Patel touched one of the buttons, and the metal underneath their feet vibrated as the platform rose to the surface. Ia seethed in silence while Brinn was on the opposite side, arms crossed, refusing to make eye contact.

A strange anxiety flooded Ia's chest. Fighting was second nature to her—the physical, hard-knocks-on-the-head kind, and even the kind that ended in a flurry of name-calling. She had gotten in hundreds of shouting matches with sky pirates over the past few years, but this fight between her and Brinn was different.

Maybe because she actually cared?

Light trickled in from above, and Ia caught a glimpse of Aaron's face. Half of the skin textile on his head was burned straight off. But what was most troublesome was the fact he stood alone, without a certain person by his side.

"Where's Geoff?"

Aaron's head swiveled clunkily toward her. "He's not here. Isn't that obvious?"

Great. Even the borg was giving her the third degree. She would have knocked Aaron on the side of the head if his face didn't look so pitiful.

"Who took him?"

"Slavers. They penetrated our defenses within minutes. He was trying to help a group of cadets when the nets caught him."

"With that core as hot as it is, the slavers were sure to find this place."

"The core was cloaked," Professor Patel snapped, her dark eyes flashing even from the shadows. "The entire level was surrounded with cryo capsules."

"Then how did they find us?" Angie asked.

"The way they moved, it was like they'd been here before. They knew every corner, every room," Brinn said. "One of them said they were looking for a girl."

The truth dawned upon Ia like fierce sunlight.

The data she had shared with Einn in the White Room included blueprints to Aphelion, as well as a rundown of their security systems.

Einn had told her he'd come for her, hadn't he? And her brother, no matter what his crimes, was never one to break his promise.

CHAPTER 46
KNIVES

KNIVES PEEKED THROUGH the jagged hole ripped into the thick sheet of metal. He couldn't see through the darkness, but he heard their whispers echoing throughout the elevator shaft. For now, he was alone.

He couldn't believe it when he first saw it. Aphelion was abandoned and burning. But Ia hadn't been fazed. When they landed, she scrubbed through the hallways, gazing into each pile of rubble. He didn't know what she was looking for until she stopped at the closed doors to the core room elevator. She peered down at the ground under her feet.

"There's someone alive down there," she said.

And just like that, they ripped the elevator door to shreds, then she snatched his windpack and flew off. Like the first time they met.

So much had changed since then.

He was still dealing with the emptiness created by Marnie's absence, and now he had lost Bastian. He tried to keep his eyes wide open. Because every time he blinked, he saw the headmaster, his blood pooling around his head like a plume of feathers.

Back on Fugue, Knives had insisted on accompanying Bastian's body back to HQ, but his father had refused, ordering him to return to Aphelion to await further commands. The general didn't realize how much Bastian meant to him, how Bastian was like the father he never had.

Knives rubbed his eyes, stopping the tears before they fell. He needed to walk, to clear his mind. He wandered down the main corridor. It looped through the entire academy like a backbone.

As he walked, he was careful not to overextend himself, in order not to break the biosealant keeping the wounds on his bicep and chest together. Before he left for Aphelion, Knives had quickly treated the injuries he received from his encounter with Ia's brother. But now the broken skin was beginning to throb underneath the wound dressings. He grunted through the pain; he would survive. The flickering lights above him illuminated the destruction around him. He stepped into the main atrium. The space was dark. It smelled of smoke and danger.

Knives tapped his holowatch and activated a light screen. The shadows stretched away from him so that he could see.

He gasped.

The sculpture of the raised fist was gone, now shattered into a million pieces of marble. And with it, so was the motto inscribed upon its wrist:

Of Progress. Of Prosperity. Of Proficiency.

He'd read those same words millions and millions of times over throughout the years. He had almost gotten them tattooed on his own wrist—to prove his loyalty and so he could be just like his sister.

Thank Deus he never had.

After her death, he fantasized about firing charge missiles at the sculpture, so he would never have to see it again. And now those words were finally broken.

An empty pit gouged right through him. He had been angry for so long now, but that wasn't what he felt now.

It was loss.

There was history here, and now it was all gone.

As if in mourning, the beams above him groaned. He looked up, catching a glimpse of the ceiling shift. It was going to collapse.

He leaped out of the way. Panels crashed down, along with pipes and rock from the surrounding mountain. Dust covered him like a veil. Coughing, he wandered back to the elevator.

He wiped the dust away from his shoulders and shook what he could out of his hair, all the while stepping carefully around large piles of debris and across deep cracks in the floor. Suddenly, he couldn't help but laugh, imagining the look on Bastian's face if he had lived to see the state of this place. Knives knew he was horrible for finding that funny. But after mungpiles upon mungpiles of mung rained down on him, he had to find humor in something.

Like his ridiculous feelings for Ia. She was a murderer, a rebel, the Blood Wolf of the Skies, but she was also something else. He didn't know what exactly she was to him, and it was making his thoughts feel light and heavy all at the same time. When this was all done, he decided he'd seek out Rx meds to put his brain back in order.

But for now, he would try very hard, desperately hard, not to smile at the sight of her.

When he got back to the elevator shaft, the platform had just settled at the top. Ia's eyes were already searching for him.

"I have to tell you something," she said. "But you have to promise not to be mad..."

CHAPTER 47

IA

"YOU SHOWED THEM how to break in?" Knives said, then raked his fingers through his hair. "How did they do it? There are defenses on every corner."

Ia knew exactly how, but she was struggling to get the words out of her mouth. She was sure he'd explode if she did.

Professor Patel interrupted. "They came in through the Origin Site. It's off the security grid."

Knives glared at her. "That day I brought you to the Nest…"

Ia's skin bristled at the rise of Knives's voice. She glanced down the hall at everyone else, hoping they didn't hear. But of course they did.

"You didn't expect me to just sit around and play Bug with you forever, did you? I took note of everything I saw, all the layouts, the security, the ins and possible outs. And that information found its way into their hands."

"So you wanted all this to happen?" Knives's voice flared with anger.

"No. Not this," she said, waving her hand at the academy crumbling all around them. "All I wanted was to escape. But I'm here now, and I can help. I just need to know who these slavers are."

Knives stared at her coldly. Finally, he nodded for her to go on.

"All slavers broadcast a signature cattle call to alert other slave nations about which territories they've claimed."

Angie's eyes widened as she tapped on her holowatch. "I found this the other day, but I couldn't figure it out." She projected the screen outward for everyone to see. It was an audio waveform, but instead of peaks and crests, it was a straight line. She played it, but all that came was silence.

"There's nothing on the transmission," Knives said.

"Wait. Let me take a look." Brinn took hold of Angie's screen, pinching her fingers on each corner and drawing them outward to zoom in on the waveform. Embedded on the audio file were a series of slight jagged peaks.

"It's a Dead Space encryption," Ia said.

"Can you decipher it?" Knives asked.

Ia took hold of the screen, manipulating the file with a series of spins, each time making specific changes to the angle of the turn. With each rotation, she extracted a layer of information meant to garble the encrypted transmission, until all that was left was the original waveform reshaped into the crests and valleys of sound. She pressed the play button.

A loud cacophony of squawks filled the air like a fury of crows blacking out the skies.

Everyone clapped their hands over their ears. Except for Ia. Her face paled as the message droned on.

The last time Ia had heard that call, she'd been contracted to lead an exodus of five thousand Viivi refugees. Viiv was about to be taken by the Commonwealth. The Viivi monarch, King Roiv, had promised Ia and her crew 560,000 NøN to move the remaining survivors safely across the Commonwealth offensive line.

They were almost to a safe zone when she caught that same raucous signal. The Armada had descended on them in a pinch formation, squeezing the spread of her convoy into one tight area. There was nothing Ia could do to fend them off.

Why on Ancient Earth would Einn send them? He had never worked with them in the past. It made more sense for Einn to send Ia's crew, and even more sense for Einn to come himself.

"Shut that thing off," Professor Patel ordered, her hands still clamped tightly against each side of her head.

Knives charged up to the screen and closed down the audio transmission, but its echoes still reverberated around them.

"They call themselves the Armada," Ia said in the foreboding hush. "Once they catch a scent, they don't stop."

Professor Patel interrupted. "Slavers know better than to attack the Commonwealth."

"No," Knives answered. "General Adams mentioned a group of slavers that was targeting the colonies. If these slavers are one and the same, then they're in league with someone powerful enough to disregard the political consequences."

"They are." Ia swallowed hard as the words passed. "My brother sent them."

Einn was smarter, cleverer than she was, which meant he could take on anyone. Her brother had made her who she was.

The bulk of Ia's most vicious plots, the ones that made her infamous, were of his design. He acted through her, used her name and her courage, while he himself kept a low profile. He was Deus-damn brilliant.

"Your brother?" Brinn asked, her voice stiffening. "The one you've been using my holo to talk to?"

"You let her use your holo?" Professor Patel voice rose. "That's a massive breach of security."

Ia's eyes shifted between Brinn and Professor Patel. She felt like she was caught in a riptide. All throughout her stay at Aphelion, she had been selfishly manipulating Brinn. And now because of her, Brinn would be kicked out of Aphelion or, worse, tried for treason.

"It's not her fault," Ia explained. "I tricked her into it. She didn't know anything about the escape plans, or of my brother's reputation."

But the worst part of it all was that Ia had lied to someone who trusted her. Normally, she wouldn't have cared. Lying was something she was good at, and if she had to do it to get ahead, then so be it. But now her lies were exposed, and she couldn't look at Tarver's face, at the hurt in her eyes. Ia had taken advantage of her kindness, and she hated herself for it.

"You really are as awful as they say you are," Brinn said as she backed away.

"Tarver, wait," Ia shouted, but Brinn was already running away.

* * *

Ia searched the halls, looking for Brinn, but she was nowhere to be found. She needed to find her and explain herself. And tell her what? That it had been her plan all along? That she had wanted to betray her? She did everything she could to escape. Lied, stole, blackmailed, and threatened. And it was easy at first. But her friendship with Tarver had changed so much. From enemy to roommate to someone Ia cared for. Someone she wanted to protect.

And she had betrayed her.

After half an hour of searching, Ia ended up on the flight deck, where she found Knives prepping the Kaiken.

Great, another person Ia had to explain herself to. She had given away the Nest's location as a possible point of entry, something she wouldn't have found out if Knives hadn't brought her there. He had opened up to her about his sister while she was only thinking of escape the whole time, even though she promised him she wouldn't.

Well, not the whole time. There was that moment while they sat in silence in the candlelight. And there were other moments. Joyriding in his Kaiken. Watching that Kinna Downton movie. There were times she worried about him. There were times that she cared.

She wasn't ready to make sense of it. Not quite yet. She backed away to leave, but then she saw what he was doing, that he was loading fuel pods into his tank and readying for flight. All he needed to do was hop into the pilot seat and take off. There was only one place he could be going.

She called out to him. "Please don't tell me you're thinking of going after them all by yourself."

He saw her, but kept on his way. "No one else here is going to do it."

"This is the Armada we're talking about. If you go up there, the next time I'll see you will be on the Dead Space Market. In pieces. Do you understand what I'm saying?" She was shouting, but it felt like he couldn't hear her.

"I can handle this," he answered.

"No, you can't. Not alone. Send your generals, your captains, your war fleets." Her voice was desperate as she reasoned with him. "Or send me. Let me deal with them."

Knives laughed.

"I'm not joking." In fact, it was their best bet. She knew the Armada's Alpha. They weren't friends, especially after he had enslaved the five thousand Viivi she was trying to relocate, but Dead Space was a small place, and there were times when they were forced to cooperate for their mutual benefit. Certainly he would be able to do her this one favor, especially if she were to break off all his digits—and not just the ones on his hands.

Knives glared at her. "Stop with the act, Ia. You got your wish. Aphelion is completely destroyed. The cadets will be sold into slavery. And I'll die trying to stop it. Isn't that what you wanted all along?"

Ia paused. She didn't know the answer. Her mind searched for words, but the words didn't come. They stayed inside, burning through her chest.

"That's what I thought. Stay here."

He was turning away from her, and she hated that above all things. To be ignored like this. To be abandoned. By someone like him, by someone she…

Her body moved of its own will, her legs running after him, her arms pulling him back so they were face-to-face.

She swung her fist back, ready to come down like a grenade. If she knocked him out, he would stay. He would be safe.

As her arm came down, he grabbed her wrist, stopping her. She pounded her other hand against his chest despite all his injuries. She didn't even care if it hurt.

"Don't be an idiot!" she screamed at him.

"I know. I'm an idiot," he said. And his lips crashed down on hers.

The world fell from underneath her, and all Ia could do was hold on to him. His hands held her hips, bringing her closer and closer. He kissed her feverishly, his tongue parting her lips, and she took him in, feeling him in a way she had never expected.

He found emotions that were trapped so deep inside her, unable to take shape until now. This fusion of desire and anger and hate for herself for not understanding what was right and wrong. It was all that was left as the rest of her fell away. There were many questions etched deep into her flesh, and he answered her without fear. Because he wanted the same thing. He wanted to know that this was *right*.

Everything she was raised upon, her actions, her past opinions, Einn and all the people who fought alongside her would scream that it was all wrong. But she still didn't want to stop.

Like a ghost, it haunted her, and like a ghost, it faded away, the kiss ending as quickly and as suddenly as it started.

Her eyes fluttered open, searching for him, for the familiar peaks of his lips, that wonderful scar along his jawline, and his cold blue eyes, marbled with gray, like the lonely memory of her home planet moments before it disappeared.

Knives was already boarding his Kaiken when he turned to her.

"I told you I was an idiot," he said. His eyes were on her, a sadness laced all along the outer rims. He tapped at the temple of his helm, and a visor fell forward.

"Knives..." she called out breathlessly, but it was too late. The heat of the Kaiken's thrusters already burned at the memory of everything that happened, and like a fool, she let them.

She stood there frozen, staring at the dark stretch of runway long after he was gone.

* * *

"Oh Deus," Ia muttered over and over. Her short legs paced up and down the hall, trying to expel all the energy stuck inside her. All because of that kiss.

She'd had her fun with boys in the past. Like Vetty. They romanced each other around the stars until they couldn't see straight. But those relationships quickly fizzled, and then she never thought twice about them. Vetty was *fun*, but Knives was hard to define. Yet she felt it, burning inside like a supernova.

Ia stormed down the hallway through the maze of wreckage until she found herself stopped in front of the med bay. The ceiling had collapsed around the entrance, giant black boulders now lying in a chaotic pile on the floor. She stared at the rubble, waiting for the satisfaction to rush over her, but as much as she wished for it, as much she demanded, it didn't come.

"Miffing hell!" she screamed into the belly of Aphelion's remains. She beat at her chest, trying to stoke her anger, but only tears came in its place. Why was she crying?

Behind her, she heard rocks shift underneath soft footsteps.

"Ia." It was Brinn's voice.

Ia quickly pressed her palms against her eyes to wipe away her tears, but when she turned, she knew it hadn't helped much.

"It wasn't supposed to be like this," Ia said.

"But it is." Brinn's voice echoed against the torn metal and ragged rocks, filling the empty hollows of space that used to be whole, and vibrant, and alive. "I trusted you, and look what you did."

Ia took in the destruction around her. When she first came to this place, she had fantasized about flattening it to the ground, until all that was left was ash and debris. But that was before she knew the people who traversed these halls.

There were Aaron, Geoff, Knives, even that girl Angie. And then there was Brinn. This place had been filled with good people, people she would call friends if they weren't Bugs. She felt the greased fingers of guilt tug at her insides.

All of her decisions came with consequences. She remembered the face of the Tawny Elder after Einn had tortured him. She blinked and she saw the sad eyes of Liam Vyking, transformed the day his father came back broken from the war. With each flutter of her eyelids, the faces shifted to those of Bugs and Fringers and Dead Spacers, all those who had suffered because of her.

She looked at the academy crumbling around her, and she felt her face grow numb. She couldn't run from this anymore. She already knew what she had to do, but it was only then that she knew why.

Clenching her jaw, Ia charged passed Brinn. "I need to stop by Armaments. Grab some gear. Gotta get going," Ia muttered as she counted the list off on her fingers.

Brinn called after her. "So you're leaving again?"

Ia stopped midstep and looked back at her.

"No. I'm going up there to save them."

CHAPTER 48

BRINN

BRINN STOOD INSIDE a utility closet of the Armaments lab, trying to shake her limbs through the right sleeve of a new suit that Professor Patel had thrust upon her just moments ago. The outer material felt rough against her fingers. It was a prototype and still hadn't been marked with RSF emblems and identification.

"This suit, like all of our new prototypes, is meant for a range of extreme circumstances, whether it be the vacuum of space or unfamiliar terrain. If you insist on facing the Armada by yourselves, then I'll at least send you up there armed and equipped," Professor Patel had told her.

On the slim chance they succeeded in rescuing the cadets, Professor Patel would stay at Aphelion to ready whatever medical equipment they could for the injured. Angie would continue probing their mangled transmission devices for any contact with the RSF, while Aaron was there to provide any protection and physical assistance they would need in the meantime.

So Brinn and Ia were on their own.

Brinn was nowhere near prepared to face off against a whole slaver nation. Then again, she'd thought the same thing when the headmaster had placed her with Ia Cōcha. *That* was supposed to be an impossible task, but somehow she was still alive.

Brinn zipped the suit up over her gray tank top. The sleeves and legs fell loosely over her limbs. She searched for the buttons at her shoulders and pressed them, triggering the material to shrink and mold against her body.

She ran her hands along the seams, taking in the dark-navy scaling of the fabric. It was a color she had refused all her life, and now she wore it like her very existence depended on it. Life was weird that way, but at least now, after all that happened, she had the courage to face whatever it would fling at her.

Brinn took one last breath before the oncoming storm, then stepped out.

"Nice threads," Ia said, leaning against the wall.

The suit Ia wore was different from her own, covered in a matte fabric as dark and colorless as the All Black. Instead of taking the suit Professor Patel offered, Ia had chosen one herself, marching straight to a locked cage in the corner of the lab and picking out a metal crate buried underneath a pile of equally heavy and equally mysterious boxes. A word was stenciled on each side of the box. *Icarus*. Brinn didn't ask, but she was certain there was a good reason why Ia had chosen the suit.

Angie rushed across the room, her gaze falling from Brinn's messy hair to the dirt smudged across her cheeks. "You look horrid."

It was just like Angie to say something like that at the most inappropriate time, but Brinn was used to it by now. Angie circled around and started to wipe the ash off Brinn's face with the edge of her sleeve, but Brinn stepped away.

Angie's expression fell, and Brinn realized why she had fussed so much in the first place. She dressed it up with her usual cattiness, but Brinn could tell that Angie, the girl who used to taunt her throughout primaries, was genuinely concerned.

"It's not like you to worry," Brinn said.

"I'm not worried at all." Angie smiled so big her eyes nearly crinkled closed, but Brinn could see the sheen of tears wicking at the edges.

"I'll see you when I get back," Brinn said.

Angie nodded. "You better."

Somehow that gave Brinn courage. Now there was a promise she had to keep.

Glimpsing Ia in her periphery, Brinn turned. Ia held up a pistol for Brinn to take. "You'll need a weapon."

Brinn's gaze went from the pistol in Ia's hands to a familiar object on a nearby table. She picked up the smooth grip of one of the tasers lying in a pile on the countertop. "I'll take this."

Ia raised an eyebrow. "Are you sure?"

Brinn nodded, remembering their teamwork test, when Ia had knocked them all out. "I know how much it hurts."

Ia flashed her trademark smirk. "The Armada won't know what hit them." She turned for Brinn to follow. "Shall we?"

"Wait," Brinn called out, stopping her. "There's one more thing I need to do before we go."

* * *

Brinn set off through the halls, stepping delicately around the piles of wrecked metal and cement. She heard the tap of Ia's boots behind her. No words were exchanged between them.

The footsteps stopped at their dorm room. The door was still stuck at the halfway point. Ia gripped onto the edge and pulled it open enough for Brinn to step through.

Brinn made her way to the closet, her hands digging through the warped metal. Her fingers looped onto a handle, and she pulled out her duffel bag. Throwing it onto the floor, she unzipped it and fished through the boxes of hair dye.

"I don't think the slavers will care if they see your roots," Ia said as she peered over her roommate's shoulder.

"I want them to," Brinn said as she pulled out the pair of hair clippers.

Ia's eyes widened, realizing what she meant. The plan was to go up there as Ia's second-in-command, so Brinn had to look the part. She was still angry at Ia, but she had to put that aside if she wanted to save Liam and the rest of the cadets.

Brinn walked to the bathroom. She laid her hands on the sink's edge and leaned forward. The light above flickered from the damage done by the attack, but it stayed on long enough for her to meet her own eyes in the mirror.

She glanced over at Ia leaning upon the doorframe. It reminded Brinn of a day long ago, when Ia stared her down while she looked for stray blue hairs hidden in her brown tresses. She should be prouder, Ia had said, but now she remained quiet and watched.

"Are you sure you want to do this?"

"Yes," Brinn said, and she grabbed a handful of her ordinary brown hair.

CHAPTER 49
IA

WALKING SIDE BY SIDE to the flight deck, Ia glanced over at Brinn, her hair now shorn to her navy-blue roots.

Brinn snapped her head, eyes narrowed. "Stop staring."

"I just like it." Ia grinned. "Now you really could pass as someone from my crew."

Brinn responded with silence. There was still a distance between them. It threw Ia's head off balance, sank her thoughts like rocks.

"Before I left," she started. "I know what I said."

"We don't need to talk about this," Brinn said.

"Then don't talk. Just listen." Ia took a deep breath. She wasn't good at stuff like this. "I don't pity you, Brinn."

"Then why'd you say it?" Her question echoed through the metal archways.

"I guess I was pushing you away. I do that." Ia was good at many things. Flying. Scheming. Fighting. Arguing. Not all of them were honorable skills to have.

"It hurt." Brinn's voice was quiet.

"Yeah." Ia scratched at her arm. "I suck."

"You do."

They walked in silence for a few more steps, and Ia watched her, willing to give away all of her wealth—everything she had collected and plundered—just to erase the awkwardness between them.

"You're staring again," Brinn said, and she walked up ahead. But before she was out of earshot, she turned. "Thank you. For saying all that."

Her words dissolved the weight on Ia's shoulders, but not entirely because there was the still the fight ahead. Ia made her way to the tarmac and stopped at the edge of the runway. She remembered the first time she had peered over this ledge, desperate to escape. That day when she jumped, she was looking down into that same icy chasm. Trying to calculate whether she would live or die.

Things were different then. She couldn't wait to get out of this place, and after she had achieved it, here she was, back again. Trying to save the miffing day.

She gazed at the world that lay beyond. Outside the clouds had parted, and the sky was clear. Now she could focus on the fight ahead.

"The jet's ready," Aaron announced.

She turned to where the jet stood. It boasted a new coat of matte-black paint, erasing all the RSF markings it had once had. In addition to the black paint, Ia had told Aaron to add a few minor details to the wings and hull. Something people would notice.

"Not too shabby," Ia said as she walked around the jet's body to admire the detailing.

"I already hacked into their system. Found their blueprints," Brinn called from the top of the ramp. She stood tall and fierce, like all second-in-commands should.

"Good work," Ia said as she boarded the jet.

As she settled into the pilot's chair, Ia tapped a button below her neck, and a sleek black helmet, stripped of all RSF markings, came up over her head. She caught a glimpse of her reflection in the pilot's window. She wasn't Nema. She didn't know how to be a hero, so she was going to do it the only way the most-wanted criminal in the Commonwealth knew how.

Before takeoff, Ia sat for a moment, remembering the darkness inside her, all the rage and the violence of her life before this. The Armada had better prepare themselves.

When a Blood Wolf has its teeth out, it doesn't take much to make it snap.

CHAPTER 50
KNIVES

AG-12'S GOLDEN TERRAIN blurred outside Knives's window. Once he passed this planet, he would be upon the Armada's transport ship, parked a perilous distance from this system's sun.

Knives turned on his cloaking system, but it was no use. At this distance, the sun would illuminate everything coming their way like a spotlight. But if he came the other way, he would be blinded, his eyes unable to pick apart anything with this system's bright star as its backdrop.

He hovered on the edge of AG-12's orbit, trying to get a better look at their ship, but all he could see was a stain, a hulking shadow. And there was no activity, no movement whatsoever.

Maybe this was going to be easier than he thought.

Knives was flying closer when a row of blue lights flared from the transport ship like sharp and pointed teeth.

Oh mif.

Knives grabbed on to the controls, trying to reverse his thrusters.

But he was too late. A wave of blue light rippled past him. The lights on his console cut to black and his monitors flickered off. His ship's life systems were down. The pressure dropped to zero, and the oxygen cut out.

Thank Deus he was wearing his helmet and grav suit. Without them, his blood would have bubbled, stretching him out like a balloon.

Knives flipped at the switches, trying to reinitiate the electrical line.

Nothing.

The Kaiken was offline.

Knives grabbed a gel rod from underneath his chair and snapped it. He tossed it up into the air where it floated, illuminating the cockpit with a warm orange luminescence.

His gaze fell to the Armada ship in the distance. Silhouettes of shapes darted out from its center. Their starjets were coming after him.

His fingers felt underneath the console and popped open an emergency compartment. A wave of plastic packages flew out into the open cabin. His eyes searched through the sea of mess.

With a steady hand, he plucked out a dark-gray cylinder.

His cannons were depowered, but a grenade would work.

Two black starjets swooped toward him, their particle-beam cannons already charged and ready to fire.

He held the grenade close to his chest, his finger looped on the safety pin. Once they got close enough, he would pull it. At least he'd take a few of them down with him.

His fingers tensed.

They were almost at him.

Almost there.

Then overhead, a cannon shot pulsed past him. The blast clipped the enemy jet's wing, leaving it spiraling backward into the starjet behind it.

Knives looked around, trying to pinpoint who had come to his aid. A black jet overtook him, banking left to a stop. By the shape of its frame, he knew it was an academy vessel, but it wasn't the right color. Another symbol had been stenciled right where the RSF decals should be, the fresh red paint gleaming in the darkness.

The feather on the starjet's frame was unmistakable.

It was the mark of Ia Cōcha.

Ia hovered her starjet next to his and attached a magnetic anchor to his Kaiken. She flew forward, towing him. Not back to Aphelion, but toward the Armada. What was Ia up to?

White high beams flooded into his vision, and they came to a stop. They had arrived at their destination.

He opened up his cockpit, only to find rows of slavers pointing their guns straight at him. A whole firing squad aching to spill his blood. As he made his way down the ladder, he was glad his helmet was on. They wouldn't see him sweat.

The crowds parted as Ia stepped through. She was dressed in a webbed, black flight suit, something he had only seen in the Armaments lab. She must have been dying to steal that piece for a while now. This girl was different from the Ia he knew. She stood taller, fiercer, almost growling as she walked past each slaver. And he realized it wasn't Ia he was looking at it. It was the Blood Wolf of the Skies.

He was surprised to see Brinn Tarver behind her, clothed in a dark-navy suit. Navy was not a RSF color. And her hair was different; it was cut close to her head. The change in length wasn't what made him blink. Her hair was blue. Tawny blue.

Ia cut into his line of sight and came close to him, her face devoid of any trace of kindness. She grabbed the lip of his visor and ripped his helmet right off.

"Do you have any weapons on you?" she demanded.

Ia looked at him like she was ready to swallow him up. Nothing remained of the girl he'd kissed—who'd kissed him back—just hours before.

"Is this a joke?" he hissed.

Her hand darted forward and gripped his throat. "Answer the question."

Knives's stomach clenched, betrayal sinking into his bones. "A grenade," he coughed. "In my vest pocket."

Ia's hands fumbled through the top layer of his suit. Her fingers brushed against his chest. Any other day, he would have savored the heat of her hands against him, but now the thought of her so close confused him.

Ia snatched the grenade from his vest pocket and tossed it over to Tarver. His eyes lingered on Cadet Tarver, unsure how Ia had convinced Brinn to join her.

"I see you were able to catch a stray." A large beast of a man with pockmarked cheeks and a shiny bald head stomped toward them. A frightening tattoo of chains linked one over the other was grafted across his forehead and down his neck. He must be the Armada's leader.

Ia addressed the man, her arms open like she was serving Knives up on a platter. "It was easy. The Bug didn't put up much of a fight."

Anger flared from deep inside Knives's chest. He kept waiting for her to turn to him, to give him some sort of indiscreet sign that all this was just a ruse. A wink. That recognizable smirk.

But her face was stone.

All hope crumbled from deep within him. If this was the real Ia Cōcha, he was as good as dead.

"My second-in-command will escort the boy," she told the Armada's leader. "In case he decides to act out."

The leader glanced over at Brinn. "How like you, to choose a Tawny as your second. She doesn't seem as tough as the others though. Must be easy to keep her in line, unlike Vetty."

Ia smirked. "What can I say? I've exchanged brawn for brains."

She made her way to Knives and grabbed his shoulder. He winced away from her touch. But she snatched his wrist and drew him closer.

"Too bad this one doesn't have any brains," Ia told the onlookers. "He actually thought I fancied him."

Knives's eyes grew hot with rage.

The slavers' voices laughed in unison, rising to a cheering crescendo. "Skewer him through the heart! Jettison the bastard!"

Ia turned to them, seeming to feed on their cheers. Like the winds of a storm, she swiveled around, bringing her fist down like a hammer across Knives's face. He fell to the ground, and she knelt, grabbing his hair to jerk his head up.

"I knew you never cared," he spat at her.

"Shut up." She leaned into his ear, and her voice softened. "If you want to get the cadets out, play along."

His eyes rose, studying her. But she didn't give him the chance to fully process what she had said before she lugged him upward and tossed him toward Brinn.

Ia stepped toward both of them, her voice still lowered. "I'll give you some time. Get your people out of here."

He saw it finally, that look of truth. The real Ia. The hardness in her face softened with compassion, and worry, and care. It lasted only a breath—not even. But it was enough to persuade him.

"What about you?" Brinn asked.

Ia shook her head. "Does it matter?"

Then Ia swiveled around, that deadly expression snapping back onto her face. She scanned the crowd of slavers gathered around shouting, cursing, cheering.

She raised her voice. "Throw him in the pits. This one will sell high!"

He knew it was all an act. But she was good at putting on a show.

CHAPTER 51
BRINN

BRINN SCRATCHED at the short blue fuzz on top of her head. It felt different. Not in a bad way. Just *different*.

The hair, the clothes, the attitude. The Armada needed to believe she was as ruthless as Ia. All Brinn had to do was pretend. And that was one of the many things she was good at.

So she walked with her shoulders back, and her eyes fearless and proud. A guard guided them toward the pits, but she already knew where they were. She had studied the ship's layout on the flight over, memorizing every turn, every room.

She glanced over to her prisoner. The flight master held his head down, his blond hair shading his eyes.

"Strong grip," he murmured through their footsteps.

Brinn readjusted her hold on his arm, noticing how deeply she had been digging her fingers.

"We're almost there," she reassured him.

Ahead of them, the guard slowed, angling his head toward them. "What did you say?"

Brinn took a deep breath.

Here goes.

"I was telling the Bug not to piss himself before he gets to the pits."

"You're cleaning it if he does."

"But I'm a lady," she said with a smirk, the kind she'd seen Ia flash hundreds of times before.

He grunted and led them around one final turn. "The pits are ahead."

The hallway opened up into a large expanse of a room, lined with locked hatches on the floor. Helpless, muffled screams echoed below, and Brinn fought not to drop to her knees at the sound.

The guard stopped in front of a hatch in the center of the room. He punched a pattern onto the key sensor, and Brinn heard the click of the lock unhinge. The guard grabbed the handle to the hatch and lugged it open.

"It's a fresh pit," the guard said. "VIP treatment."

Brinn stepped behind Knives, one hand on his handcuffs and the other pushing on his shoulder. She walked the flight master toward the gaping entrance.

The guard smiled, showing off his yellowed teeth. "Shall I throw him in for you, or will you?"

She let go of Knives, his handcuffs now hanging loose. "I give that honor to you."

The guard had no time to react. Knives buried his shoulder in the guard's chest, driving him backward. With a stifled scream, the guard fell into the pit.

The flight master rubbed his shoulder. "Smart thinking."

"You can tell Ia that. It was her plan."

Brinn ran over to the pit where she had heard the screams and rested her ear against the metal hatch. Voices wailed from within, like ghosts. Racing to the sensor, she mimicked the pattern the guard had tapped on the other lock.

She waited for the clink of the lock unbarring, but there was none. She tapped in the code again. And again, nothing.

Brinn growled, bringing her fist down so it hit metal.

She needed to get them out of there. *But how?* Her mind raced through everything she had learned about starships. Reprogramming the code would take too long, but if she shorted the power circuits, then maybe…

Her thoughts stopped on a particular memory, and her eyes widened. Of course. She knew what she had to do.

"I have to go to the bathroom," she said as she backpedaled away.

The flight master grabbed her wrist, stopping her. "Now?"

Her eyes met his. "Remember the teamwork simulation I was in? I believe you were the one who programmed it."

She unbuttoned the pouch at her side and grabbed the grenade Ia had taken from him. He saw it, and she could tell he instantly understood.

"Wait here. I'll get the doors open," Brinn said as she took off running.

"Is this all part of her plan too?" he called after her.

"Nope. This one's all me."

CHAPTER 52
IA

ALPHA CRUNCH, the leader of the Armada, led her through the corridors. This wasn't Ia's first time in the Armada's fleet ship, so the walls lined with bones didn't startle her. Nor did the smell. Like rot and piss.

They stepped through a rusting door and onto the main deck, which was as dark and gloomy as the rest of the ship, even without the bones.

Alpha Crunch was a large man, dwarfing her as they walked. He had become Alpha of the Armada a few years ago after he called a Hierarchy challenge and won. The frayed cape, tan like pigskin, but with finer grain, hung from his shoulders. It was made from the previous Alpha's skin, and it swayed at his ankles as he made his way to the central platform.

"Your brother will be happy to see you." Alpha's eyes shone in the dim as he regarded her.

"Whatever Einn's paying you, he should cut it in half. You did an awful job of finding me. Instead, I had to find you."

"I see your temper hasn't changed."

"I'm not one for pleasantries, Alpha."

"Then let me see that the goods haven't been damaged." He snapped up her chin between his oily fingers. He smelled of dried blood and melted plastic, and his fingernails, sharpened to a point, dug into her skin. She jerked her head out of his grip, trying to rid herself of the feel of his fingers.

She expected Einn to make his appearance, but the deck was empty except for a minion headed their way. He approached with a platter. Centered on top was a deep-green bottle of sauvignon, a drink once favored on Ancient Earth but now rare throughout the galaxies.

"There is only one thing I love more than slaves." Crunch grabbed the bottle off the platter and plucked out the cork. He brought it up to his nose and sniffed, savoring the scent. "Each one of these bottles is equal to the cost of one hundred premium slaves."

"That's why you took the cadets? To pay for your collection?"

Alpha Crunch bobbed his head, unfazed by her judgment.

"But why them? You and I both know Bugs are tainted goods, the stuff that causes wars."

"Yet I know someone who will buy them for more than market price."

Ia knew the slave market. A man named Miracle was and would always remain the most affluent slave owner in the known universe, but even he knew to stay away from Commonwealth goods. "Who?"

Crunch's lips quirked up into a grin as he spoke. "Einn."

Her eyes snapped over to him, and she saw him savoring

the shock on her face.

"There's a lot about your brother that you don't know. Don't you think it quite odd that RSF knew how to find you so easily after failing to capture you so many times in the past?" Crunch goaded. "Who do you think told them?"

Ia shook her head, refusing to see the truth laid out in front of her. She staggered forward, her legs all of a sudden weak. "Where's my brother?"

"My dear girl, who said he would be here at all?"

Crunch leaned forward, and his smile distorted. It grew longer and longer with each second that passed. She swayed like the floor was uneven, but it wasn't.

"Cōcha, you don't look well." His voice floated like bubbles ready to pop.

Ia's hands came up to her chin, her neck, anywhere Crunch had touched. Her fingertips shook upon a slight scratch, one that broke the skin enough for the sedative to scream through her bloodstream. The world flipped sideways, and her body tumbled.

"You want to know why Einn sent us?" Crunch whispered, but her hearing faded before she could hear his answer.

The rest of the muscles on her face froze, and she threw up a prayer, hoping her whispers would reach.

* * *

As she breathed in, the cold snapped at her face. Ia sat up, her eyes opening to a vast canvas of textured white. Stalactites of ice hung from above. She was in a cave of some sort.

Did they drag her back to AG-9?

Caves had openings, ways to get out. Carefully, she

navigated through the icy spikes, but no matter how hard she looked, there were no exits. Yet, there was something familiar about this place, something she couldn't pinpoint.

"Hello, Sister." Her brother's voice, richly baritone, echoed through the cavern, flowing around her like a warm specter. "I'm sorry I couldn't welcome you in person."

She quickly realized she wasn't on AG-9 at all.

This was the White Room.

"I like how you remodeled the place," she said.

Soft laughter floated toward her, and Einn stepped into her line of sight. His hair was longer than the last time she'd seen him, but it was still him, the person she had loved more than anything. Just yesterday, she would have killed to see his face again. But now she wasn't quite so sure.

"Is it all true? About the slaves, the Tawnies?"

His eyes met hers. "You look so disappointed."

She narrowed her eyes at the tone of his voice—like he was playing a game he was certain he would win.

"But why?" Ia asked. "What is all this for?"

A journal flickered into his hand. "This."

Her eyes drifted over the familiar rich brown leather binding, the crumpled sheets of paper bundled up between its pages. "Is that the headmaster's?"

Einn tilted his head. "I told you that information was important."

She thought back to the last time they had met. Einn had brushed off every mention of the weapons she had found, but when she'd talked of the headmaster and when she'd brought up that story of Fugue, his eyes had sharpened with attention.

He had played her, passing it off as if the information he was harvesting from her was nothing. Ia wondered what kind of power was hidden upon those pages. It must be something major for Einn to go through such lengths to possess it and to keep it from her.

"I flipped through it, and you know what I found? It's not complete. Luckily, I was already thinking a few steps ahead." He opened to the last page of the journal so Ia could see. "Remember this?" Ia recognized it. It was a piece of paper that she had taken a photo of while she was alone in the dorm room one day. There were equations scrawled all over it. On the top of the page was a name written in graphite. *Brinn Tarver.*

Ia shook her head at a flash of a memory. *You want to know why Einn sent us?* That was the last thing Alpha had said before she passed out. Einn didn't order the Armada to rescue her; he wanted someone else. Her stomach lurched. "You came to Aphelion for Brinn."

He nodded.

"And me? Where do I come in?"

"You don't."

He moved like a shadow, stopping only centimeters away. Warmth spread across her belly. Her arms curled around her waist in surprise, and she felt the edge of a knife protruding from her flesh. She slumped forward, her chest landing against Einn's lean frame.

His hand came up and stroked her hair.

"Shhhh," he whispered. "Shhhh."

Ia's ribs rattled inside her chest. With each passing second, it got harder and harder to take another breath. Blood poured out of her center, and her fingers grew cold and numb. The pain was so great her mind had trouble staying in one place.

Einn laid her down on the floor. She no longer had the strength to hold her head up, but Einn had propped her head up so it rested in his lap. Her eyes drifted to her brother's face, serene and calm as if he had forgotten there was a knife stuck in her belly.

"Every story I have is also a story of you." His voice remained low like a lullaby. She felt a soft tickle on her hand as Einn traced the lines on her palm. "Like when you hunted down nuts from Galatin at all the Fringe markets so you could bake my favorite cookies, just the way Mom used to make them."

He tapped a finger against his temple. "And there's another story that I keep playing out in my head. I've never told this one to you. But this is your story too."

A delicate smile danced upon Einn's lips. "It starts with me sneaking out of my room in the middle of the night and peeking into your room. Father was humming softly to you while you slept. And I thought that it would be me next, so I ran back to my bed, watching my door until the sun came up." Einn shook his head, then gazed off into the distance. "He never came.

"That was the night he went away, the night he left behind this." Einn's fingers brushed against the white hearts pinned to his collar, their family symbol. "I found it that morning, next to your bed. You were still asleep."

Ia's eyes widened. The white hearts were meant for her, not Einn.

"Instead of a goodbye, he left me a lesson," Einn said. "The only way you get what you want is to *take it*."

She watched him, the edges of his face feathering out of focus as her vision dimmed. Yet she saw the darkness clouding over her brother's eyes, that emotion so bitter and tangled there were no words to describe it. It was a side he had cleverly hidden from her all this time.

"It's always been me and you," Einn whispered. "But there's something more important now, and this time, I'm not going to share."

He let go of her hand, and the cold licked her fingers.

The White Hearts meant family. Loyalty. Seeing Einn now as he was, she finally realized it. He'd never deserved it.

The young man before her wasn't the same brother she'd grown to love. He wasn't the same brother she would die for, but now, it seemed like she had no choice.

"Close your eyes now," he told her. "I'll stay here with you until the end."

The White Room was a virtual construct, meant to trick her mind into thinking every sensation, every cut and injury that occurred inside was real. So as she bled out onto the white, icy floor, she felt it entirely, and when she would finally slip into death, it would take her mind with it. In the real world, her body would no longer be hers, but an empty husk. There would be no undo button, not when it came to this.

CHAPTER 53
BRINN

THE GRENADE FELT like a hot coal in her hands. Brinn kept it hidden as she prowled through the corridors. She had studied the maps for the ship before they arrived, so she knew exactly where she was going. The closest lavatory was near the flight deck. A couple more steps, and she would be there.

As she turned the corner, an ominous sound followed her, of metal clacking against bone. She kept her shoulders squared but quickened her pace. No matter how fast she walked, he was faster. Then the scent caught her. The sweat. The grease. The dirt.

"Hello, little Tawny," the voice purred. She turned, cringing at the sight of him. It was the slaver who had taunted her back at Aphelion. She remembered the smell of rot on his breath and that sickening smile. A blue and purple bruise flowered on his forehead where Liam's pipe had landed.

"Move along." She stood tall and pushed past him. There was a chance he wouldn't recognize her.

"Not so fast." He quick-stepped into her path, smiling

broadly, his teeth yellowed with grit. "I thought I told you. I'm looking for a girl."

He moved like lightning, his hand shooting out toward her throat. But she was already running. She huffed with each step, trying to make herself go faster, but his footsteps thundered after her. His hand wrapped around her wrist, so hard that the grenade slipped from her fingers. She moved to pick it up, but the slaver jerked her backward to face him, his cracked lips twisting upward at his prey.

With curled fingers, she swiped at his face, her fingernails biting into his cheek. His hand came up, feeling the fresh blood at his skin. He returned the blow, the back of his hand striking her with so much force her head swiveled, and she fell to the ground.

Behind her, the metal screeched underneath his footsteps, and she knew he was coming for her. She lay still, reaching slowly for the pack at her waist. Her fingers curled around the smooth metal grip of her taser, now heavy in her fist.

She waited.

A hand gripped her shoulder.

Whipping around, she thrust the taser into the soft flesh of his belly. Sparks pulsed, and the slaver went stiff, his muscles growing taut all at once. His mouth twisted open before he fell unconscious to his side.

Brinn stood still, her shoulders shaking.

Behind her, she heard people shouting a chorus of orders. One phrase repeated among the clatter.

"Get the Tawny."

She couldn't let the fear get to her. Brinn grabbed the grenade. Outrunning them wasn't an option, not with everyone on the ship trying to find her. Brinn had to get to a lavatory without getting caught. So her mind ran through all the possibilities, of everything she could do.

She turned corner after corner until the answer came to her.

Stopping by a cracked panel, Brinn's hands dug deep into the wires buried behind the walls. All the doors had been deactivated, so each hallway opened up to the next, which was against air travel safety codes. Ships needed to be sectioned off by airtight doorways in case of a breach.

Voices echoed through the hallways. They were nearby.

Brinn pulled out bundle after bundle of wires, until she located the right ones. They were disconnected from the power frame. Her hands worked to reconnect them. One wire. Then another.

"Where is she?" a gruff voice called from around the corner.

"I think she turned here."

Brinn's hands fumbled with the last wire. Sparks flew. Heat bit at her skin, and she pulled her hands away, blowing on her fingertips, the skin already bubbling from the burn.

"There she is."

Brinn swiveled her head to see a line of slavers storming through the hallway.

She grabbed the last wire, twisting it around a knob on the power frame. Just fifteen feet away from her, metal screeched from above, and a large door slid downward, blocking their path.

Fists pounded on the other side of the doorway. It would only take a few moments until they figured out their way back in. That didn't give her much time.

Brinn tore through the entrance of the lavatory. She ran to

the last stall and kicked in the door. She grabbed the grenade from her hip bag. Just like the teamwork test, she told herself as she stared down into the dingy toilet bowl. With her burned fingers, Brinn plucked out the pin and dropped the grenade.

3

Her legs pumped, and she was out the door.

2

Past the corner.

1

BOOM.

CHAPTER 54

IA

IA FELT A TUG, like cords inside her head had snapped. Her body tore upward as if she were flying. Her brother stared up at her, and with each second, his face grew smaller and smaller. Soon his smile was gone. Flickered away. And so were his body and hers, along with the rest of the world. She felt light, as if she had no weight.

Am I dead?

Her body hit the cold metal ground as she fell face-first onto the grated floor. A sob escaped her mouth, and she rushed to suck it back in.

Shaking fingers tumbled through her hair and onto the damp skin at the base of her neck. She grabbed the cord and yanked it out.

She was alive. But how?

Her eyes fluttered open to the color of red as warning lights strobed from the ceiling, and she knew the answer. The ship's main power source was out, severing her connection with the White Room.

The whole place was running on backup gennies. It wouldn't be long before the entire ship shut down.

Around her, smoke veiled the air, thick and suffocating. Yet even under its cover, she knew she wasn't alone. Boots shuffled around her. She was surrounded, but she was only thinking about one thing.

Einn had almost killed her.

She looked up into the barrel of a gun. Many of them. All pointed at her.

But there was no fear. Only a darkened cloud swallowing her up within her center. She felt anger, loss. She felt rage.

"What to do," the slaver chanted at the other end of the weapon. "What to do…"

His finger was on the trigger, but she lunged, her elbow cracking his forearm in two. She grabbed the pistol, and through the smoke, she fired. Her aim always hit its mark.

She fired again. And again. Bodies fell until all that was left were the screams of one man. She ambled toward him, her body swaying like she was possessed, yet her arm remained steady as she raised the gun to his forehead.

She had no one. There was nothing left.

"Please don't," he bleated like a scared lamb. "I was only following orders."

"What to do, what to do…" she mimicked sweetly.

She pulled the trigger and savored that wonderful sound.

Ia exited the holding chamber, her legs swaying like wood stilted by a large weight. If she was going to burn, she was going to bring everyone else with her.

Einn wanted to kill her?

He should have.

CHAPTER 55
BRINN

THERE WAS ONLY SILENCE.

Brinn's eyes fluttered open to a murky darkness. Shafts of light fell around her, crisscrossing through a web of metal, pipes, and wreckage.

She tried to sit up, but she couldn't. Slabs of grating laced across her torso, jamming down against her rib cage. If she tried to wiggle free, the whole weight would come crashing down.

She lay tense, her lungs shaking with each breath. Slowly, her hearing returned, taking in a chorus of creaking metal, the rage of electrical wires, and a voice.

"Tarver!" It was the flight master. "Where are you?"

"Here!" She cried, and the smoke invaded her lungs. "I'm here!"

Above the crumpled metal, footsteps rushed toward her. The weight on her chest lightened until arms scooped her up, pulling her closer and closer until she was blinded by the sudden rush of life.

"I have you," a familiar voice whispered.

She blinked quickly, trying to get her eyes to focus, and breathed in his familiar scent. Like the wildwood near her house.

"Liam?"

His eyes shone through the hazy dim. Sweat and dirt smothered his face, and on his cheek, blood had dried from a gash near his ear. But it was Liam. *Deus be, it was Liam.*

"I like your hair," he said with a smile, and she wanted to break out into a sob.

As her eyes adjusted, she saw the group clustered around them. The cadets, their faces weathered with smoke and bruises, but alive. There were others she recognized. Professor Jolinsky was there, and so was Geoff. Ia would be happy to see him. Even Nero was with them, and the look on his face as he stared at her blue hair didn't even bother her.

"Let me through." The flight master parted the crowd.

"Sir." She placed her fist on her heart in salute.

He nodded for her to follow him, and she hobbled to a more private corner, away from everyone else's ears.

"That was quite a plan, cadet."

"Thank you, sir. It looks like you didn't have any troubles."

Knives nodded, keeping an eye on an empty hallway. "Luckily, everyone's too busy getting out of the ship to care about us anymore."

As if on cue, the floor rumbled beneath their feet, and Brinn pitched forward. The flight master grabbed her by the arm before she could hit the ground. The vessel creaked around her, like it was about to be torn apart.

"Warning," a computerized voice announced. "Depressurization in ten minutes."

A chorus of unrest sounded from the group behind them. Knives faced her, looking her straight in the eye. Not as her instructor, but as her peer.

"What's the plan, Tarver? You know how we can get out of here?"

"I've seen the maps, sir."

Knives addressed the rest of the cadets. "If you want to live, you follow me. No talking back. No questions. Just follow orders. Is that clear?"

The cadets murmured, not knowing exactly how to respond.

Knives shook his head and yelled, "Are we clear?"

"Yes, sir!" they responded in unison.

Knives nodded to her. "Lead the way."

"What about Ia, sir?"

The flight master's brow furrowed at the weight of her question. "I don't know."

Her breath caught in her throat. That wasn't the right answer. Not for her.

She pointed down a hallway to the left. "The flight deck is a straight shot that way. There are enough escape pods to get everyone out."

"Tarver, don't. The whole place is falling apart. Come with us, Cadet."

Brinn had to find her. She owed Ia at least that.

"I can't do that, sir."

Knives nodded, a new decision emerging from the depths of his eyes. "Bring her back, Brinn."

"Leave it to me, sir."

And she took off through the gaping mouth of a hallway. She had no idea where Ia could be. But she did know the layout of this ship. She could take this place apart, bolt by bolt, panel by panel. If anyone could find Ia, it was going to be her.

CHAPTER 56

IA

IA PERCHED ON TOP of a pile of crates, listening. She knew Crunch would come to the cargo bay. All she had to do was wait.

"All because of a malfunction in the lavatories?" Ia heard him complain to his surrounding crew. "All of you, carry as much as you can, and be careful. For every bottle you break, I'm taking off one of your fingers."

Ia watched as his men started moving, but she needed to get to a higher vantage point. She jumped onto a nearby chain hanging from a cargo crane mounted to the ceiling, the sound of metal jangling as she climbed up to the rafters.

"What was that?" a whisper came from below.

They were too daft to even realize what she had left for them, to distinguish that old smell of earth. Not many could recognize it, because there was no longer much use for it. But when she had found it in the academy Armaments lab, her eyes had lit up. She had swiped the bright-red bottle and swept it into her pouch, knowing it could come in handy at a time like this.

She stood in the rafters and sprinkled the rest of the bottle's liquid contents over everything below.

Let them burn, a voice whispered within.

She hummed along to the words singing inside her.

Let their bones sizzle and sear.

On the deck, everyone grabbed bottles and boxes of the sauvignon, their hands and suits unknowingly becoming slick with a deep amber-colored liquid. In the low light, it was easy to think it the same as Alpha Crunch's cherished sauvignon.

But it wasn't.

It was something far more precious.

The people of Ancient Earth called it *gasoline*.

She gripped her pistol, aiming the crosshair at a large slick of a puddle pooled underneath everyone's feet. Her finger hooked around the trigger.

Click.

And just like that, the whole cargo bay was alight with fire, orange tongues burning away at every surface, raging at every wisp of oxygen.

Ia watched Crunch run through the flames to the center of the mess. His knees dropped to the shattered bottles as the last remnants of his sauvignon disappeared through the holes of the metal grating. *Pathetic.*

She landed behind him, her knees bent to absorb the impact. But even then, Crunch hadn't noticed her.

Her boots squished and squeaked against the slick floor. She twisted open a bottle she had saved from the inferno, the sound of the popped corked reverberating throughout the space. Crunch turned.

And only then did he see her. *Pathetic.*

"No more goodies." She smiled brightly, flashing the whites of her canines. He was such a foolish man. So many flaws. So many mistakes.

She kicked him, and his shoulders cracked against the floor.

"Please, Cōcha. I had to," he pleaded. "Einn would have killed me if I didn't do what he said."

"Oh, Crunch," her voice sang, the tone rich with dissonance. Ia leaned forward until she could see the veins trembling in his eyes. "Einn isn't the one you should be scared of."

"Please..." His eyes flickered to the bottle in her hand. "Have mercy."

"Yes," she replied. "Mercy." She tipped the contents of the bottle so the fermented liquid smothered his face, and she watched as his lips pursed to slurp it all up.

"Thank you, Cōcha," he cried. "Thank you."

Pathetic.

Ia threw her pistol—now empty of its charge—to the floor and kneeled, plucking two hand-forged slaver knives sheathed at Alpha Crunch's chest. She stalked out of the storage bay, the heat trailing from behind. She crossed into the hallway. The doors closed swiftly behind her. With the butt of one knife, she broke the door sensor so no one else could come in. And no one—not even Crunch—could come out.

She should have been satisfied. But she wasn't even close.

Keep going, a voice sang inside her. *Keep going until there's nothing left.*

CHAPTER 57
KNIVES

THE FLIGHT DECK was as empty as an abandoned sky hull. The Armada only cared about their own hides. Most of them had already taken escape pods to get themselves out of the implosion radius.

By the time they got there, there were only five pods left.

Knives moved fast, reprogramming the navigation systems on each unit to land on AG-9. He waved the first- and second-year cadets into each of the escape pods, trying to cram them with as many passengers as possible. There was room for twenty-five in each of them, but he pushed in a few more in order to get them all back to Aphelion.

"Don't breathe too much," Knives barked. Their oxygen reserves would be strained by the additional heads per vessel, but the trip was quick. They'd get to Aphelion a little short of breath, but that was better than being dead on arrival.

After sending four escape pods off, there were only twenty-five cadets and Marik Jolinsky left. All he had to do was get them onto the last pod. He led the final batch of passengers past a line of scouting jets and then spotted the escape pod's telltale red and white stripes inlaid on its door.

"There!" He pointed. "Hurry and strap in!"

The cadets rushed past him but stopped at the sound of gunfire. A group of slavers appeared from the shadows, pistols in hand.

"This is our ship," one growled. "So this is *our* pod."

Knives held up his hands, ordering his group to stay still. If it were just him, he might have tried to take them down, but here, too many of his people would be caught in the crossfire. It was too big a risk.

So he watched as the slavers filed in, guns still pointed. By the time the doors had closed and the pod had departed, he had already counted the number of seats over and over in his head. There had been at least fifteen extra spots left inside that escape pod.

Those selfish mifs.

He ran his fingers through his hair, pacing away from the rest of the cadets.

"Sir, what are your orders?" Cadet Vyking called after him.

Knives stopped in front of an Armada scouting jet.

"We fly."

There were enough flyers in training to pilot everyone home. Each scouting jet could hold two additional passengers, at most, and fortunately, the slavers hadn't bothered to lock them down. Knives quickly separated them into groups of three, one group for each jet.

"Marik, you're riding in here." Knives patted the side of

his Kaiken.

Marik straightened his vest. "At least I'll be with a decent pilot."

Knives clapped him on the shoulder. "Sorry to tell you this, but I won't be flying."

"What?" Marik stopped in his place.

"Get in." He pointed up at the cockpit where another cadet was already strapped in. Marik eased into the extra seat and eyed him warily.

"Don't worry, Jolinsky," Knives called out. "She'll take good care of you."

"She?"

Knives tapped at his holowatch, engaging the voice activation system. "Autopilot on. Ready all systems for launch."

The canopy lowered, and he took one last look at his Kaiken. "Go home, girl."

The Kaiken's thrusters activated, taking off soon afterward. He waved for the other pilots to follow, and one by one, his flyers took flight. Their takeoffs were clumsy, but he didn't worry. As long as they followed her, they would all get home.

Once the last of the ships had disappeared into the distance, he sprinted over to the RSF training jet that Ia had piloted in.

This would be his getaway vessel.

But instead of getting inside, he waited.

CHAPTER 58

BRINN

"WARNING. DEPRESSURIZATION in three minutes. All personnel must evacuate."

Brinn looked up, blinded by red and white lights flashing in warning. Dry heat nipped at her face, a sign that climate stabilization was gone. Next would be the oxygen supply.

She was running out of time.

Brinn turned the corner, and in the shadows, a low, throaty howl rose up in agony. It was a man's voice.

"Stop," he whimpered. "Please."

But all Brinn heard in response was the sound of bones cracking.

Brinn's instincts told her to turn back, to avoid, but she kept going. She knew who the man was pleading with.

"Ia!" Brinn cried. She shouted until her lungs creaked inside her. "It's me. It's Brinn."

Before she could take another step, the man stumbled out into the light. His body off-balance, he crashed to his knees.

Even on the ground, he held his shattered arm close to his chest. Both of his eyes were bruised, and his lips were split against the edge of his teeth. She crouched to help him, but he was already scrambling away.

Now alone, Brinn faced the darkness at the end of the hallway. She took a deep breath in the infinite stillness, waiting for Ia to appear.

"Baby Bug," a voice called from beyond the haze. Then, through the churning smoke, a figure hurtled toward her, passing through the dim. Her face was splattered with blood.

"Ia!" Brinn shouted, but the girl kept after her. Two blades glinted in between her fingers, both pointed at Brinn. Brinn peered through the shadows, past the dried blood on the girl's face. It was Ia, but something about her was different. Gone was her swagger. Gone was that trademark smirk.

Ia swiped, her arm circling wide toward her.

"Stop!" Brinn backpedaled.

Ia's arm flung forward, and a flash of metal spiraled toward Brinn. She pivoted, but still the blade sliced through her suit. She grabbed onto her arm, her skin growing slick from fresh blood.

"Why don't you run?" Ia screamed at her.

"Because you don't scare me."

"No?" Her remaining knife flashed as she twirled it through her fingers.

"No!" Brinn screamed back. "You annoy me. You're cocky. Arrogant. You never listen. And don't let me get started on the state you left our room in." Brinn pointed a finger at Ia. "You make my life so difficult, but you don't scare me, Ia."

Ia stood before her, her body swaying slightly. "You're a fool. I could kill you. I could slash your face so you can no longer see. You think I won't?"

Like a specter, Ia swept forward, grabbing Brinn by the ear.

Brinn bit her tongue at the pain but kept her eyes open so she could see. She wasn't going to run away like she did in the past. She had to face this.

The tip of Ia's knife pricked Brinn's neck, and the slick warmth of new blood trickled down her skin. She swallowed down her fear, trying to stay strong.

"And now?" Ia asked. "Tell me you're afraid."

Brinn looked up into Ia's eyes, and all she saw was pain. It reminded Brinn of her own sadness, of that familiar, unshakable weight, and she instantly remembered the first time she saw Ia's face broadcast across Olympus. Brinn thought she would see someone hideous, marked with scars and deformities, a face that would repulse her. But instead she saw a girl.

A girl, just like me.

Brinn's fingers fell lightly on Ia's wrist. Ia glanced down at her touch while Brinn eased the blade away from her throat.

"You can keep at this all you like, but you can't fool me. You're not a monster," Brinn whispered. "You're my friend, Ia."

Brinn wrapped her arms around the girl before her and hugged her close to her heart.

CHAPTER 59

IA

IA PUSHED AWAY from the warmth circling her, but the girl wouldn't let go.

"Don't," Ia screamed, digging her fingers into the girl's shoulder, trying to hurt her, scare her, anything to get away.

The girl didn't flinch. She endured the pain, and Ia hated her for it.

"Stay away!" Ia screamed. The girl just hugged her closer, all the while humming softly. It was a light melody, trilling up and down with freedom.

"No," Ia whispered. "I don't want to hear it."

The song continued, and her mind reeled backward. Back to a time before the war. Before she was a killer. Before she was called the Blood Wolf, the Rogue, and the Sovereign.

Before he went away...

A lost memory blossomed inside her. It was dark, and she was locked up in a small bedroom while a storm raged outside. Einn sat with his eyes on the door, quietly waiting for the thunderheads to pass. But Ia was never as strong-willed as her brother. She was the one who always cried.

Arms scooped her up, cradling her tiny shoulders and legs, not yet marred with the scars of living. Long, dark hair tickled at Ia's cheeks, wispy strands that had come loose from a rough braid. Ia peered through the locks of hair and watched her father's face.

"Tell the dark to go away, Papa."

Her father hummed, so softly that Ia had to place her head on his chest to hear. And soon she was lost in it, her fears quieted by the melody.

"There are times when the world will grow black. And you will feel there is nothing else," he whispered as his fingers lightly combed through Ia's soft black hair. "That's when you have a choice. You can stay put, so it can do what it will to you." He opened Ia's hand and placed a crimson feather upon her palm. The feather was light and tickled her skin, but there was a warmth to it that reached deep. "Or you can rise above the clouds. And fly."

Ever since that day, that feather had meant freedom. She heard its wings beating in her ears, pushing against the ties of gravity like a fight against nature. Without the struggle, you could not rise.

It was years later, when she saw the creatures ruffling their wings in the fighting pits, that she found out her feather was one from a Blood Wolf.

"I'm right here, Ia." It was no longer her father's voice. She felt Brinn's fingers lace between her own. "I'm right here."

With those three words, Ia felt the anger inside ebb away

until she could see herself again. If Einn had been her anchor, then Brinn was now her sails. There was no point staying in one place her whole life. Things had to change.

She leaned her chin on Brinn Tarver's shoulder. She had never felt so vulnerable in all of her seventeen years in this universe.

"I'm sorry," Ia said.

That was the first time she said those words. All this time, she thought it a sign of weakness to utter that phrase. But saying it right now, she knew she had been completely wrong. Instead of feeling weak, she felt strong.

She felt new.

Brinn leaned her head against hers. "I'm sorry too."

So this was what it was like to have a friend.

This is what it was like to fly.

"How did you know that song?" Ia asked.

Brinn smiled. "You hum in your sleep."

CHAPTER 60
KNIVES

WHERE THE MIF WERE THEY?

The ship was going down, and Knives was the only one left on the flight deck. Behind him, the jet was prepped, the engines and MOS active and ready to go, but he couldn't leave. Not yet.

He stood on the entry platform, watching, waiting.

They sure were taking their Deus-damned time.

He stepped down onto the flight deck one more time, pretending to inspect the wings and test the pressure of the wheels. Even though it was all ready and done. Even though he could fly out and escape whenever he chose to.

Ten seconds. That was all he was going to give them. No more, no less.

He peered out into the smoke. The red lights flashed from above with each second that passed.

No sign of them. His count was at five seconds. Then four. He wished time would stop.

He kicked his foot against the hull, stained with muck and burnout. His eyes dropped to the emblem painted on the side.

The red paint had dripped down sloppily along the curve of the ship like a bloody gash. It was an awful paint job, but it was easy to see what it was. A feather. For the past six years, he had seen this feather flash upon his holowatch at the top of every hour. A warning sign to all; if anyone saw that feather, they should run.

But he was drawn to her. Like she was a natural disaster, and he couldn't help but stop and look. And now he was stuck in the thick of it, waiting because he didn't know how to pull himself to safety. What was scarier was that he didn't want to.

Two seconds.

One.

Time was up. That was all you were going to give them, he reminded himself.

"Warning," the speakers screamed. "All systems shutdown activated."

At the end of the sentence, the red lights above stilled to darkness. He backpedaled onto the training jet's platform as he fixed his helmet over his head. The siren of the alarm stopped, giving way to a horrible silence.

The pressurization systems were off.

His body flew backward into the cockpit of the training jet. He grabbed on to an overhead handle, trying to keep his body from cracking into the front windows, his arms aching as he held on. The leftover scouting jets, wrenches, screws— everything came crashing toward him.

He needed to get away from it all if he wanted to live, so

he twisted his body and jumped into the pilot's seat. With one hand strapping himself in, the other yanked hard on the throttle. His head flew backward hitting the foam of the headrest. He couldn't even look back if he wanted to.

CHAPTER 61

IA

THEY WERE ALMOST THERE. Almost. Ia could see Knives waiting. She was about to yell out for him when the shutdown happened.

The air ripped out of her lungs, and her body rocketed forward, flipping midair in time to see the look of fear on Brinn's face before being thrown in the opposite direction. With quick reflexes, Ia slammed her fist onto a button at her collarbone and immediately her helmet slid on, quickly calibrating so she could once again breathe. She bit down a scream as her body twisted and turned, over and over until she was sure her bones would break. Her body crashed into one of the walls, coming to a stop between two columns inside the docking bay. She groaned as pain seared through her shoulder blades, but at least she was now wedged into place. Her eyes zipped everywhere, trying to find Brinn.

"Come on, Tarver," she murmured. "Where are you?"

But Brinn was nowhere inside the ship. It meant only one

thing. Ia's eyes snapped out into the All Black, where the rest of the debris had been rocketed. Her gaze landed on an Armada scouting ship. It was cracked in half and spinning out in the void. She caught a shape pressed close against a broken wing, and as she stared at the outline longer, the blood drained from her face.

Ia squinted her left eye and clicked onto magnification mode. Her image zoomed in, and her fears were confirmed. Brinn clung on to the edge of the jet's wing like it was a lifeline. Brinn's grav suit and helmet would help her stay alive, but not for long. Ia's breathing quickened as she watched Brinn's body grow smaller as she soared farther and farther away. People who were jettisoned into the All Black rarely returned. This would be the last time Ia would see her friend.

She wasn't going to let that happen.

Ia clicked through the modes of her artificial eye until a target arrow popped up in her vision. She had to be as precise as possible. The calculations weren't a sure bet. Anything could go wrong, anything. But it was better than nothing.

And thankfully, she had something else in her arsenal that would come in handy at a time like this. The suit she'd insisted on wearing came from a big black box with two words painted on its side. *Project Icarus*. Professor Patel had warned her against it, claiming the ignite system was unpredictable and the suit was too dangerous to wear. But Ia paid her no mind, because there were times when you had to put all your bets on danger.

Her fingers clicked a button at the nape of her neck, and she felt her suit vibrate as two small ionic thrusts popped up near her shoulder blades. At the same time, two thrusters assembled at her ankles, angled for flight.

She had no idea how to operate this thing, but now wasn't the time to worry. With a huge kick, she activated the thrusters.

CHAPTER 62

BRINN

BRINN'S HEAD BANGED against the visor of her helmet. She had managed to slide it on in time before the pressure completely collapsed around her, rocketing her out into the All Black. She was lucky, but her brain felt like it was being squeezed inside her skull. And because of that, she couldn't think. Deus, she couldn't think. All she could do was hold on.

She spun through the air, hanging onto the wing of a slaver jet. With each rotation, she was traveling farther and farther away from the Armada battleship, and even farther away from the chance of rescue.

The realization paralyzed her. She was going to die.

A notification chimed inside her helmet, and then Ia's voice. "Tarver, you hear me?"

Her throat was almost too tight to speak. "Help me."

"I'm coming for you. But you have to stay calm." Brinn grabbed on to the sound of Ia's voice. "Listen to your heartbeat. Do you hear it?"

Brinn closed her eyes, blocking out everything around her, until all she could hear was that drumbeat inside.

Ia's voice drifted in, guiding her. "Find that picture in your head, of something beautiful, something peaceful. What do you see?"

The rhythm inside her ebbed up and down, and soon she was flooded with a wondrous blue. Blue like her mother's hair, blue like her own. She saw ripples of water, the up and down of waves. Brinn had never been here before, but it was unmistakable where she was.

"It's Tawnus," she breathed.

The oceans of Tawnus stretched as far as her mind could see. It was beautiful.

Brinn's fingers fluttered through the water around her, warm as it lapped against her skin.

"Do you trust me?" Ia asked, her voice drifting into Brinn's thoughts.

"I do."

"Good. Open your eyes, and jump," she ordered. "Now."

Brinn ripped her eyes open as the world came flooding in. She loosened her grip from the broken wing and pushed away from the metal frame of the ship. The momentum of the spin rocketed her body backward. She backflipped, over and over, until she couldn't tell where she was. Faraway stars blurred into stripes. She broke out into a cold sweat as her body grew numb.

Then suddenly arms circled around her waist, and she was stopped, staring into Ia's visor. She glanced down at the thrusters on Ia's ankles.

"You're flying."

Ia flashed her trademark smirk. And for once, Brinn was happy to see that smile on Ia's face. She even caught herself doing something she seldom genuinely did: she smiled back.

"Now what?" Brinn asked.

Ia nodded over to a ship in the distance.

"We hitch a ride."

CHAPTER 63
KNIVES

BEEP. BEEP.

Knives glanced down as a tiny blip appeared on the radar. Probably some debris that broke past. Yet, there was something strange about the way it moved. Its trajectory was different, not a straight line like most of the wreckage out there. Instead, it swooped and arched, like it was *following* him.

Knives tapped on the blip, trying to read the ship's signature. It wasn't the Armada. And it wasn't a Commonwealth ship.

He activated the rear cameras. Debris from the wrecked slaver ships hurtled into the nearby sun, creating ripples of solar flares that blew out the camera lens. He unstrapped and ran to the back of the ship, but there were no windows. There was only one other way to see what was coming. He buckled a cord from his suit to a nearby clasp.

Knives pulled down a metal lever near the enviro tanks, and the cabin slowly depressurized. His toes lifted off the floor, and his body stretched toward a glowing blue button.

His palm pushed down on it, and he watched as the platform angled open.

At first, all he saw was a small shadow in the distance. Dark like a phantom.

Eyes squinted, he realized there were two of them soaring toward him. And as they neared, his heart leaped into his throat.

As she flew closer, he saw Ia's face. It reminded him of the first day they met, when she ran down the flight deck and jumped right off a cliff. She was reckless, he had thought.

And brave.

And brilliant.

And since then, he couldn't take his eyes off her.

He reached his hand out for her, waiting for her to take it.

CHAPTER 64
IA

IA SAT BY THE WINDOW of the RSF training jet and stared out into the All Black. Beside her, Brinn was asleep, her head resting on a cushioned wall panel. Ia looked down at her lap, at their fingers laced together.

It felt nice.

She never had a female friend before. In fact, she never had *any* friends. As the Blood Wolf, she had to keep people at a distance to hold that power, even her crew. But after everything that had happened, she could no longer claim that title. Her followers would shun her once they found out she had helped the Bugs. Even if Ia knew what she had done was right, others out there were not going to see it that way.

It didn't matter. Because now she had another mission. Brinn was the only person who understood and could finish Headmaster Weathers's work, and Einn wasn't going to stop until he had her. Ia had to protect her.

She gave Brinn's hand a squeeze, then looked toward the

pilot seat, her eyes landing on Knives's head tilted back onto the headrest.

Gently, she unlaced her fingers from Brinn's. With one last look to make sure Brinn was resting peacefully, she stood up and made her way to the copilot's chair.

She wasn't sure how to start a conversation with him, after everything that had happened. And she didn't mean what had happened with the Armada.

That kiss.

She wished a thousand times over that she could do away with the memory of it, but it lingered, tickling deep inside her brain. Flashes of his touch, his scent rushed at her like oxygen to a fire.

These were dangerous thoughts. Completely dangerous.

Knives broke the silence. "It's never a dull moment with you."

"That was nothing," she said, trying to settle into their natural back-and-forth. "You should see what it's like when I have more time to plan."

"You saved us," he said, his gaze resting on her.

His long, slender fingers darted toward the autopilot button and then came back to his chest, his fingers tugging at his zipper. His hand disappeared inside his suit, and he pulled out a silver object the shape of a small egg, a sensor diode flashing at one of the ends. Knives swiped his finger on the other end, and a small image projected between them, fading up from black. *Her heart.* It pounded and pulsed in steady rhythm. Upon its surface shimmered a net of wires, sparking slightly with each heartbeat.

"I don't know if the general told you everything this

little thing can do," Knives said. "This sensor monitors the Commonwealth tech implanted inside you. It can pinpoint exactly where you are in all the known galaxies, and with one button, it can stop your heart cold."

Ia understood. She had led Einn to Aphelion, gave him the layouts to tear the place down. Cadets had died. These were her crimes, and they couldn't go unpunished.

"There's one more thing it can do," Knives continued. He flipped the sensor over and slid open a hidden section. Underneath was a switch. "It can deactivate it."

With his thumb, he briskly flipped the switch. She felt a murmur in her chest, and her gaze lifted to the holo-image hovering before them. The webbed lights faded away until all that was left was the beat of her own heart.

"You're free."

"That's it," she whispered. "That's all it took."

A rush of immeasurable joy flooded into her, and everything looked crystal clear and absolutely perfect. But then she glanced over at him cautiously, on the probable chance this was some awful joke. "You're really letting me go?"

She waited for him to laugh in her face, but there was none of that. He looked her straight in the eyes. "I'm giving you the freedom to choose. After everything, you deserve at least that."

Ia gazed off into the All Black, feeling the infinite wonder of the void before her. She was free. *Free.* And she could do whatever she Deus-damned wanted.

She could kill him. Escape back to the Fringe. Find her crew and remind the entire universe who was the Blood Wolf of the Skies.

But instead, she leaned in, so close she could see his beryl-blue eyes, cold as the mountain she'd found him on. She held his gaze until his eyelashes fluttered.

"Chocofluff," she said. "As much as I want."

He raised his eyebrows. "Really?"

"You asked me to choose."

The right corner of his lips turned up, but then lowered back down into his usual glower. "You're joking, aren't you?"

"Nope." She clasped her fingers behind her head. "If there's one thing you Bugs do right, it's chocofluff."

"Are you sure about this, Cōcha?" He angled his head at her, giving her a moment to think it over. But she was already certain. After all, every journey had a new horizon.

She smiled at him. "Yes. Let's go home."

* * *

It had only been a week since the attack, and everything was still in disarray. With Aphelion still running on backup gennies, the High Officer's quarters were dark and gloomy. And also very easy to break into. Ia had decided to slip in when she saw the general's cruiser land on the flight deck. The last time she'd seen the cruiser, its bright-white hull had retreated up into the sky, the clouds edging in on it like a closing door. She'd been so angry, so eager to escape.

How much had changed.

She walked throughout the High Officer's quarters, dragging a hand across the surface of the general's desk. Earlier, she had seen him walking into the headmaster's office to talk to Knives. She knew it would take a while because the general loved to talk.

And now she waited, hiding in the shadows, finding a position by the storage cabinets that was in perfect view of the entrance.

She wanted to see the look on his face as it all settled in.

A beep came from the door, and it slid open, letting in the flickering light from the hallway. The general's figure filled the doorway, and as he moved inside, she heard the medals jingling on his chest. Each step was slow and methodical, and his calculating gaze swept across the room. He stiffened at the sight of his desk, at the papers ruffled by her touch.

Finally, his eyes fixed in her direction, his voice calm.

"I know it's you," he said.

Ia stalked out from the shadows, her body lithe and predatory.

"Did you come to Aphelion to say hello?" she asked, her voice slippery. She studied the general. The squareness of his jaw was much like his son's, and his eyes were the same shade of blue. She hadn't noticed the similarities until now.

"What do you want, Cōcha? Congratulations for a job well done? You're lucky that we're not throwing you in prison for leaking information about Aphelion."

"That's not why I'm here." She leaned against the wall and crossed her arms. "You have something that belongs to me. I know you have it on you. You're the type who loves trophies."

His eyes narrowed, shifting as he studied her face. "I didn't think you'd come for it so soon."

The general strode toward a metal cylinder resting on a gray side table. The container was big enough to fit a skull. He rested his fingerprint on the top of the cylinder, allowing the scanner to confirm his identity. The metal sheath lowered, revealing a dark black helm, scuffed from wear. Etched in its center was Ia Cōcha's feather, bright red like freshly spilled blood.

General Adams grabbed the helmet by the lip of its visor and kept it well beyond her reach.

"If I give this to you," he said, "what will *you* do for *me*?"

Her lips quirked up in a smirk. And then she lunged at him, her palms shoving him back. The general stumbled backward, his hand already reaching confidently into his coat pocket. He whipped something out, dangerous silver flashing in his hand.

It was the heart tracker, the original.

He flipped it open and pressed his thumb on the sensor in the middle, his eyes already glimmering with a look of victory.

Nothing happened.

Except for the smile that rippled across Ia's face. "Knives didn't tell you?"

The general's eyes widened in realization. "The damn fool," he muttered.

"You thought you could keep me leashed forever," Ia growled. She quick-stepped toward him, swinging a kick at the side of his knee. He crashed to the ground and hit his head. She moved toward his crumpled body.

"I could kill you right now," she growled at him, anger ripping through every cell of her body, but then she eased off. She reached into her pocket and tossed him a handkerchief.

He eyed her as he wiped the blood dripping from his temple.

"Lucky for you, general, it appears we now have the same goal," she said.

He coughed. "What are you proposing?"

"A truce," she said, learning forward as if she were going to pounce. "But only if you allow me one thing."

"And what's that?"

"My brother," she said.

"Don't tell me you want a plea bargain." His voice rose. "We're not letting him off."

"I know." An ember of fury burned deep inside of her. "And I'm going to be the one who takes him down."

The general grunted in approval and tossed her the helmet. She snatched it out of the air and stared at the feather on the visor, blooming red in the night. It was a symbol of the Blood Wolf, lost but now returned.

Standing tall like a statue, she slid the helmet on.

She was Sovereign of Dead Space, the Huntress of the Wastelands, the Blood Wolf of the Skies.

She was Ia Cōcha.

And now she was fighting for Olympus.

ACKNOWLEDGMENTS

I would like to thank my wonderful writer friends, especially Liz Arrendondo, for being there since the very beginning. Thank you for reading each chapter-like thing I sent you and giving me the most thoughtful and game-changing notes. I am constantly in awe of your talent when it comes to story-telling. Thank you to Anna Rabinovitch, my ultimate writing buddy, for all the times we shared green tea lattes, griped over grammar questions, and talked about K-pop in between writing sprints. Writing this book would have been so lonely without you.

An immense amount of gratitude goes out to Logan Garrison Savits, who plucked this manuscript out of her slush pile and truly believed in Ia and her adventures. You will always be my champion. To Seth Fishman and Jack Gernert, and the rest of the team at the Gernert Company for all of your never-ending support.

To my amazing editor, Eliza Swift, for being my ultimate

story navigator. Your guidance has gotten me through some surprise plot holes and logic obstacles, and I don't know where this story would have ended up without you—probably in another galaxy where nothing makes sense at all. Because of your enthusiasm and collaborative spirit, the whole editing process was a great adventure filled with only the best discoveries. A million thanks and even more hugs to everyone at Albert Whitman, for standing behind this story and welcoming me into the AW family.

Thank you to Gabe Sachs for being an awesome mentor and for imparting a generous amount of career advice throughout the years. I've learned so much about writing and "the biz" from you.

To Ryan MacInnes, my BFF, for reading all of my projects and encouraging me to keep going with my writing. If I'm stuck (storywise and lifewise), I know that I can always talk things through with you. Thank you for being there for me.

To Jessika Van, for being on the cover. You are an inspiration. You have always been my Ia Cōcha, since the very first chapter.

To Isaac Hagy. *Ignite the Stars* started out with a girl whose name no one would ever forget. Ia Cōcha would not have her name without you.

To Romina Garber, Kass Morgan, Robyn Schneider, Robin Wasserman, Marie Lu—thank you so much for all of your kind words and incredible advice at crucial times.

To Charles Haine, the Hochheim family, Joie and Max Botkin, Anna Ellison, Eric Greenburg, and the rest of the LA crew for being with me on this journey, and for always overlooking my mysterious disappearances while I'm on deadline.

Shout-out to the Electric Eighteens, the LA Electrics, and the Book Therapy group—we're doing it!

To my mom for not just believing in me but also being proud of me, even though I'm not a doctor, or a lawyer, or have a career with built-in health insurance. Thank you for giving me the chance to be brave in my decisions.

And to my weird dog, Thor, for just being you.

Last but certainly not least, to all the readers who've found this book. My wish for all of you is to feel as strong and bold as the Blood Wolf of the Skies.

ABOUT THE AUTHOR

MAURA MILAN grew up in Chicago but now resides in Los Angeles, where she works in video production. She can be found in cafes drinking green tea lattes and writing and writing and writing. In her free time, Maura enjoys watching Korean dramas, collecting K-pop gifs, and hanging out with her dog, Thor, who she believes should become a professional comedian. She received a BA from USC's School of Cinematic Arts and has placed a number of short films in festivals all over the United States. *Ignite the Stars* is her debut novel. Visit Maura online at www.mauramilan.com and on Twitter at @mauramilan and on Instagram at @mauraisdoomed.